THE DREAM LAND

THE DREAM LAND

Long Distance Voyager

BOOK I OF THE DREAM LAND TRILOGY

Stephen Swartz

TANGENTIAL BOOKS

In Association with

MYRDDIN PUBLISHING GROUP

UNITED STATES · UNITED KINGDOM · AUSTRALIA

ISBN-13: 978-1-939296-22-1

ISBN-10: 1939296226

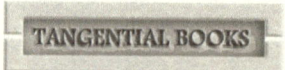

In Association with

www.myrddinpublishing.com

Cover by Marta Swartz

To sleep: perchance to dream: ay, there's the rub.

William Shakespeare, *Hamlet*, Act 3, Scene 1

THE DREAM LAND

Long Distance Voyager

Stephen Swartz

PART ONE

Kansas City, Missouri,

United States of America, Earth

June 1986

Chapter 1

Threshold

"I was face up in a vast snowfield, sun on my face, and all around me were hundreds of half-buried skeletons. The yellow sun was glaring off the snow, blinding me, and the blue sun was winking at me from the horizon, but all I could think of was 'I'm freezing to death!' They took my greatcoat, and I didn't have any boots. In fact, I couldn't feel my legs below the knees. I wanted to check them, but I was too frozen to move. I wanted to cry out for help but I was afraid of calling the ones who did this to me. I kept thinking 'It's all a mistake' and 'I don't belong here.' Then I looked up at a small branch stretching over me. I followed the branch to its end and there was a single drop of thaw hovering there. It was about to fall. I watched it for a moment—then it fell! Straight down to my legs! It hit my legs—which were frozen solid—and they shattered into a million splinters! There was nothing left but stumps! And I cried my brains out in pain—but there *was* no pain because everything was frozen! And I was wondering how the hell I was going to get home without my legs."

Arctic winds pick up, rushing against him, attacking like a line of mounted lancers, spear points jabbing.

"Is there anything that can be done?" the man asks. Desperate tears tumble like ice cubes. "I was captured and tortured, then left for dead. Can't you do anything, Doc?"

The other man sits up, feeling the wind in his face, too, gray beard brushing against his jacket collar, red necktie rumpled and out of position, wire-rimmed spectacles slipping down his long nose. He reaches up and scratches his cheek, thinking of somewhere else he'd rather be. A scan of his watch tells him twenty minutes remain in the life of this patient. If he were to fail, he would need to fashion a comforting speech to give to the family. He smiles, knowing this unfortunate soul has no family—none, officially, that is. He can be left wherever he drops and no one would care. Still, as a doctor he has been trained to be compassionate. Over the next minute and a half he decides to follow through with his oath to first do no harm and, second, to try to help the stupid bastard make sense of his twisted life.

"Doc? You there?" asks the patient.

"Yes, Mister Talbot." He reaches for a fresh pad of paper. "Go on."

The patient lies still, shivering against the cold.

"But...that's it."

Seven minutes of silence pass, each man counting from competing timepieces. The snow melts, the ice thaws, the winds drop. Outside, hopeful cheers arise from children on the school playground and mix with the rough hum of city traffic on a Monday afternoon. Dinner will soon follow.

"It could mean quite a number of things," says the bearded man with the note pad. "Most importantly, I will say, this is not an unusual occurrence for someone in your condition—someone who has faced trauma as you have. So I don't want you to place too much faith in whatever your dream might be referencing."

"Dream?" The man on the couch clears his throat. "I never said it was a dream."

"Not a dream? But I thought...."

"Actually, I'm not sure." A moment passes. "Was it just a dream I had last night, or was it a long-lost memory that keeps intruding on my consciousness?"

"That's a good question, Mister Talbot."

They regard each other across the Persian rug in the center of the office as sunbeams stream in through the windows. The patient wears a wrinkled white dress shirt and faded blue jeans.

12

Two pens are clipped inside the shirt pocket. On his feet are leather shoes, worn down into three shades of brown. Yet another client sent to him by law enforcement authorities. He didn't seem dangerous, just confused.

Perhaps he is only playing games, thinks the doctor.

"You have several key symbols: the snow, the freezing, the ice, the whiteness, and the skeletons. And the sunlight—did you say there were two suns?"

"A large yellow one and a small blue one."

"I see." The doctor writes. "And you had the feeling of being abandoned, fear of violence against you—"

"And freezing to death. Don't forget that, Doc. And icicles."

"No, we shan't forget that." He writes more. "Tell me, Mister Talbot. What do you think it means?"

The patient yawns theatrically, sits up on the couch, swinging his feet to the floor.

"You tell me. You're the psychiatrist here. I'm just the deranged mental patient."

"You're not a deranged mental patient," says the doctor. "You have experienced a trauma and I have been appointed to assist you in returning to a functioning role in society."

"A functioning role in society?" The patient laughs, but to the doctor it seems quite an artificial thing, perhaps intended to be mocking. "You mean, like my night-shift job at the IRS service center? A silent clerk digging through stacks of papers at the desk in the corner? Is that supposed to be my functioning role in society? A convenient cog in the system? Is that the hole I'm supposed to crawl into and just accept?"

The doctor releases a long exhale, trying to restrain audibility so as not to irritate the patient. Not that it matters now. He is easily aroused to anger, it seems. Of course, there is good reason, what with all the events happening, the questions, and the constant surveillance. He is lucky to have any job, and the fact that the job he holds is somewhat off the main avenue of society should be something beneficial to his recovery. And to society. The doctor makes notes of his thoughts, as required; an evaluation report will be due some day.

"I'm not crazy, Doc."

"You need not consider yourself that way."

Before the patient can respond further, the doctor retrieves a thick hardcover book from a nearby shelf and searches through it. He stops at several pages, takes mental notes, continues. Finally, he closes the book and sets it on the desk.

"According to the key symbols we've identified, you are likely to suffer unforeseen troubles. Or you believe that you will. The ice thawing indicates a fear that you will be cheated by friends...." The doctor pauses, dares to smile. "Ah! I see now why you are so concerned. It's beginning to add up, all these wintry symbols in your dream, especially here in June. You see, many aspects of your dream relate to loss: friends, loved ones, even legs and knees, perhaps also the suggestion of *peace* that you are seeking. It's very common after what you've been through. You have experienced loss, and here it is June once more. The anniversary of your wife's murder."

Fourteen minutes of deep regret fills the room.

"Does that still bother you?" asks the bearded one from his throne.

"And I felt such a comforting peace flowing through me the whole time," says the patient, the wine turned to vinegar. "Even as my legs were shattering. Breaking off at the knees. Like I was glad to be rid of my legs. That's got to mean something. Right, Doc?"

Thirty-two seconds of silent bliss. A timer produces a soft *ding*.

"It seems our time is ended for today," says the doctor, *thank goodness*.

Standing with as practiced a manner as any ballet dancer, the patient adjusts his clothing, flattens a wrinkle in his shirt, adjusts a pen in the pocket, and grabs his green, canvas jacket.

"The air-conditioning can get rather cold by the end of the shift," he says.

"Until next time, then," intones the doctor, standing.

"About that...." The patient turns to the doctor, half way between his chair and the door. "I'm beginning to believe that I could probably fix myself, Doctor Liebowitz. Well enough, at least, to be a functioning carcass of society—oh! I mean *cog*, not carcass. Sorry. Yes, if I read the right books and think deeply,

14

profound answers are bound to come. I'll have light bulbs bursting over my head and everything will be all right."

The doctor sets his note pad on the desk and faces the patient, hands on his hips.

"As your court-appointed counselor, I wouldn't advise that. We *are* making progress."

"It's not like I'm required to be here." The patient shakes his head. "I'm not crazy. You agree with me on that. And interpreting my silly dreams is done easily enough with a few cheap books. I hate to take your valuable time, Doc."

"Mister Talbot, there are other things to consider."

"Everything is fine. When I'm awake." The patient chuckles, a sound that grows sinister after two seconds. "At night, it's different, of course. I can't let myself sleep. That's when the dreams come. So I never sleep."

"You see how you continue having difficulty adjusting to your new life? That shows up in your dreams. Your fears, your desires. It's common. However, let's work on that, Sebastian. That's the reason you were referred to me. We should meet as usual next week."

Sebastian Talbot, the patient, nods two and a quarter degrees.

"We'll see if I'm available."

Chapter 2

White Collar Workers in Blue Jeans

Despite alarm clocks, automotive engines, and shouting children, Sebastian Talbot often slept, and he frequently awoke. However, he knew there would be a last time for each of these and he could never predict when that might be. So he waited, usually with the lights on. But the waiting would make him drowsy, and he would drift off to the wasteland of his memories. No matter what he did, no matter how long he stayed awake, no matter what drugs he pretended to take, psyching himself into believing he was high— always, always, always he slept: dragged down to a world where laughter sparked ambivalence and heroism was passé. The shadowy demons waited for him. Sometimes they would let him make the first move, usually not. They often cheated.

"Hey, Perfesser, what're ya gonna dream about tonight?" It was Michael Fenning, the office playboy, calling to him in the parking lot of the IRS service center.

The third shift was over and everyone was heading home, racing the sunrise. It was becoming a comedy routine for the two of them, following the script whenever they were leaving. The fact that he was called 'Professor' seemed at first derogatory, yet he accepted it. After all, he had been a teacher in a previous life. When he'd asked his co-worker about the odd moniker, he learned that Michael thought he seemed like the professor character in the TV show *Gilligan's Island*. Nobody knew anything about him, Sebastian Talbot considered, yet here was an idiot calling him smart. So he let it go on.

"Don't know," the Professor replied to Michael across the cars between them. "Have to wait until my head hits the pillow."

It didn't matter to him whether or not any of his co-workers asserted that, for him (the strange, lonely man who never participates in the fun and craziness of the department), the line between fantasy and reality was irreparably blurred.

In the sprawling IRS service center, his desk was stuck in the corner, facing the wall, his back to the world. He preferred it that way. He could get his work done quickly and accurately. The other advantage was that he could weep without drawing any attention. But he seldom did that now. Still, they all knew he was crazy—or on drugs. Once or twice he was suspected of such, but they found only aspirin in his desk and cold tablets in his locker. He swore he'd never taken anything else, but still they watched him.

Actually, it was a lie. There was a time long ago when he went around boasting of all the hallucinogens he had survived. He insisted that he was only trying to blend in with the bedheads and deadheads around him through the effervescent nights of indiscriminate youth. He had managed to become high nevertheless, simply breathing the air in the room. That caused him to withdraw deeper within his aura, leaving him to peer out through the steel turret windows of his head at the fools rolling on the floor, beating their heads against the wall, making love on the cat-peed couch. All the while he'd sat there on the cat-soiled carpet, work-stiffened back against the dartboard door, taking it all in, with his tired feet crossed, weary arms crossed, burning eyes crossed, and a cross look on his haggard face, staring hard across the room at the wooden cross tacked on the wall, noticing that Jesus was cross-eyed, too.

So very long ago, he sighed. He noticed a black mechanical pencil in his hand and tax forms on the desk before him. He remembered where he was, did not wish to be there, yet the clock was ticking.

✳ ✳ ✳

Out of the mists she appeared, like a ghost condensing into view, there above the gray, red-tufted grasses at the crest of the rusty knoll, the sky black and stormy behind her, emerald lightning crackling soundlessly against the dark horizon. The beast she rode was piebald: a grayish three-toed hoofed carrier, with splashes of black across its rump and a mane of dreadlocked cream and charcoal whipped wildly against the tawny dewlap by the storm-draft. And the young girl, her own mane long enough to cover her unclothed body, rose up on the back of the beast, scanning the landscape for her lover.

Instead, she saw him, the refugee from the tax center.

With no surprise on her blood-painted face, she parted the thick bundle of red-streaked hair tumbling from her head. Her bare flesh was tarnished gold in the subdued light. Framed between her scarlet locks, her blood-red breasts mocked him, challenged him. She seemed to believe he was the one sent to take her as wife. He knew to keep his distance: this was a Zetin girl.

Her scarlet hair was not a matter of birth, nor was her crimson flesh. Today was her wedding day, he understood, so her hair and skin were dyed in the blood of a specially-bred sacrificial slave, usually from the Sogoiji people, known to possess a particularly bright shade of red. She rode the beast nude, clothed only in her blood-soaked hair, awaiting her husband: the warrior who would savagely take her on the mountaintop, then drag her to his village, leaving her beast dead on the hill, its heart eaten raw by the two of them after sealing their union.

He looked away. To be seen would not only disrupt the solemnity of the ancient rite, but her husband-to-be would have to kill him, too—then kill her for allowing the stranger to see her.

So the man from the Internal Revenue Service Center rode away on his own beast, what the locals called *Jêpe*, as fast as he could. On the wind a scream cut through his ears and he knew that the maiden was now a wife. He clenched his teeth and dreamed of home.

✳ ✳ ✳

Skinny, blonde Tammy Tucker was grinning as usual, leaning against the wall by the pencil sharpener, her anorectic figure not hidden much under her spaghetti-strap sundress. She was rumored to have three or four children by five or six men, but how she could be so skinny no one understood. She nodded as Sebastian spoke to her, as though she were really listening, at the same time poofing her blond curls, making her hair bigger. That was the style in 1986; everyone in the music videos on MTV had the same big-hair, and so he let his hair grow out, too.

He did not expect she was listening, twirling her blond locks between her fingers, but this time the girl who Michael Fenning hit on most frequently really *was* listening. Feeling a bit embarrassed at his long professing, he stopped. Tammy's smile did not change, did not increase, decrease, or show in any way that his sudden silence affected her at all. The mouthful of teeth, fifty or sixty of them, continued to grin, framed by the forest of casually tossed hair, golden like Michael's.

Sebastian excused himself to go to the canteen for a drink before their midnight lunch break was over. He was not attracted to her, but sometimes he needed a smile—anyone's smile. Hers was constant. Something he could count on, like night and day—and always having to sleep.

Michael had been watching them from his desk, loafers up, arms back. He was jealous that the Professor was taking Tammy's time when she could be grinning at him. As the Professor stepped away, the lanky Michael sprang to his feet, smoothed his leisure suit, and strode on over to her.

"What was he telling you?" he boldly asked.

Tammy was caught off-guard. "What?"

"What did the Perfesser say?" asked Michael. "He never says much, ya know, so I was just, uh, interested."

"He was talking...about how he came to...to work here."

Tammy tended to put a funny lilt into anything she said, rising inflection often on the wrong word. Or she simply paused in the middle of a sentence, as though thinking what to say next. Then it all came out in a rush. Michael tried to be patient with her.

"Yeah? And why's that?" he pressed.

"Well, you know…he got fired and couldn't…find another job." Tammy suddenly began to giggle. "Just like you, huh?"

"Yeah, a little like me," he conceded. "Did he tell you *why* he was fired?"

"Well, no…."

"Did he tell you what he did before coming here? His other job?"

"He was…a teacher, right?"

Michael laughed. "You weren't listening, were you?"

"What?"

"He probably told you he liked the job security. Nobody gets fired here. I mean, unless it's something like stuffing tax returns in the restroom trash to meet production, like Burton did last year. They canned him faster than he could say 'Taxes-R-Us'."

"Well, he…said that."

"But he didn't tell you the real reason he's working here? Why he got fired from his teacher job?"

"Well, no…. Why would he tell you?"

Michael shook his head, exasperated. He glanced around, stepped close to her and lowered his voice.

"He killed a student."

Tammy's mouth fell open. "What?"

"He was fired 'cause he killed a student. He told me that. That's why he was fired."

"What? No way. You're kidding."

"No, I'm not."

"You're not?" Tammy crossed her arms over her chest, striking a defiant pose. "Why would he tell you something like that?"

Michael shook his head again. She could be so dumb sometimes. Heck, she was already three times an unwed mother. Other times she asked way too many questions when she should just accept stuff. He couldn't stand it. Women. Can't live with'em, can't live—

"Because he was drunk when he told me!" He shook his hands in frustration. "See, I went into McGilley's one night—in the

21

morning, I mean—"

"You were…drunk yourself, Michael."

"Listen. I went in—I was surprised, too, ya know. I never thought, of all the jerks here, it'd be the Perfesser getting smashed, right? But there he was, a bunch of glasses on the table, slumping in the booth."

"Well, maybe…he was sick?"

"No, not sick." He wanted to slap her but swore he'd never hit a woman. "Geez, he was *drunk*, I said. I know what drunk is."

"You sure do."

"So I went over to him, ya know, kinda surprised to see him there, right? I said 'hi.' He said 'have a seat.' So I sat down. Then he just starts talking, and pretty soon he's telling me all of this weird shit, like about being a teacher, right?"

"So what happened?"

"I'm getting to that, just wait a minute!"

"Don't have a minute. Look at the clock."

Michael grunted. "Okay, I'll tell you after work. Meet me at the front door."

* * *

Mountaintops dappled with snow, stabbing through the cloudbank, gray world suddenly twisted into kaleidoscopic confusion, he is thrust down on his back, a clap of thunder smashing against his head, battered ears bleeding and eyes bursting with horror. A spear falls unexpectedly beside his outstretched hand.

In a flash he grabs the shaft and flings it upward to receive the oncoming breastplate, hurling the Zetin warrior up and over his own body and letting it crash to the rocks behind him.

He turns, rolling in the snow, seeing the trailing crimson strings of viscera running from the open cavity of the warrior, struggling to escape, crawling with one hand damming his seeping guts. The spear protrudes from the sternum, where it ended its journey, and bounces back and forth with every crooked step, like a metronome counting down a life. The

22

warrior's blood-dripping fists clench the shaft and jerk it free—
then tumbles to the ground, spinning on one knee and sinking
face first against the frozen gray mud.

Raising the lance, posing as if to catch a glimmering ray of
sunlight, something to mark his victory, he brings it down with all
of his strength into the Zetin warrior's body, trying to split the
planet in half. The warrior lurches, pushes up from the ground,
lingers on his hands and knees, even as the spear is roughly
removed and readied for another stab.

He waits, regarding the complete disintegration of the
warrior's body, and observes the spasmodic hand wrenching the
stubby, curved knife from a scabbard at the hip. The warrior rips
it forward, up to the warrior's own face. Blood splatters across
the snow, drops in thick globs as he finishes his death mask:
slicing the flesh from his skull so the enemy will not see his final,
painful grimace.

The Zetin warrior flings the skin aside and the Professor,
satisfied that he has done his duty in allowing the honorable
ritual, tosses the lance aside and takes a deep breath, languishing
in the exertion, savoring the struggle. He welcomes the excited
cheers of his men as they rush wildly down the slope to meet him,
calling "Captain, my captain!"

Except they did not shout "Captain, my captain," Sebastian
knew. They had shouted "*Serpan, Êr Serpan!*" at him, using their
native language, Ghoupallêan. It was a language he also knew, had
learned over the course of several years through various
experiences, never attending a class or studying books. That
probably was the reason fluency remained elusive—mostly due
to the endless list of confounding pronouns. *Damn crazy
grammar*, he cursed, slamming his pencil down on the desk.

A few of his co-workers glanced at him as he got up and
marched out.

"Not again," he grumbled, shoving open the heavy double
doors at the entrance to the service center and bounding down
the steps to the walk that every night led him thankfully away
from his functioning role in society.

He went down to the end of the walk, just past the corner of
the building, his favorite break spot. He breathed deeply, rolling

his head in lazy circles, trying to relax, trying to tear himself away from the reality that was intruding upon his other reality. The headaches were beginning.

Chapter 3

Methods and Procedures

In the small hours before the sun burst forth over the east end of the service center and bled into a pale morning sky, Sebastian stood in front of the service center, gazing skyward. There was a strange chill in the pre-dawn mid-summer air and the silence of the night was disturbed only by the distant hum of morning traffic on the highway. He would join them soon enough, when the shift ended. And as the day spread over the city, he would shut himself away inside his apartment, shades drawn, daring himself to close his eyes.

I don't belong here, he thought as a tear bloomed in his left eye and slid down his cheek. He wiped away the second tear, blinked back the others.

He stared up at the sky, searching for a particular star. A little to the left of Eternity. She was still there. She was living her life, just as she wanted. And he was here. But this was not the life he wanted to live. He chuckled, feeling the irony swell in his gut. This surreal time of the night, just before dawn, was when he felt most alone, when he missed her the most.

Gina Parton was tall and blond, wore simple fashion, and, while attractive to him, he had to admit she would never be mistaken for Homecoming Queen. She was the smartest girl in the senior class, however. He was a sophomore, clumsy but well-intended. Sebastian Talbot was the name he carried, not one to sit well with the more athletic denizens of the school. She was never shy in calling him by his real name, and she did so lovingly. She was different from the others, he noticed from the moment he first laid eyes on her in Chorus, she a mezzo, he a baritone. He stood behind her on the risers, a step higher, which at first made them equal in height. After a few weeks of clever remarks whispered back and forth between songs, they dared to go out together for a movie and a pizza. That was the beginning of a romantic relationship, criticized by both upper- and lower-classmen. He would have liked the whole school to be concerned, even disrupted, by their breech of custom. The truth was that nobody outside of a couple of science clubs ever cared what they did. Until she showed up at the Senior Prom with a sophomore boy. Surely someone, anyone, would say something, make a complaint, perhaps cause a ruckus. But no.

They also shared Physics and Calculus classes and eventually were able to sit together and share notes, which led them to a final project on the probability of the existence of interdimensional realms, a project which their teacher wanted them to enter in the state science fair. They refused, calling it a wistful dream, an exercise in hyperbole. However, their teacher borrowed their playful idea and subsequently used their final papers, uncredited, for a Ph.D. dissertation—which, Sebastian learned years later, was rejected for lacking enough hard data. Apparently their teacher went mad trying to prove their theory and was forced to retire early, spending his remaining days at the old science museum on Gladstone Boulevard, or at the main library downtown, constantly recalculating their high school class equations.

But in the early hours of the night following her graduation and the accompanying party, she told him of her future plans. Her announcement took the form of abstract deliberations about quantum physics and the supernatural, tinged with mythological allusions and mathematical equations scribbled out on whatever paper was handy. He took it all in, partly because he actually was interested in the science she was explaining, but more so because he knew he was hearing her farewell address.

There was more to it than what she told him, certainly, and in the years after she left for college somewhere to the east, he continued his own calculations based on the theory they had developed. He hoped to ascertain exactly where the fabric of the universe might best be unraveled. It turned out to be practically in his own backyard. An abandoned quarry some two miles from his family's house seemed a perfect place to conduct experiments. The hilltop indentation, hidden by a thick forest, was perched on the edge of suburbia, ready to collapse into the black hole he calculated was on the opposite side of the universal curtain—a metaphorical curtain that could, like thread-bare cloth, be torn apart.

His own college was paid for by a music scholarship and he pushed himself through it, keeping a low profile by becoming a series of statistics in a file he regularly accessed to maintain his grade-point average. The formality of higher education became a distraction to his learning. He was too busy with the Theory to bother with mere essays and exams. However, it was preparing for Secondary Education in Social Studies that eventually became his ticket to graduation.

Gina returned in the summer but she was different from the girl he knew in high school. She confessed love affairs in various states, and admitted to sampling many kinds of recreational drugs—not surprising given the popularity of such activities in the '70s. What most astonished him was that she had given up her research. He showed her all the work he had done, yet she was hardly impressed, saying that none of it mattered, not when considering the corrupt, materialistic world in which they lived.

He felt betrayed, scientifically more than spiritually. Finally, she showed some emotion and felt bad for him. She knew how much he idolized her and laughed. She made him a bet and he took it. They would put all their efforts together and give it their best shot. For the summer. Then he would see that even if it *were* true, even if one *could* pass to some other dimension, what was the point of hassling with it when they could be satisfied living in the dreary land of their birth? She had everything she needed right there in Missouri.

"Why? Because that's the challenge of it," he insisted, jumping up and waving his arms, disturbing the silent dawn. "It's because the mountain's there. Because that's where the money is. That's why we do it! We search for the joy of searching. We fight for the thrill of the fight. We dream for the sake of the dream—and for the hope, however distant, that the dream might somehow, sometime, somewhere, be twisted and hammered into some kind of reality."

"And suppose something is off?" she asked. "If even one little calculation is off, we could be in deep shit: at worst dead, at best standing out in the field with our thumbs up our asses." He was finding it difficult getting used to how she spoke after a year in college.

Gina got him worked up thinking of the Theory. Now she was mocking him, telling him it was a joke! But here were notebooks filled margin to margin with equations, charts, graphs— everything to prove her *correct*. And she was not interested. She wanted to continue her carefree college life learning how to treat mental illness with music.

"It's Music Therapy," she told him firmly, "and it's a real subject."

"What does music have to do with anything?" he asked. He was her equal as a musician, they both knew. "It's nice and I enjoy it. Remember my scholarship? But despite making life more pleasant, what does it really have to do with anything important in the universe?"

She shook her head, blond hair tossed by the breeze.

"You talk about the universe as though it was your own private garden, something you sow and hoe every day!"

He gazed at her, trying to remember the girl he once knew. His sweetheart.

"Sebastian, you can't see the damn forest because of all the rotten logs falling on top of you. Can't you put the tiniest figures together long enough to see that music is more than some song you hear. It's math. It's more than math; it's the rhythm of the spheres. Planets spin to music, comets shoot to music, suns go nova to music, the whole freaking universe is sewn together by zillions of musical strings—like a curtain with interwoven threads. That's why we study music—not because it helps us get through our days, not so we can boogie whenever we want, but because it makes the entire universe exist. It's all connected; it all *is*! It's the same thing. You know that. Don't you?"

He sat dumbfounded. Too many theories were crashing inside his head.

"Take middle-C, for example," Gina continued. "Its frequency is 558.15 Hertz. If you double it, you get an octave higher, right? If you double it forty times you get *light*. Understand? Specifically you get the color of light we might call *indigo*. It's the same with other pitches, other colors. Play with sound, with the light spectrum, and you're playing with the universe. Then you can hear colors and see musical tones!"

✳ ✳ ✳

Night shift workers were streaming out the front doors for the last break. Their chatter tore away Sebastian's concentration and the scent of tobacco on the breeze stung his nose. He would be docked for the time he was away from his desk. He would have to claim illness. He needed fresh air.

In a white T-bird parked across the lot from where Sebastian stood stargazing sat his two co-workers, Michael and Tammy, engaged in their own stargazing.

"It's not as good as the second one," Michael was explaining to Tammy. "They got these teddy bears that fight the Stormtroopers. Totally ridiculous. Darth Vader has a change of heart so his ghost is a good guy. And we find out that Luke and Leia are brother and sister, so she gets to marry Han Solo after all. I swear I could play that dude. I look just like him, except I got blond hair."

"That's so...sweet," said Tammy, watching Michael fumble with a pack of cigarettes.

"Anyway, we can go see that *Risky Business* flick when it comes out." He glanced down at Tammy's bare knees, lighting his cigarette. "I hear it's raunchy. About a guy like me who gets a girl like you." Michael took a quick puff from his cigarette, leaned to kiss her.

She jerked. "I don't...wanna kiss now."

"Why not?" asked Michael. "We've done it before."

"You were gonna tell me about the Professor. You went to a bar and got drunk."

Michael exhaled loudly. "*He* was drunk, not me. I just went there, he started talking. I didn't drink nothing. Just a beer. At the beginning. So he's talking to me about all this shit, ya know. He was a high school teacher, like, five years, and there's this kid that's always causing trouble, beating up other kids, smoking in the classroom, shit like that. So it's the end of the year and they have the big exam. This kid just sits there not even trying to answer the questions."

"Well, maybe he…knew the answers already."

Michael shook his head. "He was expecting the Perfesser to give him an A, ya know, 'cause he threatened him. See, if the Perfesser didn't pass him, he was gonna do something. Anyway, the Perfesser gives him an F because he didn't answer a single question. And he never did any homework, neither. So the kid freaks out, waits for him after school, says the Perfesser better change the grade or he's gonna kill him."

"Wow! What he do?"

"He didn't change the grade. So the kid flunks and can't graduate. The kid goes to the Perfesser's house, breaks in, and his wife is home, ya know—"

"He's got a wife?"

"No—not now, anyway. So he's not home. The kid beats the shit outta her, then rapes her, and she dies later at the hospital. They catch the kid, but he gets off with, like, just probation or some shit like that, some easy sentence."

"That's when he…killed the student?"

"No—listen. Next school year, the kid has to repeat, ya know, 'cause he didn't graduate. He ends up back in the Perfesser's class. So you *know* he's gonna freak seeing that kid in his class. And that's what happens. They get into a fight, right in the classroom. Other teachers come, police come, but they can't tear them apart. The Perfesser's strangling the kid to death, so they fire him. But he got off the murder rap, ya know, like involuntary manslaughter or some shit like that, I forget the word."

Michael sat back in his seat, feeling proud at having a secret to tell. He looked at his watch. "Break's almost done."

Tammy kept muttering "Wow...."

Michael could not decide if she was really amazed or if she was just being an airhead. "That's what he told *me*. So whatever he told *you* before must've been a lie."

"Well, he said...he *hit* a student...and they fired him."

"Okay, so that's the story. You wanna get something for breakfast after shift, or just go back to my place and fool around?"

Chapter 4

Sines, Cosines, and Tangents

After he and Gina made love, as they often did in those sultry summer weeks in '75, they again fought over the Theory. It was always the same argument. They both knew it could never be settled until they arrived at the right calculations, fine-tuned their machinery, and actually proved it.

He pulled on his shorts and stared at the electronic keyboard at the foot of the bed as she bent down with a screwdriver, her naked butt awkwardly raised in the air before him as she adjusted the tuning.

"So all it takes is this cheap little keyboard?" he asked, gently directing her bottom over to the left.

"Quiet—I'm tuning." She pressed a key, heard the pitch, turned a pin to modulate the decaying tone. "Yes, this is it. Best we have available. But we have to change the pitch up a few octaves."

"You'll have the dogs howling for miles around. How're we going to keep it secret then, huh?"

"It'll be too high for dogs. Maybe even cause people heart attacks, or the veins to burst in their brains. Who knows? Good thing we're going up to that quarry where we can't hurt anyone—hah, nobody but ourselves."

They had checked out the quarry twice, seeing in its central semi-circular depression and smooth limestone walls the perfect auditorium for capturing and reverberating the sound waves they would create. It was also shielded from view and earshot of anyone coming by on the country road at the base of the hill. On their first visit, they climbed up the hillside through thorn bushes and oak trees before they found the gravel path once used by trucks but now overgrown with grass. Gina quickly stripped off her tanktop and cutoff jeans and stepped into the shallow pool of rainwater collected on the quarry floor. The water only went to her ankles. As the sun blazed down on them, Sebastian enjoyed seeing her beauty, but she had lost that innocence, or her appearance of innocence, that he had loved.

The next time they visited the quarry, they both stripped and reclined on a flat rock off to the side of the central arena, as they called the main area. The hot July sun burned his back as he covered her, making love.

"There's still a lot of rock here to be quarried," Gina remarked afterwards. "I wonder why they stopped digging. What do you know about this place?"

He turned to look at her from where he was wading in the rainwater pool, seeing her reclined on the rock like a goddess, arms tucked back under her head, breasts bronze.

"Nothing," he called to her. "It was long abandoned when my family moved out here."

The next day he went straight to the library looking for information about any events happening there and eventually found a newspaper article on microfilm about some teenagers being arrested for partying, shooting fireworks, taking drugs at the quarry. Another article on the same subject. Then a third. No wonder the chain was put up across the gravel drive. In all the years he had passed by it on the school bus, he had never seen anyone going up there, never saw any vehicles parked at the entrance, nor heard of any disturbance there. He went over to the county office of land management and asked a few questions, was routed back and forth among several offices until he landed in one with an old man filing papers into the drawers of a wide, metal cabinet. When he asked the man his questions, he finally got straight answers.

He returned to the quarry with Gina, filled with the knowledge that some geophysical phenomenon had occurred there. They studied the walls of the quarry, every stone, every crack, looking for anything strange. He especially searched for fracture points in the walls but found nothing unexpected. Workers who were interviewed by the newspaper reporters claimed they had seen ghostly images moving about the quarry. The workers tried to talk to the ephemeral entities but they seemed not to hear them. A few certified ghost hunters visited the site next but by then the ghosts had vanished—if they had ever really been there.

The workers must have been using pneumatic jackhammers, he considered. The heavy vibrations they produced, and the accompanying pounding on the auditory spectrum could have thinned the 'fabric' enough to allow faint visual contact with the other side. Gina agreed, liking the metaphor. Positive space on one side, negative space on the opposite side, a curtain dividing them. A curtain too worn in places. She did some research and made a few calculations with her slide-rule to determine the range of frequencies generated by such a power tool. That frequency would have to be duplicated, she explained, but without the actual noise.

"If there was a weakening of the fabric some place, as some kind of natural phenomena," said Gina, "and *then* you put a jackhammer to it, the vibrations would affect it. I mean the *tangent*. Whatever point in three-dimensional space it happened to hit with vibration. It wasn't the jackhammers themselves. No, I think the vibrations acted like an earthquake, flaking off layers of the 'curtain' in ever-increasing amounts, chipping it thinner and thinner until it was thin enough to literally see through."

"Are we going with fabric and threads as our metaphor or rocks and chips?"

"All right, Sebastian!" She wanted to slap him. "Let's go with *curtain* and *tangent*."

It was not easy lugging the equipment up the hillside through the thick summer flora. He complained every few steps. Estimating it would take an hour to assemble everything and run one test, they had left his house early, driving past the quarry's entrance several times to check for other people. Then they stopped and quickly unloaded everything, hiding it in the bushes while he drove to the 7-Eleven a mile away and jogged back to the quarry entrance to help her carry up the equipment.

In the curved, stone arena where the shallow pool had dried up in the summer heat, leaving thousands of crisp clay chips, they began to set up their experiment. The keyboard went on the flat, lovemaking rock, and the rest of the equipment was set up on nearby rocks. He pulled wires and cables from his knapsack and she connected them with painstaking care. Then he stood watch, listening for anyone coming up the gravel drive. He paused to help her properly position the speakers. At Gina's direction, he pressed the keys as she checked the settings, listening at a normal pitch through big headphones, adjusting one here, one there. Then she dropped them down several octaves.

"We're ready," she sighed wearily. "Finally, I can be done with this project of yours!"

It was late and the orange sunset silhouetted the trees. Venus blinked in the eastern sky and a crescent moon held a ghostly presence on the horizon, awaiting complete darkness.

"Your negative attitude is going to ruin this project," he teased. "You know how sensitive these kinds of phenomena are to negative vibrations. You have to keep happy thoughts. Send out positive vibes. Think success."

"Look at you, Mister Clean Aura," she laughed. "Don't worry, I *am* thinking positive thoughts. Work, work, *work*, dammit! How's that?"

"Better," he laughed, "much better."

"Put your shirt on, big boy," she called, tossing it to him, "it's time to rock'n'roll!"

Rock'n'roll, he mused, standing outside the service center, feeling the seductive tug of time-passed and the quick slap back to present reality.

He saw Fat Ken getting a quick smoke. Cassie and her girlfriends were sauntering back inside. Break was over. He had not spoken to anyone all night, he realized. Michael and Tammy were absent, too. Nothing to amuse him, only his memories, which were never amusing. He thought of himself ten years in the future, still standing on the walk at the corner of the building, still staring up at the stars wondering what Gina was doing, if she were all right, or even alive. For a moment he compared the different realities he saw in his mind, weighing them.

Rather than go inside and return to his desk, he walked over to his car, got in and started the engine. He paused a moment to determine if he were actually going to leave before the shift was done. How much would they dock his pay? Smiling to himself, he knew some things were worth more than money.

He put the car in reverse, backed out of the space, and turned toward the street. He lingered at the traffic light, then drove away. While he was rationalizing his departure, he had intended to go home and call back that he was ill and would take sick leave the rest of the night. But half-way home he changed his mind and directed the car out Highway 40 to Pink Hill Road. He was heading to that abandoned quarry he had long ago abandoned, pulled by some feeling he could not explain.

※ ※ ※

Dawn was cracking over the horizon as Michael escorted Tammy out of the service center and over to his car. Most of the sky was still black although most stars had been put away. He helped Tammy into his T-bird, taking care that her dress rode up on her boney legs. He turned on the 8-track deck, the cartridge full of Top-40 songs, at maximum decibels. Tammy jumped, settled back in her seat crying for him to turn it down. He did, then gathered materials from under his seat and began rolling a joint in his lap.

"So what do you say?" asked Michael. "We gonna get some breakfast or go straight to my place?"

"I need to get home before my kid goes to school," said Tammy.

Michael examined his handiwork, showing the reefer to Tammy. He punched in the lighter in the dash. When it popped, he took it from the dash and lit the reefer dangling from his lips. He took a quick puff then handed it to Tammy. He held his breath as long as he could.

She fumbled the joint, dropping it on the floor. He scrambled to retrieve it.

"Sorry," she said.

"Okay, okay—still lit. Shit, Tammy—"

"Well, I said sorry."

He sucked it back to life, offered it to her again, holding it for her.

"There," he said. "Get a buzz on that? You have to hold your breath longer."

He watched her cheeks balloon out and almost laughed.

"Okay, here's the deal." He exhaled. "You said you wanna find out more about the Perfesser. I know where he lives. We can go over, break in, look around, see what kind of shit he's really into."

"We can't break into somebody's home."

"Why not? Burglars do it all the time."

"But we're not...*burglars.*"

"I have a plan, see. Only, we gotta do it when he's here at work. So you and me'll have to call in sick. You got sick leave, dontcha? I know ya took off a couple weeks ago, when your kid had the flu. Got any left?"

"I don't wanna break in anybody's house."

"Tammy, you said you wanna know what he really does—or did."

"No, I didn't. That was you...remember?"

"Okay, maybe. You said you wanna know more. I got it on tape."

She laughed. "No, you don't, Michael."

"So, are we gonna do it or not?"

"Not."

She laughed again. He leaned over and planted a kiss on her cheek to shut her up.

"Michael, goshdarnit! Don't...*do* that!"

"Come with me then." He softened his tone. "I really need you to come with me, babe. You can be the lookout. I'll do the hard stuff. You're just as curious as me what the Perfesser's really into."

"No, I'm not...not so much."

"Look, the guy's got two college degrees, so what's he doing working in a place like the goddamn Internal Revenue Sewer Center? He's gotta be into some bad shit, ya know. He's laying low. Maybe he's hiding from the mob. Yeah, Tammy—that's it!

He's probably one of them, uh, witness protection people."

"No, he's not...well, probably not."

"But we gotta find out for sure."

"Why? So we can blow his cover?"

Michael thought for a moment, smiled slyly. She had an interesting idea for once.

"I never knew anybody in any witness protection program. Wouldn't it be cool to pop his secret identity? We could do it. That'd be really cool!"

"Michael, you're...crazy."

"That's what you like about me. You're coming, right? Let's make it Sunday night. Then nobody'll suspect nothing. He never misses Sunday—all that Sunday extra pay."

"But *I'll*...miss Sunday pay."

"You get money from all your kids' dads, dontcha?"

"Only one...dad. And only one kid."

"I thought you had more. Everybody said you had, like, three."

"No way. But I did...I miscarried last year," she said, then paused dramatically. "They said I was too underweight. That's why—"

"You got only one kid? Shit, everybody's got you wrong."

"Why's that?"

"That kid I met? What's his name?"

"Chuck."

"Chuck. His dad's the cop, right?"

"Yeah."

"He pays child support, don't he?" He snorted, realizing he was wasting time. "Just leave the kid at your mom's. Sunday night. Now, gimme a kiss to seal the deal."

She frowned for most of a heartbeat, then waved the smoke away and stretched her lips across the space between the bucket seats and whisked his cheek like a breeze, touching only the warmth rising from his skin. But it was good enough, Michael decided, to seal the deal.

Chapter 5

The Tearing of the Universe

Sebastian sat on the flat rock at the side of the quarry, gazing up at the moon, not sure why he had driven out there. The night was warm and humid, just like the night he and Gina did their experiment. He pulled off his moist shirt and crossed his legs, remembering laying against Gina on that same rock many years before. It had been so long since he last visited the quarry. Too many strange memories. It all felt like a dream he once had, a dream he was still trying to forget....

The shimmering lights began to blink into existence, like reflections off waves, dancing and flickering, twinkling like distant nebulas, spinning and whirling ever so gracefully, shifting like layers of heat on a desert horizon, bowing and rising at random then rushing together like slithering comet tails only to then stretch apart, like soft taffy, like his old lava lamp, like millions of ethereal amoebae strengthening and weakening until they seemed to be stabilizing, moving elegantly within a narrow range, back and forth in magnetic arcs, as a filigree world evolved into view: a ghostly image, the crossing of TV signals, the CB channel cutting in on FM radio, seeing both at once, then separate, together again, apart once more, the ghost images growing until they supplanted their view of the limestone cliffs that had been behind the focal point of the sonic apparatus.

Gina gasped, waving her hand at him to hold the tuning dial exactly where it was. She would never have made a trite remark, like *We did it!* or *It really works*. They knew what they had done, and what the other was thinking. She carefully stepped back to the machinery, not daring to take her eyes off the horizontal bands of flickering blue and gold lights, mere pinpricks of color, shot through with incandescent flashes of red. She felt for the rocks, found them behind her, then reached out for his hand.

"It's...glorious," she whispered, and he was surprised she could be so taken in by her own experiment. He had to agree, touching her hand and giving it a reassuring squeeze: it was beyond their expectations.

In the darkness, her eyes spoke multitudes, perhaps gratitude for finally persuading her to put all of her intellectual energies into the project this summer. His eyes returned the compliment, but held back amazement for more certain, measurable phenomena.

"Let me have the controls," she spoke in a hushed but excited voice.

He picked himself up from the ground and took a step back from the machinery. Gina slid into his place, not removing her eyes from the dancing lights. Released from his duties, he stepped toward it, careful not to walk between the sound waves from the speakers and the colorful phenomena they had discovered.

"I'm going to narrow the focus," she announced softly, as though her voice might blow the lights away.

He nodded, unconcerned whether or not she could see him in the dark. In pinpointing the sonic focus, the projection beam would be strengthened and in their theory it would then tear the curtain.

And the other side?

He could see the effects of her fine-tuning, the lights growing more intense and moving closer toward each other. He believed the flickering of the light spectrum was merely the crashing together of positive and negative ions—those of this world with those of the other world, through the *tangent*. He realized then that he could see something through the brightening lights, something white, and smooth, hilly, like a snowscape or a desert, some kind of a ghost land. He shivered, a little frightened by what he did not understand and could not explain.

Gina's hand directions told him to move around behind "it"—and only then did he stop to consider that it was a three-dimensional phenomena, a single point in space, hovering in the air, with the rest of the quarry remaining visible behind it.

He stepped gingerly to the right and circled behind it. Something like a pillar of fire. He could walk around the point where the twinkling spits of light brightened. From behind it, he could see Gina illuminated by the lights; he presumed she could see him. But when he stood to the side and stretched his hand behind it and searched for his hand from the front, all he could see was the ghostly landscape between the bands of lights. He could not see his hand.

The lights themselves had shifted into vertical bands, blue-yellow-red, stretching from his shoulders to his knees. The lights were tightly compacted, and becoming tighter as Gina attempted to manipulate them. They seemed to be trying to push apart. Gina's manipulation of the sound waves prevented their scattering, he reasoned. He watched until they had spread to nearly the width of his chest. He stood less than arm's reach from it, and felt something like electricity flowing across the opening to him.

"The opening," he heard Gina mutter and glanced back at her.

She was approaching him. He straightened up, ready to hold her back.

"We don't know what this is," he said, hands up to stop her.

"We know exactly what it is. It's the opening. This is one of those damn *tangent* things we've been calculating. It's the gateway, the doorway, the tearing!"

"Of the curtain?"

Even in the dark, with the twinkling lights covering her face, he could see the glimmer in her eyes. Sometimes science was better than sex.

She stepped forward and swiftly thrust her hand forward toward the breech.

"Don't," he called.

"Relax, I'm just checking it."

"If you get too close, you might be electrocuted."

She was too enraptured by the sensations to think rationally, he decided.

"It's not exactly electricity," she said, thoughtfully.

After a few more breaths, he said, "This is enough for one night, don't you think?"

She was transfixed by the twinkling phenomena.

"We can try it again another time," he said.

"No, it's just starting."

"What is starting? What do you think happens next?"

"The adventure."

"What adventure? We did something, sure. Now we need to go back and write up what we discovered, every step, before we forget what we did. We're going to be famous."

She snickered at him. "Silly boy."

He took a deep breath. "What are you going to do?"

Her smile widened. "What's on the other side? What is it that we're seeing through this light show?"

He gazed into the space—*through* the gap, what they called the tear of the curtain. It was like looking into a mirror, but a mirror with great depth. His own image was a thin sheen on the surface, an image which did not completely obscure the deeper view of something else. If he ignored his face he could clearly see another image: a barren landscape that definitely was not the opposite side of the quarry. The quasi-electric sensations held him, locked him in fascination. He tried to break himself away but saw something new at that instant, something entering the picture right in front his gaze.

A hand—Gina's hand—sliding through the opening, its image distorted as if her hand were underwater. He panicked, thinking her arm was melting as it passed through the force field. He jumped back, alarmed, and felt the tingling sensations gripping his aura a moment, then melting quickly away.

"Gina, stop!" He almost falling backwards in his hurry to escape.

She did not seem to notice him, standing as she was, balanced on her back foot, leaning inward toward the sparkling opening. Her left arm was inserted up to the elbow.

Then panic overcame him.

"Gina, what's happening? What's happening to you? Tell me!"

A wide grin of pleasure spread across her face, and her head fell gently back in ecstasy.

"It's like...sex," she mumbled, "like the rush of climax but...it doesn't end. It's like...like energy is flowing...all through me. I can't tell...where it's coming from. I don't feel...tired...or any effect of these electrical sensations. I feel...relaxed, calm...yet my senses are...heightened. It's...I think it's calling me...I think. I feel something pulling me, but...I can't see anything...it's touching my hand...pulling me...in...."

"Gina, come back!"

"Don't worry, it's all right." Her voice was a hollow echo. "It's a new world—you know, a brave new world. And I...I have to...explore it."

"No!" He rushed forward to grab her but halted as he brushed up against her, fearful of knocking her through the gap—the *tangent.*

In a flash he regarded her through the eyes of a scientist: half of her body was poised in the flickering lights, her aura illuminated by a golden, skin-tight halo, while the other half had disappeared. He shouted again for her to return but heard only his echo. Only then did he notice the loud roaring sound, like a freight train, like a tornado, and he dropped down on the rumbling ground, feeling the earth quivering. He still saw her bare left leg, the rest of her leg and her entire body hidden by the snowing of electricity.

The machines were out of control, he concluded.

He ran back to turn them off, thinking that would make the opening dissolve and he could free her. But as he ran, looking back over his shoulder, he tripped over the wire connecting the keyboard and amplifier to the power pack. It came unplugged and he could hear the roaring noise whirling down to a finish. He shot a glance where the opening had been, saw its illumination fading like a TV picture tube going out as Gina's sandaled foot was slipping through.

He bolted up and desperately dove toward her ankle, grabbing at her foot. He fell, hitting his head on something, a rock perhaps, maybe her heel, he did not know which, but he felt dizzy for a second before he passed out.

At 22:44:38 on 26 July 1975, the fabric of the universe was torn.

Chapter 6

Eternity Road

It was the third winter of July when he awoke, held in the arms of his lover, and in the spaces between his breaths and feeble heartbeats, in the gaps between the blinks of his eyes, he found the world he had long imagined: a passionate, pleasantly warm place, full of sunshine and greenery, happy people and quiet, contented children, and all the great fears of past days vanquished and sweet silence sitting on his shoulders, like a precious parrot calling '*Master! Master!*' Was someone addressing him? Who was he—a god? And as he stretched, reaching for the crystalline blue sky, his muscles and sinews were filled with vigor, and he knew that he was indeed the master, the commander, the captain of his destiny—

"Hey!" someone shouted.

His head snapped back, feeling cradling softness against his neck. High overhead, a pale gray sky curved, and he searched for angels. Beneath his weary back, the white ash of Hell stretched forever, he saw, rising to the far distant horizons in every direction, soft, soapy flakes which when he took them between his fingers and squeezed disintegrated like melting snow.

"Are you all right?" asked the voice, a woman's.

He thought he heard the cry of a bird, searched the sky, found only streamers of blond hair falling over his forehead, and there a face was framed above him: smile set regally in the center with cheeks rosy and plump with happiness. He had found one of the angels.

"Can you hear me?"

"Yes," he murmured automatically, wanting to rise but finding himself held down gently.

"We made it," the girl said, and he studied her expression, memorized her voice, deciding it belonged to Gina.

"We did?"

"Yes, Sebastian. Can't you tell?"

After a moment: "*What* did we make?"

"The curtain," she told him. "We tore the curtain. And we stepped through to the other side. We did it."

He struggled to sit up. Regarding again the barren landscape, he became light-headed and dropped back into her lap. She wrapped her arms around him, pressed his head into the soft void of her halter-top, her breasts a pillow for his head, and rocked him back and forth.

"Where are we?" he managed to grunt, from deep within her embrace.

"Well, Sebastian," she spoke in a low voice, "I don't exactly know."

He nodded his acceptance of her answer and shrank further into her arms, hiding from the new world, afraid to come out, fearful of the sight of it, the challenge of it, distressed at the thought of no return.

* * *

Standing in the open-air corridor on the third floor of the apartment complex, Michael pulled a key from his shirt pocket.

"What's that?" asked Tammy, having fun and about to giggle.

He shushed her. "It's from my brother." He glanced in each direction but no one was out at that late hour except for two third-shifters from the Internal Revenue Service skipping out of work for the night. "He's a locksmith. This is a universal key."

He struggled with the key, pushing it, trying to turn it, but it would not go.

"Does it work?" asked Tammy.

Michael stepped back, shaking his head. "Guess not."

"Serves you right," said Tammy. "We shouldn't be doing this."

Michael went over to the stairs and looked around the side of the building. "Come on."

Tammy followed him down to the ground floor, and around the courtyard to the bushes below the open window of the Professor's apartment.

"We gotta get in or we won't have any place to get *funky* tonight."

"Michael, goshdarnit. I *told* you I'm never gonna, ya know, have sex with you. I said 'no'! N-O spells 'no'. I mean it."

He shushed her again, pointing up at the window.

"You're climbing up there?" Tammy almost shouted.

"Quiet!"

"Michael...what if you fall?"

"If I fall, just *don't* scream, okay?"

Michael parted the bushes, climbed up onto the porch railing of the first floor apartment. From there, he held on to the drain pipe coming down the side of the building and the rough, overlapping wooden shingles on the side of the building, inching his way up to the next balcony. He paused there to check on Tammy, motioned her to go up to the Professor's door and wait for him.

Michael climbed over the railing onto the second floor balcony, caught his breath, and started up to the third floor balcony, cursing himself for bringing her.

He stretched up for the third floor balcony railing and pulled himself upward. He tried to swing himself over the railing as he had done for the second floor railing, but as he grabbed for the thick wooden slab with his other hand, he heard his shirt rip under his arm. He slipped and his body swung out and hit the side of the railing. Frustrated, he heaved himself over the railing onto the balcony. The open bedroom window was off to the side. He sized it up and, holding his scraped ribs, decided it was impossible.

"Are you in?" Tammy called quietly from the breezeway,

waiting at the door.

He shushed her again, studying the wall.

"Michael?"

He cursed and searched again for a good foothold. Only a real die-hard burglar would go to the trouble of skinning himself on those shingles.

Balancing himself on the railing, Michael stretched across the wall to the open window, his chest pressed against the coarse shingles. He got his fingertips on the open windowsill. Suddenly, he found himself swinging from the sill, holding his scream. He pulled himself up and dove through the window into a dark room, landing in a pile of clothing.

Hearing the tapping at the front door, he fumbled through the dark apartment, bumping into furniture until he found his way to the door.

"What took you so long?" Tammy whined when he opened it.

"You have no idea." Michael grunted.

After Tammy stepped inside and closed the door, Michael flipped on the light switch. The living room was cluttered, the floor spread with papers and boxes. More papers were stacked in chairs. One side of the room held the usual TV, VCR, and stereo system. Cheap junk, thought Michael after a glance. Against one wall, a scratched up old desk stood with a Tandy computer system on it, green dot glowing on a black screen. Another corner was filled with weights. On another wall was a shield with a couple of swords. Decorative, thought Michael, then found with his fingertip that the swords were quite sharp.

"Michael!" Tammy shrieked, startling him.

"What?"

"You're bleeding."

"Yeah, I know." He saw the bloodstain on his shirt, touched his fingers to his ribs.

"We need to get you a Band-Aid."

"Go look in the bathroom."

She found the bathroom as Michael scanned the paper-strewn living room. "Looks like the service center, all the papers out of place."

"Here," she said, returning with a box, "let me fix you up."

Michael lifted his shirt and Tammy applied several Band-Aids to his scraped ribs. He had her wrap one of them around the tip of the finger that had tested the sword.

"Well, what're we looking for?" she asked.

"Drugs."

She seemed surprised. "You're looking for drugs?"

"Yeah, drugs." Michael was already surveying the living room for good hiding places. "Let's see if he's got anything cool stashed around here."

"That's what you dragged me here for?"

"And to see if there's anything about any crimes he's done. Like the student he killed. You know, court papers, shit like that. Anything that looks private."

"Private? But why?"

"So we can mess with him!"

❄ ❄ ❄

The polite thing for him to do was to give her the shirt off his back. Then, in gratitude, she dragged him across the sands, away to a destination they could only fear to find. And with every step he cursed and complained, fighting the long march, reluctant to go forward without knowing where the exit was, unwilling to experience the new land.

"Come on," Gina snapped at him, gaily. "Life is for the experience. We're not here just to live and die, or perform rituals to superstition. We're an accident and it's just a coincidence that we spend so much time thinking about it."

He jerked her arm back as she was leading them, made her stop.

"That's not what I'm talking about," he said. "I don't think we should've left the spot where we entered this world."

"Worlds," she corrected him. "This must be the second or third we've traveled through."

"How can you be so sure?"

"Didn't you feel it? Didn't you notice the change?"

"What did you feel?"

"The air pushing against me, squeezing me. Just like the first one back at the quarry."

"I felt that, too."

"Like walking through Jell-O."

"Or being born."

She laughed. "Yes! Being pushed out of a womb. *Now* we are alive! *Here* we are alive. This is our life. Not that snuggly, warm cocoon you call Earth, full of something called normal life and reality! That's all that came before our birth."

He pouted. "Gina, we just slipped through another doorway to another tangent, on another world. So this is our third since Earth?"

"We're on our third planet in what? ten hours?"

"By your count."

He grinned, somehow embarrassed. This was not what he wanted, not what he expected when they started the experiment. He was supposed to start his sophomore year in college in a couple of weeks. If they could ever find their way home again.

"We have to explore," she insisted, consoling him with a touch of her hand on his bare shoulder. "That's what explorers do. We can't just sit down at the first tangent and call it a day. We don't have time for any daydreaming. *This* is the reality, Sebastian!"

"We should have called it a day after the first hour, after I woke up. I could've been really injured, you know. We should've returned right away."

Gina smiled, sincerely, lovingly at him. "Don't worry, big boy."

He gazed into her eyes. "How are we going to find it again? And what about what's up ahead? You've seen every sci-fi movie ever made. What can you imagine up ahead that would be worse than any of the monsters and aliens we've seen in the movies?"

She laughed. "Relax, will you! Here, in this world, *we* are the aliens. And we aren't so bad. We come in peace. We mean no harm—"

"That's not what I mean!" He started to pace. "Look, Gina, over the next hill, just a few steps away from us, at this very moment, could be hideous things, creatures that want to *eat* us, or Hell's Angels, or terrorists! We don't know. I seriously believe we should be adopting a more cautious attitude to our situation."

"We'll deal with any trouble when we encounter it."

"Well, then, what about food? And shelter? That's another problem," he said, vigorously gesturing. "We have no food, no water, nothing. And we haven't *seen* any food or water for...for almost ten hours now. We're going to get hungry soon enough. We need to find a safe place to sleep, too."

"Ten hours, you say?" She went over to look at his watch. "We've been here ten hours? Feels like only one hour."

He pulled back his hand, checked his watch himself.

"Well, I don't remember what time it was when you went dancing through all of those Christmas lights and landed here. I was too busy trying to save you."

"You were knocked out for about two hours, I think."

"Great! That means we've been here—and *here* and *here*—for twelve hours! With no food or water, no shelter, no wind, no cold, no heat, no weather, no—"

"That's it! Listen to yourself, Sebastian!" Gina playfully slapped his chest, then hugged him tightly, holding his head against her shoulder.

"What's wrong?"

"Don't you see? Look at this place." She released him and spoke in a whisper: "This is *Limbo*. There's nothing here because this is *no* place! Maybe we're not really anywhere. You said there's no cold or heat, or even wind. Look around us and there's only this kind of white ash or sand stuff that melts when we pick it up. Look above us and there's no clouds. There's no wind. Have you felt a breeze? I haven't." She moved her hand in front of him. "Not even when I wave at you."

"That's crazy. Of course, we're someplace."

"It was midnight when we tore the curtain. Now it's mid-day. We haven't had any food or water for ten or twelve hours. But I don't feel hungry. I don't feel thirsty, either. How about you? If we were walking in a real desert for that long, we'd be plenty thirsty."

He pulled away from her and regarded the trail they had made extending behind them, then scanned the sky, stuck a finger in his mouth and held it up. Nothing. There was no sound, no sensation, no life.

"And yet we're fine here, aren't we? I mean, we can breathe the air, can't we?"

He had to admit she was right. "But where are we, if we're no place at all?"

"Maybe we're just dreaming this. This is just some... some *dream* land we're in."

Gina pulled off the shirt he had given her and set it on the ground, spread it out and dropped down on top of it. She gestured for him to join her. When he sat down, she leaned over and kissed his cheek. He grinned, so she kissed his mouth.

"All right, we're in some kind of limbo," she spoke after several minutes to contemplate their realizations. "It's like we're walking in a cloud. And if we continue for another ten hours, what are the chances that anything will change? More of this same white sand or ash stuff, the same sky, the same lack of weather."

"I'd really prefer to go home now," he said with a groan. "I have business to take care of, you know, things to get done. I'm glad we proved something. But this isn't fun anymore."

"Relax, Sebastian."

"How can I relax? I'm in Limbo."

"Lay down here," she instructed, motioning. "Like you were before."

When he assumed the position, his head resting in her lap and her arms around his shoulders, he turned his eyes upward to watch her. She leaned down over him, her breasts cradling his head.

"Now what?" he asked.

"Think of home," she whispered. "There's no place like home...."

"There's no place like home," he repeated.

"There's no place like home...."

"There's no place like home...."

And the sky burst open with the same blue-gold-red flashes, a celestial fireworks laser-light show, the ash and sand breaking away like crumbling cookies and the weather returning with a sudden fury that tore them apart and threw them forward in time and backward in space, whirling them within an invisible tornado and depositing them roughly in a marshy patch of flora with few bumps or bruises, yet eyes spinning and heads dazed, hearts beating wildly and guts in knots.

"What was that?" she asked him when they lay still once more.

"I think we just passed through another one of your goddamn tangents."

Chapter 7

Elixir of Love

Michael flipped on the light in the bedroom, saw the mess he had created when he dove through the window. He straighten the clothes that had fallen, hanging up the khaki jacket and red-striped khaki trousers crumpled under the window. As he attempted to smooth some of the wrinkles, he paused to study the clothes. It was some kind of military uniform.

"Tammy?" he called. "Come here, will ya?"

"I found something interesting out here," she called back.

"Just come in here!"

When she arrived, she was smiling as if she had a big secret, but he ignored her, pointing to the uniform.

"How about that?" said Michael.

"What?"

"The uniform—army, probably. It ain't American."

"He don't seem like a soldier."

"I don't think so, neither," said Michael. "Maybe the Perfesser ain't even American. He talks like an American but he could be one of those dudes who can play different roles, ya know? A spy. Or secret agent. Sure, he talks okay. But he don't say much, does he?"

"He keeps to hisself," Tammy agreed, reaching for some fallen clothing and moving them from the floor to the bed. "But he sure got a messy home."

"Yeah, that's it," said Michael. "He don't wanna give away his accent, so he just says short stuff. Like 'yes' and 'no' and other shit. You don't have to pick up all the clothes. He might wonder if the room is suddenly neat."

"You're right." She dropped to the floor the armful of clothes she had gathered. "If he's not American, where's he come from?"

"I dunno, but look at these crazy patches." Michael lifted the shoulder and sleeve of the jacket. "Never seen anything like it. Look at this writing. Must be Russian. It's written in one of them Commie alphabets. Look at this eight-pointed star with the crazy writing around it. That's the kinda alphabet they got, wherever he's from."

"Looks kinda…Chinese."

"No, no, no!" He snorted. "Chinese's a lot more complicated than that. This looks like Russian, or maybe Arab, some language like that. Definitely not Chinese."

"So he's…a Russian?"

"Could be."

"Then how could he work at the IRS?"

"He must be a spy. I told you he was not right."

"But why would he wanna spy on the IRS?"

"I dunno. To see how we do taxes? Does it matter? He's hiding out."

He set the uniform on the door hook.

"Michael, I found interesting stuff, too."

"What is it?"

He followed her back to the living room. She pointed to the chair that had been positioned in the center of the room to preside over the piles of papers spread around.

"I think…they're love letters."

"Yeah? Lemme see one."

"I guess he's sorting all these papers."

Tammy handed him the one she was reading when he called, a five-page handwritten letter on crinkly beige parchment. It had been resting on the chair.

"Looks old," Michael said, taking it from her. "What's the date on it?"

"Beats me."

"Who's it from?"

"His girlfriend, I think...or somebody else he used to love."

"Yeah?" Michael started reading. After the first page, he turned to the end hoping to see the signature. "*My Everlasting Love, Gina,*" he read aloud.

"Gina? Who's that?"

"Maybe that's his wife."

"You mean...the one that was killed by that student?"

"Maybe," he muttered, reading silently.

"Well, what...does it say?"

"Okay, here's an interesting part: *I planned it this way so you wouldn't have time to talk me out of it. My lover has agreed, but it's not a suicide pact. I'm so weary of life. Three hundred years will do that. How much time has passed with you? You and Linda should be married by now so I—*"

"Who's Linda?" asked Tammy. "Is that his wife?"

"I dunno. Look, he's just sorting out old letters—must be hundreds of'em here. We don't have time to look through'em all. Let's get back to looking for more valuable stuff."

Michael gave her the letter and headed back to the bedroom.

"But—Michael?—it's a *suicide* letter," Tammy called after him. "Did she go ahead and...and kill herself?"

"How should I know?" He turned in the hall. "It said he was gonna marry a chick named Linda, so that must be his wife. I don't know who the hell Gina is, but she's kicked off already, so who gives a shit?"

"But, if this Gina...if she committed suicide, and then he got married to that Linda...is she the one who...got killed?"

He stepped back toward the living room. "Tammy, forget it. Nobody cares about that kinda shit."

"But ain't that...that's what you're looking for, ain't it? Interesting stuff about him? Well, he had a girlfriend who committed suicide...because—well, maybe—he was in love with Linda and gonna marry *her*."

"Geez, you women're all the same," said Michael, raising his voice. He turned and went to the bedroom. "Always going gushy-gushy over any romantic shit!"

Michael dug around in the walk-in closet, discovered a small alcove at the rear where the Professor had put in a bookcase. On its shelves were several small, ornate boxes. He opened one and found it filled with several glassy spheres that looked like marbles. Other boxes had more marbles. They seemed to be sorted by color and size. Boxes on the lower shelves were filled with undistinguished odds and ends, nothing of value or importance, knickknacks most people threw away: a button here, a buckle there, a patch off a uniform, a broken knife.

He picked up some strange photographs with a sepia sheen to them. When he regarded them at an angle, they had a 3-D effect. He flipped through the photos, seeing the Professor grinning back, mostly posed with three different blond women and one dark-haired girl, one with other men in uniform. Michael didn't know who they were, didn't care. A few of the photographs showed strange horse-like animals, striped on the rumps, with men riding them or posing next to them. No drugs, anyway.

He returned to the living room, checked his watch: only an hour had passed.

"You're supposed to be looking for drugs," said Michael in a scolding tone, seeing her sitting on the chair reading more letters. "Nothing in the bedroom. Nothing that I could find. But, hey, I sure wouldn't hide any shit in *my* bedroom. He probably don't, neither. I'll look in the kitchen."

Tammy was busy reading, ignoring him.

"Hey, it's not some gothic romance story, ya know," Michael called to her. "Put it down and look around. Look behind the TV, see if he's put anything back there, okay? Check behind the stereo, too. And see if those cassette boxes actually have cassettes in them, or if he uses them to store drugs."

Michael glanced around the kitchen, a few dirty dishes in the sink but cleaner than his own place.

"Let's see what he's got to drink," he called out, opening the refrigerator. "Only a bottle of water, looks like." He closed the door, began opening the cabinets and saw some liquor bottles. "Ah hah!"

He pulled down a couple of bottles.

"Hit the jackpot, Tammy! Look at all the booze he's got here.

The Perfesser must be a real wino. Alcoholic to the max."

All of the bottles were different in size, shape, and label, yet their contents looked the same: a thin, brown liquid he took to be whiskey or bourbon. He took a smaller bottle from the back of the shelf and held it up to the light. It was slightly darker than the liquid in the other bottles. Thinking the Professor would not miss this small bottle from the back, he set it on the counter and returned the other bottles to the cabinet.

"Michael," Tammy called, excitedly, "you gotta read this! It's really—"

"Yeah, what is it?" he called back as he examined the bottle's label. The lettering was a bit similar to what was on his uniform. Whatever country he was from, he had brought back some of the local brew. Michael smiled. "Let's have a try," he said, inviting himself as he heard Tammy in the next room telling him something.

He tried twisting the cap, then used a bottle opener on it before he saw the small spring mechanism on the cap which flipped it open easily. The scent wafting out was fruity yet musky. Not unpleasant. He sniffed it more closely: watermelon?

"Hey, Tammy, you want some of this? It's some booze from his country—wherever the hell that is."

"Listen, Michael," Tammy sang out, "I'll read ya some," and she started in before he could shout at her to keep it to herself.

He sniffed the contents of the bottle, sweet but not like wine. The more he studied it, the more it looked like just a bottle of water with some brown food coloring in it. He noticed a few very fine bluish streaks, like some kind of vegetable fiber, running through the liquid, most of the strands collected at the bottom of the bottle.

Pulling down a coffee cup, Michael poured enough to cover the bottom, raised it to his nose, sniffed it. He put it to his lips, flicked out his tongue to taste it. Not bad, he decided, whatever it was. He drank it down. He waited for something to happen. No buzz, no burning. Maybe it *was* just brown water.

He poured himself another cup of the brown liquid, deciding it was good. The aftertaste was tangy and left a slight tingle on his lips. It did not seem to have any alcoholic effect, however, so he thought he might as well quench his thirst.

It did have a unique flavor, he agreed, and poured a cup for Tammy.

"Here, have some of this," he offered, entering the living room.

"What is it?" She took the cup.

"Some of his brew."

She lifted the cup to her lips, sampled it with the tip of her tongue, then took a swallow.

"Not bad," she admitted. "*Looks* bad...huh?"

She finished it and Michael took the cup to the kitchen for another drink.

"Listen to this, Michael," said Tammy, raising her voice so he could hear her in the kitchen.

He only heard her words like an uneven mumbling as his attention was drawn more to the new drink.

She paused. "How about some more of that juice?"

Michael arrived with another glass of the brown juice and handed it to her. She gulped it straight down.

"It's good."

"See? You did like it."

"But make sure...you don't get drunk...cuz you're driving."

"I don't think it's alcoholic," said Michael.

He went back to the kitchen, poured another cup, then started looking in the cabinets and drawers again, searching for anything contraband. He reached back into the corners and around all of the dishes and condiments, certain he would find a stash of marijuana or a bag of pills, or something serious like cocaine—not that he dared try anything that strong himself. Maybe he could sell it. All he found were a couple of roach motels.

Tammy continued her reading, adding background 'music' to his new dance. Feeling energized, he wanted to move around. Something in the drink was starting to take effect on him. Finally. He downed the last swallow. Warmth spread through him, especially in his stomach. He could feel it moving up to his head, and down to his groin. Funny sensation.

"This stuff's really good," he heard Tammy giggle, and he wondered if she was getting tipsy already.

"Are you okay?" he called. "Ready for us to finally get funky?"

"No, Michael," she called back, "It's not a good time. Not this week."

"Never a good time," he mumbled, shaking his head, closing a kitchen cabinet.

"You wanna put on some music?" she called out.

"Okay," he said and heard her turn on the stereo, followed by the mystical synthesizer prelude to The Moody Blues' *Threshold of a Dream* album.

No sooner had he poured himself yet another cup of the magic juice then Tammy came sauntering into the kitchen holding her empty cup, looking for the bottle. She started to grab the bottle but Michael took it from her, playing the gentleman.

"Find any drugs?" she asked. Her voice was slurred.

"Not yet," he replied.

He refilled her glass, thinking her breasts looked larger than usual. *Am I hallucinating?* he wondered. The bottle was almost empty, he saw.

"Thanks," Tammy sang cheerfully, smacking him on the lips before dancing out of the kitchen.

He was surprised: she had never initiated a kiss. If she was drunk, he pondered, this was not a good place to do anything. Even so, he was feeling strange sensations below his belt—no, he had to be careful.

With the music going, she returned to her reading but he could not hear her clearly with the music going. Then the LP came to the end and stopped.

Tammy was still reading: "*...the way I remember you: with a gentle smile, a strong will that was compassionate, a love that makes me feel guilty, and an inner peace which transcends material body and envelopes the souls of desperate lovers lost between eons of time and light-years of space....* Michael, that is so beautiful...."

He was downing another cup, already addicted, feeling the strange heat coursing through his body. It was pleasant, and stimulating.

"She's a poet, ya know...a *real* poet, I think," called Tammy, "and he was in *love* with her. Don't you think? She said they had a child. I can't see why he'd go and marry that Linda. Right, Michael...?"

He did not answer her, distracted by the pleasant warmth becoming a burning sensation. Something unusual was happening. His pants were tight, his crotch enraged. He heard Tammy talking but he was not listening. He needed some relief—definitely. Feeling uncomfortably restrained, he quickly unsnapped his trousers.

"Michael...?" called a woman from the next room.

Clenching his teeth, his hands clung to the counter top, his knees weakening, body shivering and shaking. Fire was racing through his veins. He had to let himself go free or his pants would tear open. No matter what Tammy would think. Sometimes a man had to do what a man—

"Michael...can you...hear me?"

He pulled off his shirt and saw how flushed his skin was. He was burning up. There was something in that strange, turbid brew, he knew then—staring down at himself in panic and disbelief. He pulled his sweaty shorts down to his quivering knees. Kicking his pants off over his feet, he stood before the sink buck-naked. His skin was red like a bad sunburn. He had to cool down, had to stop the huge swelling between his legs or he'd burst. He turned on the faucet and splashed cold water over himself.

"Michael!" Tammy's voice was stressed.

In his embarrassing circumstances, he just prayed she would not come into the kitchen.

But she did. And there she stood: her damp blouse limp in one hand and her soaked bra and panty draped across the other hand. She stood as naked as he was. Her tortured eyes said it all: scared to death, and Michael saw why. Her normally small breasts were now swollen tremendously, nipples sprouting. Michael saw how moisture was running down her thighs. Her muscles were spasming—the same as his body was doing. And her skin was burning—just like his.

"What's *happening* to us?" she cried out.

"I don't know!"

He felt himself moving toward her until they were thrust together—like *yin* and *yang*, lock and key—unable to pull themselves apart by their strongest effort. Electric sensations shot through their bodies. The drug had energized their bodies and their sexual secretions were running like rivers freed from burst dams. Their minds were caught in a frantic whirlwind of runaway passion—moans and groans and cries emanating from their taut, manic throats—screams rattling the walls and exciting their fervor. They could not stop—not after the first climax, not after the fifth, nor the others....

Chapter 8

Lost in a Lost World

Sebastian could not hold back his smile, thinking about the first trip he and Gina took through the rip in the curtain, what they called a *tangent*. He felt like Alice chasing a White Rabbit named Gina.

On Tangent 3, they had slept in each other's arms—there beneath the five-leaved palm trees, each long olive drab frond drooping down to the mossy, emerald ground—and did not awaken until the rustling of the feathery blue grasses stirred them.

"What are they?" Gina asked him, yawning. The thick overhead canopy had blocked the morning sunlight, from a large red sun that filled half the sky, and let them sleep on.

"They're alien creatures," he said, "like I told you to expect. We'd better watch out. They could be poisonous. We don't have a first-aid kit with us, you know."

"Poor thing," she chuckled. "It looks comical."

The squat-legged, olive quadruped was vaguely reptilian, but sported white tufts of hair on each of its joints—five joints per leg—and down along its high-crested spine. No horns, no claws, no long fangs could be seen. But they noticed its tail was stubby and bulbous—like a knockwurst, he suggested.

"Funny looking monster, if you ask me," Gina said, nearly

laughing.

"So is the cuddly little critter of Arizona, the infamous Gila monster," he responded. "It has a deadly poison in its bite, you know."

A second, similar creature soon arrived loudly through the brush, and the two circled each other, sneering back and forth, flinging orange spittle at each other, ignoring the two Earthlings observing them. The first one had the thick stubby tail but the second creature seemed to have no such tail. He suggested that it was probably bitten off during a fight. She laughed at that, seeing the two creatures backing against each other.

"Look! They're mating," she exclaimed in a hush.

The two creatures, rear ends pressed together, twisted their heads backwards to stare down each other, the thick orange saliva dripping over their scaly olive chins and running down their lumpy throats, grunting and slithering in frantic passion.

"I wonder what their foreplay is," he asked, amused, and she shushed him.

He followed her gaze, seeing the female start to rise off the thick mossy ground, almost floating, as if being inflated by the pumping effort of the male. As they watched, the female became untethered from him and drifted away. The female creature rose slowly, gently into the air, turning around like a balloon but without appearing to be bloated, sailing upward half-way to the trees' canopy.

"What's it doing?" he asked, cautiously.

The floating female creature burst, completely disintegrating and leaving only a cloud of milk-white spores which the heavy breeze pushed through the forest. The male creature paused to see them off, transfixed, before he went on his way.

He and Gina jumped up, covering their mouths and noses, and crashed through the brush, trying to escape from the drifting spores. Eventually, they came to the edge of the forest. They stopped just inside the cover of the forest, staring out across a wide, treeless landscape of tall yellow grass.

"I don't think that was a real creature," he said, breathing hard.

"Of course they were real," Gina responded.

"Not bursting like that."

"That's how they do it here, I guess. Different worlds, different creatures."

"Different mating habits."

"Aren't you glad I don't float away and explode after you're done with me?"

He grinned. "I'm happy you stick around for next time."

"You expect a next time?"

"If we can get home!"

She slapped his shoulder. "Again with pooh-poohing our adventure!"

He was too tired to argue with her and instead hugged her.

"I think the female creature was a plant," he said. "A plant that's designed to mimic the female of that animal species—"

"To get a male creature to inflate it," Gina exclaimed, "so it can spread its spores! That's actually brilliant!"

"And the male creature is none the wiser."

"He thinks he mated with one of his own kind. He got off, all right—so he goes on his merry way, satisfied. Males are so dumb."

He nodded. "We'll do anything for our females."

"So easily led," said Gina, her gaze fixed on the grasslands outside the forest. "Follow me, Sebastian!"

Looking out on the golden pasture, they spotted a small herd of reddish, antelope-like beasts, three-pronged horns rising from the foreheads. The animals were grazing, unconcerned by them. The grassland seemed safe, the stalks rising only to their knees, so they stepped out of the forest and made a line for another forest far off in the distance.

Crossing the open savanna, the grass became short and brown. They came upon a troop of orangutan-like creatures, their fur distinctively olive-green with flecks of white hair around their faces making them look like Santas.

They passed carefully across the plain, the grass gradually changing to a vivid, olive-green landscape, the tufts shorter now. They noted the line of flying creatures passing overhead—monkeys with bat wings in place of forearms—then proceeded toward the next forest.

With their next steps they came not to the next forest but to another day.

"It happened again," he sighed.

"Tangent four?"

"I presume so."

He looked back over his shoulder, gazing in the direction they had come and found a range of barren mountains rising where a step before had been the thick forest.

They walked through the knee-high red grasses, occasional head-high white flowers on light blue stalks sprouting from the ground. Some of the flowers seemed to be guarded by fist-sized bumblebees in blue and purple stripes. The sky was hot pink.

"Do I need glasses, or does everything look brighter here?" she asked.

"Yes, I think it *is* brighter."

"No, I don't mean brighter," she said. "More intense. It's the colors—everything is so sharp and clear. They aren't brighter shades but they're more distinctly defined and vivid."

"Like a cartoon, almost."

"Exactly! Like some Disney animation."

"We're in a Disney cartoon!"

She took a hop and a skip through the grasses, analyzing their rusty hue. The shade of red was not brighter but it was very brilliant. And there seemed to be no variance in the shade, no fading in or out of that hue. And no shadows.

"And I feel livelier, too," she called to him, dancing away through the grass.

"Come back here, you waskly wabbit!"

He chased after her, playing tag—almost tripping over some olive-green yard-long centipedes hidden in the grass. Eventually he caught her and fell with her to the ground. The grass was high now so, falling down into it, the stalks bent inward and almost closed over them.

"I feel really good here," said Gina, "like I have lots of energy and I can't sit still."

"You must have breathed in some of that reptile's spores," he smirked.

"No, I didn't." She took a deep breath. "Maybe it's the gravity. And the air."

"More oxygen, do you think?"

She bounced up from the grass and the stalks playfully grabbed at her ankles. She tore free and he rushed to follow her.

"Let's get out of here!" he shouted.

The stalks reached for their ankles as they ran, trying to trip them, trying to tie them to the ground. Faster and faster they ran, leaping through the grass, heading for a line of rocks on the edge of a ridge. They would be safe among the rocks. He ran after her, feeling no shortness of breath or fatigue in his legs.

He mounted the rocks one step behind her and as he reached for her hand, he realized he was following her through another tangent, so clearly outlined at the top of the ridge in blazing, flickering lights and clouds of boiling air.

Somehow they had found their way into a cavern on this newest tangent. That cavern led them through the mountain and into another valley which, climbing down and then walking across the narrow gorge and climbing up again, led to another cavern.

"I think I'm finally getting hungry," he said.

"I'm thirsty," said Gina.

They weren't sure where they were, only that they were in the wrong place at the wrong time. Hearing what sounded like falling water somewhere inside the cave, they marched on. Turning the corner, however, they met a group of huge, hairy humanoid beings and were quickly surrounded by them. Before the Earthlings could react, the twelve-foot tall ape-men grabbed the two of them and carried them, cradled in their arms like pets, down other cave corridors. Soon they came to a large central chamber where he and Gina were gently deposited into a pen made of wooden stakes and hemp-like ropes.

"What do you think they want with us?" Gina asked him, climbing to her feet on the pliant, leathery floor strew with something like hay.

He remained in his sitting position, staring up at the many huge eyes regarding them from the sides of the pen. Their hosts were human in the most basic sense of the word: standing upright, hands with opposable thumbs, brownish fur covering most of their primate bodies. But the creatures had no protruding noses, only a double slit between their bulging eyes. Their mouths were vertical slits rather than horizontal, and as he watched them speaking to each other he deduced that their jaws moved back and forth sideways, like clapping hands.

That would be a painful way to die, the thought shot through his consciousness.

"You're not just imagining this, are you?" he asked Gina. "I'm going to wake up soon and it'll be all over, right?"

"I don't think so." For once her face showed fear.

A pair of large hairy hands stretched into the cell, reaching for them. They backed up, and the hands paused, perhaps waiting for instructions.

"Do you think we could make a run for it?"

"A run to where?"

"You memorized the passages when they brought us in, didn't you?"

"No, I thought *you* were memorizing them."

They were both gathered up into the muscular arms of their large-boned hosts and again carried through various chambers of the cave. Along the way they saw other ape-men gathered in family groups, cooking and eating, making or repairing tools, old ape-men and young ones, hairless babies, muscular warriors and chubby maidens. Then came a shaft of daylight—the exit.

Outside, they saw snowcapped mountains not too far away, smelled the odor of roasting meat, and choked on the black smoke coming from a fire over the side of the cliff, and saw below them a gathering of the clan.

"I think we've been invited to dinner," she remarked, but he did not respond, held firmly in the grip of his escort.

At the bottom of the stone ramp, they joined the crowd.

"What's going on?" he asked her, calling across the gulf between their tall masters as each was carried to opposite sides of the plaza.

"It looks like that female, the one tied to the post there," she called back, "is part of some kind of initiation ritual. Or she's being punished for something."

Two male creatures went over to the tied-up female and held her arms behind her. As they watched, a third creature brought a flint axe and quickly hacked off the female's feet, leaving bloody stumps. She never screamed, never uttered a sound, although pain registered in her eyes. When they picked up her severed feet and washed the ground where blood had stained it, she observed their cleaning activity intently, as though checking to be sure they did a thorough job. Then they released her and she dropped to her knees and dragged herself away as the crowd dispersed.

"That'll teach her to run away," said Gina, shivering.

"Not a good time for dark humor!"

"It's how I relieve my stress!"

"I don't think we're in Kansas anymore," he muttered.

The big male in charge of their handlers gestured for the new pets to be brought forward. Gina squirmed in the grip of her escort.

"I hope they don't think I'm a female!"

"They just don't want us to run away!"

"I *want* to run away! Now!"

"What're we gonna do?"

"Down there I see a river. If we could just make it down there, we could get away."

"But how do we get down there?"

"We have to make a run for it. These guys are pretty big. They couldn't keep up with us if we ran full out."

"But they have to let go of us first."

"Any moment now, I think."

"I'm ready."

"Now!"

The instant they were set down they dashed up and scrambled across the plaza, jumping off the cliff, splashing into the river below, and letting the raging torrents carry them away, away to another tangent.

Chapter 9

Interdimensional Voyagers

They sat on the gray, chalky boulder, staring at the fading sunset across a golden sea, streaks of green clouds painted with golds and pinks overhead. The sky seemed more green than the sky of Earth, a detail they could not ignore. The winds were picking up and they were tired, chilled. He wrapped his arm around her shoulders.

"Gina, how are we going to get back?"

"We're not, Sebastian, so shut up and deal with it!"

They had passed through another curtain, another *tangent* doorway, but their clothing had remained soaked by their river escape. The long hike across the afternoon—first the beach then the thick, grassy hills leading up the mountain slope—had not sufficiently dried the rags that their clothing had become. The red halter-top she had worn to the quarry was in shreds and would not stay together as she walked. His shirt was torn beyond wearing, too, even though he had given it to her. His blue jeans had been reduced to cut-offs. Both of them had lost their footwear—her sandals, his sneakers—and their feet had become blistered from walking over the hard ground.

Sitting there rubbing her feet, Sebastian decided to compliment her on how her Bermudas, torn away to little more than bikini bottoms, showed off her legs better. She punched his shoulder.

After the large, golden sun had shown itself for the last time, and the tiny blue sister star spinning around it had slipped below the horizon, they made love. It was slow because they had nowhere to go, and plenty of time to kill. Near the end they were able to forget, for a few precious seconds, that they were actually lost on a lost world.

Afterwards, they calculated the time they had been away from the quarry—if indeed they really were *away* from it and not just in a different dimension of the same physical space. Five days, they figured. And yet they had not eaten or drank substantially. They did not seem to have lost weight, nor were they fatigued beyond what would be normal for their amount of exercise. They took stock of themselves, noticing no difference in their breathing or heartbeat patterns. In every way they seemed to be at some kind of spatial standstill, as though it were only their minds that were traveling and the flesh-and-blood bodies which went along were simply the shells around their consciousness.

"I know we're not really here," he insisted, sitting with her. "I know I'll wake up in the morning, find you beside me, and realize it's all been a dream—a somewhat interesting but otherwise bad dream. It's funny how much imagination can trick a person."

"Go pinch yourself," she said, and he responded by pinching her, which escalated into a pinching duel.

They rocked back and forth against the ground until they called a truce. She kissed him, dubbed him the Dream Master and he called her the Queen of the Western Universe. They were looking west, after all. At least, the suns were setting in that direction, so it *must* be west.

In the darkness that slid over their mountaintop, they saw no moon to light their evening but there was a faint glow against the ceiling of clouds that moved in at dusk.

Curious, they climbed over the rocky mountainside to investigate and were surprised to see the familiar grid pattern of a city, its bright twinkling lines raising their spirits like a long-sought Christmas gift. They sang for joy, jumping enthusiastically and hugged each other. They grabbed their rags from the rocks and dressed themselves as best they could. Heading down the slope toward civilization, they did not stop to worry that it was still on a world that circled a pair of suns.

"Wait!" he called to her as they neared the plain at the foot of the mountain.

"Now what?"

"What if this city is inhabited by beings that aren't human? Won't we kind of stand out? I mean, we need to be careful again— as always."

"Besides, we're nearly naked."

"Let's get a look at *them* before they see us."

"All right, no more surprises—"

"Like back in the caveman tangent," he finished.

"Stop worrying—it's a real *city!*"

"Of some kind."

"Oh, I can't wait to take a really long, hot bubble bath."

"Oh...? Like in a hotel?" he said, then laughed. "Paid for with American dollars? I have a couple in my pocket, if you need them."

She did not honor his remark with a rebuttal.

They hid in bushes alongside a paved road with a metal track running down the center, leading toward the city. A few vehicles passed them, and they knew it was no illusion that they were no longer on an Earth where Ford and Toyota reigned. The vehicles were three-wheeled machines with aerodynamically scooped roofs. Yet they did not whiz down the road like something built for speed. They hummed along what seemed to be a monorail in the pavement.

Later, walking along the road in the dark, they found a signpost.

The lettering seemed alphabetic but neither of them could immediately read it. Gina said it looked Cyrillic, the kind of characters used in Russian, which she had studied in college— along with Latin and Mandarin. He, too, had picked up a couple of foreign languages in school, so between them they could at least manage in six different tongues. Gina pointed out that if she were to pronounce the characters on the sign as the letters they resembled in the Cyrillic alphabet, the sign might form words rudimentarily similar to those of the ancient Indo-European proto-language.

"Really? You studied that stuff?" he asked, unconvinced.

"Yes."

"What's your translation?"

He studied the characters a while, then declared that the sign probably identified the city ahead of them.

"Is it called *Biz-nu-ik*?"

A different set of characters, by comparison, seemed to be numerals, he decided.

"Are you sure?" asked Gina.

He grinned. "Apparently, the population of the city of BIZNUIK is, in this year of 9227, just over 300,000 more-or-less happy citizens."

"Really!" She read the characters again, left to right, ready to correct him.

"Doesn't that make sense?" he asked, pointing at the sign.

"Smart-ass!"

He gave her a kiss.

"Whoa, you sure need a bath, mister!"

"A week of running through tangents will do that to anyone."

She took his hand, squeezed it tightly to stop his train of thought, and mentioned a new possibility. Perhaps they had traveled not through other dimensions but rather through time, into the future of Earth itself. If that were so, she surmised, the characters on the sign were not alien but those of a futuristic Earth language. Maybe the Soviets had conquered the world, after all, she suggested; this could be the next logical development of their language. And the unusual vehicles they saw were merely futuristic cars, nothing too strange.

"I don't think so," he told her, and began lecturing about the different worlds they had crossed. They were too different from the Earth they knew. They could not have been on some futuristic Earth, not with the sights they had observed. The idea that they had returned to Earth at some point in the far future was absurd, he told her bluntly.

"So where are we?" asked Gina with a shrug.

"We are on the outskirts of Biznuik."

"A fun town?"

"Let's hope so."

Closer to the city, they saw people sitting on the side of the road in the back of what could be described as a truck, a larger version of the vehicles seen earlier. They were people, he and Gina saw. Real *people*. Not just some kind of humanoid, but regular Earth-type versions—with dark hair and straight noses, five fingers on a hand—

"They look like us!" he exclaimed under his breath.

"Too much like us," said Gina. "Where are we? I thought we were supposed to be on another planet somewhere."

Although out of fashion by the standards of Sebastian and Gina's 1975 point of origin, the clothing that the people they observed were wearing was not too weird. It looked Roman. Togas and headdresses for the females, puffy-sleeved shirts and leather pants for the men. Gina was already thinking ahead to the new clothing she would buy to replace her rags. He again reminded her that all they had were a few dollars that thankfully were still stuck in his pocket.

"I've got a few of those marbles from the crab-claw ape-men's cave in my pocket, too."

"Why'd you keep them?"

"I collect rocks, don't you remember?"

Realizing the state of their appearance, they hid from the truck people, waiting until the truck-thing moved onto the road and headed off toward the city. Once out of sight, Sebastian and Gina scrounged the picnic leftovers for any food they thought was edible.

"We can't walk into the city like this," she insisted, quickly finished with the snack.

"What are we going to do, then?" He looked up and down the road. "There's got to be some place along the road, somewhere we can get some supplies to help us blend in."

"We need to steal things?"

"Clothing, at least."

They continued walking along the road, heading in the direction of the city, and ducked into a ravine and dashed behind some bushes whenever vehicles passed by them.

As they trudged back out to the road, he stopped.

"There!"

Gina saw the building off the road, dark and apparently abandoned. He led her across a field to the adobe hut. They entered through the ajar front door, made of wood, and he felt for the light switch he expected to be on the wall beside the door.

"Remember where you are, big boy."

"Do they even have electricity here?" he asked.

"They have cars," Gina analyzed, "so they should have electricity."

There was no moon to give them any light so they felt around in the dark for anything that could possibly be useful. They bumped into a table, something like a chair, a cabinet, some things that felt like toys, squeaked like toys, then something like fabric.

"I found some cloth," Gina cried out, "maybe a robe, it feels like."

"Great, now find one for me."

"You've still got your shorts, dear. I need something to cover myself. Don't want to get the local boys all excited."

"Yeah, right!"

"You don't think aliens would be attracted to me?"

He froze, remembering high school. "Of course. Who wouldn't be charmed by your obvious, uh, charms?"

"Good answer, Sebastian."

They continued feeling around the hut. Eventually he found another piece of cloth.

Outside, they tried to see what they had stolen but it was just as dark. They threw the fabrics around themselves like Roman togas, following the suggested fashion of the truck-people. Returning to the road, they continued toward the city, glowing over the horizon.

"We'll just say we were at a Toga party," she offered.

"If people here know what that is!"

Not more than a mile down the road, what felt like a mile, they were picked up by an elderly couple—a human couple, smiling, their eyes full of concern. They pulled up in their three-wheeled machine and called to them. The two Earthlings stepped over to the car. After learning the two did not understand the language, the man tried to indicate that a ride was available. The Earthlings, in turn, told their story by drawing in the dirt with a stick. It was a tale of hiking in the mountains and being attacked by wild animals; in escaping, their clothing was torn to pieces. The elderly couple seemed charitable and waved them inside. They were taken to the next town, which lay over a few more hills.

"I wonder what country we're in," he asked Gina, and the woman turned to look.

"I'm wondering what language they speak," Gina responded.

The elderly couple were entertained, it seemed—as the automated vehicle drove them to their destination without need of direct operation by any person.

Once in the town, the couple took them to their own home and offered the ragged youths some hand-me down clothing. Probably from their grown children who no longer lived with them, Gina considered. Sebastian tried to show their appreciation for the couple's kindness by offering them the prettiest of the colorful stones he had brought from the previous tangent. He thought they would at least see his pitiful attempt to compensate them.

However, the couple seemed to think such a small stone was too much payment for a short ride and a few used clothes. The elderly man dug in the purse dangling from his waist and gave them a handful of oblong golden disks, which seemed like coins. The elderly woman pointed them to an inn where they could use their stones and "coins" to get a room and some food. Then the woman pointed down the street to what was clearly a transportation terminal of some kind, where they could buy tickets to Biznuik, or anywhere else they cared to go.

"Will it take us back home?" asked Sebastian.

In exchange for some of the loose stones, they were able to obtain enough alien money to purchase a few sets of new clothes in the latest alien fashions and a couple of bags to carry them in. They had several fine dinners at a fancy inn, enjoyed an outdoor concert of bizarre musical instruments, and bought plenty of souvenirs. The spherical stones were a half-inch to an inch and a quarter in diameter and looked to them like rough-cut agate or opal, some solid and others striped or occluded, mere children's marbles. However, they were something of value on this new world. Some of the rough stones would still cover them for a week of comfortable living while a particularly bright, perfect, flawless stone might buy them a whole mansion, or more.

"*Gealan*," the elderly man said, pointing to one stone in Gina's hand.

"Cat's eye," she replied.

"Lucky marbles," said Sebastian.

"*Om-jê*," the elderly woman said, as the couple waved farewell.

"I hope that means 'good luck,'" he said to Gina, "because we still need some."

They would soon be walking among the wealthy citizens of this world and experience its vibrant society, feeling proud and privileged, while the simple life of college students on a far away Earth began fading into dim memories.

Chapter 10

The Dissolution of Reality

Sebastian calculated it had been 127 days that they had been on their tangent-hopping adventure, all but six of the days spent on this last world, a planet the locals called *Ghoupallesz*. Now it was coming to an end. The trepidation of a fantasy life come full-circle was hanging on the tips of his fingers, as surely as the brilliant blue and gold and red lights were twinkling behind him, so impatient to welcome him back into the sacred pit of the abandoned quarry cut into the forested hill in the western Missouri countryside, back to the unyielding line of his rightful destiny.

The doorway they had discovered on Tangent 6, the one welcoming them to Ghoupallesz, beckoned. But he hesitated, imagining he was still standing before her as he had several days prior, begging her to join him. It was almost a different person who stood there from the one he had followed through the rip in the curtain into the dream land.

"I'm sorry—I'm really sorry," Gina sobbed, "but I *have* to stay here."

She gave him a handful of reasons that quickly sifted through his fingers. None of them were very difficult for him to counter or explain away. The truth, as he saw it, was that she loved adventure, and this accident was the ultimate adventure for her.

In many ways.

"I really have fallen in love with him," she said, continuing to describe the Ghoupalle man she had met in a bazaar in the city of Siti weeks earlier. "He doesn't know about me. I didn't tell him anything. He believes I am who I say I am, who I want to be. I *am* Ghoupalle now. He loves me. You know this is—I'm sorry, but— this is the chance of a lifetime. I'm sure you can understand. I can't pass it up. I have to stay."

He tried to hide his disappointment.

"Yes, what would you be missing back on Earth?" he agreed out of politeness.

"People working from dawn to dusk," she said, thinking he saw her view of things for once. "Every day the same routine, the same tasks, identical chores, and always the sun sets with exhaustion pressing them into their easy chairs, their children screaming around them, maybe a cold TV dinner to eat, and meaningless sex once in a while. Never gaining on life—not even improving, just hanging on—around and around they go, endlessly—volunteering themselves to be the machinery cogs, the dispensable parts, having some function in society. I'm sorry, but those people are spending their lives on giant treadmills. I can't ever imagine doing that. I never wanted to give in to that destiny or accept it—even with my college degree. I've been putting off that sorry resignation while I looked for something more worthy of my talents and a lot more soothing to my soul. But now I've found it, Sebastian. Here is this great opportunity, unfolding so easily—it's the yellow brick road and I've got to walk on it."

"I know," he sighed, nodding. "I knew it from that first moment when you reached your hand into the lights. You wanted to go— you *had* to go. I understand, Gina. But—"

"Please don't be angry with me."

"I'm not."

"I *will* come back some day. I promise."

"I know you will."

She started to speak, became choked up and just stood staring at him.

"And I'll be waiting for you," he said softly.

"You don't have to wait," said Gina. "I release you from that—from any obligation. It hurts me just as much to let you go, but since you won't stay with me...."

"I know."

"We really do love each other," she said suddenly.

She meant Dassex, the Ghoupalle man, a young entrepreneur in Siti, a city on the eastern continent. He was handsome, tall and broad-shouldered, like most Ghoupalle males. He had a quiet sense of humor that even Sebastian could appreciate, and he was intelligent in a clever, skillful way. Sebastian understood how Gina could fall for him: he was like a grown-up Sebastian, he conceded. However, he knew Dassex was only her security, a protector to fall back on while she went off playing in her new playground. She would not stay with Dassex for long. It was just the experience that was what she wanted.

"I wish you a happy life," he said then. He meant it, although he thought it sounded insincere.

"Thank you."

"Live long and prosper," he intoned with a quiet snicker, trying to duplicate the split-fingered salute of Mr. Spock.

She laughed, wiping away a few tears.

Even now, her smile shone through the cool, shifting dimensions. He regarded her fading image, somehow transported to the Biznuik tangent to mock him in his final moments—as he was stepping through the curtain on the return voyage to their dusty, dirty quarry.

It was the month of *Azit*, early autumn, in the year 1927 on the *Ghoupalle* calendar in use when they arrived on the last tangent of their journey. The six others, distinct worlds each, were quickly forgotten as they assumed their roles in the new society. They learned that most nations had lopped off a full 7,300 years of history, thus bringing the calendar to 1927. The sign outside Biznuik which had read 9227 was based on the old calendar.

Gina picked up the language quickly—she had an ear for it—and taught what she could to him. She embraced the culture, absorbing it as easily as she breathed the air. The fashions and architecture were similar to that of central Europe in the Victorian era, but the people's lifestyle more resembled the optimistic 1920s in America. Their technology, by contrast, seemed as advanced as the late twentieth century in some areas yet were distinctly pre-World War I in other areas.

From Biznuik, they made their way east around the coast of the continent.

In the port city of Selauê, which Sebastian immediately loved, the buildings were tall and wide, topped with grand spires, many of the spires topped with large silver globes. It seemed no building was taller than five floors and there were no windows on the ground floors, only rows of doors. They found more ramps than staircases and the elevator had yet to be invented. Stores employed shopping attendants who followed them around and carried their purchases. They paid with the gold disks or, if the sum was great enough, with one of their precious horde of *gealan*.

Strings of colorful banners crisscrossed the avenues and the streets themselves were lined with bushes and flowers. Men in khaki uniforms and round, shiny blue helmets rode the backs of horse-like beasts with the animals' veiny dewlaps and white-tufted rabbit ears flapping and their rumps striped orange and brown. They patrolled the city and occasionally waved long, hooked staves at vagabonds and loiterers. Boxy vehicles of three and four wheels slowly moved along the streets, jockeying for position at each intersection where a man waved flags to indicate who should go. On the promenades, everyone wore needlessly elegant clothing. No t-shirt and jeans here, Sebastian noted. The women wore full-body garments for the most part, toga or sari-type gowns, while some of the younger ones wore baggy trousers with open slits along their legs and almost breast-baring vests with long feathers attached. And everywhere people walked on thick-soled footgear, some walking with decorative canes, others with seemingly useless flags held high. Children in floppy red hats and ballooning yellow suits bounced rubber balls attached to leashes, which always bounced back to them. A few people carried pets, usually some ferret-like animal or one of several kinds of birds with long, green tails.

The utter newness of the sights pulled their attention along, and Sebastian fell into the role he enjoyed: being the dapper gentleman who Gina, the love of his life, always welcomed to escort her. They fit in just fine strolling through the parks, shopping in the stores, resting on the public beds that were present on many street corners. One time, they were made to wait while a public custodian rushed over to clean the bed before they could climb onto it, spraying some disinfectant, it seemed, then fanning it dry. After the bed was prepared, the man invited them to enjoy their lovemaking, but they did not feel so comfortable doing that sort of thing in such a public location.

This new world, the cosmopolitan cities, the dramatic scenery, and the bright green skies suited Gina immediately. It was familiar enough to be comfortable, yet exotic enough to stimulate their senses. Gina bought books and collected news bulletins she tore off public billboards where the people congregated to read them. She studied the language until she could decipher the general history of the place, and customs of the society.

Their language was not Russian or any other Slavic tongue, as they had suspected at first. The linguist in Gina concluded that the script was *like* Cyrillic but their vocabulary was closer to Germanic languages, though she found many words that were similar to Latin or Sanskrit. He thought certain words sounded French. Definitely of Indo-European origin, she told him, leaving him to speculate which came first. Was it simply coincidence, or was there some connection between this new world and Earth? Was there a universal grammar which allowed different civilizations to independently create similar languages? Such connections, which soon seemed so obvious to her as her studies increased, enabled her to quickly grasp the intricate fundamentals of the Ghoupallêan language and engage in it every day. By the day she met Dassex-Saraxun in Siti, she could speak it sufficiently well that their conversation increased exponentially. The Ghoupalle man thought she was from the nation of Sekuate by her accent. Ironically, that nation on the western side of the vast supercontinent was the origin of the books and newspapers she had studied, as well as the home of Biznuik, their starting point, and Selauê, where they spent a lot of their time.

Meanwhile, their sudden and unexpected wealth from the *gealan* stones brought from the cave of the ape-men on the previous tangent gave them a life of ease: the perfect situation for the gentleman-scientist that Sebastian was, free to pursue the curiosities of the world wherever he found them. There was so much to explore, so many features to try to understand. It was clear from the maps and the books they continually perused that this was a world as rich and varied in arts and history, as detailed in its beauty and cruelty, as any period or place back on Earth—

Back on Earth, he often mused. Every morning and every evening, seeing the two suns rising and setting, he had to remind himself that he was far from home—and might never be able to return there.

Then they delved into the sciences of Ghoupallesz. The people around them were nearly identical to themselves. Their build was tall and slender, hair in the usual places—indeed, some people freely lounged nude in the parks or on the public beds—and ranged in shades of brown to gold, and was generally wavy. Many women wore metal props to hold their braided hair straight up. The people around them had straight noses, square chins, not so high cheekbones, and two eyes, one mouth, five fingers per hand, five toes per foot. Most were attractive.

Perhaps, Sebastian speculated, that had more to do with them visiting the districts where young, vigorous people came and went. There were few who were overweight or underweight, or shorter or taller than average, Gina pointed out. Since Gina was slightly taller than Sebastian, she seemed to fit in better than he did. The visual imbalance between the two of them caught a few eyes, though there was no taunting.

Sebastian and Gina both remarked on the fact there were not many people who showed signs of advanced aging. In fact, everyone appeared rather youthful compared to their official age. An older man shown in a news bulletin was celebrating his hundredth birthday yet he appeared to be only fifty. The lifespans given for many famous people listed in almanacs in the Archive building in Selauê showed lives extending a hundred and fifty or more years—*Ghoupalle* years, that is. Using Sebastian's watch, they were able to calculate the length of a day on Ghoupallesz (29.84 Earth hours). And there were 408 days in a Ghoupalle year—which, therefore, roughly equaled 523 Earth days.

"Too long to wait for my birthday cake," Sebastian had snorted.

Of course, they learned it was not the custom to celebrate birth anniversaries. Mention of that threshold was a trigger for bad luck in the coming year. The seven gods and nine goddesses were listening, obviously!

Still, Sebastian and Gina were able to sit at any outdoor cafe in the seaside city of Selauê and not draw stares. And none of the residents of the planet ever pointed a finger at them or called them "alien." Just in case, they were able to purchase modified "papers" with enough *gealan* should they ever be asked their status.

Selauê had been their second stop, after a week in the port of Biznuik. They traveled east, then southeast, on what the natives called the KOHAX—the acronym of a three- to five-car contraption which operated much like a train between cities, running on some kind of magnetic rail system, yet went more like a bus within the cities. Along the rocky coastline and highland steppe they went, arriving at another port, Selauê. There they enjoyed the larger city's wide, tree-lined boulevards and beautiful parks. From the harborside business district, the view of the twin suns setting across the sea was magnificent. So was the delicious, bountiful seafood in the small, charming restaurants there—the strange fish, unusual shellfish, and bizarre variety of seaweeds. He was certain he gained weight there, but Gina appeared not to notice. They purchased maps in a shop on a side street near an institution that Gina swore looked exactly like one in Paris she saw when visiting there after high school.

On their third day in Selauê, he declared it to be the city where he wished to retire. He repeated that idea once or twice a day to Gina, walking the streets hand in hand—seeing the natives doing similarly—and kissing in the gentle streetlamp glows, breathing in the cool, salty air, and settling into their too-fluffy hammock-like bed on the second floor of the rustic inn along the canal, just over the hill from a high-walled army fortress.

They had been told by the innkeeper that it was a military academy, so Sebastian insisted they should not go near such an establishment, where guards would naturally be more curious of strangers.

"What are they going to do, send us home?" Gina argued.

So he took the dare and, strolling with her through the neighborhood of tall, red brick townhomes, they made the detour past the slate-gray walls and found no other distinguishing features there than a soldier in greatcoat on the back of a striped horse-like beast trotting along the street.

They spread out the map on the floor of their room and surveyed the expanse of the country, the continent, the entire world.

Mostly, it was a huge single landmass, easily divided into four continents by long, high mountain ranges and long inland seas. The continent where they presently were located was called Zissekap. It was on the western side of the supercontinent. It resembled an eagle's head projecting from the larger, squarish landmass. The city of Biznuik, their first destination, sat at the tip of the eagle's beak and Selauê, their current location, was down along the throat. They were surprised to discover that off the coast of southwestern Zissekap across a narrow sea, lay another, separate continent of jungles and high mountains, apparently wild and less developed. Running the length of the main landmass from north to south was a range of mountains they calculated were higher than the Himalayas. The river basin west of that range dwarfed the Amazon. The plateaus to the east of the range approximated the vast steppes of central Asia. Yet it was not Earth, they kept reminding themselves.

They traveled north from Selauê, across the rolling hills and through the mountains to another metropolis, the capital of the nation of Feasfend—at the eagle's eye. It was larger than Selauê and lay at the junction of two great rivers. But they were less impressed with its hard, gritty, industrial landscape, and moved southeast along one river, rising beyond the cataracts and soon came to the city of Peror, settled in a deep, forested valley at the ear of the great eagle. The city was attractive, they thought, yet still they wished to explore more.

Using the only air transportation service that was available— small-fuselaged craft with very long, wide wings carrying six air-sucking engines—they joined the twenty other passengers, paying the kingly sum required, and strapped themselves in for a shaky liftoff. The craft deployed two giant balloons that lifted the aircraft upward from the ground tether and when it was high enough, the aircraft's thruster engines were fired and the aircraft moved horizontally over the city, rising gradually into the sky. It was eighteen hours of flight time—Sebastian keeping time by his Earth watch—and they stopped four times for fuel, finally crossing the ocean—called the 'Great Ocean' by the residents, for lack of any other comparable-sized body of water. On the eastern continent, they approached the lofty tether and again the balloons were deployed. Once attached, arms swung out to brace the aircraft. The passengers stepped onto a gondola which was lowered to the ground using a large parachute contraption.

They had arrived at the city of Ghoupalleme, a metropolis newer and larger than Selauê or Feasfend. To the north they could see a vast, snow-capped range of mountains and Gina wished to see them up close. Before they could visit them, however, she dragged him across the country until they arrived at a river nearly as wide as a sea, both embracing and straddled by the city of Siti. Their huge government buildings occupied several islands in the middle of the slow-moving river. It was a carefree town, designed in hexagonal shape they saw on their map, with the river slicing it perfectly in half from north to south.

Here they paused to reflect on their destiny, locking themselves away in a rented room at the top of an old inn with a good view of the river. They compiled what data they could recall and analyzed what had happened and what was likely to happen. The goal was to realize a way to return to that limestone quarry on an ugly little world off in the Milky Way galaxy they had left a few weeks before. He would not let her out until she came up with a solution.

Finally, when she was about to go mad she begged him to let her walk around. That was when she met Dassex. Never uncomfortable in the company of aliens, Gina found it difficult to remember who she was and where she was from. Looking deeply into the Ghoupalle man's soft brown eyes, however, made her memories vanish. He was, like most people they encountered, youthful in appearance; he said he was seventy yet did not look much older than a college student. As she played and caroused with her new heartthrob and his circle of friends, Sebastian remained in the apartment working through the days and nights, desperate to return to the dull routine he had once loathed, eager to see if anything had changed, and whether anyone had noticed him gone. Would life back on Earth have passed him by? The results he came to were not what he had been looking for.

The Theory had changed, he discovered. And because of that, new methods had to be employed. He tried to explain it to her, and she pretended to listen, but he could see that her mind was elsewhere, continuing to play, to journey, to experience.

So he summarized it for her: "It was never the machines, never the sonic vibrations, that tore the curtain. It was already torn. It had to be a natural phenomena that already existed. We saw it because we were looking for it. We found it only because we were so intent on focusing our equipment on that spot. The tear was always there; we just needed to see it. As it turned out, it was better that we ended up having to go to the quarry at night. In the daylight, we wouldn't have seen the lighting effects that revealed it to us."

"But can you just look anywhere and see another tear like that?" she asked, breaking from her daydream.

"That's what we'll have to do," he replied, encouraged by the return of her attention. "Given the odds on the number of solar systems with planets in the universe being one in a billion and still leaving the number of planets having intelligent life at a billion or so, then it seems that if one such tear of the curtain is at that old abandoned quarry then there should be other tears around the world. Around Earth, I mean. And around the universe, in or on many other, different worlds."

"The ancients always told about passages to other worlds," she spoke up. "That's where some of their gods came from—from those other worlds. Or where they went after death...away to those other worlds."

"That's right, Gina. Suppose the ancient Greeks' Hades wasn't some mythological place but a *real* one—a real world that existed through a tear in the curtain like the one we found, a real passageway to the Otherworld, where the dead would go, possibly to live again."

"And how about the Egyptians? What do you think all those

pyramids were really built for? To bury some tyrant king? To mark the landing pad for some ancient spacemen? I think not! What could be so important to demand that kind of manpower? I say they were built to *cover* an exposed tangent."

"An *exposed* tangent?"

"What else would you call it?" She closed her eyes a moment. "Tangents are everywhere, but certainly not every one is available to us. When one is found, it has to be marked." Her eyes opened, focused on him. "We were lucky, you know. We could've searched all of our lives for a gateway to the stars and never found one. Many people do."

"Gateway to the stars, huh?" He rubbed his chin. "A *stargate?*"

"Is that what you want to call it?"

"I guess not. That sounds too science-fiction, Gina. Besides, I think that word's been used before. We can't use that term."

"A gateway to the stars is a *stargate*, dammit, and we'll call it whatever we want to call it. We're the explorers here. Whatever we discover they have to name after us."

"A Sebastian-gate? A Talbot? You know, like *robot*? Oh, never mind."

"Definitely not."

He sighed. "Okay, it's a Stargate. *The* Stargate."

"No, *a* stargate. It can't be the only one."

"But if a stargate links two *stars*, then you'd burn your ass off!"

"Then how about *planet* gate?"

"How about Watergate?"

"Point taken. Okay, we'll call it an Interdimensional Tangent. How's that?"

"Much better, Gina. More scientific, less surreal. We could even call it IDT for short. How's that? Talbot and Parton discovered eight IDTs during the month of August in 1975. Sound good?"

"Not bad."

"Maybe people will actually believe us someday. Maybe they'll build monuments to us, and to our discoveries."

"We'll have our own pyramid!"

"Perhaps the ancient people here on Ghoupallesz built monuments like the pyramids to mark their exposed tangents."

"But where are they?" asked Sebastian.

"Beats the heck outta me! Do you think you can possibly find another one here?"

"I want to find the one that goes to the central chamber of the Great Pyramid in Egypt. Hah!—I'd probably end up in a stone cell full of rotting jungle mush in one of those Mayan pyramids in Guatemala, for all of my luck."

"You're luckier than you think."

"I guess we'll have to return to Biznuik," he sighed. "We'll have to try to find that same tangent—your stupid *stargate*—again. And then go back through each of those other five tangents we passed through on the way here. How can we ever find all of them? And how do we keep away from all the claw-mouthed ape-people and the spore-balloon lizards and the six-legged llamas?"

"I don't know."

"But we have to try," he said.

She was touched by his determination, and saddened by his solemnity.

"We have to try to find a new tangent," he said. "Or make one. We need to tear the curtain ourselves. We need to be able to summon that same super-intense concentration we had at the quarry. If you could've seen your eyes, Gina, the fire in your eyes that night. We need to find that same highly focused mental energy that we built up naturally during our big experiment."

She smiled politely, laid her hand on his. "I know it can be done."

"But where it will lead, I don't know."

"That's part of the experience, isn't it?"

She almost laughed then but he was not amused.

"I have to get back for college," he said, raising his voice to show his seriousness. "I have a career to begin. I have social security checks due to me in forty years or so, and a car with payments no doubt overdue by now, and my parents—they've got to be calling the police to search for us. There's plenty of reasons to return."

"I know...." She lowered her eyes.

He spoke quietly again, beginning to realize that the inevitable was upon him. "This kind of adventure can be fun, Gina. I agree. And it sure is educational. And it's certainly of scientific interest—though no one would publish a paper on it unless we could prove it. And we can't—not yet. But as long as we don't know we can return to our point of origin, we'll always be thinking about it. We have to *find* the way back—and actually *go* back."

She was silent.

"You're going back?" she asked.

He glared at her.

"What do you mean by that? That's what we've been talking about, isn't it? What about you? Don't you *want* to go back?"

She smiled, warmly, sympathetically.

"I'm happy here. I left nothing on Earth, nothing I really need. I like it right here, the way things are. This is my home now. This is where I want to be."

"We have to make sure we *can* go back, Gina."

"We can." She pursed her lips, waited a moment. "*You* can, anyway."

"You're not going to try? You won't help me?"

She gazed into his eyes, thinking it over.

"I'll help you go back," she said, "as much as I can, but when you finally tear the curtain and step through it"—she paused to choose her words—"then I will have to step back from it. I won't go leaping after you, Sebastian."

"So that's it?"

She saw his disappointment and she rushed to him, cupping his face in her hands.

"Oh, I love you! I really do," she cried. "I don't want anything bad to happen to you." She hugged him tightly. "You've got to understand that I love adventure more than anything. I really am crazy about this new life I've found here. I know it sounds hokey—I'm not playing the role I was born to play but, dammit, why can't a woman be the explorer once in a while?"

"You can be," he sighed. They kissed. Upon parting, he added: "Good luck."

"And good luck to you, too, Sebastian."

And have I had good luck? Sebastian pondered, sitting on their 'love' rock at the side of the quarry, gazing up at a tired, cloud-streaked moon.

Back in his apartment, locked in his desk drawer, he kept Gina's farewell letter, written many years later when, weary of such a long life on Ghoupallesz, she was planning to commit suicide. It was delivered to him by another Voyager they met named Renée. Then Gina decided to go on living, apparently, and went to a new time and place.

He remembered being angry when he first read it—slapping off the TV, disappointed with the triviality of the events happening around him.

I don't belong here, the letter began. He repeated the words.

The letter was dated 1442. The month of *Gamau* was in autumn, though she was living in the tropics at that time. The date was the twenty-second, in the last week of the month. Having no moon by which to divide the calendar, each artificial period consisted of five weeks, each of five days.

He smiled as the flood of images saturated his mind, even as the moonlight shone on his back, the swaying trees forming a shadowy dance against the limestone walls.

Of course, he had met Gina again—several times, in fact—in years dated later than 1442. In his twisted, self-abused mind, he realized that meant she had been traveling in future eras, all of them prior to her retreat to the *earlier* year where she decided living forever was no longer fun. To change time zones, she'd have to return to Earth—their quarry, perhaps—and go again through a different tangent leading to a different place or time. She wasn't really dead. She lived on in some other time period, hopping around as easily as some jet-setter on Earth flew from resort to resort. He remained hopeful of meeting her again in a different time, on some future trip, before the time of her real, physical death on that day in 1442. The touch of the parchment in his hands had given him strength.

He expelled a long sigh, remembering Gina's elegant full signature on the last page, imagining the dot of the *i* to be a single tangent in the vastness of the universe and how, if he tried really hard, he might be able to pry it open and find her smiling back at him. She had pointed out that everywhere a person could stand or sit, see or touch on Earth, on land, in the air, in the sea, were *tangents*—any point on a circle or sphere. He considered that tangents were also any points that could be imagined in a three-dimensional map of space. Not the so-called *outer space*, which was minutely explored, but all *space*—around and between, among and inside every single bit of matter in the universe from the largest supernova to the smallest slice of an atom's quarks. And every such tangent had another side, or *many* other sides, each acting and reacting in multi-dimensional space. Any point was a doorway to any other point—in theory.

In practice, however, any point was *potentially* a doorway to other points, yes, but as they discovered, there was a tendency, like gravity, toward particular alignments favoring a connection to one point over others. A viable atmosphere tangent would not connect to some toxic atmosphere tangent they could not breathe, for example. That was the reason they continually returned with ease to the same time/tangent, the same plane on Earth.

With his own subsequent visits, he came to understand that anything was possible there—but you seldom got what you wanted or what you asked for, he mused.

Gina must have known that, too. With their initial adventure they had become cosmic soul mates, partners in the Great Experiment, the Keepers of the Secret *Scheisse*, the Wisemen of the Western Universe, the two Travel Agents *par Excellence*—for themselves, at least. There could be no animosity between them if they were going to be able to move freely within the fluctuating space-time continuum, no matter who they met and had relations with. He agreed. After all, he never expected he would ever find anyone who might take her place. He believed that Gina would always return to him, like a human boomerang. They kissed like the lovers they used to be and pledged that 'soul-mate' would always outrank 'spouse' or 'lover'—no matter what world they happened to be on.

Chapter 11

Lovers and Friends

Sebastian sensed something like the approach of a thunderstorm as he sat on the rock in the quarry, waking him from the memory-trance he had slipped into. For a second he thought he was still in his apartment. Someone was knocking at the door, and he could not resist opening it. Perhaps it would be Gina, come to be with him.

Light rain began to fall so he left the quarry.

Gina....

He could not deny that what he felt pulling him to the quarry was most likely his Long Lost Love calling to him across the universe, once more needing his help. He choked back a laugh, recalling how much they both enjoyed irony. He saw himself in a flash of distant lightning as one of those science-fiction heroes in the books he had read as a teenager, all of them ordinary men snatched from their mundane existences to do battle in exotic, far-off worlds with sword and/or sorcery!

If Gina needs me....

"I have to go," he muttered, making his way down the gravel path to the road. He walked to the 7-Eleven, clothes wet, bought a Dr Pepper, and got into his car.

As he drove slowly, absently through the dark streets back to his apartment, he thought of that first lonely night when he returned, but without Gina....

The night had been unexpectedly warm when he first stepped back into the old quarry. But the sky above was full of stars that night, the moon a gray disk among wispy clouds streaking the horizon. The world around him was quiet and serene. He paused where his first step landed, feeling the energy rushing through him, the strange sensation like lightning was leaving his body. He felt the solidity of the ground beneath him, as though he had been at sea for a year. It was real. It was home. He was back.

Then he had turned his attention to their equipment. After 127 days, he was certain it would be destroyed by any rain that fell and the hot August sunshine that would beat down on it. Glancing around, he panicked, for a moment thinking he might be on yet another tangent, one which so cruelly resembled his real home. Then he found the equipment: dirty, spotted from a rainstorm, looking unusable. But it was still in place after all that time, and he felt relief.

He had chuckled uneasily, not believing he had truly returned, not believing he had truly ever left the quarry.

Leaving Gina in Siti, he had returned to the place outside of Biznuik where they had first arrived. He envisioned the walls of the quarry, remembering the feel and scent and sight of everything there, avoiding any thought or image of the other worlds they had traversed, concentrating on only the one point of origin as he began tickling the air in front of him—until he felt the invisible spot where energy swirled. He gently poked his finger into it, thinking of a dozen metaphors, dismissing each of them. The spot became a rip, a rift in the wall that gradually gave way. The curtain was tearing, and when he had rent a wide enough opening, he lifted his foot and stepped straight through to the quarry.

How long had it been? He never contemplated that there might be any time difference between the two worlds. He imagined that weeks had passed on Earth and everyone would be looking for the two of them. And yet, it seemed like it was still summer. Because they had never expected to be able to travel as they did, they made no preparation for their return. He had no money now—no dollars, just a few *gealan* stones—and he could not remember where he'd left his car keys, or if he had even brought them. And the clothes he now wore were alien fashions—a little Star Trekkie, perhaps, but serviceable, he decided. It did not matter. He still had to walk home—most of the two-mile distance was through the dark countryside where he could hide whenever headlights approached. For the last few blocks into suburbia he would have to try to keep out of sight.

As he came upon the 7-Eleven store, he saw the parking lot was empty, no customers inside. But he had no money. Hungry and thirsty, he was also curious. He pushed himself inside, the door hitting his backside as he paused there, feeling the stares of the clerk and another customer buying cigarettes.

"Halloween's a ways off, ya know," the man chuckled.

"Costume party," he responded quickly, trying to act as though everything was perfectly normal, the English words surprisingly uncomfortable in his mouth.

But everything wasn't normal. He continued to feel nervous twitches of energy running errantly through his body, strings of electric snakes wriggling up and down his arms and legs and back. The sensations, ticklish and cold, were the electricity still trying to find a way out of his body. And the colors were different—but only because he had been looking through a tinted atmosphere the past few months, seeing the alien sky in shades of green instead of blue. He felt thinner, yet every step he took seemed heavier to him.

"So, what'll it be for ya tonight?" the clerk called to him as the other customer exited.

He was walking up and down the aisles unable to make up his mind.

"A newspaper," Sebastian decided.

"They're up here."

He returned to the counter, pulled the top paper from the rack. Holding the newspaper in his hands, tightening his grip to help the electric spasm pass, he fixed his eyes on the date. It was the same year, the same month, he saw. But it was now *two* days later than when they had gone to the quarry. Only *two* days had passed! And yet he had lived 127 days on that other world.

Suddenly, he felt like he held a great secret and if he let down his guard others would be able to see it written on his face. He turned away quickly, stuffing the newspaper back into the rack. He circled through the store again.

"Excuse me," he spoke up, the store clerk watching his every move closely. "I seem to have lost my wallet—this damn costume, no pockets, you know? Could I use your phone? It's a local call."

"Can't let you use it," said the clerk. "There's a phone outside."

Rather than waste time pleading, he stomped out of the store, thinking there was a chance someone forgot their change. But when he picked up the receiver of the pay phone and jumped back from the spark, he found the sidewalk becoming littered with quarters, dimes and nickels. He gathered them up, chose a quarter to insert into the phone, and dialed his friend Jason's number.

"Jason!" he shouted into the phone.

"Hey, dude!" his friend shouted back. "Where the hell you been? Your mom and dad's been calling me."

"I thought they might."

"They're going crazy!"

"I know, I know."

"So where were you?"

"The other side of the universe," Sebastian replied.

"What?"

"Can you pick me up?"

"Where?"

"You know where."

As he waited, he imagined his mother asking him where he'd been and he would say with Gina, and his parents would quiz him about his behavior. *She's a dear girl*, his mother would say, *but did she lead you on? Did she pull you into temptation?* He was supposed to be a good boy, study hard, start a good career, meet a nice girl. To cover his absence, he was prepared to say she had tempted him. "I resisted as much as I could," he planned to say. Then he would go to his room and think about the 127 days they were together. And the last day together.

The candy red Mustang roared into the parking lot of the 7-Eleven, the engine shaking the pavement, The Moody Blues' *Question* blasting out the open windows.

"Ready to go?" Jason called out over the music.

A year later Sebastian would guide his friend to the other side....

* * *

Returning home at the edge of dawn, he wondered why the lights were on in his apartment. He might have forgotten to turn them off when he left for the IRS service center, he decided, but he definitely recalled his stereo had not been playing. Considering the possibility of a break-in, he took the baseball bat from the trunk of his car and stood outside his apartment door, listening. The door was not shut tightly, he noticed, so he slowly swung it open, ready to go to bat.

He stepped inside and made his way to the grunting noise in the kitchen, ready to swing for the bleachers—and discovered two frantic lovers violently engaged on the floor.

"Michael? Tammy?"

Seeing the empty bottle on the kitchen counter, he knew what had happened.

"What're you doing here?" Sebastian the Professor shouted, trying to startle them into halting their activity. They did not seem to hear him and did not slow their movement.

He got down on his hands and knees beside them. Their eyes were locked on each other, lips pressed tightly into what must have been the world's longest kiss. He repeated his question more emphatically. Tammy's eyes bent toward him, noticing him for the first time. He could see the frightened, astonished look in her eyes which told him their actions were not their choice. They had already had enough and wanted to stop. But it was beyond their power.

"What are you doing here?" he asked again, flashing back to that summer with Gina at the quarry when the grizzled old owner of the property had come upon them and asked the same question. Gina, busy with the electronic equipment, had simply responded, "Don't bother us, we're scientists!"

He regarded his naked, sweaty co-workers, wondering if they

were conducting their own sordid experiment.

It had been over a year since he had last used any *moussalaganê*. The thin brown liquid was distilled from the cactus-like *moussala* plant of the desert regions of Typeg, southeast across the savannas from Sekuate. Taken in small amounts—a fingertip's coating would do—it slowed the aging process. In greater quantity it produced an extended range of sensations during sex. A single drop was about maximum dosage for a single evening. Even using such small amounts, it should not be consumed more than two or three times a month. That made the elixir something to be savored, used for a special occasion. Those who overindulged, however, could find their bodies permanently harmed. Sex organs could become too strained to function normally. Continued abuse might result in the inability to function at all, and beyond that stage victims awaited a long, painful death. Those were the warnings for Ghoupalles; those from Earth who dared indulge were more easily affected, and more easily damaged by the drug's properties.

There was, unfortunately, nothing in the drink itself—taste, bouquet, or appearance—that would hold back the naïve, unsuspecting consumer.

He looked at the opened bottle, tried to remember how full it was, calculating their dosage, wondering how long the effects would last. If they drank the whole bottle, divided evenly between them, they might continue for days. He considered medical treatment. That would lead to endless questions, he knew, and he had been interrogated enough about his exotic affairs. That was one reason he preferred the quiet, simple, low profile of a government office worker at the IRS Service Center.

So he tried for an hour to pry them apart, but their hips were firmly locked, their bodies running on automatic, their minds hijacked as the sexual storm thundered on. He could hardly get a grip on their profusely sweaty skin. When he could not stand it any longer, he called for an ambulance.

* * *

Sebastian reported to work the next night as though nothing out of the ordinary had happened, but he immediately got an inquiry from Joyce about his two nights of sick leave.

"I'm feeling much better, thank you," he replied, grabbing the next stack of tax returns and sitting down at his desk in the corner.

"Did you hear about Michael and Tammy?" Eun-Sook, the Korean girl, asked him as they began the first break of the night.

"No, what?" he asked.

"They were skipping out of work Sunday night and they were in a big car wreck."

"No kidding."

Later, Kate, the plus-sized work leader of the section, pushed a pair of cards under his nose and stuck a pen in his ear.

"You wanna sign these cards for Michael and Tammy?" she said, and the edge in her voice did not please him.

"Sure," he answered and took the cards from her.

"Then pass 'em on to Felix," she snarled.

As he signed and passed, he listened to the row of young women—Latisha, Lamona, and Lafiona—talking excitedly about the crash, and modulating effortlessly to the fender benders their boyfriends had experienced—those debonair fellows sitting in their Cadillacs outside the service center at dawn when the shift ended, speakers beating like earthquakes.

Priscilla, however, was different. He conversed with her once in a while. She was always surreally positive about everything despite being practically born in the service center.

She signed the cards and passed them back to him.

"I already signed," he said.

"Awright," she sang, then called Kate to come over and get them. "I got work ta do here, ya know. Don't need to be signin' nothin' for nobody!"

At lunchtime, Joyce announced that they would take up a collection to buy flowers for their two wounded colleagues, to be purchased by Kate. Fat Ken, who never contributed money to special collections or food to department pot-luck dinners, broke with his tradition and slipped a dollar into the envelope. The

Professor, as his contribution, made a show of putting in a ten. He had, however, already made up their lost wages from his bank account and took care of their emergency room costs with cash.

Chapter 12

The Balance

Home after another delightful shift, Sebastian sat back in his lounger, the morning news on the television a blur as his memories satiated him.

The instant he had stepped back onto his familiar tangent in the quarry to the east side of Independence, Missouri, Earth, the whole experience began to play with his mind. He knew it was not a dream, yet he could not quite accept that it was real. He sure had gone somewhere; he had souvenirs.

But where was Gina? He called her parents' phone. He wanted to explain. They thought she had returned to college in St. Louis. He called her number there but no one answered.

He had to tell his friend Jason something to alleviate suspicion, so he said he had been kidnapped by bikers, taken to the Ozarks, and forced to tell them stories. His friend laughed and knew it was a lie. It would be difficult from that night forward to keep from telling lies. The truth made no sense. Those who had never experienced the wonders of passing through a tangent, a doorway to another world, and then somehow returning could never understand the truth.

"We went to a party," he said as his next excuse, "and things got pretty wild. I didn't know where I was for I don't know how long. Then I woke up in a ditch by the side of the road."

That sufficed for a while.

Earlier in the summer, it could have been true. He and Gina did go to some parties, and people did get wild. He was introduced to a girl Gina's age named Aurora Fawn Cosgrove, the daughter of hippies, but he only allowed himself to be friends with her, saving himself for the love of his life, Gina.

After he had returned alone through the tangent, he kept to himself for a week, thinking through all that had happened, trying to understand the process. He made notes, then filled in the notes. He needed to record what he had experienced before he forgot any of it. Thinking about everything Gina had said to him, he wondered if he could go through the tangent using only the powers he used to return to Earth; in other words, do it without the equipment. Twice he hiked to the quarry, examining the place in broad daylight under the blazing August sun but found nothing unusual. He could not locate the tangent in the bright afternoon light, of course, though he calculated its location: half-way from the center of the quarry to the southeast edge, three-quarters of the distance from the cliff out to the big stone at the opposite edge, and about the height of his hip. He found a stick and pushed it into the clay at that spot—a point in three-dimensional space that would have to be pried open.

Then he ran into Fawn in Independence Center, the new shopping mall that had opened a year before in what once had been pasture and forest between the 7-Eleven store and the road leading to the quarry. Tall and slim, with short-cropped red hair, Fawn had a pretty smile when their eyes met outside Macy's. She recognized him and seemed glad to see him. They ate lunch and chatted a while in the food court. When she had to leave, she invited him to another party and he said he would be there. His reaction confused her.

"Are you two broken up already?" she asked. To her, of course, it had only been a month.

He thought for a moment, searching his feelings. Gina, the love of his life, had not returned with him. She had found another lover.

"Yeah, I guess so," he replied in a voice that was so sad Fawn hugged him.

After a couple of hours of loud rock music, crazy drunken idiots acting rude, and the hot, muggy evening full of mosquitoes, he suggested they leave. He drove them out the country road past the quarry, parking before a dark side path in the shadows of the forest. He took her hand and led her back to the quarry entrance, telling her there was a magical spot at the top of the hill, up the gravel trail through the trees. She was excited, giggling, fiddling with her tube-top, and told him she was waiting for a chance to spend some time with him.

"So, to make a long story short," he told Jason later, "I concentrated on the spot, there in the dark, and it opened just like before and we stepped through."

"To where?"

"The other side." He watched his friend thinking. "To negative space—the opposite of what we know as Earth."

"But how?"

"It doesn't matter," he said sharply. "We were in some jungle at first but then we saw it was an island. And there was a group of women there—skimpily clad, of course. Well, it was one big party, and Fawn and I were taken back to their village, and we were given some sweet brown liquid, a kind of fruit juice, and it almost knocked us out. It made us super horny. In fact, I got so wasted—"

He stopped, seeing his friend grinning. Maybe he was stoned again.

"Go on," said Jason, glassy-eyed.

"I was going to say that we all had sex. Fawn and me. Fawn and those women. Those women and me. I know you don't believe me. Well, it was good at first, then it got to be too intense. Actually quite horrible. So we escaped. We didn't want to become, well, something like their sex slaves, you know. We ran to the beach, took their boat, and sailed across the sea—six days—over to the other coast, which was some kind of desert. In fact, it looked like the same kind of place where Gina and I landed during that first trip of ours. It had the grey, soap-flake stuff."

"That's far out, dude," said Jason, lifting the bong again.

"We hiked inland about a day and we found a thing like a temple. Four pillars on a stone platform, stone roof overhead. It looked like it was carved from a single huge rock. Right there in the middle of this desert. In the center was a pedestal about chest high, and it had a huge gemstone on the top, about the size of my hand. The stone was dark blue but when we put our hands on it, it glowed yellow, then red. And get this: as it glowed, we felt some kind of energy surging through us and we started to see different scenes outside the four pillars—a view of the quarry! Yeah, like we were right back home! So we kept focusing on that image and then stepped off the platform into the quarry—right onto the clay at the center of the quarry. When we looked back, there was no temple thing anywhere, just the forest on the other side of the quarry."

Jason had not lost his grin. "Then what happened?"

Sebastian felt that he had been talking for nothing.

"She thanked me for a lovely evening and I drove her home. What do you think? She was freaked out!"

They had been away 3.51 Earth days, he had calculated, even though they had spent 32 days on the other world. It didn't matter in the waning days of summer when nobody had to be anywhere. His college did not begin for another week, but he did feel guilty for being with Fawn, wanting to be with Gina more.

And the temple-thing! He had instinctively known what to do once he stepped onto the platform. It seemed as though someone had discovered the special properties of that place and decided to institutionalize it by building a *place*, marking the transformation point, around his tangent. *His tangent!* He felt proud of his discovery. Yet who would have, could have built that Stonehenge rip-off? Someone from the future? Residents of that world? Other interdimensional voyagers? He didn't know, didn't really care, as long as the possibility existed for him to return and find Gina. Then he would bring her back home, no matter how much she protested, and they would be together forever.

Smiling to himself, he moved from the lounger to the bedroom. He removed his clothes, switched on the fan, and flopped on the bed. As he drifted off to sleep, the sounds of the day dulled by the hum of the fan, he thought of Gina.

❋ ❋ ❋

A few nights later—in fact, the evening of the first day that he skipped his weekly meeting with Dr. Liebowitz—Sebastian passed the front row of desks in his section of the service center as usual after the lunch break but bucktoothed Beverly looked up from her work and spoke directly to him—for the first time in history.

"Hear yer gettin' married again," she said. Bubbling spittle slid off her front teeth.

He turned hesitantly. "What...?"

"Aintcha gettin' married next week?"

"What makes you think that?"

She quickly looked around, searching for spies, lowered her voice. "Priscilla told me."

He went to Priscilla, who turned off her Walkman and bent her chubby face up at him.

"I never told her no such thing," said Priscilla.

"Then why would she say something like that?"

"How should I know?" said Priscilla, waving her hand dismissively. "You know she's weird. She's a psycho."

"Perhaps a psychic."

"Well, just leave her alone."

"I've been trying."

"Can't keep away from her, huh?" Priscilla laughed loud enough that Lafiona had to ask her what was so funny, followed by Latisha and Lamona.

Sitting at his desk in the corner, facing the wall, he listened to their delighted squealing, now certain that one of the two who had broken into his apartment and read his letters had divulged their contents to the unworthy denizens of the service center.

He went to Michael at the next break.

"I swear I didn't say a word," Michael insisted, raising his hand to take an oath.

He motioned Michael away from his desk. That was easy. Michael was always willing to get up and socialize. They went to the northeast canteen, empty at night.

"I didn't tell Tammy anything," Michael said, sitting at a table. "She was the one reading your letters. I was only looking for, um, criminal records."

"Criminal records?" Sebastian the Professor shook his head at the odd tales these strange people could tell. "What criminal records?"

"I dunno, that stuff about you killing one of your students."

He threw his arms up in shock. *"What?"*

"Didn't you tell Tammy about the time you were a teacher, how you got fired 'cause you, ya know, did some *damage* to one of your students. After the student got off for...well, you know what he did...."

Staring at Michael a moment, he wondered if it were all a game. Perhaps he was the target of some elaborate plot to drive him insane that all of his enemies had cleverly concocted. It seemed to be working.

He blinked.

"I don't know what you're talking about."

"You don't have to be insulting," Michael said with a grunt. "I said I was sorry, didn't I? I'm sorry—again. How many more times I gotta say I'm sorry?"

Sebastian shook his head, began pacing the room.

"It was a crazy idea and I'm sorry I even thought of it," said Michael. "You know, it was actually Tammy who wanted to—"

"Shut up," snapped the Professor.

"Alrighty—"

"Silence!" He stared at Michael. "You decide to break into my apartment—just like that? And you were looking for criminal records? court papers? illegal drugs? What were you thinking? What do you think I do for a living? My goodness, Michael, I should have just called the police and have both of you arrested for breaking and entering."

Michael's face was pale. "But you didn't."

He waited for the silence to become uncomfortable, then: "No, I didn't."

Michael looked down. "Thanks, man."

"You guys have enough trouble to deal with without dealing with the police."

"I know," said Michael softly.

He expelled a great sigh, returning to the table where Michael sat.

"I'm not mad at you, merely disappointed you'd try something so stupid. I don't have any idea where you'd get an idea like that. I'm curious what you were looking for. Obviously not what you found." He lost his angry scowl. "But you had a good time anyway, didn't you?"

"Man, I *swear* we were, like, *sucked* into each other!" Michael, jumped up. "We really couldn't stop! We *wanted* to stop! We *tried* to stop! We were like, like our bodies were hijacked! What the hell *was* that shit, anyway?"

Sebastian couldn't repress a chuckle.

"That's funny to you?" asked Michael.

"You shouldn't drink something you can't identify. Especially if you find it in a stranger's house. It could've been cleaning solvent. You're lucky it was just fruit juice. And you were so clever, thinking I'd never notice, you pushed aside the ones in front and took the bottle of the pure juice. You drank the concentrate."

Michael nodded his head quickly. "Yeah, well, the joke's on me, huh?"

"It sure is, and I'm truly sorry for you."

"And I guess, well, thanks for calling the ambulance."

"Sure."

"So now what?" asked Michael, stuffing his hands in his pants. He grimaced at the pain in his groin. "Are we, like, even now? Or do I have to go on apologizing every time I see you?"

"I don't want you breaking into my home again."

"Don't worry, I won't."

"That's good to know." He smiled sincerely at Michael. "I don't keep score like that, where we have to be even, or someone owes something. The world doesn't work like that. I'm going to forget about this, but—"

"Thanks, man."

"But you won't be able to forget about it," said the Professor. "I'm not talking about guilt. I'm talking about the effects of your drug abuse." He nodded at Michael's unhappy crotch. "You're still feeling the effects, right?"

"Yeah, it hurts."

"Swollen?"

Michael sighed. "Yes."

"It'll get worse."

"How worse?"

"Difficult to say. The worst case scenario is that it eventually falls off."

Michael instinctively looked down. "Shiiiiiit."

"Yes. Like that."

"What can I do about it? The doctor in the hospital said put some ice on—"

"And you went to all that effort just to see some court documents?"

Michael laughed insanely. "Yeah, man, that's it."

"I keep things like that in a lockbox at my bank." He watched Michael frown. "Really, I don't know what the hell you're talking about, Michael. I've never killed any student. I've never killed anyone. On Earth. And I wasn't a teacher very long, either."

"Then why would you tell Tammy stuff like that?"

"I didn't tell Tammy stuff like that. You did—or somebody did—probably trying to make me out to be some sociopath."

"Tammy said you told her."

"She must have heard me wrong."

"Come on, now!" Michael grimaced, shifting uncomfortably, feeling pain again. "Tell the truth, Perfesser, what're you really into? Who *are* you? What kinda business you into? Drugs? Hey, I won't tell none of those assholes back there. But it's driving me crazy. And that juice we drunk—is there any cure, or some kind of antidote? There's gotta be. You gotta know something about it. Where'd you get it, man? I saw your papers, and your army uniform, and all those little marble things in your closet. I know about all of it—and about Gina. I know about Gina—and Linda— and the 3-D pictures, and all your—"

"All right, all right," said the Professor, waving a hand to stop him.

"You gotta give me the antidote, Perfesser—or I'll never be able to be a father! You gotta help me get back to normal! You got to, Perfesser!"

He sat down in the chair across the table from Michael. The expression on Michael's face was the most anxious he had ever seen, waiting desperately for the answer.

"I wish you would stop calling me Professor," he said, "I really hate that."

"Okay, done." Michael regarded his colleague, waiting. "What's your real name?"

He chuckled. "You don't know my name?"

"No, you never said." Michael shrugged. "And I'm not so nosy I'd come up to you and ask."

"Yet you'd break into my apartment looking for some fictional crime story?" He burst into laughter.

"Goddamn, I'm *sorry*, already!"

"Apology accepted."

Michael studied him. "So what *is* your name?"

He looked directly into Michael's eyes. "My name is Set."

Michael paused, thinking about it.

"It's actually my adopted name. That makes it my real name—but it's not the name I was born with. A dear…um, friend gave it to me."

"Wait a minute," said Michael, holding up his hand. "You really don't have to tell me any more. I was just jiving you. Forget it. I sure don't wanna be responsible for maybe telling somebody some of it sometime in the future, ya know. I mean, I don't wanna know anything that'd get me in deep shit. I don't want you coming to kill me 'cause I spilled the beans, okay? That's enough, Perfesser. Sorry, I mean Set. Mister Set, whatever."

He stood, thought a moment, then went across the room, Michael's eyes following him.

"There's nothing special or unusual about me, I want you and all of your cronies in the service center to know. I'm single. I live alone. You probably noticed that during your visit. And I have just about two friends on the face of the Earth. One of them has already died—sort of—but she might still be alive—somewhere. The other is—was—a long-time friend who's probably dead now, too. And then there's you, Michael. After going through my apartment, you probably know more about me than any other *living* person on Earth."

"Why do you keep saying 'on Earth' like that? You said it before when you were talking about killing people?"

"Because that's the most appropriate phrase—geographically, astronomically."

"Uh-huh, I see," Michael responded, nodding his head, trying not to give away whether he was accepting and believing what he heard or was merely putting on a polite face while inside he was screaming *lunatic!*

"So, Michael," he continued, "I was a teacher, but I never liked it, so I gave it up. I went traveling, went to many exotic lands. And I married a wonderful lady I met during my travels. We had some children, they grew up, and one day she died."

"Gina? The one in the letter?"

"You read it?" He frowned. "No, it was a different woman."

"Uh-huh, I see."

"Every so often I'd come back here—because this *is* my home, after all, the place where I was born. However, I couldn't ever stay here long. I'd get restless. I'd start to think about the places I've visited, and I'd want to see them again. So off I'd go."

"Just like that?"

"Just like that." He took a breath. "Almost."

"So, you were like a...a merchant marine?"

"No, not quite. More like a *mercenary* marine."

Michael perked up. "No shit? You were a mercenary? Like those guys who go to Africa, fight for whoever pays'em?"

"Similar." He grinned, feeling his ego expanding. "But I never fought for money."

"You didn't? You were into politics, huh? So, you're like some member of some terrorist organization. Man, I *knew it!*"

"No, not that. If you'd shut up, you wouldn't have to ask so many questions."

"Saw-ry," Michael intoned, and buttoned his lips with his fingers when the Professor pressed his own finger to his mouth to signal silence.

"Listen, Michael," said the Professor as he glanced at the doorway to be sure nobody was entering. "I'm going to be taking another trip soon...to one of those exotic lands...and you might be able to assist me. And, if you're interested, at the same time I can help you. Perhaps we can do something about that injury of yours. Does that interest you?"

"I don't have enough leave time for any trip."

"It won't take long. A weekend is all we need. Probably."

"Okay, then," said Michael, nodding excitedly.

"You bums jacked around long enough?" called out Fat Ken as he waddled into the canteen. "Joyce's got it bad again, you guys. Better get your butts back to your desks before she gets super pissed."

"What're you, her little meter maid?" Michael barked.

"I'm warning you," Ken replied, helping himself to a couple of candy bars as long as he was in the canteen. "Won't be my ass in the bitch's sling."

"Wouldn't fit, anyway," said Michael.

"Always the wiseguy."

"Actually, we were discussing a private matter," Sebastian cut in, though he never felt he had to explain anything to Ken.

"What, you guys making a date or something?"

"No, asshole," Michael snarled at Ken. "We're deciding whether to just roll you down the hill out back or rear-end your Pinto and watch you burn."

"Very funny."

"You like that? I got more!"

"Gentlemen," Sebastian broke in again, "shall we all return to our desks and discontinue this conversation?"

"Sure," said Ken, turning to get a Popsicle from the vending machine.

"We'll talk further," he told Michael, watching Joyce's big watchdog waddle out of the canteen, slow enough that he could keep an eye on them too.

Chapter 13

Travel Agents

Agani Island came often into Sebastian's mind as the new semester began. It was the first place he and Fawn had visited that late summer night. It was a place of exile for witches from the mainland, he eventually learned, women who were too promiscuous for polite society. He marked the point in the quarry that led to the island, anyway. Although he'd had experiences there which were alternately pleasant and horrifying, he kept it active because he could get through the tangent with less effort and energy than through others.

The *other* tangents, wherever they were, wherever they led, became his obsession. Most weekends through the fall semester he would go to the quarry and search for other tangents. Occasionally he would feel the weakness in the fabric of the universe and halt. He would mark the location with a golf flag, drawing a line on the pole at the height of the weakness. Returning later, prepared for a journey, he would test the tangent by opening it and stepping through it to whatever world awaited him on the other side. No matter where he first stepped on the other side, he gradually learned that all of the worlds he came upon were part of the same *planet*. And that planet always seemed to be the one that he and Gina had discovered on their first trip: the world of Ghoupallesz.

From one planet to the next in a heartbeat, a step, half a breath—but sailing on a boat for six days and hiking another day through the desert was not a very convenient way to visit the civilized parts of Ghoupallesz. Even so, he longed for a tangent which would lead him straight to Gina's doorstep, wherever that might be. Trips of twenty to fifty days seemed to cost him only a day or so in Earth time, occasionally only a few hours. The time differential was quite favorable then for Voyagers coming from Earth.

Then one day, Sebastian found a new tangent and arrived, quite unexpectedly, in the middle of a war between two small kingdoms, Jisilika and Foixe—where he proved his History professor wrong by perfectly executing the Napoleonic cavalry maneuver that had failed Blucher at Waterloo. He recalled the Battle of Austerlitz in 1805: the French cuirassiers versus the Russian dragoons. He knew the tactics employed in the American Civil War, too. Yet the beasts the soldiers mounted on Ghoupallesz were barely more than pack animals. The *Jêpe* was a tropical horse-like creature, strong and sturdy, having a half-striped donkey's body, rabbit ears, and a long dewlap. The *Jêpe* could not run on its three-toed hooves fast enough for the type of cavalry charge the wars of the 18th and 19th centuries on Earth demonstrated, yet the Jisilikan commanders still expected a regiment to make a straight-on charge against infantry lines.

While forced into ditch digging duty, he listened to a few lieutenants discussing the next day's battle. Not so good at the language yet, he asked his shoveling comrade what they were saying. "They plan to charge Hill #3 at daybreak," the man grumbled in Ghoupallêan. Sebastian was surprised, and remarked, a little too loudly, that charging Hill #3 on *Jêpe* was a suicide mission. The lieutenants called him out. He explained how *Jêpe* could be used in a flanking assault around the hill rather than charging up the hill. Of course, he refrained from citing examples from the wars he had studied back on Earth. The hill in question had a gentle slope on the east, protected from view, while the west side was steep and had a small gorge cutting along the south edge. Furthermore, the terrain on the east slope was packed dirt with loam, which would provide good traction. He had seen it while he ran errands for the camp. The south side, however, was rocky and the small stones would affect the *Jêpe*'s hooves and slow their movement.

How did he know?

"I've read a lot of history books and I've ridden [ahem, *Jêpe*] practically all my life," he told them in his best Ghoupallêan, "so what you want to do, since there are [uh, giant siege guns] on the top of the hill, is take two regiments, place them on the south and the east, drawing the attention of the enemy with one and attacking with the other."

They stared at him a moment, then asked further questions. He drew a map in the dirt and indicated how the cavalry should be deployed. He marked an angled charge from the east, a zigzagging pattern up the slope, hidden by the forest, that would reduce the chance of defenders hitting the charging cavalry; that pattern would confuse the defenders, forcing them to scatter, and—as Sun-Tzu stated in his *Art of War*—the battle will be won before it is begun. He pointed to the back-up squadrons and suggested tasking them with rounding up fleeing soldiers from Hill #3.

The lieutenants smiled, then introduced him to their captain.

He had ridden horses at his grandfather's farm throughout his childhood and read about every military conflict from the Trojan War up to the Second World War, especially the cavalry tactics of the Napoleonic Wars and the American Civil War, so he had good ideas to share with the officers of the Jisilikan army. They had laughed and told tales through the night and attacked at daybreak following his plan. Victory came easily and he was promoted to lieutenant, which they called *Landor*.

He also won the heart of Aisa-Evelê, a girl he met in a bar afterwards. Late into the night, talking in bed, he began to feel uncomfortable and by dawn he learned her grandmother was Gina. That was a tale for another time, certainly. But he knew then that he was on Gina's trail. Some day he would catch up with her.

About that time he started keeping a journal of his travels. His first entry came after that military adventure. He decided it was significant enough to warrant recording:

November 16, 1976. Tuesday afternoon. Active
test of Tangent A-5. Appeared in W. Gotanka, GP-
1235. It is wartime and the Jisilikan army is
badly in need of soldiers, I was drafted off
street. Sent to Feasfend for training. Due to
horsemanship skills, assigned to 39th cavalry
regiment of the 3rd army, travel to Manên for
orders, but war takes favorable turn for
Jisilika and my initiation into battle
postponed. Not sure I want to be in a battle but
can't escape. We have furlough in Feasfend--meet
Aisa-Evelê in a tavern, intimate episodes on
Rogin-23 and Pouor-1 & 4. Comrades & I leave
Feasfend for Manên, join 3rd army, march to
defend Peror, dug in for 2 weeks, Peror is
saved, pursue Filopan army into Foixe. There,
Filopan 4th army meets Foixe 2nd army, both turn
on Jisilikan 3rd army near Deliê, forced to
retreat, suffer guerilla attacks enroute to
Arôdan. Remeet Aisa there--she's been following
the army looking for me. Leave Arôdan with 3rd
army for march back into Foixe, last refuge of
Filopan 4th army, 2 week siege, victory, take
city, routing Filopan army. Nearly caught a
cannon blast in the face! Can't take such risks!
No wizard magic here if I get wounded. Meet Aisa
again, intimate on Terpa-12, 13, 14 & 15.
Jisilikan army marches to Antêa, engaging in
small battles enroute, retreat to Airazê where I
hear about Aisa's death in the shelling of the
city. Jisilikan 3rd army routes Filopan 4th army
at Pälous, return to Peror & disband. 39th
cavalry regiment & Yours Truly singled out for
special awards; given distinguished title of
"d'Elous" (the Great). They're joking but I like
it, think I'll keep it. New name on Ghoupallesz:
Set-d'Elous. Then I declare my retirement and
grieve for Aisa. Depart Ghoupallesz on Denio-
1:1235. Took 144 days there, only 4.38 days
passed on Earth. I missed the History exam, got
an F.

Writing it down did not make it true, he understood. Who would believe some college kid anyway? Who would believe he'd been to another world? He certainly was no well-funded scientist with a team of assistants blazing a trail through quantum physics. The story made no sense to him, either. He tried it on his friend, Jason, who back then was often high on dope, and got little or no response. The reality of his journey to another world made no dent. Everything was "Cool, man, cool." He gave up trying to get Jason to accept the truth of his frequent diversions.

Getting back on track in his classes was more difficult. Away for so many days each trip, it was impossible to remember what he'd read, or studied, or the last lecture. He had missed taking important notes. Susan here, or Becky there helped him. Even Kyle and Dave and Cindy in his other classes were concerned and wondered where he was when he was absent from his classes. He made excuses—helping a sick parent (no, it was benign), some job interview (the internship), an unexpected business trip (to New York, then Paris, then Rio de Janeiro), fighting the flu, just plain overslept (yes, for six full days! rare condition, doctors said)—but his expression never matched his words, and his words did not match the truth. He was a bad liar, he discovered, so he began avoiding all questions. He kept to himself more and more.

No, I am not a loser, he insisted. His GPA was a healthy 3.25, despite a lot of absences. And he was not alone. He had a girlfriend attending college in St. Louis. What's her name? Gina Parton. They were very much in love. And, yes, he was going to be very successful after college, maybe go to graduate school, probably be a well-admired History professor at some prestigious university. Or he might be a popular jazz musician, he mused as he polished his silver trombone before the Wind Ensemble's next performance, the final concert of the semester. Holst's *The Planets* was the main feature.

He did what he could to change his grades on the university registrar's files—flirting with Valerie, the student worker, helped a lot—but he still felt guilty about having to cheat. He knew all the history he needed to know. It changed every day, anyway. What he did not know was where his future lay. He needed a degree for one path. The other needed only a degree of courage.

＊ ＊ ＊

Life seemed to stretch and expand for Sebastian like salt-water taffy and he became a serious collector of calendars, just to keep track of his comings and goings.

"You've been here long enough, haven't you?" he dared ask Gina when he stumbled upon her living on the north side of Selauê in Sekuate. It was a journey he took the next year, hoping again to coax her to return with him. "It's not too late to return, pick up where you left off, get back into your life."

"I've got everything I need here," said Gina. "This is my life."

"But won't your family be worried about you?"

"They've probably forgotten me by now."

"No, they think you're back in college," he insisted, "but too busy studying to call them. That's what I told them. They call me almost every week, asking about you. They still think you're going to marry me. All I can say is that I haven't heard from you either."

She nodded, reflecting on a ghost of a memory of a ghost town life.

"You should stay here, too," she said cheerfully. "What've you got going for you back there? On your beloved Earth?"

"Well, it is my home. Where I was born. Where I expect to die. Someday."

"Not for a while."

He shifted uneasily on the floor cushion. "It seems that I want to stay home and you want to travel." He regarded her, saw her eyes looking inwardly. "I guess we won't ever get along that way. I see that. What did we ever have in common before?"

She looked up. "Love of adventure."

"Yeah, up to a point."

"You want to write up every experiment," she said with a sly grin, "but I'm anxious to get on to the next experiment. It's what happens next that intrigues me. Not what happened last time. This is like one big experiment. Life is just an experiment."

"So you're living your experiment, huh?"

"Of course!"

"Like an anthropologist...living among the natives, studying them. Is that it?"

"Okay...sure...that will do." Their eyes met for a moment, then broke away. "I suppose I am here to study this place, and the people who live here. No, I wasn't thinking it was like some researcher who went and got lost in the wilderness, but now that I'm here don't you think I should continue? Shouldn't I see what it's all about? Then someday—"

"Someday you'll return and publish your study? I don't think so."

"You're right." She pouted. "I won't come back. I won't publish a book about life on Ghoupallesz. You're right about that."

"So all of your so-called research will never be shared with anyone?"

She deliberately sighed. "Is that sad?"

"Unprofessional, perhaps."

"I'm interested in everything, but I'm not interested in writing up the experiment."

"You should keep some records," he suggested. "I've started a journal of my travels."

"Well, aren't you the good scientist!"

He pointed at the notebook beside her on the table. "Write about your adventures, then. Someday you may need to remember everything you've done."

She picked up the notebook. "I have been keeping a diary."

"Good for you." He caught himself and grinned. He hated to use her standard phrase, but he loved how it made her squint. "Hey, maybe you can have someone bring it to me when you're done writing it."

"Sure," she said without expression, "I'll leave it to you in my will."

Back on Earth, he was able to resume his life. He kept notes of everything. Whenever he would step back through the tangent, he could read what he had been doing before he left and pick up his life without pause. He also kept notes of what he did while he was away.

During the next year and a half he often stepped through one of the tangents at the quarry to see where it might lead and what he might find there. A few weeks in what he called negative space would only cost him a day or so of Earth time, a week at the most, sometimes as little as a couple of hours. He calculated the days: a total of 617 on his Earth calendars, but more than a thousand additional days lived on Ghoupallesz. That made him, for all practical purposes, two years older than his official age on Earth.

At first he was hesitant, wanting only to see if he could do it again. As it became easier, he traveled more often—in a few instances twice in the same Earth day. Besides satisfying his curiosity, he would sometimes escort his girlfriend-of-the-moment through the tangent for a little adventure—what he suggested to them was a "walk on the wild side." Merrie O'Dell was not impressed by the desert. Margie Schmidt was frightened to tears in the jungle. Melanie Bradshaw seemed to enjoy it but got a bad rash. Annie Kleberg was practically ready to be a Voyager like Gina—so, of course, he rushed her back through the tangent to Earth and vehemently insisted she'd had a bad dream. None of them were right. None of them could substitute for Gina. He could not even dream up someone who might replace her. Some nights he could not dream at all. What was the point of dreaming, anyway, when reality was like a dream?

He went in search of Gina sometimes, too, but just as often gave up whenever something else interesting caught his attention. Still, he did find her from time to time, as he popped around the years and the cities—just as she did. It was becoming a game to them, a playful chase across the tangents. He visited her, life by life, and gradually began to accept that she would always be ahead of him in this tangent game. He remembered the things she said to him each time he visited, but still he vowed to forget her and stop living a lie and not worry about what she was doing or where she was or who she might be with. She was never going to be his—never more than a good friend.

Although Gina was really only two years older than him, the next time he met her, quite by accident on an autumn journey through Tangent B-3, she looked thirty years older than him: still beautiful in a natural way, but mature now: a woman, not a college girl. He liked the way she looked and praised her appearance.

"You are so charming, Sebastian," she praised him in return.

"I mean it. No matter how weird it is to be seeing you like this, I still love you, and I want to be with you forever."

"Be careful. Forever is a long time," she said, a blush crossing her face. She remained relaxed, knowing that her latest husband, Tomak, did not understand English. "Somehow, I feel we've had this conversation before. You're still sweet. But you've got to stop being a high school boy—or a college lad. This puppy love thing is getting old."

"It's not puppy love," he insisted, feeling like a Dachshund. He became a Rottweiler: "We made love! We had sex! That means something!"

She laughed. "Of course, Sebastian. We had a good time."

"I am in love with you! I was back then, too. I *made* love to you because I *love* you."

"Lovely wordplay, darling." She saw how her words cut into him. "Oh, Sebastian, you know how teenagers are. Just having fun, no commitments, no long-term plans. We were living for the moment. That's not to say I didn't love you. I do love you. But there are at least thirteen types of love and, unfortunately, not all of them apply to you. I care about you, but I'm not head over heels, sorry to say."

"I understand," he said but did not.

"Look at us," she said. "Just look! You're still...what? Twenty-one? And look at me: in this life, I'm—well, who can say for sure? I look like I'm approaching fifty, right? If I were back on Earth. Is that the way it should be?"

"But you're still young in another life," he insisted, "a life I haven't found yet."

"Now you're getting it."

He wanted to shout to the moon the injustice he perceived, but Ghoupallesz had no moon and the nights were frighteningly dark.

"You're right," he said, calmly. "Why should I want you? Especially now? You're old. I'm still young. I'll find someone my own age to marry."

He massaged his chest, feeling a lingering pain there as her words ran through him. The years back on Earth had not lessened the hurt. He finished college, got his degree and found a job teaching. Keeping busy through the weekdays, he made trips to the other side of the universe on weekends. Occasionally his path would intersect Gina's life story and they would enjoy a few moments of nostalgia.

On March 13, Gina's birthday, he again left for what he considered was a well-deserved vacation. He did not plan to search for Gina, but he found her. In Ghoupalle year 1828, in Siti, in the nation of Ghoupallæssus, on the eastern side of the supercontinent. A butler-type fellow in a golden suit showed him into her chamber. A hot beverage was served, later a plate of small, crisp, fried vegetables with a purple yogurt sauce. They were happy to chat through the day, always keeping it light.

"So tell me," she said, reclining Rubenesque and fully pregnant on the chaise-lounge like some goddess bored out of her mind and thankful the jester was available to raise her spirits, "how's everything back home, back on that dreadful place you call home?"

"First of all, you'll want to know that your parents have stopped searching for you. They keep calling me, even so, asking if I've heard from you and all I can say is 'no.' I want to put their minds at ease but I can't say anything. Even if I wanted to say something, I wouldn't know where to begin. No one would believe me. I'll end up in some insane asylum. Or they would accuse me of knocking you off, hiding your body somewhere. But now they've called off the search and consider you gone. They filed to declare you dead. They had a memorial service. I attended."

"That's sad," she moaned lightly, "but what can I tell them that they'd believe?"

"I understand."

"So…what else?"

"Isn't that enough to blow your mind?" he exclaimed, throwing his arms up.

"Almost. I never got along with my parents, you know. It's better this way."

"Is that what you think?"

"Sebastian, I'm here now. I can't go back there. You can still tell me about back there, though."

He gazed at her, his eyes following the line of her distended belly, seeing her popped navel through the filmy white gown. This was somebody else; it was not his Gina. But he knew otherwise, deciding not to argue any more during his visit.

"Well, my parents have retired and moved to Florida," he told her. "So I'm living in the house. The same house I grew up in. That's a bit creepy. Now I'm master of the house, so to speak. I do what I want. Put my feet up on the coffee table, leave clothes on the floor, clean the kitchen at the end of the week instead of right after each meal. It's a kind of heaven, I suppose. And I sleep in the master bedroom, which is especially weird. I can't have sex there without feeling icky."

"You're having sex in your parents' bedroom?" She laughed.

"Hypothetically." He knew what she meant. She was checking on him, making sure he was not lonely. "I've been dating, but haven't found anyone. I mean, anyone like you."

"Again with the love story!"

He jumped in to cover his tracks: "So my old room is just a study now. I've got all my books in there on tall shelving. Doesn't matter. I'll sell the place someday and move to a better place. Something modest, not a huge mansion like you have here."

"Even so, good for you!"

"And, as I mentioned before, I'm teaching Social Studies at the new high school they built across town. Too many students in the district now, so they needed a new building. I was lucky to get a job there, given my grades in college."

"They're lucky to have you," said Gina with an air of certainty.

"I suppose so," he said, slowly shaking his head. "Things change."

"They sure do."

They both sighed, perhaps sensing a few regrets hovering in the corners of the ceiling or stuffed under the cushions.

"We were just a couple of kids back then," he said, turning to watch the children playing with the nanny near the back wall of her compound. "Now, look at you: You've got kids of your own now, and a husband. You married well. What's his title again?"

"He's Deputy Marshal of the Eastern District, Third Ward."

"But marshal of a big city."

"Siti is a medium-sized metropolis," she corrected him, "only a million in population."

"Well, I'm sure if you live long enough you'll continue to marry upward. You could be a queen someday."

"That's a goal to shoot for, isn't it? I think I'd like being a queen."

"You'd make a great queen."

"I would, wouldn't I? I'd be sure to be a benevolent royal, granting favors all day." She let out a pleasant laugh. "It's a lovely fantasy, Sebastian."

The pause was long enough that the butler fellow came to check on her needs. She waved him off and turned to her guest.

"I guess it's time to put away our childhood games," he said solemnly, "and start living our adult lives."

"I've *been* living my adult lives," Gina insisted, "indeed, for several, um, lifetimes now. This is my fifth family. I've had three husbands and two lovers on Ghoupallesz—outlived them all— and now I've given birth to five children. I have put away childhood fantasies, dear Sebastian, yet you—"

"It's only been a couple years for me," he announced, almost bitterly.

"I know. Yet you still seem to insist on playing the game to the bitter end. You're a Romantic! That's always been clear to me. But there's no room for being a Romantic if you're going to be an Interdimensional Voyager. You have to be tough. You have to be certain—about everything. There can't be any mush in your mind, no softness in your will, and no opacity in your view of the universe."

He knew she was right, as so often she was.

On a trip in September 1980, while studying the political movements leading up to the Gotankan revolution of 1118, he found her in a library. She was young again, proving that he was meeting her in a "time zone" more recent for her than the previous one where he'd insulted her, calling her old. She had not yet experienced that insult, so she welcomed him into an embrace.

After a late lunch at an outdoor café, they walked the cobblestone streets to her white townhouse, in the backwater district of the city of Peror. She said she shared it with a man who was traveling that week. It did not matter to him this time and she was glad he could accept it. They stayed up late, drinking and talking history and he stayed the night. Though she insisted that he sleep on a mat on the balcony, she was not shy about pulling him into the bathing basin with her the following morning.

"I've been waiting for you all this time," he said, frowning, wiping from his mouth the last bite of breakfast. "I don't think it's going to happen. I wish you well, but I'm ready to be with someone, too. In fact, I've found someone. Back on Earth."

"I'm happy for you."

"That's good to know. How many times have I been happy for you? I want *you*."

"Oh, don't be such a wimp, Sebastian! You and me, we'll always be the best of friends. And in my book the Best Friend outranks Spouse or Lover. You're the one I tell my secrets to. I don't tell them to my husband. Poor Goxon wouldn't get it, anyway, so why bother him? He'd never understand how tangents work, or how I'm able to stay young while he ages so dramatically. Oh, well, he is such a hunk, at least. Someday I must leave him. You know, before he wonders about me. It's inevitable."

"Certain secrets must be kept." He put on a happy face, felt it not sticking. "I have found someone. Her name is Linda. She teaches at my school. Math. In fact, that's how we met. I walked across the hall one day after the last period and asked her to check some equations I'd put together—"

"Always the mathematician wannabe!"

"For the tangents, not personal stuff."

"Sounds sweet."

"She is. Now that I'm looking at you, I have to admit Linda has a resemblance to you. But I love her. I think I do. And since you're already taken, it seems I have no choice. I'll be alone or I'll marry Linda and ride off into the sunset, and perhaps live happily ever after."

"That's how all good stories end."

"Then I'll do it." He studied her wistful expression, not sure if she was genuinely happy for him, or merely hiding a jealous twinge.

They talked long into the night, always one of their indulgent habits, and in the morning she had her large pet lizard wake him and lead him to her.

"Here, Sebastian," she called, holding out a small, ornately wrapped gift, "this is for you. Something to remember me by, if you want to think of it that way. Or, consider it a birthday gift— which ever birthday is closest. Or, perhaps better, consider it a wedding gift."

He took the square box and carefully opened the red wrapping, lifted off the top and looked inside. In the box sat a globe on four squat feet; it was gold and the globe held the pearly outlines of the continents and ocean of Ghoupallesz. He took it from the box and discovered that the northern hemisphere opened. It was a music box! As the music played, he regarded Gina, his long lost love, and smiled.

"Thanks," he spoke softly.

"You're quite welcome."

"It's a beautiful song," he said, a bit choked, "but rather sad. Beauty and sadness. They always seem to go together."

That was the last time he saw her, met her, talked with her. He turned twenty-five the next day and vowed never again to step through the tangents.

Chapter 14

Reality 101

Lunch break at the service center, about one in the morning.

Crazy Felix Unruh approached Sebastian in the canteen as he pulled a Dr Pepper from the vending machine. The huge bushy handlebar mustache the skinny man wore was probably half his body weight. Sebastian straightened up, turned cautiously, awaiting the inevitable confrontation that usually ensued. Politics. Felix had a counterargument for everything.

Instead, Felix extended an envelope toward him, an IRS internal memo envelope.

"This came for you few minutes ago," he softly muttered, mustache camouflaging his mouth like a ventriloquist's prop. Then he left. No confrontation. Strange.

The envelope was his pay statement, listing his income, gross and net, deductions, and payments to government charities. Behind the card was a small note that he could see was handwritten. Right then, he felt disconcerted that someone had placed a note in with his pay statement.

He drank down his Dr Pepper and went for a walk around the service center, over to another department where no night shifters worked but the lights were left on for security. There, row after row of vacant desks stood in a room the size of half a football field, banks of computers and clumps of lockers trying to partition it into separate sections, endless aisles dissecting them, the ceiling tiles going on forever. He went to the far wall, ducked into the canteen there, unoccupied as expected. He bought a Baby Ruth and sat down at a table, pulled out the note.

I know about Michael and Tammy. I know about the drugs you gave them. I'm gonna tell the police unless you do me a big favor. Meet me in the south canteen after your shift.

Folding the note up, he let out a sigh.

He was used to the unusual aspects of his dual life across two worlds, but the events that happened in the service center never ceased to amaze him. It was a world unto itself, with its own established rules and penalties, its own customs and rituals. Sometimes even its own secret language. The note was written in the secret code he had overheard spoken by various employees through the years. The people who worked third shift were especially *special*. Bored beyond reason, he surmised, their number one topic of conversation was sex. More so their own sexual episodes—or whatever they dreamed would be their ideal scenario. It was the one thing everyone had a common interest in. And many of his fellow employees were notorious for engaging in acts of infidelity, along with sexual sabotage. Even he had come under the scrutiny of some of the women on third shift.

The message, he deciphered, was from a woman who, for some reason, was threatening to expose his albeit limited participation in the Michael and Tammy affair. It was the same kind of lame assertion he often saw in movies, where someone says "I'll tell everybody that you and I made love *unless* you and I *do* make love!" The last thing he needed now, fighting the headaches from the Great Beyond, was for some woman to be nosy about nothing. She probably wanted to blackmail him. Of course, he had nothing anyone would want. Except sex. He worked hard to stay away from that possibility. He was holding out for Gina. Understanding the inner workings of the universe somehow made something like sex with a less-than-ideal partner a rather mundane activity.

He thought of his role in the episode and decided that he had no reason to worry about being connected to the affair. However, he considered whether or not this potential blackmailer actually knew anything. Perhaps it was simply a bluff—"Just to mess with me," he muttered. He had to go and see who it was and determine what the favor was going to be—if only to make sure his quiet life would remain quiet as he waited for the proper alignment of tangents. It was coming soon, he could feel.

He rubbed his temple, his head beginning to throb, and left the canteen.

※　※　※

Truth was a juicy peach running down his face, sticky and sweet. Reality, however, in all of its glory, seemed to always hit him over his head whenever his memories started to soothe him. He sat up at his desk, having dozed off for a minute and, realizing the shift was at an end, went to the designated break room to meet his fate.

"So you're the one behind this note," said Sebastian in a hard, controlled voice. He was on edge, hating the idea of being falsely accused of something and forced to defend himself.

The woman sitting at a table there looked up and smiled. He knew her, one of Michael's friends. She stood and waved at him to follow her. Out the back door of the service center they went, grinning at the guard who probably figured they were going to a car for a quickie. Instead, they stopped on the stoop where the smokers went during breaks.

"I know all about everything," said Cassie Dorfman with an angry twist of her long snout. She crossed her white sweater-clad arms over her chest.

He started to speak but was cut off.

"I followed'em to your apartment. I knew something was up. I heard Michael talking. I knew he likes that skinny bitch Tammy, and I knew they was going out that night. So I followed him over to her house, and they took her kid over to her mom's. Then I followed'em over to your apartment and I saw Michael get in through a window you left open. I went up there to tell him off cuz he's MY boyfriend, NOT hers. Then I see'em all over the floor screwing like couple a dogs in heat!"

"You went up there?" he asked, surprised.

"Hell, yes! Michael's MY man, and I sure ain't gonna let him play around on me. I was gonna give him a whole bunch o' shit. I saw your door was unlocked so I was gonna walk on in and catch'em. I only opened it a crack—'cause I heard'em making noise—and I saw it all, I mean *everything*, I wantcha to know. Michael said they took some kinda drug that was making'em do it. I told him he was full o' shit, and left."

He was confused. "So you broke up with Michael?"

"Hell, no!" She glanced around, making sure they were alone. She dropped her arms to her sides. "How could I?" She groaned, then breathed deeply a few times. "Come on, look at me. I ain't no Marla Maples, ya know. But Michael's a real hunk, in case you hadn't noticed. I'm damn lucky to have him—and I ain't gonna give him UP neither. Specially to that weepy willow! Michael—he knows I do anything for him—and he takes advantage of me 'cause of it. But—hey!—I can take some of it, 'cause I know I ain't so great lookin'—but I wanna keep him, see? But I know—I jus' KNOW it—he wants that bitch so MUCH now. You shoulda seen'em."

"I did, actually—"

"I dunno what kinda drug you gave'em, but anything that strong gotta be illegal."

He was amused, shaking his head in denial.

"First, Cassie, I did not *give* them anything. They broke in, remember? They *took* it. I wasn't even there."

"But you—

"Second, it's not anything illegal. It's just a strong, aaa, health elixir—"

"But you left it out," she insisted, shaking a finger at him. "You knew Michael's gonna see it and drink it—so he would be screwing that bitch."

"It wasn't left out." He felt a pain in his head. "It was put away. In the back of a cabinet. Out of sight—"

"It's still drugs, mister." Her scowl began to concern him. "You're gonna hafta do me a REALLY big favor to get outta this.

You're gonna hafta help me get Michael back."

That was not the favor he expected and he felt relieved. "What?"

"If you don't, I'm gonna tell all what you did to the POLICE— and also the FBI, the CIA—and anybody else I can think of. You hear me?"

The rumble of early traffic on the highway filled the pre-dawn air. A semi-tractor rig blew its horn and he turned to look.

"You hear me? You better help me, or else," Cassie cawed. "Got that?"

When he sighed, he tried not to make it sound like he was bored. "Yes...."

It was exactly the kind of blackmail he'd heard about throughout the service center. He would play along as far as he could just to keep everything under control. Later he would decide what to do. Perhaps she would forget about it after a couple of weeks.

"So what shall I do to assist you in achieving this wonderful reunion?" he asked as politely as possible.

"You mocking me?"

"Of course not."

"I wantcha to talk to Michael," she said with a victorious grin. "Tell him he'd better stick with ME—you can say how much better I am than that skinny bitch Tammy. Just *say* it. Then I want you to see to it the bitch has an accident—and it's gotta look like Michael did it—nothing *serious*, ain't gotta die or nothing, but I want her to think Michael's trying to get RID of her. Then she'll dump him and he'll come crawling on his knees back to me, just BEGGING for me to take him back."

"Well, that certainly sounds like a good plan," he said, pursing his lips.

"It is," said Cassie with a grin.

"Anything else?" It was difficult to hide his sarcasm, but she did not catch on.

"Yeah," she said after a moment of thought. "I wanna bottle of that stuff, too, what you gave Michael."

"I didn't *give* it to him."

"Whatever! I wanna bottle of it so I can drink it with him.

Know what I mean? Then, he'll never wanna leave me again. Ya got that?"

He let out an impatient sigh, checking his watch.

"How big a bottle do you want?"

Cassie smiled like she had won the lottery. "As much as you think he drunk that night. I'm gonna put it in a different bottle so he don't know what it is."

"Consider it done." He did not usually enjoy lying but sometimes it was necessary.

Cassie smiled, satisfied.

* * *

He could feel it spreading, like invisible fog, when he first entered the service center. Ten minutes late for his shift and reality was already dissolving. He was certain when he saw Tammy arriving before him—she was notoriously late—and was welcomed back by the other women in the section like a favorite conqueror. Instead of enjoying their rare praise, she burst into tears and sobbed at her desk, thinking that everyone knew exactly what had happened to her. She got up several times to go and compose herself.

Then, during his first stack of tax returns, Sebastian could no longer maintain his concentration. Razor shards of memory were cutting into his mind, causing him to grab hold of his temples to contain the pain, shaking his head to drive away the cold, difficult images taking root. He pushed himself further, checking the errors on an Iowa farmer's tax return, but just before the first break he had another attack of sensory hallucination: the white, frosty breaths of beleaguered soldiers forming milky clouds around them, padded up like big bears, weighing down their jittery *Jêpe*, awaiting the signal to strike. His body shivered to match the frigid scene, remembering that day, the dawn of what became the final desperate assault on Siaa, impregnable fortress city of northern Tebbicousimankalê. They would lose, he knew back then and recalled now. He shook it off, tried to refocus on the papers before him.

He went late on break after finishing the farmer's tax return, finding a grand total of 233 dollars and 85 cents underreported and thus still owed.

Sitting at the table in the corner of the canteen, sobbing loudly, was Tammy. Her face was beet red and a puddle of tears spread upon the table.

"Why are you crying?" he asked. The words had just come out; he was not sure what the right words would be. "They all think you were in a car wreck, Tammy. Nothing else."

She looked up at him. "What?"

"They don't know what really happened. They were all told you and Michael were in a car wreck. I came along and took you two to the hospital. That's the story."

"You...mean it?"

"Of course," he said, smiling. Reality was holding together a bit longer. Suddenly he felt cold, and shivered where he stood. "I haven't said anything about you. Who'd believe me, anyway?" He added the last bit of awkward self-effacement for her benefit. It was true, however, that none of his co-workers ever believed him—some gossiped about his secret past—and who could blame them, as crazy as he acted sometimes? He took a quick breath. "Don't worry. I took care of everything."

She started to speak, stopped herself and began crying again.

"Now what?" he asked. He watched her thinking.

"Not...*everything*."

"Not everything what?"

"You didn't...take care of...."

"I didn't take care of everything?" He puzzled out her broken sentences. Then he saw her eyes turn down to her stomach. He stared at her hand in her lap.

She pouted, rolled her eyes upward like a naughty little girl.

"I'm pregnant."

He nodded his understanding, took a seat across from her. "You're pregnant?" He let the pause open his mind to a solution. "All right, then...uh...maybe I can help you."

She continued to look down. "This sure ain't...the life I wanted."

He felt sorry for her, though not understanding how he could feel that way about someone he barely knew.

"I was supposed to get married to a nice guy," she said, wiping away tears with the back of her hand, "maybe a rich guy, and raise a big family. We'd have a happy life. It was all supposed to be different. Not this sucky IRS job and all this bullshit.... It'd be like a dream. Like some frickin' dream!"

"You don't belong here," he spoke softly, then tapped a few times on the table, thinking. "I get it. Sitting here, feeling our lives going on and on, like some dream we can't awaken from."

She slowly nodded. "Yeah...."

"It's like some dream we have—good or bad, doesn't matter, it's full of vivid details and seems more real than dream. And then, as we awaken, we try to cling to the dream because that's what seems real, and our waking life seems like a dream that we don't want to have. Suddenly, we can feel wakefulness intruding on the dream world and we resist it, even as we are also realizing that the dream world *was* only a dream and not reality, even as we wish for the dream to continue—we have to see how it ends: Do we save the girl? Will we find what we're looking for? Can we live happily ever after? What do all those symbols mean, anyway?"

"I dunno," Tammy muttered.

"We know it's inevitable that wakefulness will win and pull us reluctantly from the world of the dream. Yet, even after we're awake, there's a lingering sensation of the world we visited. It haunts us, compels us to return, perhaps even follows us through our days, making us change our actions, or make choices based on our blind hope that we'll be able to return to that dream world— because *that* is our reality. But within an hour or two, or perhaps by the next day, we've forgotten it—all of it—as though the dream never happened. Sometimes the dream merges with reality, becomes another event in our lives, has power over us. Sometimes we don't know which is which. Sometimes—"

He regarded Tammy: tears wiped away, staring at him like she'd seen a ghost.

"Well, that's what my shrink says, anyway."

He felt the urge to wink, as though he were divulging secret information.

"You mean one of them psycho-ologist doctors?"

He pursed his lips. "I don't actually go see any psychiatrist," he said. "I simply—"

"Psychiatrist—that's it."

"I get into some good conversations, however," he finished.

After a couple heartbeats, she giggled. "Yeah...."

"The dream we have for our lives is like a sleeptime dream. It just hovers there, teasing us. Like the horizon. It's the difference between what we want and what we get. What we end up doing in our lives, that's the reality we want to escape from. We want to be where everything works out for us. We don't want the sucky IRS third-shift job. We want to be kings and queens, heroes and heroines." He paused, listening to his echo. "I'm not supposed to be here. I was meant to do other things, but I—"

He stopped, wondering if he were about to say too much. He lived such a solitary life he seldom had deep conversations with people. It felt strange.

"This isn't what I should be doing," he continued. "I preferred my last job, but that's no longer possible. I've moved on."

"Huh?"

He had to grin, seeing her eyes darting about, searching for answers.

"People want the dream world, not the reality they're given. You and I are stuck here. In this reality. Alcohol, drugs, meditation, whatever—they're attempts to return to that ephemeral state of being we call the dream world." He grinned. "For me, that doesn't happen. My dreams are real, and I do remember them. Maybe you do, too."

"I never dream."

"You should," he said. "You don't belong here either."

She became flustered. "I don't want to work here, but it's the only job I can get."

"No, Tammy. I mean you don't belong *here*." He waved his arms around to indicate the entire universe. "In this reality. You deserve better."

"No, I don't. I'm just a—"

He slapped the table. "Tammy! Look at me. I want to help you."

She met his eyes, sniffling back fresh tears. "You do?"

"Of course. That's why I'm talking to you now."

"Then...how?"

He stared at the ceiling for a moment, thinking.

"All right, Tammy. That's a fair question." He shifted his eyes on her belly, then up to her tear-streaked face. "The first step is very simple. Decision number one. Do you want the baby or not? I think that you...umm.... Let me guess: this situation is the result of that night you were with Michael in my apartment? Is that right?"

She grimaced. "Well, Professor, I'm—"

"Call me Sebastian."

"What?"

"I wish you'd call me by my name."

"Really?"

"Yes."

She stared at him. He grinned, thinking of the next thing to say.

"What is it?" she asked.

"It's Sebastian."

"That's your name?"

He nodded, gestured for her to continue.

"Okay, Se-bas-tian." She forced herself to smile. "I know it was an *accident*, but it—it wasn't—well, you know...."

"I understand. Accidents happen. But the results are something we have to deal with."

"No!"

"What's no?"

"That's not it." A tear slid down her face. "I guess...I *mean*.... Oh, I dunno!"

He reached across the table and put his hand on top of hers.

"Listen to me, Tammy. It *was* an accident. He gave you some of that drink, which wasn't meant for you. He didn't know what it was. But after you drank it, you felt pretty good, right? You were turned on, right? You *did* feel like having sex? Just not with *him*."

She almost smiled, decided it was not proper for showing her disappointment and resumed her crooked, weeping pout.

"I don't—I'm not in love with him...with Michael. I never ever *wanted* to, ya know, I mean.... I'd rather make love to *anybody* but him."

"I get it."

"But I—I don't wanna get an abortion because I…well, I think it's wrong, ya know. But I can't have another kid, too."

"Have you thought about adoption?"

"What? I already *have* a kid."

"No—" He had to hold back his frustration "—I mean, giving it up for adoption after it's born. How about that?"

"Oh…."

"Actually, Tammy, I have some kind of plan."

"You do?"

"I started to mention it to Michael—"

"You did?"

"I began but I didn't finish." He glanced around to be sure no one else had come into the canteen. "Do you want to hear it? The plan? I'll tell you, but it has to be a secret—our secret—or it won't work."

"It's not…abortion, is it?"

"No," he replied, wondering if he really felt so much obligation to help her and Michael. He thought of the past, and the future, saw nothing that fit. A warmth began to grow in his chest, a sensation that told him he was doing the right thing. Or it was Gina calling him to help her. Either way, he knew he could not stop now. He cleared his throat. "In this plan, Tammy, you can go ahead and have the baby. We will then find someone who will adopt it and give it a loving life, and he or she will never want for anything. And—"

"But everybody'll know about it!" she exclaimed. "I'll get bigger. They'll see my big belly and know I was—"

"And no one will know about it," he finished, ignoring her outburst.

"I can't quit this job, ya know. I need the money. Specially now."

He squeezed her hand and she looked up, met his eyes.

"Tammy, listen." He took a deep breath, not sure what he was initiating but feeling he was meant to get into trouble one way or another. The voices were whispering to him from inside his head. One of them was Gina's. He regarded his co-worker again, noticing for the first time very minor details of her face and figure, her fashion sense, or emotional state, her humanity. "Michael's heard the plan, and he's willing to help me—help us. So, unless you absolutely hate him and he disgusts you right down to your toes, he has to come with us. For one thing, he's the other person who knows what really happened. And, two, he also needs help. He has a type of affliction, too. I need to get him some kind of treatment. So I thought we could take care of both of you at one time, in one trip."

"Well, Michael doesn't, ya know, disgust me down to my *toes*. I mean, he's funny. Sometimes, but.... How's he gonna help us?"

He felt himself smile. "I haven't told him yet—because I haven't worked out all of the details. Soon, though. I need to check some data, run a prediction analysis, and other things to make sure...."

She stared glassy-eyed at him. She didn't need to understand everything, he decided. It was enough to escort her, as a good friend—no, as the hero, as the only person who could take care of the problem.

"You agree with the idea?"

"I dunno."

"It's the only solution."

"You sure?"

"We'll work out the details later." He saw her face relax. "Of course, it would mean you never see the baby. Because of the adoption."

She began shaking her head, trying to understand, and he wanted so much to stuff his words into her head, so much easier than hoping they would enter through her ears.

"But how's everybody—how're they not gonna know? They're gonna see me—see my big belly—"

"I'll take care of it," he said, a little edgier. "Nobody will ever know anything—unless *you* tell them. I said I'll take care of everything and I will. We're going on a trip. To a wonderful place—a resort, you might call it. You'll be living there for a few months, until the birth. Then you'll return to work as though nothing happened. Because nothing here *will* have happened. Not here. So nobody will know you had a baby. It will seem like nothing happened to you. Or your belly. No time will have passed here."

"I don't get it. You telling a story? Michael said y—"

"It's kind of like time travel." He chuckled. "It's science. Very technical stuff. You don't need to understand it. All that matters is you'll come back before the event ever happened."

"*Time travel?* Are you outta your mind?"

He shushed her. "Just trust me. I said it's *like* time travel. That's an analogy."

"A what? A now-low-jee?"

"Analogy—it's another way of looking at things. Like when you have a dream that makes something more clear in your waking life." He smiled at her. "I'll take care of everything. It'll cost you nothing. And there's nothing illegal involved. Or permanently damaging—probably. You'll be back before anyone knows you were ever pregnant." He gazed into her eyes. "Will you trust me, Tammy?"

She toyed with a smile again. "Awright. I guess I gotta trust you."

"That's the first step."

Chapter 15

Shaman and Storyteller

Somewhere in the frozen night, with thick swirling snow blocking his view, he called to his men to ready themselves for battle.

"*Halen-ga!*" he cried, giving the order to mount up, hearing the *Jêpe* begin shuffling over the hard-packed snow, his troops unslinging their ATs, preparing them for firing.

Line 32 on Form 1040 was definitely wrong, he saw, and wondered why he had missed it before. He punched the adding machine keys again, double-checking it. Usually he could do the math in his head. He must be losing it, he surmised. Ever since he returned from his lunch break at the all-night 7-Eleven, he could feel it coming on like a cavalry charge.

They trekked around the sloping hillside, hidden among the vast whiteness that nearly blinded them—so invisible in the white parkas that covered their khaki uniforms, riding the white-cloaked beasts. They came out unexpectedly behind a small encampment of Tebbi army reservists. The camp included many recruited Zetin warriors, he could see. In the later stages of the war, the Tebbi government had used Zetin mercenaries against the Sekuateans. Before he could give any command to his troops, one of the Zetin spotted them, shouting in a rough, crackling voice: "BIT'GN-SKN! SEKUATANK-SKN! L'GAN GOL-SKN!"

He bolted back in his chair, pounding the keys of the adding machine harder, tapping his pencil furiously on the desk. He shifted in his seat. Trying to ignore the images frozen in his head as they bulldozed through his mind, he grasped his pencil tightly to keep his hands still, but the pencil broke. He flipped the tax return over, focused on the figures at the top, trying to add them quickly, forgetting each digit as soon as he read it.

His men dived from their *Jêpe* into the snow, frozen as it was, some of them hitting barefaced and screaming as their cheeks flash-froze. He threw himself from his saddle and fired in the same breath—which raised a cloud around him to mark the target for the Zetin. He called to his second-in-command, who rushed to his side with a bag of explosives. Together they began tossing them down the hillside, the long cylinders tumbling easily down the icy slope, down between the legs of the Zetin warriors. The first one to be sprayed into violet gelatin, blood freezing instantly as it spurted from torn bodies, was a Tebbi officer just coming out of his thermal tent.

His co-workers were soon aware of the disturbance developing in the corner of their section. They turned, one by one, watching him grit his teeth and mumble obscenities under his angry breath, louder and louder. He even tried his old trick: adding numbers from the tax forms on the adding machine, simultaneously multiplying them in his head, then subtracting the smaller from the larger on the adding machine, dividing the same number by *Pi* in his head. He hit the adding machine with his palm, snapped another pencil on the edge of the desk, and let out a cry like a wounded animal.

Falling back against his chair, it tipped over and sent him sprawling across the tiled floor, where he began thrashing about like a fish out of water.

"There he goes again," Joyce the section manager remarked, looking up from her desk. She regarded the episode over the top of her glasses. "How long this time?"

"I dunno," Kate replied beside her. "About six months, I guess."

"Six months? Hmph! A new record. I about forgot he did that sorta thing."

"Guess he'll be taking off," said Joyce, reaching for the leave book. "He always does after a seizure."

"You wouldn't think he was epileptic," said Kate.

With each thundering explosion from the grenades, his body jerked against the floor, his head feeling as though it was swelling and might burst. His muscles were taut. He was racing down the hillside, sword drawn, slicing through Zetin like they were snowmen and his blade blue with fire. His soldiers overran the encampment and took seven prisoners—all Tebbis; the Zetin never allowed themselves to be captured. Later, having no personnel to guard them nor place to keep them, he was ordered to kill them. They regrouped and pressed on, making their rendezvous with the 7th *Treskand*, a battalion-sized unit, for what would be the last assault on the weak northeast corner of the city. In about seven hours, as the twin suns showed themselves briefly at dusk, the Sekuatean armies would declare victory and raise their eight-pointed star over the city of Siaa. Then, five days hence, the Tebbi forces that had been held in reserve all winter would sweep down on the city, surprising the exhausted Sekuatean forces. The next few months would be a frantic, disorganized retreat across the broad peninsula of Tebbicousimankalê, chased by the Tebbi army, harassed from every corner by Tebbi allies.

But he would not live to see that.

His *regêlad*—the 200 soldiers he commanded—would be duty-bound to follow his orders, which were to keep to the secret passages to the coast. There they would make their escape. And his men would not be grateful to be saved from certain death. That was his defining moment, he concluded: when the universe ground to a halt and waited impatiently for him to make the decision of his life, the kind that kneads new character in a person. It was not until they entered Selauê under cover of night and spirited away their families to the silent hills before the final onslaught by the arrayed armies of the Northern Alliance that he realized it *was* his defining moment. His own family was long gone. No one waited in Selauê for him.

He awoke in the nurse's office at the service center, many days or hours later. He did not know which, not until Michael poked his head in and inquired about him.

"How ya doing?"

"*Gaum-da? Zetinê-y-ke?*" he asked, sleepily looking around.

"There you go with them freakin' words." Michael chuckled. "You can go home now. Shift's over. Good timing. We were getting into some tough shit, too. Joyce was giving us some instructions about this new kinda form but nobody was listening. Then Fat Ken farted right in the middle of it and everybody cracked up. You missed all that. Hell, I shoulda thought of the same thing, but I don't have the guts to pull it off. Making it look real, I mean. Do we still get paid if we have fits?"

Sebastian sat up on the cot as the nurse returned.

"How're ya feelin', dear?" she asked him, bending down to wipe beads of sweat from his forehead. "Anyone I kin call for ya, ta pick ya up?"

"I can take him home," Michael offered.

He waved his hand through the air, struggled to rise but settled back on the cot.

"I'm all right," he spoke in a rough voice when his head cleared. "Just a little too much—too much—"

"Stress?" Michael suggested.

"Ya don't seem to have flu symptoms," the nurse said, "not what's goin' 'round."

"I'm all right, I said."

He braced his arms, raised himself to a sitting position, then took a deep breath and pushed himself upward until he stood tall. Michael caught him when he tottered, held him up so the nurse would see that he could go under his own power.

"You really had us scared, Perfesser," Michael said, almost laughing. "What kinda booze you been drinking?" He turned to the nurse and grinned. "Just kidding."

"Uh-huh," she nodded with a wink.

Michael helped him out of the office and through the maze of corridors to the front lobby and sat him down.

"I'll bring the car around," he said.

❋ ❋ ❋

"So what's wrong with you, anyway, man?" Michael inquired once they were safely within the confines of the Professor's apartment. He had not dared mention it during the drive, not wanting the Professor to flip out in the car. "You see why we're always wondering about you? Almost forgot you went goofy like that. We all did. And then, there you go—back to normal. Jumping on the floor and wiggling around like that."

He smiled weakly, slouching in his easy chair where Michael had dropped him. Staring at Michael sitting on the edge of the couch across from him, he took a long deep breath and slowly blew it out. Home again.

"I didn't mean to alarm all of you."

"Alarm us?" Michael chuckled. "Hell, Joyce and Kate were practically laughing, sitting back in their chairs, watching you spaz on the floor. They got so used to it, didn't even faze'em this time. The triplets freaked out, though. Guess they never saw you do it before. And Crazy Felix said you're an epileptic. Is that right?"

He took a stronger breath, then spoke: "Michael?"

His co-worker leaned forward. "Yeah...?"

"Shut up, will you?"

Michael sat back, waved his hands apologetically. "Hell—sorry, ya know."

"It's been a rough night and I'd like to—"

"Hey, man, I brought you home. I took care of you. 'Cause you're gonna take care of me, right? I'm just curious what the hell's the matter with you. Don't want you to forget I'm helping you. Trying to show a little compassion for a fellow human being. You are human, aren't you?"

He waved Michael off. "All right, thanks."

"You are human, aren't you?"

He nodded. "Sometimes."

Michael waited for an explanation, starting to doubt the obvious. "So what've you got? Some nervous disorder or some shit like that?"

He shook his head slowly, trying not to show his exasperation. He wanted to be left alone now, to wallow in his misery, to hide from his public embarrassment. He wanted to prepare himself for the inevitable journey he must undertake. This time would be different.

"It's not epilepsy," he said, "so don't worry about that. It's just—doesn't matter. Even so, it's something I've had for a few years. It comes and goes. I don't quite know how long, a few years. Whenever the—" and he stopped himself from using the terminology he and Gina had invented. It would not be appropriate to divulge all of the truth to the uninitiated.

"A few years?" Michael seemed to count in his head. "That's how long you been working the service center, ain't it? It must be stress."

"No!"

He immediately regretted allowing his irritation to show, too tired to censor himself or maintain his usual facade of self-control.

"What the hell's wrong with you, man?"

"It's not stress. There's no stress for me there. That's the reason I work there. It's a break from stress—the stress that's out there!" and he jerked a thumb rudely toward the window, indicating the neighborhood or the whole city, the world at large, or maybe the entire universe. Michael could not catch which one. "*That's* where the stress is. And sometimes—once in a while—it comes up behind me and stabs me hard in the back of my brain."

"Like one of them migraine things?"

"No, dammit!"

"Sorry, Perfesser. I mean...hey—what'd you say your name was again?"

He raised his head and stared at Michael, aimed his dagger eyes straight into his.

"Shit, man," Michael cried out, rubbing his eyes, "you're freakin' me out! I just asked your name, no reason to get angry. Now, what did you want me to call you? Was it Sit—like 'sit down'?"

He stood, surprisingly strong and vigorous now, his stern countenance regarding the human seated before him, the man's shoulders shrinking and aura folding inward.

"My name is Set. Derived from the name Seth, or the even the older form, Sutekh. But never, *ever* 'Sit' as in 'sit down.'"

Michael cracked a grin. "Okay, man. I didn't mean nothing.

Relax, will ya?"

He dropped into his chair with a hurricane sigh.

"I'm tired of relaxing. I'm tired of this waiting. I'm tired of this entire petty, simplistic, routine, little world. I've been here too long. It's time to move on. Again. That's what tonight was about. It's almost time to leave. When it's getting close I can feel it. It intrudes on my consciousness. It vomits up my memories, then stabs me. What's it been, two years? I thought I was done with that. Now it returns, trying to pull me back to the abyss. Yet it's a good thing, really—or so I want to believe. I've been waiting a long time."

Michael looked concerned. "Waiting for what?"

He took a long breath, held it a few heartbeats, getting his thoughts under control, then turned and met Michael's serious eyes.

"Waiting for a certain alignment to arrive."

"Alignment...?"

"Yes."

"Of...?"

"The universe."

Michael froze a moment. "Oh, you mean like the planets? Like that Shirley McClean chick talking about how all the planets are gonna be in a straight line, causing bunches of catastrophes on Earth?"

"No!" he erupted. "Michael, just listen."

"Okay, you're the Perfesser."

He leaned forward, lowered his voice. "I'm going to tell you some things you may find hard to believe, but just hear me out and try to keep an open mind. Don't start judging until I say you can judge."

"How long's this gonna take?"

He shook his head slowly, disappointed. Was his plan going to work or not? Was this character suitable for the mission?

"Michael, is there anything more important to you than learning how you can get your penis fixed? Is there?"

"I guess not."

"Maybe you do have the time."

Michael nodded, slowly, as though he had come to some

conclusion about the state of the universe or his place in it.

"I've been watching you for a while now, at work, you know," said Michael suddenly, in a different tone, his face unusually tense, rapping his fingers loudly on the end table. "You think you're better'n everybody there, dontcha? I know you do. I can see it in your face. You don't think the rest of us is even dog shit, am I right?"

"That's right: I *don't* think that."

"Then I guess you feel *sorry* for all of us stupid idiots, huh?" Michael stared at him. "Like, how could we be working for the goddamn Internal Revenue Screw-us. Like, how can we add and subtract even. Like we're all such losers. Ain't that right?"

"What are you talking about, Michael? I don't think that." He examined his thoughts. "All right, I do think some of our colleagues are lucky to have the jobs they have. Not you, and a few others. You should get better jobs. You could be successful at other jobs. I know why I'm there, but you...I don't know why you're there. You always dress like a manager but you're doing the same paper-shuffling as everyone else."

"You gotta dress like the job you want," Michael responded.

"All right, that's good advice. And it makes sense."

"I heard it on a motivational program—"

"If I've said or done anything to give you the wrong impression, then I apologize. To be honest, I seldom give anyone a thought. I'm too busy distracting myself from the outside world to judge anyone. I simply observe. In fact, I've often wondered about *you*, Michael, why you're working there. You seem an intelligent guy, a charming sort of fellow—charming like a used car salesman. Why aren't you working in a better job?"

"Well, Perfesser, I'll tell ya...things just don't work out for me, ya know?"

"I'm sorry to hear that."

"Yeah," said Michael, head lowered, "me, too." He squirmed in his seat.

"How about we go get some breakfast?" Sebastian offered.

Michael was slouching on the sofa. "Yeah, whatever."

"I'm sorry, Michael." He stood and stretched. "I'm hungry. Come on. Let's talk over breakfast. My treat. You drive."

On the drive down Highway 40 a police cruiser followed, then quickly passed them and the Professor had seemed concerned.

"You *are* hiding out," Michael laughed, slowing for the red light at Noland Road.

"Not from the police," was the Professor's response.

The back booth in the Shoney's on Noland Road was removed enough from the noisy pre-dawn pancake crowd, but Sebastian paused whenever the waitress came around with more coffee. He tried not to be friendly so she wouldn't stay and chat, but Michael, while swabbing up his leftover syrup with a piece of toast, was happy to flirt with her. So Sebastian poured another sugar packet into his fresh coffee, stirring it, waiting for the waitress to leave.

Sebastian waved Michael to let the waitress go.

"Tonight, I was trying to finish that file of returns," said Sebastian, "and I began making mistakes with the math. The shifting was interrupting my concentration. The alignment, I mean. It's coming soon. When the alignment approaches, it's like a curtain between our present reality and a dream world becomes thinner, so they almost merge, and it's hard to tell them apart. I was surrounded by my memories there at my desk, like I was stuck in a theater and reliving something that happened long ago. You can't imagine how frightening that is unless you've experienced it. Tonight, it was the same event from my past, from a battle I was in. All the sensations I felt back then returned to me. Every action, every movement, every thought—it felt so real as I sat at my desk. And you know what happened next."

"So you thought you were back in the war, huh? It's like that Vietnam thing, isn't it? What's it called? Post-hypnotic stress disease—or something like that."

"No, it's not that." He thought a moment, watching Michael dab a napkin to the corners of his mouth. "I suppose the symptoms are similar. I've had times when the memories were pleasant, too. Those intrude just as much but are naturally easier to deal with. So when I fell out of my chair, I really thought I was falling off my *Jêpe*. Hitting the floor was like hitting the snow on the ground—"

"Falling out of your *jeep*?"

"No, it's *Jêpe*. That's 'Jay-puh'. It's like a horse." He shook his head. "You don't know me. And I don't know you. We work

155

together. That's all. I observe you, you observe me. We are not friends. We are co-workers. Only that. We wouldn't have anything to do with each other were it not for the random circumstance of being employed in the same place at the same time."

"Yeah, I get it—"

"And yet, because of that proximity, you and I have managed to cross paths, and because of that crossing something unexpected happened. Now you're wounded, and so is Tammy—in a manner of speaking. Now I'm involved with you two when I never expected to be. But at the same time, I have to do something—a project, let's say—something which is very hard for me to do. It's been a while since I last did it so I wonder if I can even do it now. I feel weak and I could possibly fail. I don't know anyone else. Apparently, fate has brought us together in such a way that you can help me at the same time I help you—both of you."

"What do you have to do?"

"I have to go on a trip."

"Oh, yeah?"

"And you and Tammy are coming with me. If you want help for your problems."

"Where're we going?"

"It's far away—"

"I gotta check my personal leave. I don't have no vacation days left."

"Stop." He stared at Michael. "This is not the usual kind of trip people take. We are going to visit a place where I must go to take care of my problem. While we are there, we'll take care of your problem and Tammy's problem. Then we'll come back here and everything will again be in balance."

"Where is it? The Ozarks? St. Louis?"

"You've never been there." He saw the waitress approaching with the check. "And I don't want to go there again. But I must go."

"And we get to go with you," said Michael, smiling. "That's cool."

He grabbed the check, scooted to the edge of the booth. "Let's get out of here."

Michael winced as he climbed out of the booth. He grabbed his crotch.

"Problem?" asked Sebastian.

"None of your business," Michael grumbled.

"Painful, is it?"

Michael straightened up. His pants were stained. "Yeah, sometimes."

"It's starting. The damage is quickening."

"Yeah, guess so." He made a painful grimace.

Sebastian paid and they left the restaurant.

"You're gonna help me, right?" said Michael at the car. He unlocked the door and they climbed inside. "I was starting to look like some super stud, then it started to hurt, and it has some weird discharge—"

"There are micro-tears occurring which let the pus leak out," said Sebastian the Professor. "The swelling will continue. It'll continue to grow, but not in a good way. Eventually the blood flow will be compromised. Then it'll turn gangrenous and you'll really h—"

"Shit!" Michael exclaimed. He started the engine and they drove away.

"For now, put some ice on it. No Earth medicine will help, so don't take any, no matter how much it hurts. Or itches. Or swells."

"Geez, man, what am I gonna do?"

"We have to get you to a doctor, one who knows how to treat it."

"And you know where the doctor is, right?"

"Right."

"And it *can* be treated, right?"

"I think so."

They turned in at the apartment complex, parked.

"At least, I hope so," said Sebastian, stepping out of Michael's car.

"Dammit, you gotta fix it!" Michael grunted.

They went up to the apartment.

"It won't be easy but obviously it must be done," said Sebastian, going to the kitchen and returning with two glasses and a bottle of purple liquid.

"No more of that poison you have, man!"

"This is just wine. Real wine." He poured, handed a glass to Michael. "It all started back in the summer after I graduated from high school. See, my girlfriend and I decided to hike through the woods one afternoon and find some secluded spot to make love. We were just teenagers, of course. Instead, we happened onto an old, abandoned quarry...."

PART TWO

GHULAD-6:1440
FENULA, KISH-A-TEK, NOG-MEGANK—

She joined in marriage with Sartan-Tek the Fourth, the Ruler of Kish-a-Tek, the modern nation named Fenula. Therefore, she was a queen. And she had borne the royal heir, a son who would never be king, who would never sit on his father's throne. What wealth they had managed to send out of the country when the invasion came would be all that they had to live on, a small fortune only. Her maid, the Lady Renée, hired the warrior Set-d'Elous from the land of UR-THA, and he prepared the queen's guard to redeem themselves for allowing her to be captured by the Zetin bandits. As the mission was successful, the warriors each were honored and rewarded appropriate to their achievement. Their leader was presented the highest medallion of the House of Kish and Tek, by the Queen herself, and she bestowed upon his cheek the royal kiss of gratitude.

> —from Fenulan historical records; found transcribed into the journal of Gina Parton, Interdimensional Voyager, First-Class, *Oak-Leaf Cluster*

159

Prologue

It was a simple operation, perfectly tailored to his particular skills of spatial deduction. He and the hand-picked band of mercenaries from northern Gotanka and a few of the queen's guards easily scaled the stone walls of the old Zetin monastery and quickly found the room where the Lady was being held captive. She cooperated; only her two female Zetin attendants were killed, silence, as it was, being golden. Then, under cloak of darkness, they hurried through the corridors, past the sleeping guards, and exited the crumbling structure well before dawn, returning to the safety of the mountain forests above Fenula Lake by midday. They had lost only two men, sacrificing themselves in the slaying of the awakening Zetin guards while a dozen bloodied corpses littered their trail.

The Lady Jinetta was thankful, though she kept mostly to herself as they all made their way south. Whether exhausted or famished, no one could tell. Only their leader, the cold-hearted warrior Set-d'Elous, could speak with her, using their own private language. Still, she never smiled, wrapped in blankets. Later, when they returned to the capital city of Têfos, it seemed as though the people had never known their queen had been stolen and held for ransom by the Zetin. That was the plan, Renée had told him: the people should never know about their queen's unfortunate fate, otherwise war would surely result. And no one wanted war. War came later, nevertheless, but at least the Zetin's intended first casualty was already free.

His long lost love Gina and her friend Renée were able to escape from Têfos as it came under siege, taking her infant son with her, hidden in a peasant's wagon, riding east toward neighboring Herêbout, where they would eventually find sanctuary.

At Gina's persuasion, he was given rewards in addition to those of the Royal House. She convinced Renée to turn over to him controlling interest in her *gealan* distributorship. All he had to do was dig up the small, shiny mineral spheres that back on Earth would be considered glass marbles and sell them to a contact in Selauê. Since she would be with Gina until they were safe, she would not be able to keep up the business. She only asked that he hold twenty percent of the profits in reserve for her. Someday she would come for it.

Such an on-going operation, he considered, might require him to establish a proper domicile nearby. It also might require him to finally accept the need to return through the tangents he had sworn off since his last meeting with Gina.

So Sebastian Talbot—a.k.a. Set-d'Elous—would come to reside in Lyas, a city in the southern half of Sekuate, close enough to *gealan* digs for convenience but far enough away for them to remain hidden. He would make regular, repeated visits to Ghoupallesz, he knew then, accepting the deal. And once there, he would be making routine visits to Selauê, then back to the desert kingdom of Aivana where the sandy fields that held *gealan* were found.

On that day of *Pouor-12*, in that Ghoupalle year of 1441, he wrote in his journal that he had collected his first profits from his initial labors: 721 *merin*. In those days, the monetary unit *merin* bought about as much as 100 dollars did in Missouri. Therefore, if some bank on Earth could do the exchange, he would have more than $72,000 for a few days' effort—a lot of money back in the early 1980s. Converting the *gealan*'s value to gold in Selauê enabled him to transfer his wealth back through the tangent to Earth, where he would exchange the gold and deposit the cash into his account at the Blue Ridge Savings & Loan at 39th Street and Noland Road.

Chapter 16

Patient Virtues

Her name was Zaura-Matousz. She was a desert goddess dressed in filmy, flowing amber robes woven of Typeg *sembour*. Sebastian could see her healthy figure easily when sunlight shone through the cloth. Yet it was some hidden force holding him in a trance, a feeling which had nothing to do with the tepid summer climate of Lyas or the spicy *erbän* fragrance wafting on the breeze from the courtyard garden below them.

"*Emai Zaura*," she spoke, her voice soft and cool. Her words bathed him in a radiant shower of sensations.

He understood what she said that first day they met, standing in the open-air corridor of his new apartment block. The glass skylight directed saffron rays down upon her shimmering golden hair, the light running down her robe to her sandaled feet. In his many journeys through the varied landscapes of Ghoupallesz since the day he first parted with Gina and returned alone to Earth, he had noticed the consistent beauty of Ghoupalle women. And yet, until that single perfect moment when that particular woman addressed him, he'd never been so completely consumed by beauty. It was a glow that extended beyond her flesh. It pressed across the green paisley tiled floor between them and tugged at his senses, playfully at first then with more insistence. If she had been a statue or a painting, he could have stood there for days feeling the electricity striking his brain with punches of pleasure in regular rhythm. The blink of her eyes, an aqua richer than the Soguirê Sea, cracked his paralysis.

He had to acknowledge her. He did not wish to be thought rude. But his poor Ghoupallêan language failed him and came out as the mumbling of a child.

"Ghou'n däl-farnim mêtik?" she asked. Did he have some illness?

He was too entranced by her to reply but she went ahead and smiled politely, bowing her head slightly in greeting or farewell. She moved off along the corridor with smooth, heavenly grace.

Locked inside his new residence, he felt he would burst with happiness. His lodging agent had moved him into the small apartment next to hers, in a two-story pallid adobe building in vaguely Roman style with a central courtyard filled with a lush garden. The city of Lyas was perched on the edge of a deep river gorge, the city streets wrapping around a pair of royal blue lakes on the tableland. He only wanted to use it as a base of operations while engaging in the lucrative *gealan* trade. The spherical stones were plentiful in the arid canyons and plateaus of southern Sekuate.

"Emai Zaura," she repeated, seeing him on other days as she came and went. Her smile was always wide and welcoming, her eyes gleaming with interest, her golden hair cascading down to her waist, curling around her face, framing it like an angel's portrait.

One day, with his back turned and his mind occupied calculating the value of his most recent harvest, he had responded spontaneously: "How do you do?"

When he turned, the puzzled expression greeting him told him that his English had slipped out again. Not only that, he had failed to respond politely for yet another time. She might not bother to greet him the next time, he knew. He quickly forgave himself and realized that she was introducing herself. He bowed his head to hers, foreheads touching, as per Ghoupalle custom, then held out his right thumb, his fingers curled into his palm.

She pressed her thumb to his and he felt a sizzle of arousal. She went further, greeting him as someone of more importance than a mere stranger; as her new neighbor, he was someone she'd be dealing with daily. She wrapped his body in a cozy embrace, a position in which each person brought one arm up toward the back of the other person's head while the other arm dropped to clench a buttock, heads held right cheek against right cheek, bodies chest to chest and hip to hip. He was dumbfounded yet quite excited. Too excited to respond in kind. When he failed to respond properly, she released him and retreated a step, recognizing him as a foreigner. More and more people from the north were coming down to take in the warm, sunny climate, after all—as she had a few years before. She apologized for being too forward and exited.

He was out during the days, but his solitary evenings were stained by the sounds of love emanating from her apartment. Trickles of laughter came through the wall, sometimes musical notes, or excited chatter—or the occasional dull bell-like motif sounding with meditative precision. He wondered what sort of people visited her. He never inquired about her occupation. When he would stay in during the day, storms passing overhead, or waiting through holidays or other business arrangements, her apartment was quiet.

They frequently met at noon, each going out or returning. She was always kind to him. Her soft, luscious invocations always melted any resilient anger tattooed on his soul from ancient days—when he had left Gina back in Siti to return to Earth, vowing never to return. Then he returned. Many times.

He would never admit that Zaura had any passing resemblance to his former lover. Once when she invited him to accompany her on an errand, he floated beside her almost like a feather, held so gently in her magnetic aura: that invisible cloud surrounding her within which her senses could reach out and affect her environment, including the foreign man walking beside her. He knew something about auras. Russian scientists had proven that all living things, plants and animals, had an energy field surrounding them. He heard that some people could train themselves to expand the range of their aura and thus their sensory perceptions. Whenever he was even within sight of Zaura, however, he could feel her aura embracing him as vividly as her body and arms had when they first met. The effect of being beside her also made his aching muscles relax and the pain of digging for hours in the sand melt away.

Her aura (*hæ* in her language), it turned out, was her job. Even among Ghoupalle people, hers was especially wide. Recognizing her natural ability, she had been sent for formal training in *senzenaxii*. As a *senzenor*, she used her natural abilities to affect the mental processes of her patients for a variety of purposes: relaxation, stress elimination, stimulation of intellectual centers in the creative mind, even fixing sexual afflictions caused by psychological imbalance. He had to laugh. His new neighbor was some kind of faith healer? But it was not so simple, he came to learn. Her 'gifts'—on Earth they would be called 'God-given' but on Ghoupallesz they were assumed to derive from her link to the planet's own energies—did improve the lives of her patients without being either obscene or illegal. He understood that intellectually. Although he'd always believed his mind to be open, he had difficulty accepting his growing attachment to his neighbor.

Her standard rate was seven *merin*—traditionally the measurement of one day's wages but in modern times fixed at a specific amount of credit. Because they had become so close, she would not accept payment from him of his largest and most valuable *gealan*: a one-inch sphere whose exterior had a silver sheen but when viewed more intently held a purple hue so deep that he often found himself gazing into its glassy depths for a long time. It was the only one he had, found in the rich deposit southeast of Aivana, his most lucrative field. He vowed never to sell it, though his dealer estimated its value at around 1000 *merin*.

She began inviting him into her apartment as she prepared for her evening's work. They enjoyed talking, and he found that she had opinions about everything. He could never understand all she said, of course, but it was enough that her musical voice soothed him and her aura bathed over him, cleansing him. He wanted to be her customer; he desired to have her aura drain the tension from him, lift fatigue from his mind. But that was not allowed; he could go to another *senzenor* across town, but not her. He would have to be satisfied with watching her exercise as she readied herself to become the instrument of healing. She stretched her legs, raised her arms, bent her back, flexed her muscles and through it all breathed rhythmically. It was a stately dance, set to the bell-tone music she played by releasing a pair of balanced hammers, letting them strike the bells alternately until she stopped them. She arranged the materials of the room, underwent her own purification ritual, sat herself down on the cushions to meditate, and had a light lunch—always the same two or three particular fruits and a kind of mineral water—followed by a nap, which he learned was a custom among Ghoupalle people: to nap after a meal, every meal. He watched over her during those nap times, stroking her hair with his eyes, caressing the curves of her figure with his mind. Sometimes she would react in a way which enabled him to imagine his own aura had touched her, had given her the sensation of physical contact.

After her nap, she would rise and bathe in the Ghoupalle style bath: a small circular tub set flush in the tiled floor with a wide lip for sitting and sponging. She asked him to rub this or that perfumed oil into her skin, and he relished the task. She spent the afternoons cleaning the side room where she performed her healing, making sure it was pure, setting out all the necessary materials. She never allowed him to help her there, explaining that it was ritual space and only she could enter it. The purification, it seemed to him, was more symbolic than physical. He saw no way the room could be completely cleaned, in every little nook and cranny, without the aid of a vacuum cleaner— which had yet to be invented in the Sekuate of 1441. He realized the time zone of Zaura was almost five hundred years *before* he and Gina would step through the curtain for the first time near Biznuik. And yet, for him it had been three Earth years and 27 trips after the first trip.

He observed the cushioned bench, the maroon drapery hanging around the pastel pink walls, scanned the shelf of oils, perfumes, powders, and juices she used, the rack of towels and other cloths, each with their own ritual purpose. He saw all of it and could come to no other conclusion than his neighbor really was some kind of prostitute. A sacred prostitute, sure;

nevertheless.... Every evening when he heard the laughter, the songs, the bells—he knew someone was enjoying her in ways he longed to. It served to alter his mood, widening the gap between the highs he experienced when with her and the lows that swallowed him when he was alone, listening to her work.

It did not take long for him to pack, and when he heard no further sounds coming from her apartment, when the dark sky was melting into the cement gray of dawn, he wrote her a note as best he could and stepped from his apartment, quietly closing the door. The note tacked to her door announced that he had spent too much time with her—though he'd enjoyed it—and had neglected his business. His choice of words was simple and direct since he was not fluent enough for subtle nuances. He hoped that she would feel the implications he left in his fingerprints on the parchment: he was too much in love with her to ignore her evening episodes with those other men and women. Then he left, taking the KOHax bus-train out of Lyas, traveling to Aivana to dig for *gealan* in the coastal beaches.

After he had collected enough to fill his small cloth bag, he went north to Selauê and sold them. The market was down so he settled for the 175 *merin* his dealer offered. He returned to Lyas to put his apartment in order and pay for the next year, in case it was that long that he might be absent. Zaura-Matousz was not there when he stopped by. That did not matter, he told himself; she was someone he enjoyed knowing but now had to forget. Like Gina.

He used the *merin* to purchase the two-inch gold ovals at the exchange in Sairel, a city at the base of the gold-rich mountains that ran down the center of the continent of Zissekap. Then he carried what he could back to Earth, where he resold it for 16,442 dollars. He put that into high-yielding Certificates of Deposit. That was the only way he could transfer wealth between his two worlds.

※ ※ ※

"You've told me all about this *stargate* place," his friend Jason said. He raised a short glass of bourbon as though making a toast and propped his sneakered feet up on the ottoman. Sebastian did not mind the casual rebuke to his furniture, apparently. Jason grinned. "But when do I get to have a look at it?"

The spontaneous answer, 'It would only bore you,' he quickly pushed back down his throat, and sought a more honest answer for his friend, mechanical wizard and automotive freak.

"It's complicated...."

"You gonna tell me, or what?" Jason filled his friend's glass. "I mean, man, I'm always hearing all these weird stories about everything you do there, and for all I know it's just some freakin' dream outta your head, man."

"You're absolutely right," he confessed. "It *is* like a dream. Also, it's dangerous, and it'll certainly be a problem for you dealing with the culture and language. You'll feel sick right after the transfer, maybe suffer ejaculation from all the electric sensations. But if you want to go, I'll take you there."

"Ejaculation?"

"It happens sometimes."

"Far out."

He gave Jason a disapproving smirk.

"When do we leave?" asked Jason.

"I don't know. I have to check the time differential. You don't want to go for a short hop through the curtain and come back to find you've lost your job because nobody's seen you for three years, do you?"

"Can that happen?"

"All the time."

Jason paused a heartbeat. "I got some vacation time coming up."

"And that's how you want to spend it? Not keep on building your dragster?"

"Naw, I need something new."

"But can you deal with that?"

Jason grinned. "I can deal it like a royal flush, man."

After he left the Ghoupalle woman, Zaura, he discovered that barely three days had passed back in his hometown on Earth. His stay on Ghoupallesz had lasted two of their months. He returned to work the next day, claiming migraine as an excuse for his absence. The supervisor frowned, recognizing a slacker when she saw one. She had to put up with him, though, because of some special arrangement.

He had returned in time for his date with Kristen, too. It was marked on his calendar: Saturday, October 12. He had forgotten about it completely during the months spent on Ghoupallesz. With a couple hours to spare, he showered and dressed, then drove to the university where she taught music in the evenings. Gazing into her warm, brown eyes, he knew, would cause all of the frustrations he felt with the strange Ghoupalle woman in Lyas to slip away.

Kristen, a blonde Nordic beauty, was a cellist in the orchestra. He was the tuba player. As her skill increased with every passing concert, she moved closer to the first chair position and further from where he sat in the back. A music teacher in her home by day, she taught strings at the university three evenings a week. Her last lesson was with him, though he was not a very good student.

They talked music during rehearsal breaks and over coffee afterwards, sometimes other subjects. Without trying, she reminded him of Gina, but he could not move their relationship to a deeper level because she was married—though unhappily. He longed to take her away from the work-aholic husband, who spent days on end in the office and returned home only for sexual relief and a battery of punches intended to prevent her from even considering leaving him or being unfaithful. Yet she had never been unfaithful. He felt it was coming, however. Only a time and place was needed, and some reasonable assurance of privacy.

Toying with her food at Los Fuentes, she broke the silence to ask him about his wife. She received only a hard stare. It was still a forbidden subject, she guessed, though she already knew about the murder. He was so hurt, she could see. She only wanted to draw him out, open him up, help him move on. But he would not allow himself to fall under her magic spell.

The back seat in his car was not large enough for them to make love comfortably, but the act was still completed with some degree of passion. He drove her to her car, parked by the auditorium where they met for orchestra rehearsals. She kissed him tenderly, talked about what they should do after the next concert. He had to come up with a plan by then.

In the evenings when he considered practicing his tuba, knowing how much his downstairs neighbor would enjoy it, he dreamed of Kristen: her long flowing blond hair—incredibly blond, almost white—her perfect face, with the cute dimple on her left cheek.

The dimple was on the right cheek for Zaura.

He began to develop a new plan. The time he spent on the other side of reality had given him more than a few insights. And more than a few hideaways. No one could ever follow him there. He knew many scenic places and welcoming towns where he would not mind living the rest of his life, especially if he had Kristen with him. The question uppermost in his mind, however, was how to tell her so she would not think he was crazy. It was possible to run away with her, but she had to understand and accept it or it would not work. The resistant mind closed the curtain.

Zaura's simple manners were similar to Kristen's., he found himself thinking in an exposed moment.

Kristen spoke English, which was a plus.

He would lie awake each night—before he began working the night shift. Unable to sleep, he would invent future possibilities and playing them through in his mind, seeing how they would turn out. Always the scientist.

The best option was to take Kristen with him to Sekuate, perhaps Lyas where the climate was warm and sunny. He had already begun his business there, so he needed to return occasionally anyway. He needed to check on his operations, do some prospecting himself. A good collection of *gealan* from a week's concentrated digging in the rich fields of coastal Aivana could easily pay for a year of freedom for them in Lyas. Or, subtly transferred to the commodity of gold on Earth, a few months of comfortable but not too luxurious suburban middle class living in yet another new city on Earth.

Sure, he could run away with her to another state, another city on Earth, but they would still be vulnerable to her angry husband's pursuit, and to the law. They would have to move constantly to keep their freedom. They would never be able to settle down, get married, have a family, or enjoy their lives in peace. Her husband, jealous as he was—abusive and vengeful— would never grant her a divorce. The one time she mentioned it, she had to miss a concert because of a dislocated shoulder.

His course of action was clear.

* * *

It was early spring when he and Jason, partner in crime, arrived in Lyas. They stayed at his apartment, and for the entire week his beautiful neighbor was away. He wanted Jason to meet Zaura most of all—some way to prove himself worthy of having an exquisite neighbor such as Zaura. Even so, he worried that Jason would not be able to contain himself and insist on staying to look for a woman like Zaura for himself. Perhaps it was best she was gone, Sebastian decided, and took Jason out to the *gealan* beds in the desert. He explained the procedures he had to go through to convert the *gealan* into something he could use on Earth. No one else but his friend Jason could possibly have listened so calmly, so patiently, and yet believe everything.

"And you just dig in the sand here until you find one of these marble things?"

"That's all there is to it," he responded, holding a smoky golden orb up to the yellow sun, examining it for flaws. "But you have to know where to dig. And you have to know which is a good one and which is a bad one. You have to be careful, too. They're so delicate. One scratch and it's ruined."

He taught Jason some of the language, a few words and phrases—enough to order a drink in a tavern. Close enough in pronunciation to get his face slapped by a dark-haired Rouê woman in the market.

Despite his hippie trappings and his drug-wasted act, Jason was several notches above average. That was how he managed to dissect a drag racer's engine and through spatial dynamics design improvements that brought him countless drag strip trophies and prizes. He was naturally interested in the motorized vehicles of Sekuate but they had passed to a time when the automobiles were of very primitive quality. They had electric-powered vehicles like buses, and the military did use a kind of truck to move supplies, but the soldiers rode *Jêpe* for more efficient cross-country campaigning. If they were going to stay longer, he promised, Jason could ride one of the airships.

The period of safe transfer was coming to an end.

"I think I could fix the motor they're using on that truck," Jason would say, hearing the rumbling of the pot-bellied engine compartment at the rear of the flatbed, the driver sitting in front with control levers reaching back to it.

"I'm sure you could, but you might get rich off the patents," he replied, fearing that he was encouraging Jason to stay. "Be careful what you wish for—because you might get it."

"Hell, no," Jason snorted. "Can't live here. No pizza."

"That's right."

"We could invent that, too, ya know?"

"And after that? A chain of restaurants called, say, McDonald's? And the formula for Pepsi?"

It was only a short trip: twelve days in local time, eighteen minutes of Earth time.

The warm desert air was unusually humid when he next walked into his Lyas apartment on the late summer evening of *Shae-14*. He could hear laughter and music from the neighboring apartment and knew that Zaura still lived there. He calculated he had been away from Ghoupallesz for thirty-two days, but found he was off by one. The electronic sensors he set up in the quarry on Earth were working well.

On his way through town, he stopped for dinner and contacted his dealer in Selauê via a kind of telegraph, the *maxa-d'anno*. The news that *gealan* prices had risen pleased him. For once, he had returned at the right time. It was just about the only time in his many lives that he would be in the proverbial right place at the right time. His investment—something like fifty thousand dollars in assets—had risen more than a hundred times in value. It was hard for him to calculate dollar profits in *merin*, but there was no doubt that this was the time to return to Aivana and gather as many of the marbles as he could carry.

As he was stepping out, dressed for the desert, his comely neighbor entered the corridor, her sweeping *sembour* gown swaying around her legs. Greeting him, she asked about his health and invited him to her party. With a bunch of strangers? No, sorry—he had business to attend to, he responded. Next time. Then she told him she had wondered if he moved away, and apologized for—in English it would have meant something like 'leading him on'. He understood her, anyway, and said he never felt that way. It was the first of many lies he would tell her.

"*Alan santor'n ashê emai-tu sevêm ga es-qath ge-gilen*," she said in her lilting voice, coming up to him, welcoming him into her embrace. Her spicy *erbän* scent intoxicated him. 'When you return, please call on me and we shall play together'—the literal meaning. He took it as only an idiomatic expression. To be polite. Then he left.

The sands were wet from a rare desert shower, but he found his markers and knelt down to begin digging for his wares. By late afternoon he had uncovered sixteen, half of them of near top quality and only two not worth transporting back to Lyas. The larger sun broke through the dingy brown clouds and began bearing down on him, drawing streams of sweat from him, then dried the moisture and reddened his skin. By dusk, the smaller blue sun was showing on the near side of its twin, hovering in the larger yellow star's corona. He packed his bags, the *gealan* carefully wrapped and separated by class into four pouches, the highest class numbering 22. Based on his dealer's information, they could bring him seven or eight thousand *merin*.

With that money, he could purchase a much better apartment for Kristen to live in.

❄ ❄ ❄

"Hey, dude, when're we gonna go back to that place you always go to?" Jason asked, looking up from under the hood of his drag racer, listening to the engine rumbling.

"First of all," he said, handing Jason the necessary socket, "I don't *always* go there, and second, it's not a good place for you to hang around—or, for you to know too much about."

"What about you?"

"I'm already too far gone to stop."

"You're always having fun there."

"I do not."

"Well, I wanna go back."

"Why? It's not such an interesting place after all, didn't you see?"

"What the hell you talking about? Those chicks there are so fine, man! We gotta go back."

He laughed.

"What makes you think you'll be any luckier there than here?"

"They're easier. Take that hooker next door to you."

He slapped the side of the car.

"Watch it, will ya?" Jason exclaimed.

"Zaura is not a hooker," he stated firmly but without his own conviction behind it. "She's really a nice girl. She's just a...a masseuse."

"Same thing," Jason concluded, not looking up. "They all get around to sex sooner or later. It all depends how much you're offering."

"You are warped. If you don't offer money, it's not prostitution."

"If there's no money, then she's a whore."

"Where do you *get* these ideas?"

The hood crashed down, and his mechanical friend stood up straight, cracking his back.

"From *you*, dude!"

"I don't talk that way. You've gotten everything twisted around in your mind. No wonder you strike out all the time. You come on like that and of course you'll get slapped. You better watch yourself. Especially those women down at the plant you hit on."

Jason turned away, grabbing a rag and wiping off his greasy hands.

"Don't worry about me, dude. Just get me back to those Lyas ladies. That's all I ask."

"You want me to be your travel agent for your sex tour of the other dimension?"

"You got it, dude."

"Give me a break, Jason. I can't do that."

"Why the hell not? You do it for yourself."

"That's the reason, to tell you the truth. Hey, I strike out there as much as back here—about like you. In fact, the only girl I ever had any relationship with there was Gina."

"Come on, man, no way! What about Margie? You took *her* there."

"That was a mistake."

"And that Kristen chick? You gonna take her there?"

He was caught by surprise. "No, of course not."

* * *

Two months after Zaura invited him to play, he once again found himself returning to Lyas through the rip in the curtain. She was waiting for him. She had put a note on his door, which he could not read other than her signature. He had just opened his door when she suddenly appeared, calling to him. The standard greeting followed, there in the corridor, and an elderly couple passing them happily remarked on the frivolous spontaneity of young lovers. Her hands slid down his sides from armpits to hips, as though she were a cop frisking him. She pressed herself against him, rubbing her aura all over him. He did not push her away, she saw, and she knew it was safe to have further relations with the foreigner.

"*Qath-se paisen-gal*," she whispered behind his ear, and let her long tongue slide out of her mouth and tickle his cheek, inviting him once more.

Inside her apartment, he was welcomed onto the couch reserved for paying customers and was lightly caressed by the beautiful, sweet-smelling goddess who watched over his soul while he was in Lyas. The oils she spread over his skin were scented in tangy *taira* and musky *vimak*, and the salts with which she softened the rough places on his body were bittersweet *sannadin* from the Sosou Isles. In the luxurious fog that enveloped him, images of angels settled around him, invoking that magical, mystical time when he had first languished in the limbo of tangent bliss with the one he most wished to love. Now, though, his thoughts vanished effortlessly and were quickly filled with the savoring of the tactile pleasures bestowed upon him. And when he chanced to open his eyes they fell upon the golden countenance of his benefactress, posed in her natural glory without her uniform, as stately and serene as the best his imagination could ever invent. When she lowered herself to kiss him, she used her slick tongue to massage his moist lips. And the pointed tips of her conical breasts pressed against his chest. And the scent of her *olar* perfume engorged his nostrils. And she lay beside him, her flesh pressed tightly to his, two becoming one. Her aura ran over him like syrup, her senses merged with his. He was in ecstasy.

The spell was broken for only a moment, when she stretched up to retrieve a bottle from the shelf on the wall. Grasping the narrow, extended neck of the stone-carved bottle, its walls so thin he could see the liquid swimming inside, she pulled off the cap. He watched her intently as she tilted the long bottle until a small drop of thin, brown liquid fell on her fingertip. She gently ran it across his lips, pressing her mouth to his to ensure that he would accept the strangely sweet potion. Another moistened fingertip was placed on the tip of his tongue, and her lingering kiss allowed their tongues to entwine, wrestle, dance—until he began to feel unusual warmth flooding through his body and his freshly powdered skin began to tingle. She was not alarmed so he presumed that his condition was normal, especially when she twisted herself over him, opened herself to him.

It was his first taste of *moussalaganê*, the elixir of love, drawn from the spiny *moussala* plant in the deserts of Typeg and Sandou. When the moment came—and it was forever spiraling upward to climax, prolonged on plateau after lofty plateau—what he had firmly thought was an ecstasy beyond comprehension was continually thrust to greater heights of intensity. She held him as a precious pet, shaking with him until his riveting began to subside. He did his best to appear unfazed by the power of the *moussala* extract. Dignity had long ago been lost in this ritual of pleasure, and if losing it meant this, then he never wanted his dignity again.

Chapter 17

Prophets and Sages

Zaura was transfixed by the stream of foreign words. She did not understand what this strange woman was telling her lover, but she thought it best not to appear insensitive to what she believed from the tone of their voices was a serious matter. So she excused herself, going to her sleeping room to pull on one of her gowns. In polite conversation, especially with strangers, it was proper etiquette in Sekuate to cover a sexually flushed body.

The month of *Gouo*, at the advent of the autumn season, was traditionally when everyone took new lovers. Before the month of pleasure could end and their brief compact expire, a visitor had arrived from a distant land. Reluctantly, Sebastian bid her enter, offered her the expected sensual hospitality. Then, refreshed, the woman, Gina's friend—whose name was Renée Simon—told him casually about the approaching tangent shift. Born in the early years of the twentieth century in Trois-Rivières, Québec, she'd had a lot of experience with tangents. At such a time, she explained, the stressed fabric of the space-time continuum would pull apart "like the wax globs in one of those old lava lamps" and leave the passageway through the curtain broken "like a bridge being washed out."

That was not news he wanted to hear, and in fact had never heard before. He tended to believe that the time differential was more or less the same between the two worlds. He told her he'd found figures in his research that led him to postulate on that effect.

But, if he remained on Ghoupallesz, said Renée, he might be stranded and never be able to pick up the reconnection later. Yes, reconnection was possible mathematically, but it was extremely difficult to predict. He took it as a kind of put-down of his tangent-ripping skills. She was adamant: Even the tangents they knew well and used often could shift suddenly and never be found again.

"Don't listen to me, then," said Renée. "I don't think you're understanding at all the importance of this effect. The whole thing is like a giant taffy. You pull it back and forth and every pull makes it softer, until finally it's soft enough to chew—if not, all the caps on your teeth come off. As for what you and Gina call *tangents*, they're pulling against each other—like a big string of taffy with each end attached to opposite sides of the universe. They're stretching thinner and thinner. That's why the time differs as it does: thinner means they're closer in sync with each other—until finally they *have* to pull apart. Just like taffy—the loose ends swim around until they bump into each other and stick together. Then the pulling begins, and the whole thing starts over. And where will you be then?"

"What's wrong with staying here and just riding it out?" he asked, but immediately saw she was perturbed by his apparent naïveté.

"Because, my dear, it may not end. There's no way to tell until it does end. That may be a day or a year here, but it could also be a hundred years. How long in Earth time? None of this has ever happened before, never in the same way, so it's unpredictable. This could be the last break, and you'd never get back again. Do you want that?"

His eyes met hers, felt the weight of her persuasion.

As much as he was enjoying this trip to Ghoupallesz, he could not sever his ties to Earth. Not now, maybe not ever. It was still home to him. That was the reason he'd returned even though Gina wanted to stay. He would never have abandoned his high school sweetheart, but she made a choice. Now the choice was his. So his visits would be short, his return home often. The very idea—the words his mind used to tell him the idea—sounded so bizarre to him that he had to confirm to himself that he *was* so far away from home.

For now, a singular loop in the fabric of the space-time continuum had paired Earth with Ghoupallesz. In the same narrow blink of real-time sat the recent past of Ghoupallesz and the late twentieth century of Earth. Renée had left her home in Québec quite by accident in 1922, found her way back when it was 1969, saw what had happened to the world during her absence, and was quite happy to return to Ghoupallesz permanently. Now, some three hundred Ghoupalle years later, she would likely die of old age if she ever returned to the home of her birth for long.

He looked up at her, standing there before him, and reluctantly nodded his head in agreement.

As he made his way with Renée to the tangent among the barren hills outside of Lyas, he told her that he planned to stay on Ghoupallesz but needed to make one last trip to Earth to tie up his affairs once and for all. Because he had chosen a life on Ghoupallesz, she mentioned a vacation cottage she owned. He liked the idea of weeks of pleasant isolation with his new Love, and so he allowed her to talk him into buying the cottage on the island of Karluk, up north in the Megank territory—providing he was able to return.

He then posed the question of what to do about his girlfriend, Kristen, and his plan to bring her to Ghoupallesz. Renée stopped, grabbed his arm.

"What about that Ghoupalle woman you were with? I thought she was your wife."

Renée was right. Who was Zaura to him? Neighbor? Playmate for the month of Gouo? Whenever he was out of sight of Zaura, his mind returned to normal and he resumed pondering Earthly matters. Kristen was the one he was meant to be with, no matter what enjoyment he had shared with the Ghoupalle woman.

"You'll get over it," she told him. "The more time you spend here, the longer you live here, the more attuned your mind and body will become. You'll soon forget everything you had on Earth. You'll forget that sense of right and wrong. Morality will be a handful of water, ungraspable. Life here will be magical."

"And is it for you?" he asked.

"Yes, I'm a perfect example. But I'll give you another example. You know those fish that live down at the bottom of the ocean on Earth, ten miles underwater? The pressure down there is so great that if you brought them up to the surface they'd explode from the *lack* of pressure. If you brought them up slowly—in geological or evolutionary time—they could adapt and be able to live on the surface. It's the same for us."

"If we go home too quickly we explode?"

"No, but we do get used to this place the longer we stay. I'll tell you—since we're all like a fraternity here, all of us who travel the dimensions—you'll know when the time comes, when you've adapted reasonably well, well enough that you can think of yourself as a native. That's when you start feeling the universe pulling you apart—"

"Oh, you mean the headaches?"

"You have them already?"

"Like gravity working in opposite directions."

"That's what it feels like," Renée responded with a half-hidden congratulatory smile. "You are on your way to becoming a first-class Interdimensional Voyager."

"And when the tangents are closing—which is when I can pass most easily between them—that's when the headaches are worst."

"Maybe you are already first-class."

"If having more painful headaches is all I can expect, then I don't want to be a damn First-Class Voyager."

"Then stay one place or the other. Since you've already started having them, I suggest you stay here. It will be easier for you to return home from here than come here from your original dimension. You will be all right, then. But you will have more and more trouble going back."

The cottage on Karluk came up when he said the Ghoupalle woman was only his neighbor and it was the month of *Gouo*, something about their customs. He did not fully believe it himself. Zaura was wonderful—she had the *aura*: Zaura the Aura, he nicknamed her, and laughed. Renée asked why the laugh. He lied and said he was thinking about the look on Kristen's face when he told her where they were going.

"If you do it right," Renée advised, "you can have her up there on Karluk Island and she will think she's living off the coast of Norway. It's beautiful there."

It was his for a thousand *merin*, two ferry tickets included. He saw the idyllic life that faced him in a romantic hue. The simple life. Just him and his beloved, deeply in love. What did they need with civilization, no matter where it was? All he needed was Kristen, away from the people that hurt them both. Yes, he said, and gave Renée the payment in *para* notes, ten to the *merin*, from his knapsack.

"You'll love it up there, I promise," she said. "The perfect honeymoon getaway. Nothing to do but make love. That's where I got away to with my fifth husband, Laguad. What a lover he was!"

"I hope the bed's been cleaned since then."

"What bed?"

✳ ✸ ✳

When he met Kristen at the university between music lessons, she was grinning, a big secret hidden behind her smile.

"What's up?" asked Sebastian.

"I have good news," she replied, almost singing.

He contemplated in a heartbeat the odds of one person's good news being another person's bad news, and felt they were stacked against him. They had been before. Her news was that her husband had finally seen the error of his ways. He had apologized. He had begged her to forgive him. He had cried. They had reconciled. He was treating her again just as he had during their honeymoon and she could not be happier.

"That's wonderful," he lied. It was becoming easier, he noticed.

She was so bubbly, telling him about her wonderful new situation, he could not believe that it was not true. There could be no other reason for her to act so contrary to her usual, reserved persona. She explained how it happened, and, yes, he could see how it *was* possible to make up with a monster. And spouses—being what spouses were—were always more willing to try and improve a bad situation than abandon it as hopeless and admit failure—failure in marriage, failure in love, failure in life. He understood.

The result was the same: once alone, always alone.

*　*　*

The tangents mended quickly and Sebastian was on the first flight back.

In Lyas, he could barely cross the town without tears coming to his eyes, thinking about his rejection. How he could lose so soundly to another loser, he could never accept. He swore he would put Kristen out of his mind forever. And his neighbor, Zaura, so resembled Kristen that he had to leave. Zaura was not home when he was moving out of his apartment, paying the landlord. He told himself that perhaps it was for the best. He wanted to revel in his melancholy.

Taking the KOHAX bus-train up to Selauê, he rode the airship to the city of Elêna on the northwest coast of Tebbicousimankalê and caught the ferry for Karluk Island. On the voyage, the crisp northern air revived him, brought back his lust for life. It was spring again. He dropped his suicidal contemplations.

Snowy mountain crests were his first sight of the island, the peaks penetrating the low ring of clouds. Soon the rickety old pier greeted them, along with the collection of shacks and warehouses, the fish cannery and the old Zetin temple on the hillside. There were the Zetin people, lining the wharf to receive the latest news and supplies from the ship that docked only once a month.

He was shown the cabin by one of the town officials who doubled as lodging agent. No, it was not a cute little cottage as

Renée had let him believe. It was a cabin—rather worn, too, but he could see the potential in it. The view of the coastline and the sea from the front door was spectacular. He waved away the persistent thought that it would have been a nice honeymoon cottage. He moved in, not changing much, and slept a long sleep.

Some villagers soon learned of his heartbreak and conspired to keep him healthy against his will. It was a nearly impossible task, they soon discovered, fighting against his best efforts to kill himself through sloth and vile self-indulgences. He slept all day, drank all night. The days in which he did rise before dusk, he would usually chase the bushy-tailed *grael* up and down the hills. He hated their baying, but gradually he lost his hatred, and soon became exhausted running after them, satisfied to regard their quick, animated frolicking.

The various seeds villagers gave him he eventually planted in the small plot beside the cabin, and then watched them daily for signs of life as they sprouted and grew through the brief summer months. He harvested the odd vegetables and took them down to the village to share with the other islanders during their festivals. The haunting melodies of the village band bore into his brain and sucked out the anger he had managed to bury there.

The melancholy tunes—the sweet plectrum sounds of the *arkôt*; the soft twang of the small bowed *goul*; and the cool flute-like *uel*—provided a black magic that transformed him into the maniac that he always knew he was. In an unexpected rage, he tore up his garden, frightened the *grael* away to the upper pastures, stormed through the village streets in the middle of the night, breaking into the temple before he knew what it was. In his drunken fit, he knocked over a lamp inside and burned the Zetin holy book on the stone mantelpiece before he could put it out. Horrified by his actions, he charged back to his cabin and threw himself from the cliffs.

The jagged rocks below moved out of his way and he splashed head-first into the icy waters, baptized.

Rising phoenix-like to the surface, he had the first of many conversions. He caught his breath and felt his long-sought sanity welling up within him.

Once back in his cabin, wrapped in blankets and warmed by

the stove, he knew he had been on Karluk long enough. It was time to move on, to get on with his life. He sat back and pondered just how lucky he was: to take a few months to sort through life's priorities and still come back to Earth with only a few hours lapsed.

Returning to Lyas, he found his way to his former apartment building, only losing directions twice. How long had it been? Only a year since he first made love with the woman named Zaura. He wanted to be with her again, to be within the hold of her aura once more. That was as good as being in heaven.

He stayed with Zaura just long enough to observe her lifestyle, much the same as it had been when he first met her. She loved to be loved. There were parties, and there were her customers—patients, they were called. Once she gave him a few *para* bills and sent him off to the new *têprexi* show in town, a ritualized song and dance performance, when a special customer was coming to see her. He paid double, she told him. The businessman was from Sairel, the main city of the eastern plateau, a garden oasis. She said his company was involved in processing the *moussala* plants. He did not wish to know any more about him. He did not go to the concert but watched her apartment from outside.

When the lights went out, he headed toward the hills out the east side of town where he knew he could find the right tangent. How he wanted her now, he confessed to the vast panorama of stars. Different stars. Alone in the universe, he sighed. He was merely a stranger in a strange land, lost and abandoned, doomed to listen to others' laughter, to see the happiness that other people shared. He did not know how much more he could take. But if he left that night, he conceded, he could never return with any clear conscience.

He turned around and by dawn was back in town, let in by a sleepy Zaura. She could not understand why he was always running around in the middle of the night when everyone was supposed to be safely stowed away in their homes, safely asleep on their *qala*. No wonder he always looked so tired. He needed his beauty sleep, too. And he needed friends, she told him. Friends were as necessary to good health as proper diet, and to that end she would have a party for him. He would meet many wonderful new people, and some of them he "may want to ask for a love test"—the translations were becoming tricky. If he met a lady who pleased his belly and feet, Zaura explained as gently as she could—more tricky translations—then he should declare his desire for union at once—and boldly.

Gazing straight into her aquamarine eyes, the words choked in his throat.

It was a surprise party, he discovered, walking through the doorway. He had spent the day working on his *gealan* business, examining his wares, pricing them, keeping the books accurate, and now that he was mentally and physically drained, here was Zaura's party waiting to eat him. He saw her handsome guests, twenty men and women, doing strange dances throughout her newly decorated apartment. Everything was pale blue now. The theme seemed to be exotic feathers.

And Zaura? There she was, face to face with a tall man in flowing robes like hers, both her palms pressed against his palms, arms raised above their heads, engaged in some kind of pushing match. They raised first their right legs, then their left legs; dipping nose to nose, wiggled their butts back and forth; leaning back, they waved their elbows like birds flapping their wings. It had to have some meaning, he supposed. The music sounded rather ornithological: hammered plucking on the *arkôt* and birdy squawks from the clarinet-like *bul-hann*. He called it the Funky Chicken.

A willowy girl named Seasö, one of Zaura's closest childhood friends, tried to teach the dance to him, but he never caught on with his three left feet. When the thin, brown-haired girl had talked him out of his *blaxan* tunic, he finally began to relax. But laying skin-to-skin beside Seasö in the dark, forced to listen to Zaura talking with another Ghoupalle man—didn't catch his name, didn't want to—was not an equal turn of events, he decided. They talked as she strummed her fingers across his nipples. He tried the same with hers but she disliked it—or he was doing it wrong. Everything felt awkward. Seasö did not use any *moussalaganê*, either, though she did try to turn him on by screwing her skinny fingers in and out of his ear canals. It didn't work. Neither did licking the back of his elbows.

In the middle of the night he left.

Chapter 18

Love on the Rocks

Sebastian Talbot, tax examiner, wasn't sure he could put up with the drudgery of his new job. Just back home from a Thursday night overtime shift at the IRS Service Center during the peak of the tax season, he was ready to stretch out for a marathon of sci-fi movies he had been recording off the cable TV during the past month. Then Renée visited him.

She did not even knock on the door but tore through the curtain straight into his bedroom. He heard the noise, thought it was another stupid burglar. Prepared to practice his curve ball swing, he found instead a woman tangled in the long cords of the window shades. He lowered the baseball bat.

"You're getting to be like a Ghoupalle," he told her, half joking and half irritated.

Renée apologized, explained her reason for dropping in unexpectedly. It was Gina, she said. Gina was near death, lying in a hospital in Kipzon. There was no accident, no injury or disease. It was old age, plain and simple. Renée had been living a relaxed, slow-paced, contemplative lifestyle. Gina, on the other hand, was a candle burning at both ends, always grabbing as much Ghoupalle gusto as she could, for as long as she could. Now her body had given up. If her situation was like the sci-fi movie he had just loaded into the VCR, she could simply transfer her soul—with all her thoughts, memories, and personality intact—to a new body right off the assembly line. That was not the way things were done in Ghoupalle year 1443.

"I thought she would live forever," he cried out, unable to accept that her death was so near, so real.

"She has," Renée explained, "but her body has lived all of its years. She's had a great career—lived many lives, had many loves. But at this time and place, it's come to an end. It just happens to be in the time *there* which is right *now* here on Earth."

"What's that supposed to mean?"

"I mean, she still exists elsewhere, in other time zones. She's still quite alive *somewhere*. This is only where the voyage ends. Like her character dies in chapter ten but we still read about her earlier adventures in the remaining chapters. We can see it *now*— and maybe, in your other journeys, you will meet her again. It will be her past but your present."

"My future," he sighed. "I won't be going back. I vowed never to return."

"That's up to you, but if that's your plan, then you should make at least this one last trip to see her off properly."

"To the Great Beyond? I thought we proved it doesn't exist."

"We all die, even Interdimensional Voyagers."

"Well, I won't let them say I refused to attend another Voyager's funeral."

＊ ❋ ＊

She lay as he expected to find her, sheets pulled up over her old, frail body, a nozzle from a breathing apparatus hooked into her nose. It was not too different from people dying on Earth, he thought. But then, he had never known anyone who died, not personally. All of his relations on Earth were alive still. Gina was his first death, and the one he least could accept.

She opened her eyes at that moment, when his breath grew quicker, and he suddenly took her all in: the paper-thin flesh hanging wrinkled on scrawny limbs, deep-sunken eyes, knobby cheeks, toothless jaws, hair fallen from her head—

"You came," she uttered, interrupting his remorse.

"Yes, I—"

"I knew you would."

He glanced at Renée, who stepped back until she was against the wall.

"You're still handsome," said Gina, "a handsome boy...forever young."

What could he say? He had not seen Gina for years—his years—and had scarcely heard about her for almost as long. Now she was suddenly transformed into a crone, a hundred Earth years, maybe a hundred-twenty she appeared to be. It was a different person he had loved and been loved by, in a far away time, in a strange and exotic place called Earth. In a flash it seemed like only yesterday they were lugging their equipment up the gravel drive to the abandoned quarry. They were making love on the flat rock. He suddenly recalled when the old man caught them trespassing. And the next time, when they finally tore the curtain—

She had been speaking to him, her voice unusually clear, her spirit strong yet.

"I have a secret to tell you," she whispered.

He leaned down.

"I will see you again," she said, "many times, in the future— and we will be lovers once more. We will have a child, you and me."

"We will?"

"A daughter."

"That's a nice wish," he said, being gracious.

Somehow, gazing into her dull eyes, he could not feel confident in her statement. Would she be old? If that was what she meant, how could he be her lover? How could they have a child?

"Listen to me," she said, her voice fading. "I can't tell you...all of the times...when we meet but—we *will* meet again—*when you're a free man, when you're a free man again....*"

She was singing the last line of the Moody Blues' song, he realized, from the *Seventh Sojourn* album. He had it sitting in his cassette deck when Renée arrived to fetch him. Gina's last letter had included that line—when she beckoned him to remember her the way she was that one special summer long, long ago. It was just eight years ago, he counted. She committed suicide after writing that letter, he believed—yet he had forgotten it until that moment. No, she did *not* kill herself there in Liêta, with her husband out fishing on the lake, as she had written!

"You killed yourself, Gina—in Liêta," he cried, shaking with anger. "I have your letter. Renée gave it to me a long time ago. How could you be dying now—in this hospital bed—in Kipzon?"

Her dry, contracted lips began to smile, turned up at the corners in a wide death grin.

"That's my secret," she said with a chuckle. "That's your mystery to solve."

"Mystery...? You mean what happened after you decided not to commit suicide?"

"Yes—"

He just stared at her, regarding her in her glory and her triumph, feeling again the bonds that had merged their souls. They were becoming one now—again—but he could feel hers weakening, drifting away. Soul mates forever.

"I love you, Gina," he mumbled, "I always have."

She closed her eyes.

"I always will...."

* * *

A box of papers was turned over to him in the hospital's archives. He took it solemnly, not looking through them at all. Renée told him some of what they were: property deeds, letters of credit, certificates of this and that, royal decrees, charts and maps of her travels, lists of relatives past and future, declarations of marriage, several phony death certificates, and the real one. At the bottom was a letter. It was sealed and was thinner than her suicide letter had been.

Opening it as they rode south on the KOHAX to Lyas, he scanned the first line:

I have lived three-hundred and seventy-six years on this world, loved one hundred men, and given birth to twenty-two children.

He turned to Renée sitting beside him, reading over his shoulder, and they both smiled as they read the second line:

Catch me if you can!

He gazed at the plateau of Ilait as they traveled to Lyas, the wall of stone rising there on his left for several hours, the cradle of Zissekap civilization, the Atlantis of Ghoupallesz. It was now a scattering of rugged canyons perched atop the towering mesa. He imagined Gina as their queen, the mother of all Ghoupallesz, and he felt joy in his heart. He would see her again, when she was younger, when she was in her vibrant, exciting youth. She had said so. She knew it. It would be when he was able to achieve whatever his most dynamic possibility would be. General? King? God? That pleased him. It inspired him. There on the ramparts of ancient Ilait, where Ghoupalle civilization was born, he would stand with his queen, and together they would rule the known universe. They would be the sovereigns of their ancestors' many worlds, and be the benevolent gods the races had so long desired.

"What are you thinking?" Renée asked him.

"Nothing."

When they pulled into Lyas, they parted. Renée changed to the KOHAX for Sairel, to connect with her jungle tour of the Galguin Basin. He sat down his bag, overflowing now with Gina's papers and personal effects. The bright autumnal day conjured dreams of immortality that he was reluctant to tuck away in his pocket. But vouchsafe them he did, for a rainy day. Such days did not often come to the dry, chaparral of Lyas. Therefore, he mused, his dreams were protected for a long time.

"Time to change my life," he told himself.

In long, gray jerkin and *Buiske* trousers, boots of *kann* leather on his tired feet and a long, triangular crimson cape thrown over his left shoulder as was the fashion, dressed too heavily for late summer heat, Sebastian—a.k.a. Set-d'Elous—returned to the apartment where his Love resided and stormed past the shocked party guests. He took Zaura of the House of Matousz firmly in his arms, singing a song of melancholy and placing his single silver/purple *gealan* in her soft, open palm and curled her fingers around it, pressing her fist to her heart. On his knees—which was not a Ghoupalle custom—he turned his face to hers, taking her other hand, and cried out to her the words which made tears drop from her eyes and land on his cheeks:

"*El-in vem-stae ne-puzend madexon-se gah art uelen-tas lous-se nasser-defomen qant elmai zu laen qâm Ghoum.*"

He waited for her reply, repeating his words in his head—they sounded correct enough: 'I can no longer endure the waiting, and watching the lights turn out without me beside you.'

"*Zil, Kalmonê,*" she spoke, barely above a whisper, before he could finish even half of the full statement he had prepared and memorized. 'Yes, Sir.'

"*El aven-y'da rik jumai-se il elr qala,*" he struggled on through her joyful tears. 'I must have you in my bed.'

Thus it was that Sebastian Talbot—known to this Ghoupallean woman, Zaura-Matousz, by the rather odd name of Set-d'Elous—begged for the right to join with her in partnership, a literal translation of the Ghoupalle words, on the twentieth day of the month of *Shae*, in the year 1444, in the city of Lyas in Sekuate-sotos. It was recorded so in the city archives.

For the ceremony, it was easier for them to return to her hometown of Selauê.

Once there, he had to bear the scrutiny of her large family—five brothers and five sisters, and her parents: mother Basha-Ym and father Metour-Matousz. The eldest sibling, Rasek, immediately disliked the 'mucus-leaking-nosed weakling-of-outland-places'—direct translation (colloquially: 'snotty foreign wimp')—but others in the family tentatively approved the union. It was Rasek's duty to protect his younger sister, of course. However, Zaura was not the eldest child, nor even the eldest daughter, so she was expendable, free to mate with a foreigner, even one who was shorter than she was.

To the great archives of Selauê they went. The gray stone monstrosity was a labyrinthine combination of library, public records office, and science and history museum. It was the place where couples went to file marriage papers, where new residents arranged their legal and social matters, where students did research. It was a genealogist's dream: records of anyone and everyone who had ever lived in or passed through the city were kept indefinitely. That presented a rather awkward problem for him when it was their turn to complete the form on family history, required for a partnership certificate to be stamped to initiate their new joint record.

Zaura was born on *Joäon-1*, the first day of the year 1411, so he chose 1405 as the year of his birth. Since his real birthday on Earth was in the spring, he selected a suitable month on the Ghoupalle calendar and used the real number of the day. His betrothed was alarmed. She had thought he was younger than she was. Superstitious folk believed it was bad luck for the man to be older than the woman. A five-year difference was deemed most desirable.

He asked her if that made a difference to her, quite willing to change the year on the form.

No, she replied, yet it would be difficult to keep it from her family, who would review the paperwork prior to the ceremony.

Her parents could not, however, change anything or prevent the marriage now that she was above the legal first-marriage age of twenty-five. That seemed like a long time to wait, but considering the normal life-span was easily a hundred years, twenty-five did not seem so long, he decided, and since physical maturity arrived by twenty-five for females and thirty for males, it made sense. On Earth, he would be credited with only twenty-seven years, while she had thirty-three Ghoupalle years now, although she appeared to be twenty in Earth years.

His place of birth was Lyas, he wrote, but when that surprised her, he quickly explained that his family soon moved to Siti in Ghoupallaessêa, the city where he and Gina had spent most of their early days. By his accent, Zaura believed him.

He would continue making up his life, something he wished he could have done back on Earth: his nursery school, his primary and secondary schools, and his university, his military career—which he could give more weight to because of the time he mistakenly spent in the service of the Jisilikan army, more than two-hundred years earlier. More recently, he could claim the mission for which he won the award from Gina—The Grand Medal of the Royal House of Kish and Tek, or something like that—presented to him personally by Queen Jinetta. It was the highest honor the nation of Fenula could bestow upon anyone, citizen or foreigner, and it was his. He would have saved Gina's life even without the medal, and with no consideration of her rank as first-queen by marriage to the fourth Sartan-Tek.

That he was a military man surprised Zaura. He had no boisterous scowl or arrogant swagger like a soldier. He took it as a compliment. He only did temporary assignments, he said—"only every fifty years or so," he added under his breath in English. She told him that her family would be proud that she had "caught" a military man. Now, if he could only be assigned to the Selauê garrison nearby, their life together would be perfect. His smile told her she was right.

The things people found out about each other when the wedding day came!

The actual day was *Batou-10*—after the three busy days filling out papers. It was easy for Zaura, whose memory was typically Ghoupallean, a storehouse of everything she had every done. His, however, was a paint-by-number picture of a crudely fabricated life, which he changed and substituted freely, never to be set in stone. Zaura did not mind; they were in love. They would "turn out the light together"—as her mother kept saying.

Early on the wedding day, he and Zaura were loudly paraded around the neighborhood park, white flags waving to call attention to the disgrace the Matousz family must endure. Another daughter of theirs was going to be raped—and by a foreigner, too! Please have sympathy for the family, and give gifts and food to help them get through the tragedy! That's what they were chanting to people on the street. Some who watched them bowed low in respect. One fellow cried out the same disgrace happened to his family. Others pulled money from their purses and handed or tossed them to the family members or the hired substitutes for family members who could not attend the parade. He was embarrassed, understanding only half of what was being spoken. Zaura smiled, however, letting him know it was all part of the customs—old traditions that were not dying hard at all.

After twenty laps, they entered and at the center of the park the procession halted. The wedding couple were pulled down from the cart and separated. To his right stood Zaura, his bride, and her sisters were cutting away her clothing, knives ripping the gown to shreds. At the same time, the men of her family were similarly removing his clothing in a rather violent way. He tried to resist but he saw Zaura was laughing at her experience. Soon they were without clothing. Her father came to him and with a brush painted a red strip down his chest. Her brothers spun him around and the painting was repeated down his back. Zaura wore a blue strip down between her breasts and down her back. For a moment their eyes met and he knew everything would be all right—if he could just get through the ceremony.

They were led off by leashes attached to ribbons encircling their waists and a few blocks away were sat down at opposite ends of a long table.

An outdoor feast was prepared. A family feast! Many of the relatives were on hand to inspect both the bride and her foreign groom, both in their nakedness. Most relatives offered the traditional sympathy for the family's loss. It will be better, they said, after children are born and grow up to do great things. Only then would the family's honor be restored. Some of the male relatives easily joked how they wished they were not related to the bride, while some of the female relatives took close gazes at the groom's particular apparatus—one cousin in a rather scientific examination, others with a giggling reaction to his blushing.

Something like toasts were spoken and food was shared— except with him or his bride. They were fasting, it seemed. One young girl teased him by holding a piece of meat in front of his face and snatching it away when he tried to bite it. You'll get your turn tonight, the girl laughed.

When the feast was done and the tables cleared, the relatives again formed a procession and went down several more streets—the happy couple paraded with them—to the temple. He knew it was a temple by the large golden symbols on the roof. The seven gods and nine goddesses would welcome them inside and bless or curse the union. The outcome was not yet decided. There were tests to perform, he imagined.

Relatives inquired about his family. Where were they? Were they dead? Did he hate them? Didn't they want him to be united with a *senzenor*? Poor man!

He had to make excuses for his family. He said he was an only-child and his parents were now deceased. They believed him—except for eldest sibling Rasek who swore to investigate his soon-to-be brother, a man of relatively short stature from a distant land.

The others were happy to assist in the ceremony, helping to collect the ritual ingredients to be mixed in a large silver bowl: samples of saliva, blood, urine, hair, and skin. The bowl was held aloft by Zaura's mother as solemn words were spoken by a man wearing a heavy yellow *raelor* robe and wearing an amulet shaped like the Cyrillic alphabet character G (Г) next to the P (П). He could not understand the words, but learned later that they were ancient words of which no one but the priest knew the meaning. Naturally, he thought. It made perfect sense that the marriage couple should not know what they were getting themselves into, should not know what promises were being made. Certainly, he had no doubts about Zaura, only about the bureaucracy he was being led through to be able to sleep with her. As he listened to the droning voice, he came to realize that the Г and П had special meaning: symbols of the words *Ghou-Palle* (Ггω-Пɕʮ), which meant "Paradise of the Gods." The people who bore the name *Ghoupalle* had fallen from that paradise, having angered their sixteen gods and goddesses in some way.

The silver bowl holding the potion of their combined bodily samples was blessed by the robed man and set afire by Zaura's father. Thank goodness they did not have to drink it, Sebastian sighed. When the contents had been consumed and the fire extinguished, it was filled, without cleaning, by what he thought was a kind of wine. It was not; it was *moussalaganê*—straight and pure. A lethal dose! Kneeling together on the white mat in the center of the room, he and Zaura took turns drinking from the bowl. The juice had the wedding couple ranting and raving like wild animals on the floor in front of everyone within minutes. When the first act was completed, the guests cheered and popped open real wine, pouring it for each other even as the wedding pair continued coupling without pause until they finally lay exhausted on the floor some time later. The guests had long returned to the party, only occasionally watching the show on the floor. More cries of sympathy from relatives and other onlookers at the ceremonial ravaging of their poor daughter. The parents accepted their best wishes and hoped they would overcome the shame soon.

Zaura's eyes were shining, her face warm and glowing in a hue that reminded him of the most beautiful sunset he had ever seen.

This is my wife, thought Sebastian and kissed her quickly on the mouth, despite the act being very much against custom when in a public venue. She grabbed a sitting cloth from one of the seats and drew it over their heads. Now they could kiss in private.

The guests soon gathered them up and took them outside where the naked, sweaty, *moussalaganê*-flushed pair were set atop the *Jêpe*-pulled carriage for a ride to their home. In their case, it would be the house of Zaura's parents. They would stay there through the honeymoon—all the better for Zaura to be advised by her mother.

Three of the relatives brought a large brown cloth and other relatives helped pull it over the wedding couple, grabbed arms and legs, and helped enclose the pair inside the cloth. When he got his head out a hole, he was hit in the face by a drop of rain.

The sky was darkening, turning green. Another bad omen, Rasek declared. Then the rain began to fall: fat, green plops like paint shaken from a brush, followed by a steadier, lighter shower. The air was warm, the rain refreshing—except for its color, which was merely the reflection of the sunlight.

He did not mind being paraded around town with his new wife, wearing the brown garment designed for two, a long double-shirt. One more symbol of their life together, he cursed. It was cramped, though he enjoyed their moist flesh sticking together beneath the rough *raelor* fabric.

After another festive twelve-course dinner, the couple were escorted to bed for the night, with Zaura's mother sleeping on the floor near Zaura's side of the *qala*. Instead of the usual four-legged furniture of Earth, the typical Ghoupalle sleeping device was a thin yet firm hammock-like bed suspended from the ceiling by its four corners. Her mother awakened them twice when they had fallen asleep, concerned that they were not using their time engaged in doing what was expected of them. They were supposed to mate constantly for the first day—a 29.84 Earth-hours day. The first hundred-eleven times were the most crucial to assuring a fruitful family, she reminded Zaura.

In the morning, the mother reported the couple's lack of enthusiasm to the others, and Zaura's father had a long talk with him about his daughter. Through the words he was able to understand—the man spoke in a thick, country dialect—it seemed that, although she had been a *senzenor*, a profession where she used her aura to heal people, she was not too delicate to be taken as...what was the word he used? As a *jalo*, something like a bear with horns, the animal most descriptive of rough and persistently bold sexual activity in Ghoupalle lore. He assured Metour-Matousz, his "bride-father," that he did not think Zaura was too delicate; they were merely too tired from the day's activities.

"*Mêmo fasuen-kal?*" Metour cried out so the whole family could hear him.

They all laughed at his inquiry about their fatigue, some of them covering their grinning mouths. Perhaps they should try again, the family suggested. Basha, the mother, offered to go out and purchase a bottle of top-grade *moussalaganê*, but Metour stopped her, saying that the couple needed to be able to do the act without any assistance or it would not be real. Any child that resulted could be deformed or an idiot. Real passion made the best grandchildren, he told the woman.

The new husband was behind schedule; only ninety-three more!

Zaura was crying, upset over all the trouble. She wanted to

please her family, whom she had not seen much in three years. Now it seemed she had failed miserably. Her new husband went to her and comforted her, as gently as he could. Soon they were making love again, naturally and passionately.

Metour listened from outside the door, giving a play-by-play report to the others—and loud enough that he was sure his daughter could hear him—chastising them, insisting they were too quiet. He joked that they must have fallen asleep again.

I will do my best to empty him, Zaura called to her father through the door, of course in Ghoupallêan.

Zaura kissed her husband. They regarded each other solemnly, knowing the truth of their pleasure. She suggested they had better make some noise so her family could get on with their lives. The next night was loud and kept everyone awake, the couple's intentional moaning and groaning making her father wish he had not advised the foreigner to be rougher with his delicate daughter.

After almost two weeks, they had met the goal and were allowed to depart. Her family was pleased and had a final feast for them. They were not painted and were allowed to wear clothing this time. They sat together, white ribbons linking them neck to neck. Rasek stood in the corner most of the evening, staring hard at him.

In the morning, Set-d'Elous and his wife, Zaura-Matousz, were relieved to finally leave Selauê on the KOHAX for Lyas. They were the happiest mixed couple on the planet, he guessed, although he never stopped to consider the consequences of marrying an alien.

Chapter 19

Idyll

With a crystal green sky curving overhead, he laid his tired body against the supple, emerald hillside, content to let the *grael* graze unwatched, listening to distant cries of *sangi* as they darted through the springtime air.

From his lunch box pillow he could see the village below, at the far end of the long, scooped valley which slipped down between the two ridges that met as towering cliffs at the northern end of Karluk Island. A ship was coming in, he saw, would take another hour to reach the wharf. He had watched more than a few come in during the past several months. A life of pleasant ease was what they had, he and his bride, Zaura-Matousz.

He scanned the high meadows for any *grael* that might have wandered too far, letting his mind sail off and land wherever it happened to fall. He had already forgotten what day it was, though it ceased to matter. His life began on *Batou-10* the previous year when he married Zaura. He numbered everything from that day. Such was the simple peasant life. He smiled, knowing the year 1445 would be the best year of his life.

Zaura tended the garden and he herded the *grael*. Their cabin he had bought from Renée to hide Kristen away in had become the honeymoon cottage for Zaura. Now that cottage would be the birthplace of their child in a few more weeks.

She had not wanted to move away to far off Karluk at first, even hated it when she first arrived. Since her career had ended rather abruptly upon marriage—no such thing as a married *senzenor*—she was content to try something new. Not truly understanding what had happened, he was secretly glad of it. It affected her powers somehow. Perhaps he had become too used to her; her aura seemed weaker. Or perhaps it was only because of her pregnancy. Either way, he thought, it was an inevitable development, as certain as long winter nights result in summer babies.

They had arrived in autumn, one of the last ferries before winter set in. The four months of isolation the island endured during winter only served to solidify their union. They had to help each other. It was a test. Now that spring had blossomed on the island, there could be nothing more perfect: the cool, crisp northern air and the gorgeous rainbows of morning showers, the thick gray grasses the *grael* loved to eat, and the round woman who waited for him every evening. He should have married her much sooner, moved to Karluk earlier, dived into this simple life a long time ago.

He did not need his *gealan* business any longer; he had closed it out in Lyas before they left. He still had a partnership in the business, but he fully expected to be cheated out of his share. And that was all right; if he were able to gather any of it, it would be all the profit he ever wanted. He already had enough from what he had collected over his short career. Running a calculation through his head—momentarily distracted hearing his ragged shepherd, the dog-like *hanno*, chasing down a stray kid—his *merin* account in Selauê was at 72,000 when they stopped there heading northwest to catch the ferry from Elêna.

Karluk Island had greeted them on a clear, golden afternoon when snow already blanketed the upper pastures. They had stayed in the village for a week until they could get up to the cabin. He bought *grael* from another shepherd, the same man he sold them to when he left Karluk before. The seeds now growing in the garden were gifts from the villagers. They had plenty, and could only look forward to the day they would become bored with the pleasant, peasant life.

He stood up, seeing the ship at last sliding against the dock, telling himself that day would come. It came before when he was here and it would surely return. Until then, they were bursting with joy at every sunrise, savoring every sunset, and worshipping the intimate moments between. Every meal he sat down to; every time he turned back the blankets and found his warm, loving wife waiting for him; every day he saw her hanging laundry on hooks along the back of the cabin and thought her waist might have grown a little larger—everything reminded him of his happiness. If he ever asked for a dream to come true, it was the world he was experiencing now, at that very moment—"At this given second, as my heart beats," he cried out, and a few *grael* trotted away, startled by his outburst.

"Is festivarê in villajê," his pregnant wife told him when he returned at dusk, driving the twenty *grael* before him. She spoke broken words of the language he had been teaching her. He enjoyed hearing her try to speak English. There was a festival down in the village tonight, she said. Ah, he was tired—from sitting on the slopes and watching the goat-things all day. He got up early to milk them before breakfast, too. He always felt energized sitting around the bonfire with the villagers, watching the dances and listening to the music, hearing tales of Zetin myths and magic the shaman told. The people of the island were like one family and gathered frequently to feast. It was something he looked forward to no matter how tired he thought he was. He regretted only that Zaura was too pregnant to dance around the fire with the other women as she had done when they were new on the island.

He made sure all the *grael* had entered their pen for the night, then trudged to the entrance of the cabin, pulled off his dirty clothing there and stepped over to the washing place. The only plumbing was the bucket they used to take water from the barrel where it collected, over to where it was needed. He stepped on the wooden palette beside the cabin, looking up at the stars, thankful that, among everything else, it was no longer too cool to shower outdoors.

"Is *ne*-good *emai*, my *jiji*," she told him, pouring the water over him. He smiled at her. It was more difficult for him to understand her when she mixed the two languages, but he knew she was telling him she did not feel well. He could go down to the village alone if he wanted to attend the festival.

"I can't leave you here by yourself," he answered, seeing her trying to comprehend his words, then repeated them in Ghoupallêan.

She kissed him and proceeded to dry him off in the folds of her wide apron.

"*Ju* go to, *Eben* stay—is good-*kal*?" she said.

Sending him inside, she began preparing her own bath. That was something he never could get used to. Ghoupalle customs were generally not too bad, but one which he hated was that pregnant women were supposed to sleep separate from their husbands. Zaura told him it was the custom, and he laughed, wondering what the big deal was, even if he promised not to touch her. She could not be seen unclothed in her pregnancy, either. He was not allowed to witness the birth of the baby either. Customs were customs. What he called The Old Ladies Society oversaw the birth of all babies on the island.

"When on Ghoupallesz...," he mused, dressing to go down to the village.

The sky was growing dark, the stars above forming the *Qannor* and the *Dikondra*. Then, hearing the water splashing outside the closed window, he promised to bring back some of the red candied *frûmkin* that old lady Uz'A always made.

The village was dancing when he arrived, welcoming the ferry and the latest allotment of wares. Everyone was rejoicing at the arrival of spring and the renewed ferry shipments. The crew and six passengers were invited to take part in the feast. A huge dinner was laid out before the chief's house. The reason, he quickly learned, was that the eldest son of the chief had returned on the ferry, away two years at the university in Loulê, capital of Tebbicousimankalê. After greeting the chief and his son, he sat down among the shepherds and farmers, his far-flung neighbors, and was busy enjoying all of the excitement when Uz'A came and told him to go to the temple.

Puzzled, he thought only that there must be some chore to do, perhaps one more table to be brought for the extra people. Instead, he found only one person there, standing in front of the thick wooden doors with the street dark except for an oil lamp two houses down. He stepped closer, curious but hesitant, and saw it was a woman dressed in ankle-length robe, a long cowl covering her head and shielding her face.

"I'm sorry to sneak around like this," she said before lowering the hood to reveal her identity, "but I didn't want anyone to see me talking to you. Probably some of the elders would still recognize me, even after all this time."

The only person who could speak fluent English and was likely to turn up on Karluk Island was Renée.

"What are you doing here?" he exclaimed in a hush, as surprised to see her as Gina.

"You're married now, and we both know how utterly conservative these Zetin are," she spoke quietly, "and if they only saw us speaking they would brand me a witch and call you a wizard—or whatever words they use—"

"In English, it's hooker and john."

"Listen to me, because we only have a short time and I'm taking the ferry back in the morning. I came to tell you about the next shift of the tangents, and it's important because it's going to be a big one."

"You always say that, Renée."

"Listen, if I'm going to be wrong, isn't it better to err on the positive side? I'm not telling you for your info, like before. This one's going to be big, I said. Big enough maybe to be the real break, the final one of this whole grand loop."

"What do you mean? If it breaks this time it won't come back together again?"

"That's right. You've got to trust me on this because I didn't bring anything with me to prove it. The sensors are rocking back in my house in Têfos. It will happen sometime in…at the earliest, the last week of Gouo."

"But that's months away."

"I know, but this is when I have the chance to come out here and tell you. I still have fifteen other Voyagers to contact. You're in my region of the planet so I'm responsible for you."

"You're like the Interdimensional Voyager secretary."

"And it also gives you the time you'll need to settle things before you go. I had to track you down from Lyas, which wasn't an easy task, I want you to know. You move around too much. You should feel privileged; you're the first Voyager on my list this time. You're the farthest from a working stargate of anybody I have to contact. You'll need all the time you can get."

"Renée, I can't leave. And I don't want to leave." He glanced around, checking the shadows, the music and laughter from the festival echoing down the lane. "You see, I've got a wonderful life here with Zaura. She's going to have our baby in a few weeks. I can't get up and leave now—not her, not now."

"That's your decision. I'm not telling you what to do, only what's going to happen. In case you *do* want to do something— like get away in time."

"How about you?"

"Me? Don't you already know about me? I'm here for the long haul. So this could be goodbye for you and me. That is, if you leave and I stay on Ghoupallesz when the cosmic bridge washes out. That will be it. No more interdimensional voyaging."

Finally, he thought, something to crack the perfect mirror.

"I know this is only a temporary link we're using," he said, "and that it's happened before and that it's broken before." He shook his head, thinking. "But how long could it really be—until it comes together again?"

"This time I can't say. I will guess—just for you, because I like you—it will be no less than a year, Earth time, and here? Oh, I can't even make a guess!"

"Try!"

"I can't."

He grabbed her by the shoulders. "Try!"

"It could be three months or it could be forever." She pulled away. "Or long enough to seem like forever. It could be the end. Which world do you want to be left on? If you ever want to visit your home again, if you have the slightest urge to return for even the most remote, wildest reason you never considered before, you'd better go. But if you do return, you may find yourself stuck there, back on Earth."

He lowered his head, feeling the heavy weight of decision pressing down on him once more. That was what he thought he'd left behind in Lyas and in Selauê. And on Earth. He did not like decisions.

"All right," he said, taking a deep breath, expelling it. "I have eight more months or so to think about it, right? And I will. Do you have a place to stay tonight?"

"On the ferry; there's no inn on Karluk."

"You don't want people to see you here, but you can come up to the cabin and stay with us. Zaura met you in Lyas, so she knows you. I'm sure it's no problem."

"I don't think that's a good idea. These Ghoupalle women can't stand having other women around."

A torchlight flickered down the lane and she pulled him back into the shadow of the temple. The torch danced along the street, paused, turned away.

Pressed together against the stone wall, he felt her warm breath on his neck. The light passed and he felt her hands start to lift him away, hesitantly, as though she was not sure she wanted to. Her hands held him, brought him close again, felt him.

"People will be coming this way soon," she said.

"You won't be able to get back to the ferry."

"The way is blocked now."

"They will see you."

"All right, I will go with you tonight."

In the darkness the trail was difficult to follow and they tripped over stones and stepped into holes as they went. The only light was from the glow of the fire in the center of the village behind them. No moon illuminated the night. Turning to look back, he lost his night vision and stepped on a loose stone which sent him tumbling off the trail into the grass. Renée rushed to him, held his head in her hands, asking him if he was injured. She ran her hands over his body, checking for injury, but settled against him as he tried to rise.

"You're not hurt," she whispered to him, her breath once more tickling his neck. "I can tell it's been a long time." She rolled off and lay beside him in the cool grass, her robe falling open. She leaned over and kissed him.

"What about Zaura?" he asked.

"Listen to me: I don't love you, and you don't love me." She pressed against him. "It's only sex. It doesn't have anything to do with her."

"It does, Renée."

She reached for him and he decided to let her.

"It's been a long time," she said. Her sigh sounded like the wind. "For me—and, I guess, also for you, with her being pregnant."

Her hand went to his trousers and he grabbed her arm. They wrestled a moment then lay still.

"All right, Sebastian, dear, I think—"

"It's Set-d'Elous on Ghoupallesz."

"That's better," she said with a laugh. "Let me make love to Sebastian then and Set-d'Elous can remain faithful to the end."

She pressed against him and he did not resist. As she continued, he slowly slipped into the dark ocean with a soft splash. He found himself swimming alone until he managed to reach the distant shore. Only then, pulling himself out of the water and collapsing on the beach, did he notice he had gotten wet.

To the east was the constellation *Ugalê*, to the south spread the long *Vanourrin*. A cool breeze blew over them and she pulled him tighter as he reached out and threw her robe over them.

"I think you should stay on the ferry tonight," he said, sitting up and looking at the now dark, quiet village below.

She rose and kissed his cheek.

"If you have any plans to stay here for a long time—maybe for hundreds of years like me—guilt is the first thing you learn to forget. You have a lot more to learn, my dear, and I'm the one to teach you. I want to teach you everything I've learned. You can be the great Voyager you have the potential to be. Join me, and be my student."

"Your student?"

"And my lover. I haven't had so many, really—not like your friend, Gina. They all died naturally, of old age. I'm very faithful. Generous, too."

He realized the late hour that it was, seeing the constellation *Tumori* turning around the night sky. At that instant he knew his idyllic life had ended. An explanation would be due when he returned to the cabin. If he lied, said he was in the village, there was nobody there to corroborate his story. UZ'A knew he went to the temple during the banquet.

"You should go back to the ferry," he announced, standing and leaving her in the grass. "Perhaps it would be best if you didn't tell me about any shifting tangents in the future. I'll take my chances. If I'm stranded here, well, so be it. And if I never return to Earth, then that's the way it'll be."

She jumped up. "No, you can't end it like this." She ran to him as he started up the trail. "I can teach you so much. You're throwing it all away!"

He turned and ran up the hill, far ahead of her. When at last he saw that she was not following him, he paused to catch his breath. He could make out a figure moving down the trail, back toward the village. It was still far from where their cabin stood, and he worried that the door there would lead him not into the safety of Zaura's arms but into another dimension, one where he would never find happiness.

He gladly closed the book on the month of *Pouor*. The spring days grew warm as they busied themselves preparing for the birth. Once *Denio*, the month of mid-summer, arrived, the Old Ladies Society marched up to the cabin and carried Zaura down to the village for her birthing. He had to believe she was in good hands, all of their combined experience cradling crying newborns.

On the tenth day of *Denio*, late in the afternoon, he thought he heard distant screaming, then sobbing. He waited with the *grael*, tense with the fear that something had gone wrong. When the son of the woman assisting Zaura arrived on the slope out of breath, he learned he was the father of a daughter. Now he had five days to name her. Once the ink was dry on the birth record he signed, he would be allowed to see his two ladies. After two months of the UX'THA—a Zetin word meaning something like 'bonding'— they would return to the cabin.

There on the high pasture between earth and sky, the wind gods dizzying him into stoical contemplation, his idle time made him think again about Renée's visit. The time when the universe would tear apart was approaching. And yet, everything still seemed so normal, so routine. Somewhere outside the reach of his senses a fantastic astronomical event was going to happen that would seal his fate like the nailed lid of a coffin.

He had already made his decision to stay with his dear Zaura on peaceful Karluk Island. As the time for catastrophe drew closer, he began to worry that he really would be cut off forever from the world of his birth. He was, after all, still a dedicated employee of the Internal Revenue Service most of the time. How long had he been away from that life? A week? A month? He still had an apartment filled with valuable items. He had been on Ghoupallesz for more than a year of Ghoupalle time this trip. It was possible that life on Earth had already passed him by, that even now some weird new employee sat at his desk in the corner of the service center, a new tenant resided in his apartment, all of his possessions, valuable or undistinguished, relegated as inheritance to no one. It was possible he was already being mourned.

The strongest force in the universe, he knew, was not the pull of tangents, not the flash of quasars, not even the vacuum of black holes sucking galaxies into compressed *gealan*-sized spheres. No, the strongest force in the universe was curiosity. The power of that simple human affliction was the only force that could rip him away from his idyll.

He lied to Zaura when he visited her at the home of UZ'A in the village. It was about him needing to check on his business back in Lyas. At first she was surprised, thinking it had been closed down completely, then she remembered he still held on to a small share. In fact, he should visit right now, she agreed, while she was staying in the village and people could care for her and their daughter. He could let the *grael* run free on the slopes, the naturally rough terrain keeping them from straying too far. Once back in Lyas, he also could get anything they might need for their daughter's first few years. He could go and be back in two weeks minimum, a month at most. He would collect what he was due and then turn over the remainder of the business for the last time, he promised.

To his innermost conscience, he confessed—on his last day on the upper slopes with the *grael*—he was going to return to Earth. It would be a quick voyage, he insisted to the clouds and the rocks. Long enough to see what had passed and, if it could be salvaged, to settle his affairs and prepare the way for his family and friends to accept his permanent relocation to...hah, another planet, another dimension. He would be back before Zaura was returned to the cabin, and long before the collapse of the tangent bridge.

In the morning he saw the storm clouds building as he boarded the ferry, but he did not understand the omen that a Ghoupalle would have clearly noticed. He bedded down in one of the forward cabins, no one to see him off that early, not even Zaura whom he told to sleep in. They said their goodbyes the night before, he and his wife, and their new daughter.

They had named her Aisa after an ancient Danid queen. And the pixie, dark-haired like her father and sucking at her mother's breast, carried the name of *d'Elous*. It was the custom that first-borns take the father's surname, alternating with the mother's surname with subsequent children, regardless of the sex of the child. He would be back before his little daughter, Aisa-d'Elous, could learn to answer to her name.

On the second night out, the clouds thickened and turned stormy. The crew was fearful and ordered him to stay below as rain lashed the decks and winds howled against the bulkheads. He overheard the crackling radio in the communication room. Making out the words clearly, some freighter was notifying any nearby ships that it was foundering in the rough seas. They were signaling *Mayday*, crying that the holds were filling and that the hull was breaking up. The storm grew louder, covering the radio noise, and he held on to his stomach. As the night wore on, he felt the seas become calm, the winds dying away, and he fell asleep at last. When he awoke, he was in another world. He walked in his sleep through the city of Elêna, boarding the airship, which rose from its tether and turned south.

Arriving at Selauê, he changed to the KOHax to Lyas. He did not pause there but rushed to the hidden hill he had almost forgotten, and stepped through the curtain, realizing how late he was for his work shift. In the service center, someone's promotion party was in full swing when he came around the shelving and sat at his desk. No one noticed him. The large calendar hanging on the wall showed him that he had missed only a weekend and the first hour the next night, so he claimed car trouble.

Chapter 20

Brother and Sister

The rain was green in the lamp light as it fell around him, over him, standing there soaked in the midnight streets of Selauê, the smoky windows on the red brick townhomes bolted shut. As the once-and-future tax examiner, he did not seem to feel any of the chill or wetness, consumed as he was in his agony. He collapsed to his knees, felt a moment of pain as his kneecaps crashed against the cobblestones, then dropped to his haunches and tumbled over, sobbing into the puddle near his head. The end had come, finally, after many prayers sent over many years that he would be freed of his entangling interdimensional desires. Now it had come and though he welcomed it as inevitable, his heart and mind still felt time was on his side. For this evening, while the news was still fresh, he was duty bound to submit to his mourning.

When he returned to the countryside east of Kansas City, Missouri on his home world, away from the quiet isolation of Karluk, he languished in the perverse paradise of the Internal Revenue Service Center, simple life that it was. He felt safe in the knowledge that he had more than a few months on Earth before he had to return to beat the tangent shifting, When he'd satisfied himself that nothing would be missed, he packed his bags and returned quickly to his new homeland, to the charcoal hillsides of

Lyas where he had met his future. From there he had rushed to the sacred isle in the northern sea where his family awaited him. Upon setting foot there on Karluk and being battered by the astonished stares of the villagers, he had hurried up the trail to the old cabin only to find it gutted by fire. He came down to the village and was told the story: when he did not return for her, Zaura decided to move back to Selauê, her and the baby. The fire happened later—a bad omen, they all knew, to have lightning burn down the cabin where the young couple had made their first child.

Uz'a remembered him when they took him to see her, now ten months on her death bed, and told him about Zaura. When he had set sail on the ferry, the storm that followed him had hunted him and swallowed the ship. A string of bad omens from the start, and Zaura heard the news that his ship had sank in the storm, no survivors. It was too much for her, the old woman said, and she chose to flee the island where her memories fought with her every waking moment, seeing his face in every green sunrise, hearing his voice in every whistle of wind. She stayed only two months after the news, Uz'a said in her cracking, weak baritone. Then Zaura took the ferry to Elêna with the child, saying she would live in Selauê with her family.

"How long ago did she leave?" he asked the woman in his broken Zetin speech, seeing her becoming exhausted by his interrogation. He had to know: "A month, two months—a year?"

"Xaa-jz," she replied, shaking her head. Her voice crumbled. Requesting a drink from her younger sister, wrinkled with age herself, she asked her about the date.

"Gsut dromrü dot', baxo'et zaxj' st-raye dem tonn kaxj'," the sister said. 'I remember the cabin burning; it was a month after she left.'

Uz'a smiled, satisfied her memory was still intact, then spoke in a stronger voice.

"Bax zaxj' chinn-saz'az'," she said. 'It was ten years ago.'

The three-day voyage on the ferry back to Elêna was not enough time to sort out what had happened, certainly not long enough to decide a course of action. He knew then that he had to have a pretty good story for Zaura when he met her in Selauê. It was less than six weeks of Earth time he'd been away, and he'd calculated that to be about one Ghoupalle month—plenty of time to return through the Lyas tangent and rejoin her on Karluk, long before Renée's prediction of breaking tangents would occur. The long anticipated shift had come early, though, throwing the time loop free. When it finally reconnected itself, it was ten years into the future. Ten years—in the blink of an eye!

In the Selauê of 1455, at the Matousz family house on Lane 49 Block 12, in the older back-bay district, he was 'greeted' by eldest son Rasek. The word would not exactly apply to the phrases uttered at the sight of the foreigner who'd spoiled his sister and then ran out. He knew what they all must think of him, but there was no explanation he could give which allowed the truth to be known. They would think less kindly of him were he to tell them he was held prisoner on another world by the fickleness of universal laws governing interdimensional travel. Quantum physics was just magic to them. And magic was a bunch of lies. He had simply lost his way and could not return as he had planned. No, that would not do. He was captured by Zetin warriors when he arrived at the port of Elêna and was forced to fight in their army, yes! In Fenula, he told them at last—since there really had been such a war in the interim.

Although they seemed to believe him, there was nothing they could do to help. By Ghoupalle custom and Sekuate law, they were automatically unwedded on the first anniversary of the last day she saw him. She was free to marry again. And she had done so—although it was four years after he sailed away before she again took the *moussalaganê* in a House of Union. He felt some comfort in that: she seemed to have mourned his passing.

But what could he say to her after the time that had passed? He had to see her.

Rasek refused to say where she was, but her mother told him, fearing his rage were she not to divulge the address. Zaura lived now in the city of Sairel in Sekuate-sotos. Up in the highlands east of Lyas, in the oasis of a man-made lake, in the heart of the *moussala* fields, she was the wife of Tolour-Frêdin, a dealer for a company which processed the desert plant. He recalled the name: the same man who visited her regularly when she had been a *senzenor* in Lyas—her special client.

At the moment the Matousz door closed on him, the light extinguished from his heart as the light was from their porch lamp, he began telling himself that there was no point in seeing her, meeting her once more, or disturbing the new life she had found after his tragic demise.

Then the green rain began to fall, the night turning darker, until he found himself in a neighborhood that was unfamiliar to him. It was an omen, he knew. He was as lost in life as he was in this block of old brickfront townhomes, laying against the wet cobblestones, crying into the puddle that absorbed his tears as fast as the rain fell down upon him.

Reality had dissolved completely.

The long-haired girl playing in the yard had to be Aisa, he thought. Even from across the street he could see her resemblance to him. Then his eyes regarded the house behind her, set away from the street and partially hidden by a garden of summer vines, ferns, and rows of large violet flowers. It was a home Zaura deserved, he conceded, and the businessman who had been her favorite customer was able to give it to her. He had given her a rustic cabin on a far-away island! This businessman had been willing to take in the lonely woman with the foreigner's daughter at her side, to give her his home, to share his life with her.

He stood at the gate feeling envy welling up within him, so fixed on the image before him that he did not hear the girl calling to him.

"*Hama'n g'edoren-y'da kal?*" she was asking him when his trance broke. 'You want to meet Mommy?'

The woman she brought outside had cut her hair short and wore a simple-style *qanliin* dress that was the housewife uniform in Sekuate. She started down the walk, expecting that once again an old client wished for help with a problem. It was not uncommon, but she always sent them away, telling them politely that she no longer did *senzenaxii*, and if they persisted, she would be more direct and confess that her powers of healing had diminished to the point of ineffectiveness. Then she would march back to the protection of her home and wish away the tears that came whenever she thought about her former life, when she could help people merely by the touch of her hands, by feeling their thoughts. That led her to ponder how her life would have been different if her husband had not been lost in the angry fist of the northern sea.

This man looked familiar to her as she approached, still thinking it was a former customer, but before she could reach the gate, she was halted as if by an invisible wall. Her daughter cried out, worried that her mother had suddenly turned ill. The blond woman, still quite attractive even in her older persona, fell to her knees on the walk and her daughter ran to her. The man tore open the gate and came toward them, and the girl jumped up to protect her mother. The man took the girl in his arms—strangely, it felt to her—and with his other arm tried to embrace her mother, there on the hard pavement, together on their knees. The girl could not understand why her mother was weeping so much, not until she was told that this stranger was her father. Her mother had thought him dead, lost at sea, for ten years, and now here he was, his face in her cradling hands, their lips crushed together.

The boy was cute, playing soldier with his friend in the side yard, and when he came indoors, he was introduced to his sister's new father—or old father; he was confused. He was Samot, the son of Zaura and her second husband, who was away on a business trip. The boy was curious but since the stranger was friendly to him and seemed kind to his mother and sister he accepted him as well.

After a simple dinner, she tucked the children into their *qala* and extinguished the lamp. He wanted to stay and watch them, but Zaura took him away from their room and turned him toward the sleeping room she used. It was hers, she explained, because since they married her aura had decreased further and Tolour was not satisfied that his wife could no longer give him the wonderful pleasures she once had. He continued to provide for her but they had come to live separate lives, each in a separate wing of the large house, crossing paths with frequently kind words empty of any lingering bonds. Zaura professed that she was happy, content with her life. But her lover's return had changed everything.

In the morning she rolled back the sheet on the *qala* they had shared and began conducting the special techniques she still remembered from her days in Lyas. On the foreigner who knew everything, they still worked, she discovered—perhaps because he always had suffered the effects more strongly than any other of her clients had. That brought joy to her heart.

For several days they were a family together, yet held apart by the one who was absent. Zaura released the tension that was weighing them all down, and gave him the answer to the question she sensed he wanted to ask. They would never be apart, she announced, and he suggested they move back to Lyas where they had once been happy. The only thing to do was to forget the ten years of separation, try to resume their life together as it was meant to be. They agreed. Ten-year-old Aisa understood and declared she wanted to live with her true father. Five-year-old Samot struggled to interpret the results of the meeting around the tiled hearth where they sat to eat their meals. The *tabli* was barely dry and the plate of *sebal* hardly eaten when they broke from breakfast and began packing.

He told a concerned Aisa that, yes, she could bring her *grisso* doll, a stuffed raccoon-like animal common in the plateaus around Sairel. Samot took his *holka*.

✻ ✻ ✻

He remembered the girl, Seasö, who was Zaura's best friend. They stayed with her in Lyas for six days. Then a friend from Sairel sent an urgent message to Zaura. She had told her friend in Sairel of the circumstances of her departure, but she was not prepared for the news. When she told him, he could not believe it either, but somehow he knew to expect it. Her brother Rasek, suspicious of his motives in reuniting with Zaura, had taken it upon himself to track him down and keep him away from his sister. Rasek, who towered a head taller than him, had arrived in Sairel looking for Zaura, asked her neighbors and was told that they went to Lyas. He was on his way at that moment.

She paid the courier, who had brought the message from the communication office, and immediately told her children to pack again. Uncle Rasek was coming.

The vehicle they drove was given to Zaura by her wealthy husband, Tolour-Frêdin, but she had little experience with the machine. It was called Etur, an anagram of the longer, unpronounceable scientific name for a 'common self-propelling steam-powered machine of personal transport'—something like that. The word *etur* was, in another context, derived from the verb meaning 'to roll.' Since that was what it did, those people who could afford to indulge in the latest mechanical contraptions called it by that name: hence, it was a 'roller.'

Preparing to leave Zaura's house in Sairel, he had gone to the 'Etur-house' and examined the machine, realizing that it was only a prototype of the sleek vehicles he and Gina would cruise down the highway someday in the future. Instead, this one had the small engine in back and the 'pilot'—in the Ghoupalle lexicon—worked two levers, one in each hand, and one foot petal. Filling the vehicle's fuel box with the maximum number of fuel capsules at Seasö's house, the first puffs of excess steam looked green in the afternoon sunshine. After a moment, the engine was humming, the steam almost clear. Then they climbed in and he pushed forward on both levers until the engine slipped the necessary pin back into gear. He moved the left lever to the side and the vehicle turned out of the driveway of Seasö's apartment building. He eased the Etur onto the street, getting the hang of its quirky movements, but paused for a man riding a *Jêpe* to pass.

The road to the east was barren, and as they drove, mostly in silence, Zaura told him the address of a friend in Typeg, the city-state between two rivers cutting through the Zissekap desert. Typeg prospered on trade between north and south, and dealt in everything. Gina had lived there a while. When they arrived they rented a room in a small adobe inn that reminded them of their apartment building in Lyas. The children played under the swaying *jibal* trees as they sat at the table in the courtyard deciding their next course of action, awaiting a reply to the message Zaura sent back to Seasö.

Rasek had visited Seasö, the return message came finally. He had stayed barely a *peth* before continuing on to Typeg.

Her brother sure was determined to make a fool of himself, he remarked, but his literal turn of phrase went over her head. He comforted her then, her worries about their confrontation merging with her feelings of guilt at running away with him. He could not do much about that, though. He did not see how Rasek could find them in a city of a million people, but Zaura insisted on fleeing once more.

They took the road north, the long highway that traversed the Saunicêa plain between the Zissekap Mountains on their right and the high plateau of Ilait on their left. Pausing only for overnight rests at inns along the way, they arrived in the capital of Filopêa. The city seemed like Las Vegas to him, all of the lights shining at night, all of the gaming houses. If he had any knowledge of their gambling sports, he would have been tempted try his luck. Zaura was not fazed by the entertainment readily available. She kept them all together in the room they rented for the night.

"What are we going to do?" she asked him in very polite Ghoupallêan. "We cannot continue to flee from him; he's my eldest brother."

He had no answer for her, none that would help their situation. She wept against his shoulder and the children came to hug their mother. A solution had to be realized soon.

After two nights they proceeded north. He was driving by maps he could not read, listening to Zaura's uncertain directions. He turned onto a highway leading to Foixe, intending to continue straight north and cross the border into the Kingdom of Bezua-hü. Zaura believed that her angry brother would not follow them into that country, with its reputation for immoral excesses. Instead, they found themselves quickly approaching the capital of Foixe after two days. That was fortunate because their fuel was almost out, the steam dwindling in the engine, the gears slowing. He had considered gathering some plants from the side of the road to burn in the fuel box but the instructions printed on the fuel box cautioned against trying to burn living materials to produce steam to run the engine.

The city of Foixe drew close as they drove through a park on the outskirts, a hilly area that seemed rather familiar to him. He was having Ghoupalle *déjà-vu*, he thought, and pulled the ETUR over to the side of the road. There were monuments on every hill, plaques on some trees, and tall statues along the paths among the hills. It *was* familiar, he suddenly knew. Hill #3. He had been there, on that very hillside, among those same trees—or trees that had grown back after the fighting had stopped. He paused before the statue of a soldier on a *Jêpe*, pointing off in the direction they had charged one autumn morning when the Jisilikan army returned to counter-attack the Foixên forces.

He had been there, leading them, the rank of lieutenant on his shoulders, the cheap glue barely dried on his patch of promotion. There in the Ghoupalle year of 1235—having survived a blast from the enemy *sirambola* which could have ended his interdimensional voyaging just as it was getting started—he had wished so intensely for the battle to be finished that he lead his men over the hill to attack the flank of the Foixên troops, drawing the attention of the Foixên away from the frontal attack that was about to occur. The Jisilikan forces were victorious, but *he* won. They made him a captain—*Serpan*—and gave him a medal for valor. He gazed up at the bronze statue of the *Jêpedor*—the horse soldier—who seemed to have a slight resemblance to him. He thought of Aisa-Evelê, the girl he'd returned for after the battle only to discover she had followed the army as they campaigned and died in an artillery barrage.

As they continued driving north to the city of Vith, near the border with Bezua-hü, the grinding noise from the engine box could no longer be ignored. He slowed but kept going. When they stopped at the first fuel agent they found inside the city, he asked the mechanic to check the engine. The mechanic suggested he get one of the gears replaced whenever he could stop for a longer time. He thanked the mechanic and hoped the gear would operate properly a few more days. Zaura warned the children to stand back from the rear of the vehicle lest their hands be burnt by the expelled steam. He purchased a box of fuel capsules, supposedly enough to last 200 *radit* at moderate speed, and stowed them in the back. Scribbling some numbers in the dirt beside the ETUR, he calculated they could go about 150 miles.

The children were becoming restless as the *radit* passed by, and Zaura was anxious to hurry on, though they did not know where they were going. They believed that if they simply continued running, eventually Rasek would give up and leave them alone. He told her it was a nice wish, but not likely to come true.

"He hated me from the first moment he saw me," he exclaimed in Ghoupallêan, not concerned with being polite.

Driving through the city of Vith, he pondered the sight of his statue, his own personal war memorial, and it strengthened his resolve. There was only one answer, he knew, but he could not tell Zaura.

Zaura inquired about his idea, seeing the children asleep as they approached Milipour, the largest city of western Bezua-hü, deep inside its borders, knowing somehow that Rasek still pursued them, probably also across the border now.

He parked the ETUR in back where the *Jêpe* were tied up, and got a room in the run-down old inn, requesting a room in the back, up on the third floor. Zaura asked why, but he only shook his head and took their bags in without replying. For the children, the sense of excitement in their family trip across the continent of Zissekap had long been lost. They felt the tension cast by their parents. The end was coming soon, so they prepared for it.

"The only solution is to end this flight," he told her in Ghoupallêan. It was after they had made love, but without the usual attendant *senzena* activities. "I came back into your life—a life in which you had already settled," he said, holding her hand. "I'm the one out of place here. So I will be the one to solve this problem—by sending you home to Sairel. In the morning, you should go back with the children. I will stay here. Your brother is more interested in punishing me than in keeping us apart. I'll wait for him—and you'll be on your way back to your life. The life you are meant to have. Maybe you'll arrive in Sairel before your husband returns; then none will be the wiser for our adventure."

She tried to speak but her words fell out only in tears and desperate caresses. Though they stayed awake until the sky warmed into dawn, it was not long enough to say all of the goodbyes they wanted to tell each other.

"How can I part from you a second time?" she whispered in Ghoupallêan. "Never to see you again—after ten years of absence already, Lover?"

"I know how your heart feels," he said, knowing that no words in any language could accurately express his pain and feelings of regret. "Mine is broken, too."

When sunlight from the large yellow sun broke through the window, she awoke the children and helped them pack. They were going home, she told them. He could hear her words, standing behind the door, and he felt a tightening in his chest. For the first time in more than a hundred days he thought of the easy life he had back on Earth, working the graveyard shift at the IRS Service Center, and wished he were on his way there, just making the start of his shift. Someday, he would look back on this adventure and laugh.

Leaning back on the chair beside the open window, a thickly forested slope outside, he pulled out his weapon: one XG-48, Zetin army standard issue handgun. As an old-fashioned projectile weapon, it was an artifact given to him by Gina as a souvenir from his rescue mission. He kept it in working condition for a special occasion. He carefully wiped off his fingerprints with a soft cloth, held it in his lap as he pushed the four pyramid-shaped slugs into the chambers and loaded the long tube of propellant. As he worked, he listened for the creaking of the stairs, the knock on the door, the thundering voice of the devil in Ghoupalle clothing.

The man burst through the door, *kaldo* firm in his hand, raising the curved blade either as protection or for his attack. He did not know which. He remained on his chair, realizing that he had been lulled into inattention by the long wait.

"You have traveled too far," said Rasek in his rough, uneducated Ghoupallêan, trying to sound important, "too far to meet your misfortune in this shabby inn."

"This is where I've been waiting for you," he retorted in Ghoupallêan.

"Where's my sister?" Rasek asked, gruffly. "Have you destroyed her—all of them—in your ignorance?"

"I sent them back to Sairel. I'm alone."

"That's good. Zaura shouldn't see your ending."

Rasek stepped forward, lowering the *kaldo* in front of him, looking every bit as though he expected to walk the blade straight into the foreigner.

In a flash he was off the chair, swinging the chair up at the raging maniac. Rasek swung the wide blade, catching the chair and snapping it in two. He scrambled away, his antique pistol nearly slipping out of his hand as he dodged the flying pieces of chair.

He raced into the next room, hearing the shouting from below. Probably the manager of the inn calling the police. He hoped.

"You shouldn't've come back," Rasek cursed. "You shouldn't've tried to break up her good marriage—a marriage to a good man, a steady supporter, a Sekuatean."

"It wasn't my fault I was gone so long."

No conciliatory words would help, he knew.

Rasek stalked him through the apartment's rooms, certain of his ultimate victory. There was no need to hurry. The foreigner would be backed against a wall somewhere. The cut would come from beside the ear and run diagonally across the neck and shoulder. He would slice him open with the *kaldo*, pull out his heart and stuff it into a jar he had down in his ETUR for that purpose. Later he would show it to Zaura, and offer it as a gift of his undying brotherly love, and she would be glad that he had saved her from the dirty little *süggor*—the rat.

"Hey, Rasek!" he cried out suddenly in English, seeing the man so absorbed in thinking about what he was going to do to him. "Don't count your chickens before they hatch."

Then he raised the XG-48, never before firing it, and pulled the trigger twice.

Chapter 21

Sins yet to be Confessed

In the end he was doomed, as sure as the large, yellow sun would rise before the small, blue sun, as sure as winter followed autumn, as sure as his name was not truly his own. This time, he accepted it all too easily. If the events had climaxed in any more spectacular fashion, he probably would have had his conversion sooner. As it was, that moment of humbling would have to wait another century. Only once in a hundred years—pick any calendar—could he be allowed to face the real death. That was another rule. Magic would not save him.

"There he goes again, taking another break from reality," someone said—and he heard Michael and Tammy, over by the drinking fountain, giggle.

He could do nothing to defend himself.

"Bad dream?" Priscilla called to him.

"No," he grumbled. "No dream at all."

"Then what's the problem, hon?"

"Too much reality."

The memory of the previous week's trip hung over him like a night of drinking and he swayed as he stood, thinking back to Milipour and how he'd jumped from the window of the inn after he shot Rasek—with the innkeeper and constable pounding on the door. He twisted his ankle when he fell, found out later it was fractured. Dragging his foot behind him, he struggled up the wooded slope, tripping, falling down the opposite side. Through the forest he hobbled, believing everyone in Milipour was after him, and found a highway leading north into Rox. He dared to flag down an ETUR. The pilot's name was Mamna-Srenno, a nurse at Third Hospital of Voro—farther up through the tiny mountainous nation of Rox and east into the Furank Republic. A hospital was what he needed, seeing how his foot was bent—

Rolling his head up off his crumpled arms, he saw Michael had arrived, looking anxious.

"Break over yet?" asked Sebastian, stretching.

"Almost. You got a couple more minutes." Michael cleared his throat. "By the way...."

He stretched his arms, stood up. "I need something to eat before I start in on that stack of returns. Walk with me."

They arrived at the south canteen, found a few people there from another department. He bought a Baby Ruth and an apple from the machines. Michael got himself a soda and brought it over to the table where the Professor sat.

"I thought you said you were gonna take care of...ya know, everything," said Michael nervously. "It's been over a week now, and—" More people were entering the canteen, so he lowered his voice. "And I need to know if you're serious about, you know, what you said before."

Sebastian took a bite of the candy bar, nodding.

"Well, you sure don't give me confidence," said Michael.

"Don't—worry—" he spoke between bites of the sticky nougat. "I am serious—but, I said—just have to—wait for the right time."

"When *is* the right time?" Michael was becoming anxious. "We *are* gonna go—right? Sometime soon, right? I mean, if you keep putting it off, Tammy'll be showing and—shit, I ain't getting any better!"

"Don't worry." He crumpled the candy bar wrapper, flung it at the trash bin. "Maybe next week."

"Let's set the date and get it over with."

He shook his head. They had to be patient. He could not pick some arbitrary date. It had to be the right time or they could all find themselves literally in the wrong place at the wrong time.

Michael had no ability to wait calmly. Tammy was waiting with no fuss. Or maybe she had forgotten.

"I think everything should be ready by Saturday," he told Michael.

"What the hell's there to get ready?"

"Take it easy, Michael. We *will* go and we *will* take care of your problem. It's not quite as simple as you think it is."

These Earthlings could be so demonstrative—

The sweet, young nurse from Voro was not at all that way. She had sensed he was running from the law and cared for him in her home rather than take him to her hospital. Somehow he impressed her as a man who had been wrongfully accused, and in the haze that filled his head while in the throes of pain, he believed it, too.

During the days when Mamna was at the hospital, he sat in the chair she provided, positioned within reach of everything he might need during the long hours. He sat there and brooded. The gray, misty weather that hung in the valley, midway up in the mountains that divided Furank from Bezua-hü, was perfect for his melancholy. He told Mamna about Zaura, about being away for 'a few years' because he was forced into battle in Fenula, about returning to her and being attacked by her brother. The nurse had a sympathetic ear, and her gentle Nightingale persona soothed his depression.

When he was able to get around with a cane, she showed him the sights. He enjoyed her Furank accent—a kind of Scottish lilt. One evening, she was telling him about her childhood and was finishing a short anecdote about fighting her little brother when their eyes met—

"Time to get back to work," Fat Ken announced as he wandered into the canteen as though he had business there, plunked a handful of coins in the vending machine for a bag of powdered donuts.

He sent himself home from the service center, claiming illness, then made himself dinner but called it breakfast since the sun would be rising soon. Finding nothing of interest on TV, he returned to writing in his journal. With his fingers poised over the electric typewriter's keys, the machine humming, a thought blasted through his head. The room seemed to press in on him and he closed his eyes. Another night, he sighed, so long ago yet the same.

The night stuck in his memory was several weeks after he had abandoned his pursuit of Zaura-Matousz, he knew. After that adventure, he'd had no choice but to return to Earth, to his job at the IRS service center. He was still distraught over his failure so he'd sat at his desk trying to type the latest chapter into his journal. It was late as his fingers worked in spurts to fill the page.

After a while, he stopped to read what he'd written and, feeling his mind falling blank, typed one more line:

```
How can a man summarize his life in a single
chapter, especially when that life covers two
hundred assorted years, two planets, and a
cast of millions?
```

"It's impossible," he said, sitting back.

He was alone in that dark room, lit only by a small desk lamp.

"That's not always true," a voice that seemed to be his conscience spoke to him.

"It's not?" he asked, automatically.

"It *is* possible to answer. But you'll ask that question a thousand times before you find the answer—if you ever do."

He turned suddenly, realizing the voice was not in his head but in his apartment. The movement in the shadowy corner of the room caught his attention. Someone was sitting in his TV chair. The floor lamp beside it was off and he could only make out the shape of the person—a woman, it appeared.

"Gina...?"

"Who else would it be, Sebastian?"

"Are you a ghost or real?"

She laughed but did not rise from her seat.

"We all die, you know. What's the difference? Do I look dead to you?"

He wanted to jump up from his desk, but a wave of her hand halted him, pushed him back into his place. She did not intend him to see her face to face.

"I saw you die."

"How can that be?" she responded. "I have never died—not yet—and not for a while. Perhaps you are confusing me with someone else."

He was ready to contradict her, then decided maybe he should not tell her about her life. Interdimensional etiquette.

"I only came to tell you how very proud I am of you," said the woman in the shadows. "I knew you'd marry a Ghoupalle eventually. They're so doggone irresistible. I'm sure she was beautiful, and I'll bet she made you quite happy. Renée told me."

"Was...? Made...?"

"I'm sure you outlived her. That's why you're back here on Earth, right?"

"Did Renée tell you the rest?" He cleared his throat. "How she tried to seduce me, wanted me to leave my Ghoupalle wife? That might be acceptable sometime in the future, but not now, and not on Karluk. Did she tell you how she sent me back here because of the shifting tangents? How I was trapped here? How I hurried back to my Ghoupalle wife and found ten years had passed? And she had married another man, thinking I was dead? And how we ran away but her brother followed us and I had to kill him? Did she tell you any of that?"

Gina did not answer, and the night grew deeper.... Darker.... Danker....

"You did the right thing."

"How would you know?" he snapped, turning in his chair as though resuming his writing.

"Because I know what happens next."

He spun around in his chair, leaped to his feet.

"What did I do? Can you tell me that? I try to be a good person—whatever that is—but everything I do ends up crap for me. I really loved Zaura, and I never meant to hurt her. I never thought I *could* hurt her. I wasn't even trying to be careless. Every time I go there, I screw things up. I make a mess of everything."

"That's why I call you Set—the God of Evil—Lord of Destruction—the bull in the china shop. Like the fire that cleanses, you prepare the way for new life."

"I don't want to be known for that."

She laughed, and what was once a sweet, pleasant sound in her youth had become a cynical crowing that grated on his ears.

"Don't take yourself too seriously. You might begin to believe it," she said. "Then you *will* be trouble for the other side of the universe. You should live like me: a slower, more reflective lifestyle. Frankly, I don't know why you stay here. Maybe so I'll be able to find you easily. That's kind of you, but—"

"Gina, you don't have to come here and see me. How many years has it been? Seven or so here in this time zone—a lot more for you, obviously. I don't know how you remember me as well as I remember you. We started as teen lovers. Then we were scientists together. And explorers. Now you hang around me trying to be my conscience, like you have some kind of wonderful wisdom to share with me. Well, share it if you have it. Don't just sit there mocking me for wanting to keep my foot in Earth's door."

"But is it such a good door?"

"No, but it's my door."

"Home is where your heart is, not where you sleep."

"You *do* have words of wisdom."

She shifted in the chair, almost rising out of the shadows that covered her face.

"What I do, Sebastian," she said in a tone that set him on edge, "I do for *me*. If I do something for you, it's only because *I* feel good doing it. If it makes you happy, that's a bonus. Yes, I do feel good making you happy. I always have. But don't ever be fooled into thinking I'm doing something only for *you*. I'm still doing it, ultimately, for me."

He dropped back in his seat, switched off the electric typewriter, knowing he could write no more.

"I've been around long enough to know what works and what doesn't." He forced a smile. "Yes, it's nice to see you again, Gina— especially after seeing you laid to rest a few months ago, Earth time—but all this time-popping and space-sliding makes me dizzy. I know all that I need to know."

"Oh, you do? What do you know?"

"I know that in the dream land I can be anyone I want to be. I can be the husband of Zaura-Matousz. I can be a wealthy *gealan* dealer. I can be the rescuer of the notorious Queen Jinetta. I have many options. If I want to, I can be the commander of the siege of Siaa. Or I can lead the expedition to discover the continent of Lapügh. I can be Tyuan-Da or his twin. I can be Samot-d'Ussek. I can be Brounadar at Debrek, or Tatandellus at Uisza—"

"Only generals?" she said. "You haven't learned a thing. Death and destruction are all you know. Can you also be Ghulad-Mekmel? Or U'Pê of the Ty? You say you can be anyone you want to be, then why be a general? Can't you be a healer? Or a peace maker? Can't you be somebody like Tukou-Mê or that Buddha fellow from here? Can't you be like Jesus Christ, or Queen Lutui of Rox? Or—"

He grinned soberly, feeling that night long ago as a mere hour behind him. The headaches were ceasing, he discovered, as his memories were put back safely into their album, tucked away in his head. That was both a good omen and a bad one. He was glad he no longer suffered those effects, but it also meant that the rip in the curtain would begin mending. His window of opportunity was now. If he was going to travel to the other side of the universe, with or without Michael and Tammy, it had to be soon.

It might already be too late, he considered as he arrived at work the next night. How many people in the service center knew about his plans? The only way anyone could know was through Michael or Tammy. The one with the looser tongue was probably Tammy, no rocket scientist. But then again, she would not be associating with any of those people, not with the way they treated her. Michael could have been the one, but why would he want to sabotage his own mission? No, the service center playboy would surely be smarter than that.

Thinking back to that night Gina had visited him left him unable to concentrate on his tax work. He sat with his head bowed over the papers, appearing to all but the most discriminating eyes as though he were actively working on underreported income taxes. Meanwhile, he was running the tape through his mind's video player once more: two years ago, it was, and yet that night now seemed like only yesterday.

He let loose a chuckle, realizing that the only woman he had ever professed his undying love to had been so easily replaced in his heart by the golden-haired beauty from the chaparral of Lyas. Perhaps the greatest shock to him was the knowledge that he could, if he put his mind to it, return to a time when his dear Zaura would not think he was lost at sea. He grinned. Perhaps the future could be changed, he suddenly wondered. He could no longer keep his thrilled exclamation under control—

It was almost morning at that point in their conversation and the shadows she hid in were turning gray.

"You should give yourself another chance," Gina had said that night. "Do you think I never had any problems? If I wanted to escape my life, I had to return through the tangent, then come back to a new time and place there. Different tangent, different time, maybe different place. You think that's easy, feeling your way through a field of tangents, looking for one that fits your fancy?"

"You're saying all I have to do is return to a time before the tangent shift?" he'd asked her, only partially believing her. "Then I can find Zaura again but before she remarries?"

"Haven't you been listening to me?"

"But time is already written, isn't it? We can only stop here or there and fit in with what's already going to occur. We can't really go back and do the same thing differently. We can't bring a change to what will happen later. It doesn't work that way."

"Pay attention, Sebastian," she said. "Do you remember our first voyage? I stayed and you returned. Well, I also returned."

"You did?"

"Long after you."

"At the quarry? When?"

"Oh, who can remember that far back? A couple of years after you returned, I suppose. I got worried, and I was bored, curious. I returned to check on things. Like you did. I didn't get far, however. You see, I looked at myself in the rain pool in the quarry and I was very old. I came back as a senior citizen. Poof! I'd been on Ghoupallesz too long, living my life. I panicked and searched for a different tangent. Finally, I went back through a different rip of the curtain. I was reborn, the clock reset. Now look at me."

"You do look good," he said. "For your age—which is...? Whatever it is now."

"I've spent over a hundred years on Ghoupallesz. Their years. Four hundred and eight days per year, with thirty-hour days. You do the math. I'm so damn old. But quite spry."

"Equal to five hundred-ten Earth days," he said after a moment. "Times your hundred-odd Ghoupalle years. Yes, senior citizen, all right."

"I look like I'm in my fifties, don't I?"

"Yes, you're one hot grandma."

She laughed, and her voice sounded younger.

"What about the emotional strain?" he asked when she fell silent.

"It can be difficult. Leaving those you come to love.... Moving on...."

"I know what you mean."

She watched him sinking into melancholy. She noticed her cover fading, though he had diverted his eyes from her aged facade.

"I'll have to be going now, or I'll be late for an important engagement."

She stood, hesitated, then took a shaky step toward him. He rushed to catch her.

"Are you all right?"

"No, I'm in the pink of health," she replied. "Of course, I'm not all right! It's hard on my body to make this journey. But it was important to see you. I've been here too long and now the tangents are pulling me apart again."

"Let me help you."

"I'm all right."

"I can drive you back to the quarry."

"Don't be silly. That tangent field is too old, too unreliable. I'm a First-Class Voyager, you know. I can bend stars and implode planets. I just can't walk for too long now. But I can rip the curtain any damn time, any damn place I want to. You have a very convenient one in your bedroom."

She slumped in his arms, then recovered.

"I'll help you."

"Don't come with me just to be helping me," she grinned, "but you're certainly welcome to attend my son's wedding—if I haven't already missed it."

"Your son's wedding? Which one?"

"One of them. Sartan, I think. I can't remember a damn thing without my journal."

"Me, too."

"You, too?"

❊ ❊ ❊

Now *there* was something he had not expected to see—not after all that had happened between them. There they were, in the corner of the canteen: Michael, the playboy, talking with Tammy, the girl with the permanent grin. Maybe it was about the trip. He wasn't sure. No—there—she smiled. She laughed, too, her own unique giggle.

"I see you two are talking again," said Sebastian, walking over to them.

"Well, I thought I should," Michael responded, not enjoying the interruption.

The tone of voice was not lost on Sebastian. "Is everything all right?"

"Oh, yes," Michael sighed, glancing at Tammy.

"That's good," he said. "Are you ready?"

"Ready for what?" asked Tammy.

"To go."

"On your special trip?" asked Michael.

"Yes."

"I was beginning to think you were just messing with us."

"No, tonight is the night—I mean later today, in the evening. Tomorrow night's shift. Can you get off? It should be tomorrow night, at the latest."

"Tonight?" asked Michael, anxiously. "It's Friday. We're gonna go out after work."

"You were, huh?" He let his disappointment show for their benefit. "Having fun, huh? Do you think that's of greater importance? More crucial than your swelling body part?" He jutted his chin down at Michael's injury for emphasis. "More crucial than some new life forming inside you?" He glanced at Tammy's belly, still flat.

"More important than what?" asked Michael.

"Your delicate conditions."

"It's just one night. Where're we going, anyway? You never told us."

"Yeah!" Tammy jumped in.

"Well, if I told you, you'd be telling everyone in the service center—like you have with everything else."

"I ain't told nobody nothing."

"Somebody's been passing the news around."

"Not me."

"Well—" He shot a glance around, seeing that all the people from their department had left. "It doesn't matter. Tonight or tomorrow night is the best time, if we're going. If you still want to go. If you're still interested in taking care of your problems. You can go out after work, if you like. Then come over to my apartment. You still remember where it is, don't you? I'll leave the door unlocked this time."

"Hah!" said Michael.

"Then I'll take you to where we're going."

Michael's face showed his seriousness. Once again, he understood the Professor's instructions. It was finally going to happen. Well, something would happen. He didn't know what it might be, but...okay, it could be amusing. Besides, Tammy was starting to come around to his way of thinking. Maybe things were turning out for the best, at last.

❋ ❋ ❋

"Okay, I just got the scoop!" Bertha Bigelow shrieked in her hairy voice. She rushed down the busy aisle in the mail room, all of the women looking over or around the sides of their twenty-tray mail-sorting desks. Her body was jiggling in fifteen different ways. "Tonight's the night. She's gonna go over to the Perfesser's, and Michael's taking her."

"Well, that can only mean one thing: the three of them are gonna do it together."

"Can you *believe* it?"

"That's creepy—I mean, with the Perfesser."

"Yeah, but with Tammy? Hell, that girl's so skinny, how kin she take care of two guys?"

"You girls are really crude! All you ever talk about is sex, sex, sex."

"That's all we wanna do is sex, sex, sex," Big Bertha responded, and the room roared.

"So, what're we gonna do?"

"What we always planned to. Follow'em and spy on'em, if we can."

"Well, listen up, gals!" Bertha exclaimed. "I heard'em say they gonna go to the Perfesser's, and he's gonna take'em somewheres else."

"You mean like one of them bypass motels?"

"Even easier. Boy, I'd love to see the look on her face when we knock on the door, they open it, and *flash goes the camera!*—catchin' the three of them in the sack together. That's what I wanna see."

"Yeah, we could blackmail'em," said Bertha.

"What for? Ain't got nothing we want."

"Then just the fun of it," Bertha giggled. "Hell, don't nothing ever happen 'round here. This the best thing to happen since they started up the night shift again."

※ ※ ※

"Okay, what's going on here?" Joyce asked everyone in the Underreporter section after the midnight lunch break. "You all having some party I'm not invited to? First, Michael wants off, then Tammy." She looked over at Kate. "Now *you* want off, too? You know we can only have three gone at a time in this

240

department. You'll have to wait your turn."

Kate leaned over to her manager.

"I know what's up." She lowered her voice: "They think there's something going on between Michael and Tammy."

"That's nothing new."

"Yeah, but the Perfesser's helping'em with something. Ever since the car wreck."

Joyce shook her head. "Come on. He was the one who called the ambulance. That's why he's involved."

"No, Joyce, there's more."

She sat back, waving them to return to their work.

"You see, we've been putting it all together, me and some of the girls from the mail room and over in Data Processing. We think there's something else going on besides."

"Can't you leave those two alone?"

"Not until we find out what they're really up to after work every night."

"Kate, you've got a bad habit there, following people around."

"Don't ya wanna know what's going on?"

"I'm not the curious type like you," said Joyce. "What people do on their own time is none of my business—and none of *yours*, neither—no matter how weird it might be."

"But you don't *know* how weird it is."

Joyce scanned the room, seeing that both Michael and Tammy were not yet back from break. The Professor was not back, either—and right before he was taking off a few days! She thought for a moment, then turned to Kate.

"How weird *is* it?"

Sebastian had pulled on his adopted name, wore *Set-d'Elous* with confidence as he stepped out of the bushes and found himself in a city park somewhere in Lyas. He remembered Lyas was particularly dry on that spring afternoon when he escorted Gina through the curtain into the municipal park, set between blue Lake Zarmê and green Lake Orosz. The two of them slipped out and in two steps blended with several other couples passing by, admiring the flowers.

Regarding Gina, feeling her hand clasping his, he could not speak.

"What's the matter with you?" she asked him.

"You're young! Look at yourself. You're not the age you were in my apartment."

"I'm a First-Class Voyager, I told you." She laughed. "Someday I'll teach you that trick. Or maybe not."

She took his hand and led him through the park. The woman still looked older than him, evidence of her longevity on Ghoupallesz, but she had shed about twenty years during the passage through the tangent. He saw her more like the queen he had rescued from the Zetin, the same girl he had kissed in high school. It was still Gina, no matter what appearance she had.

"The first thing I always do, no matter how much of a hurry I'm in," she told him as they crossed the street to a news bulletin board, "is check the date. Then you'll know how to act, and what to do."

He stared at the paper tacked up, realizing the language had faded somewhat in his memory.

"My goodness! It's 1472!" he cried.

"Relax."

"B-b-but the year was 1455 when I returned for Zaura last time. That was seventeen years ago? I lost ten years with her the first time. Now I've lost seventeen more years?"

"I said relax." She linked her arm in his. "You don't have to stay. You're just helping me come back, like the Eagle Scout you always were. See me over to my son's wedding and you're free to go."

They walked along the avenue, catching stares from the people they passed who heard them speaking English.

"But you're not old now, Gina. Can't you go by yourself? I don't want to be here. There are too many bad memories for me."

She shushed him, gave his hand a playful slap, pulled him along.

"Why don't you indulge me this one afternoon," she said. "Look around us. Here is a fine spring day, perfect weather, not a yellow cloud in the whole green sky. Are you looking? The trees are in full bloom, and—look at that *stighal* over there, the way its long pink petals droop all the way down to the ground. What's that, about forty feet? You won't see anything like that back on Earth. You see the beauty here? the harmony? Look at the *lugê-feq* with the big, orange *roso* on its branches. See the *halêl* flying over the roof of that townhouse? Why can't you just relax and enjoy this day? If you leave here by tomorrow, you won't have missed more than an hour of your precious Earth."

He looked around as much as her impatient tugging would allow. She was ushering him quickly down the walk, certain that she would be late for the wedding. Everything was passing by him too quickly, and her words were like breezes, part of the environment.

"Here we are," she announced, pulling up in front of the red stone House of Union.

A priest in the traditional yellow *raelor* robe stood outside and welcomed the people who were arriving. The priest seemed to recognize the flustered woman with the younger man on her arm. Inside, Set scanned the group of Ghoupalles—and he presumed they were scanning him, too. He sat beside Gina, the place of honor for the groom's family. They were the only ones there, he saw. The bride's family was nowhere to be seen.

"Wait here," she whispered to him. "I'm going to find my son."

He waited, in that conspicuous seat at the front, closest to the wedding mat. Feeling curious stares sticking to his back, he realized he still wore his Earth clothes.

The ceremony was about to begin and Gina had not returned. He tried to remember what had happened in his own Ghoupalle wedding, thinking if the parents had been out front or backstage. Some bells were rung and the priest came to the dais to address the group. They all stood, and he followed, turning to welcome the groom, led hand in hand by his parent. That was the custom, he vaguely recalled; he'd had no parent in his ceremony. Gina looked quite handsome—about forty, he decided. The young man was about twenty-five in Ghoupalle years but looking like any fresh-faced Earth kid of sixteen. His bride would be older.

The bride arrived. He could see the dark-haired girl was beautiful but, more than that, possessed an ethereal familiarity.

Perhaps he was only attracted to her matrimonial nudity, walking tall and proud down the aisle beside her mother. He came to focus on the woman holding the girl's hand. His eyes followed her until she was even with him in the aisle. She gazed ahead at the priest. She did not notice him, but when her daughter had been given to the priest who bid her kneel beside the groom, she saw him out of the corner of her eye.

The woman gasped, clenched her chest, lost her balance, regained it as he jumped up from his seat to help her. She let him assist her to the bench where their eyes finally met.

The ceremony paused as everyone stared at the disruption. What was wrong with the bride-mother? the guests were wondering.

The warm orbs he had gazed into a millennia before, he gazed into once more. She was breathing fast, still clenching her chest, not because her heart was weak but as a gesture of shock. Her golden hair was still short, the same as it had been when they'd met in Sairel. Now, as they regarded each other, her face held a quiet maturity which he could feel, a glow that lit his own face— which blinded the whole assembly with its brilliance, shining upward through the red tinted windows high on the walls of the room.

"Zaura...."

Her hands took his face and pulled it against hers, there on the bench, with all fifty or so people watching, not caring what they thought, wanting his touch never to leave.

"*Fan-mosta Ghoum ben pitend-se!*" the new bride laughed afterward, held in the three-way embrace with her new husband, her mother, and the father she had thought lost forever. 'What a spectacle you made of yourself!'

Zaura wept, afraid to release him, keeping one arm around his waist, her other clasping one of his hands like a favorite pet. Her head stayed within breath of his face, and she regarded him every other *pii* as she received the congratulatory sympathy from the guests.

The newlywed couple was proclaimed "Aisa-d'Elous, in partnership with Sartan-Tek the Fifth, of the House of Kish-a-Tek"! The young lady shouted her happiness. She declared her father's return was the greatest wedding gift she could have imagined. The young husband took his hand and shook it vigorously, seeing for the first time the man his mother, Gina, had told him about on many occasions. Here was the great warrior Set-d'Elous who had rescued her from the Zetin. He had come to the wedding! That was clearly one reason he was so taken with the daughter of his mother's great friend. It did not matter so much then that the groom and his mother were no longer royalty. The nation of Fenula had no monarchy following its victory over the Zetin, but the family still had some of their wealth—at least that was what his mother told him, and Gina seldom lied.

"*El nejê-sethend hoven-y'da,*" Zaura whispered in his ear so he might know her foremost thought among the din of the crowd. 'I never gave up hope,' she told him. She had heard about her brother's death and said she prayed to three of the high gods that he was safe from harm somewhere. She thought he and her brother might have killed each other.

He whispered to her: "*E nejê-laeforen ju-se mosanne-poreg se apesen,*" telling her he would never again leave her, no matter what happened.

"*Ashê ga eli delen ju-zu biae Tolour-dexas,*" she told him then, and quickly described her second husband's death. He winced in her embrace, hearing that the man was bitten by a *sünra*—the basketball-sized mountain spider—while in Saunicêa inspecting *moussala* fields.

"*Fasê-in kal?*" he asked. 'When was that?'

She pressed her face into his shoulder and he could barely understand her words. Raising her face to him, she repeated them: "*Lêr eqapra-se Sairel-kem esraogend.*" She smiled faintly, embarrassed. 'It was the same trip we ran away from Sairel.'

Suddenly he felt ill and Zaura held him tightly. Her second husband had already been dead when they gave up fleeing from Rasek in Milipour.

"Everything I try to do, I screw up," he reminded himself, using English so his anguish would remain private.

"Please come with me to Selauê; I'll introduce you to Aisa's brother," Zaura whispered into his ear. He heard her Ghoupallêan words but his mind had instantly translated them into English.

Thinking her memory faulty, he said he had met the boy before in Sairel. She continued: "I named the boy after you, his father; he was born in *Keruk*, the next year, so we are four now."

The weary but still astonished Internal Revenue Service employee turned and searched the crowd for another woman he wished to thank.

Gina was standing at the edge of the congregation, beside the exit. Her eyes met his, a knowing wink sailed between them, and she waved her hand in farewell. She stepped through the doorway and disappeared, as surely as if she had stepped through a tangent right there. Perhaps she had.

"Throughout all of my years," he said, turning to Zaura, his voice hot and intense, using his most carefully chosen Ghoupallêan, "there was only one woman in the world I thought I could love, and who I wanted to love more than anyone else, but you—you, my dear Zaura—you have made me forget her at long last, and forever."

PART THREE

The world was all before them, where to choose
Their place of rest, and Providence their guide:
They hand in hand, with wandering steps and slow,
Through Eden took their solitary way.

John Milton, *Paradise Lost*, Book XII

Chapter 22

Return of the Native

They were married on *Shae-1*, barely four months after their daughter's wedding. This time, however, there was no ceremony, simply the registering of their names at the Archives in Selauê, their new home. However, their children arranged a small celebration in their home in Selauê, Aisa being the ringleader, assisted by her new husband Sartan, her twenty-two year old half-brother Samot, and her eighteen-year-old full-brother Set-*jousta*, named for his father. A few bowls of *frol* and several plates of assorted *ulae* and *qann*, a couple bottles of *gor*, and a large red and white *del-fex* for good luck were placed on the table. Zaura's family—her parents and siblings—refused to attend. Indeed, they learned of the return of the native only from Aisa. The couple believed there was no point in bringing up the conflict over Rasek's death again, and they were right.

As Aisa innocently explained to her brothers, whenever Father came to visit Mother, they would have a new brother or sister the next year. He learned it would be true that same month. A child was due the next spring. They would all come together once more for celebration.

Until that time, though, they went to their own lives. Aisa and Sartan lived nearby, where he managed his family's overseas businesses—those trade connections that survived the Fenulan invasion. Samot, who called himself the outsider, returned to Sairel to attend the university on his father's education fund, intending to continue Tolour-Frêdin's career. Set-*jousta* was at the preparatory school attached to the Selauê Academy, living in the dormitory.

That left the small apartment to themselves, and for the first weeks together they rarely left it—and, within it, they barely left the sleeping room. Zaura looked down at her long-lost husband and remarked that he finally looked younger than she did. That pleased her; they would appear as a normal couple. But it concerned him. Over time he would remain closer to his Earth age while she aged at a pace normal for her. He knew her age in Ghoupalle years and he knew what it was, mathematically calculated, in Earth years—fifty-seven—while he had recently turned thirty.

As she slept, snuggling against him on their *qala*, all he could think about were the wasted years when he was away. He had seen his daughter shortly after her birth, then again for a few days when she was ten, and not again until she was getting married. In all, it was only a month. Perhaps Ghoupalle people had a keener sense of familial relationships, he pondered. And Samot, the son of his opponent in the battle for Zaura's affection, he would go out of his way to treat fairly, to welcome him as a member of the family—which he was, of course. He was Zaura's son and he loved anything that was hers, so he would be loved as much as his other son, Junior. Still, he could not deny his pride when he admired his strong young son preparing to enter the Selauê Academy, the most prestigious university in all Sekuate.

In alternate moments, however, he would sigh a lowly sigh, trying not to awaken Zaura. So much time passed by, so many days together erased before they could happen. He vowed to make up for them. As he was falling asleep, the images of his own childhood crept into his dreams. Scenes of grassy yards, of football with the Hawkins twins, of hiking through the forests at Scout camp with Jason, of lazy summer afternoons and star-filled nights—and he was seeing them from the arms of his Ghoupalle wife, one hundred light-years by spaceship or ten seconds by the tangent.

"Ah, when a boy, the summers are endless," he mused. "For a man, the years pass in the blink of an eye. So does a whole life: the courtship lasts forever, but the years of raising a family are over in a flash."

Basha-d'Elous, named for Zaura's mother, was born on *Keruk-9* in 1475, as the spring term was concluding at the Selauê Academy. Her elder sister, Aisa, had given birth to her first child, a son, two months earlier. And Sebastian the Professor, better known as Set-d'Elous, was a *real* professor at last. He now taught classes in military history and cavalry tactics, but he was able to get away from the final examinations for the birth of his daughter.

His son, Dunas-Matousz, was born a year later.

"What's all this?" Sebastian asked, arriving around the shelving, into his section at the IRS service center. The first break was still on and most people were away from their desks.

He referred to the banquet set out on the table nearest his desk. That always annoyed him. All during the night people would be stopping by to snack on the goodies their co-workers brought.

"What's the occasion?" he asked Priscilla, who had her desk moved next to his, away from the new guy who smoked three packs a night.

"You didn't bring nothing?" she asked, listening to him with the earplug out of her left ear, continuing R&B through the right one.

"Bring anything? I didn't hear about any party."

"It's Ken Davenport's birthday," she replied with a slight sneer.

"Fat Ken?"

"Awright now," Joyce spoke up from her seat at the back, "there's no need to be snotty. You'll have your turn at a birthday party—if you put your birthday on the paper I sent around last October."

He sat down at his desk, began arranging his tools for the night, his pencils sharpened just so, his unused eraser, the staple puller, the pen with official government black ink, the one with red ink, and the essential Walkman cassette player and ear piece.

"So what did you bring?" he asked Priscilla, feeling the first curly tongues of smoke floating over from the new guy's desk.

"I brung what I always bring, Salamander Salad," she said in her syrupy voice. Her specialty was a lime gelatin with lots of fruit, nuts and other things suspended in it. Some could not tell what it was and refused to try it.

She saw his brown paper sack on the desk. "What'd you bring, honey?"

"Me? I brought what I always bring: tuna salad on wheat bread."

There was a commotion. The ground was moving, and they heard Joyce announce that Ken was coming back from the errand she sent him on while they set up the table.

"Happy Birthday!" Joyce and some of the others shouted when the pot-bellied man rounded the end of metal shelving stacked floor to ceiling with boxes of tax returns.

Fat Ken acted surprised, and his eyes widened at the sight of the banquet.

"Bet he's gonna start right in," Priscilla snickered.

The others shuffled back to their desks to begin their work for the night.

When the lunch break came at half past midnight, the line had already formed. Fat Ken had two plates. A true artist, he could fill a paper plate to his chin without it breaking under the weight of the food. Others stood back to make room for him to pass.

Sebastian stood up.

"Here you go," he said, offering his sandwich.

"What's that?" the birthday boy asked.

"It's a tunafish sandwich."

"What're you, some kinda wiseguy? What're you tryin' to say? That I need to go on a diet? You sayin' I need to eat *tuna*?"

"No, it's what I brought tonight. Happy birthday. Here's a tunafish sandwich."

"What an asshole! You know what you kin do with your shitty tuna sandwich, dontcha?"

"Ken, I just forgot to bring something tonight. This is the sandwich I brought for my own lunch. And I'm giving it to you. It's not big enough to share with everybody."

"Ya know, you're one sorry-ass individual!"

Ken sat down his plates of food and was about to say something harsher when the Grand Exalted Night Shift Manager of the whole service center came strolling by, wearing his three-piece suit, joking with two front office ladies who were slumming.

Sebastian the Professor could not quite catch what Fat Ken said but he knew it was something he did not want to hear. The others continued helping themselves to the buffet, but the confrontation left a dampened silence over the section. No one dared raise a voice above a low hush, not wanting to disturb the solemnity of the occasion.

"Really, I didn't mean anything by that," he told Priscilla. Then he thought for a moment and added, "I thought he'd still have room for it."

"I hear that," she responded, "but, hey, those three"—meaning Fat Ken, Joyce, and Kate—"they *should* share your sandwich. They gettin' much too big now."

He felt a pat on his shoulder and turned, fearing it would be Ken. It was Michael, just returned from his lunch break across the service center in one of the canteens, ignoring the birthday party. He crouched down beside the desk.

"Hey, man, heard what happened. Sure wish I could've seen Fat Ken's face. Way to go."

"Way to go? I wasn't *trying* to insult him. It just happened."

Back to work after lunch and running the calculator, he thought about the upcoming trip. Once more through the tangent. He wondered if he still had the touch, if he could still sense the energy vortices. He thought through how the plan would unfold the next evening. Finishing the batch of tax returns he had been examining and setting the last file in its bin, he rose to get another batch of tax returns. A bundle of about twenty would be enough to last the shift.

Ken was in charge of delegating files, loaded on wheeled carts, one of dozens of full carts forming a line spiraling around the desks in their department and down the hall. He thought he would try to break the ice as he took another batch. He would let Ken know he really had not meant any offense, but the big man's ugly sneer spoke several paragraphs of verbal abuse.

"That's all right, Ken," he grinned, forcefully. "I have more important things to do—like go fix the damn toilet for my wife." At that moment he had been thinking innocently of a long-forgotten incident with Zaura, and the words had just come out.

"What're you talking about?" Ken said, catching the Professor off-guard. "You're not married."

Priscilla perked up, peeked over the carts.

"Shhhh! Don't be so damn unsensitive."

Ken looked at her. "Oh, yeah—almost forgot."

He handed the Professor a box of files, estimating that it contained thirty.

"Thanks," he muttered, taking the box and returning to his desk. He did not want to show that Ken's remark was eating into him. It was common knowledge by now that his wife had been murdered.

"My pleasure," said Ken, then under his breath, "I'm gonna get you for that tuna shit."

Sitting at his desk organizing the files, Sebastian felt himself slowly being overtaken by another headache. It was not a good time for that, with the trip scheduled for later the same day, the next night's shift. He only hoped Michael and Tammy would be ready.

❉ ❉ ❉

He pulled into a parking space at the far edge of the shopping mall, built on the edge of the farmland, and ordered his colleagues out. They gathered their bags from the trunk and started off after their leader. Across the vast empty pavement they went, and down the clean, white sidewalk that ran along the country road waiting for suburbia to meet it.

"How much more is it?" Michael complained after ten minutes.

"That hill," the Professor pointed out.

The hill they saw was crowned with forest but he knew that hidden behind the thick summer vegetation was a quarry hewn from limestone. Around the hill lay fields of corn and soybeans, and the road running between them went past the gravel drive leading up to the quarry. On geological survey maps it was called Pink Hill, but he called it *Rü-kel*—its Ghoupallêan translation.

His guests were surprised when he pulled out a key and unlocked the padlock on the chain that held the gate closed. He explained that he'd added it for better security after he bought the property from the son of the old cowboy who caught Gina and him experimenting years before.

"You own this land?" Michael asked, impressed.

"I was trespassing so much that it seemed best to just buy it," he replied.

"No shit. How much?"

"Not expensive. The quarry's panned out."

"Where'd you get that kinda dough? Not working for the service center."

"I used to sell…commodities," he answered, thinking of how he sold the *gealan* in Selauê, bought gold, and changed it into dollars.

"Why you work for the IRS, then?"

He did not answer, instead closed the gate and locked it. Of course, anyone who wanted to could easily climb over the gate but at least it prevented vehicles being driven up the road for wild parties. He was most concerned about his sensitive equipment and the carefully set monitors he had there. And the wire grid with flags marking various tangents.

Standing at the entrance, where twin stone pillars rose on either side of them, he knew that something was wrong. He ran toward the depression where a pool usually formed in rainy weather and found that the wire grid had fallen over. The grid, an intricate system of wires that he had constructed, marked the points of several tangents among the three-dimensional space of the quarry. The top left wire intersection of the grid, which would have stood about four feet off the ground when it was in place, was the tangent for Lyas. Further down and to the right was the point Gina had aimed at during their early days of experimentation. That was how close they came to hitting Lyas on the first try instead of blundering through six other tangents.

"What's wrong?" Michael asked, helping Tammy off with her knapsack.

"The grid is knocked down, maybe from the storm the other

night."

"That's bad?"

He nodded, kneeling beside the crumpled wire, trying to determine if he could simply bend it up and have it still in proper alignment.

"I had the places marked," he said. "Now it's blown over. I don't know if I can fix it. At least, not quickly."

"What're you talking about?" Michael asked, walking over and looking down at what he called the Hollywood Squares.

"I'm talking about the points where the universe can be torn. I told you last week—when you were so damn eager to go."

"You mean you're serious about all that shit you were hypnotizing me with?"

He straightened up and Michael turned away from the angry face that confronted him.

"Well, ya gotta admit it sure sounded kinda hokey," Michael said. "I mean, you almost got me there, but—"

"It's real."

"What're you talking about?" Tammy interrupted.

"Is this just some weird dream of yours?" Michael exclaimed, throwing his hands up. "You're putting us on, right? Where's the hidden camera?"

"Will you listen to me?"

"Man, somebody somewhere's laughing their asses off seeing me out in the middle of the night here in this damn quarry of yours. And you bought this place?"

"Is everything...okay?" Tammy asked.

"No, it's not," said Michael, turning to her. "The Perfesser's weirded out all a sudden. He thinks there's some invisible doorway to another world around here someplace."

"There is," he insisted. "I had it marked with this wire grid, but it's out of place now. Throws the whole system off."

"You're full of shit. There's nothing here but old rocks. You got a perfect excuse not to have to show us how it works. 'My damn grid's outta place.' Yeah, sure."

He dropped to the ground wearily, sat cross-legged before the bent wire, listening to Michael's cursing as he and Tammy went and sat on his and Gina's 'love' rock.

The night was full of bad omens, right from the moment Michael showed up at his apartment dressed like he was going to a disco.

"I always gotta look good, no matter where I go," Michael had said.

But regarding Michael's emerald silk shirt opened wide at the collar, the gold chain around his neck, baby blue polyester suit and polished tan oxfords, his blond mane blow-dried big and fluffy, he had to respond: "Where do you think we're going, Las Vegas? Don't worry, you do look good, but nobody's going to care where we're going."

When he went down to get Tammy while Michael changed into rougher clothes from his duffel bag, he found her 'weekend trip' luggage filling the trunk of the car. Lugging the two suitcases up to his apartment, he made her sort through them and choose only one extra outfit to take. It all had to fit in the small knapsack he gave her. Anything else they required he promised they could buy when they arrived at their destination. When he told them they would have a ten-mile hike, Michael complained so much that he wanted to call the whole trip off. One reminder about his problem was enough to keep him on track. The man had no sense of adventure, he sighed, disappointed. But he would need Michael's help when they got to Ghoupallesz. Stowing the suitcases in his bedroom, they left for Pink Hill and the world beyond, where the key fit the gate but not the door.

"Back up and turn around," Cassie instructed Dodie, her cousin, pulling up to the metal gate at the side of the road, hidden among the trees. "I think this musta been where they went. It's the only other road out here, the only place they coulda disappeared like that."

Dodie maneuvered the car around.

"You wanna get out and go on up?"

"Are you kidding?" Dodie exclaimed. "Look how dark it is up there. Too creepy."

"I thought we was gonna spy on them."

"You was, not me," said Dodie, afraid of the dark and the night noises.

"Well, if you're chicken, I'll go by myself, but you're gonna miss all the fun."

"Fun, what fun?"

Cassie retrieved the paper sack from the back seat, opened it for her cousin: fireworks.

"Cassie! What're you gonna do? Looks dangerous."

"Ain't dangerous. Just gotta be careful. It's all legal stuff. But I gotta get up there before they finish their foolin' round or I'll miss my chance to get'em. It's payback time for Michael Fenning and that bitch. And that goddamn Perfesser, too! They can all go to hell, far as I'm concerned!"

She climbed out of the car, checking her pockets.

"You got any matches?"

✻ ✻ ✻

Squeezed behind the wheel of his Pinto, Ken stared out all four windows as he drove along the dark road leading between the hills and into the unknown countryside. He was desperately searching for any sign of the Professor. He saw him pull into the shopping mall, but while he went around the building to keep out of sight, his co-workers had disappeared. He caught a glimpse of them walking down the road but then they were gone again.

"Where the hell *are* they?" Ken muttered, soaked in sweat from the humidity outside.

Then he saw a light down the road, just a flash. A car was parked there on the side. So that was their plan! They had arranged for someone to pick them up and get away so nobody would know where they were really going. Now his curiosity was piqued, more than for his act of revenge.

Ken had planned to let the air out of his co-worker's tires or scratch his car with keys—something like that, not caring if he would be suspected or not. He suddenly had a much better idea. He turned his Pinto around and headed back to the 7-Eleven store he'd passed, cursing his wiseacre co-worker. No one got away with calling him fat to his face!

"Stop laughing, we're getting close," the girl driving the station wagon cried out.

Two women from Data Processing, Kate from Underreporter, plus three from the mailroom packed the car. Inside, Big Bertha's hearty guffaw was like an explosion of TNT. The women cackled like geese. Only Kate had any perspective on the illicit adventure they were commencing. The idea they all had was that their weird co-workers were going out to the woods to indulge in their wildest fantasies. Kate believed the only fantasies being played out this night were in the minds of her fellow service center workers.

"Better shut up. They'll hear us coming," Wilma warned.

Chapter 23

An Officer and a Gentleman

There they stood, stiffly at attention, saluting the *Berron* as he passed in review: red cuffs flashing in the somber sunlight, golden eight-point stars on his shoulders, a length of braid down his right arm, the peaked cap with the coat of arms of Sekuate, the flowing blue cape laying over the rump of the auburn *Jêpe* he rode, black calf-high boots glistening and reflecting the grim faces of his army as he passed, as he passed, as he passed by them. Soon would come the action, the bloody fighting, the holy combat, there on foreign fields and under distant skies where none would know their fate save the winds stroking their cold corpses. Medals and ribbons, new swords with bunting, promotion in rank, the admiration of friends and comrades, the honor of cheering crowds, the peace at last in the arms of loved ones—was that payment?

He broke with tradition and suddenly looked away, almost heard the assembly's hushed breath, and tried to find his family among the thousands who lined the great parade ground.

"*Kanê, seren-tas,*" his young second-in-command whispered hurriedly, urging him to face forward even though the *Berron* had already passed them.

First Officer of the Republic, Chief Commanding General, the *Berron*, Katoum-Armag was in the twilight of his long career and the wars he had fought had taken their toll on his mind as well as his body. He was the longest reigning *Berron*, a position as powerful and full of honor as the monarch himself. Born in the capital city of Seas, down the street from the palace, the fourth but only surviving son of another *Berron*, he excelled at the Selauê Academy and graduated one year early, joining the cavalry corps. His commission in Ghoupalle year 1398 was the same year he, Set-d'Elous, had rescued Queen Jinetta. He was amused to realize he technically out-ranked Katoum-Armag, having achieved the rank of *Serpan* before the man became *Landor*. Katoum-Armag was promoted to general in 1428, however, appointed commanding general of the First *Coraesz* of the Sekuatean army soon after. He became *Berron*, the supreme military commander, in 1440, the same year Set-d'Elous met his Ghoupalle wife. Since becoming *Berron*, Sekuate had lived peacefully with its neighbors and the general had grown gray and cynical, fearing that he would be remembered as a general of peace.

Armag's day would come, he imagined—at that time not yet knowing the future of his adopted land. War would come, inevitably, but he would flee before then, he and his family. The old general would die with a sword in his hand and an arrogant grin on his sagging jowls, great mustache and goatee stained with the blood of his enemies. Even now, on this day, he was playing the part of the inspector on the occasion of his army's departure into action, albeit improbable combat. He loathed the ceremonial role, riding along the parade ground with his color guard, the pale blue flag of Sekuate waving, the golden eight-point star at its center emblazoned with the imperial crest of the king, the *Mexas*, Tomodon of the House of Sarrêban.

In the uplifting notes of the national anthem, words full of encouragement and pride in the nation and its long history, he heard only the cries of men dying and the snorting of *Jêpe*, the blasts of cannons, the whistle of mortars, and the anguished blare of trumpets in retreat. He closed his eyes, held them shut until the music stopped. His head was full of thundering explosions and he wished the ceremony would end so he could press his hands to his temples. But the band continued. His second-in-command,

Serpan-1 Rasek-Kalanou, was becoming alarmed but resisted moving from his staunch pose.

He was not ill, not stricken with the paralyzing *taerou*, not weary of military ceremonies, nor was he bored with the proceedings. He, the captain—the *Serpan*—commander of the 102d *Jêpedor-regêlad*, of the 5d *Treskand*, 2d *Rasselad*, 2d *Berêlad*, 2d *Coraesz* of the Army of Sekuate; he, who was a full-time professor at the Selauê Academy, instructor of military history and modern cavalry tactics; he, with appointment to the *Coraesz* 'special services' detachment involved in covert operations (his team had successfully affected the coup in Sogoê, installing a more favorable priest-king)—no, he was merely deep in thought reviewing the six years he had lived in the pleasant aura of his wife, Zaura-Matousz, she and their two daughters and three sons, all of whom made him proud.

Now they were called to defend the nation against internal aggressors, members of the self-named Gangus Army, a surprisingly well-organized band of revolutionaries. They had taken over a town to the north of Selauê; the town's *Bojar* requested assistance in driving them out. The task fell to the Second *Coraesz*, headquartered in Selauê, and passed down to the Fifth *Treskand*, which included his regiment. It would likely be a simple assignment but he loathed disciplining his adopted country's own people. He did not like being apart from his family, either.

Despite the trips he'd made back to check on his hometown Earth—only a week had passed the first time, after two years with Zaura in Selauê—he no longer considered Earth the place of his retirement. He had lost a week's pay at the service center but he held onto his job—mattering less and less with each year he lived with Zaura, commanded the 102d *Regêlad*, and taught at the Academy. What was real and what was the dream land to him now? One was becoming the other. On his short visits back to Earth, his dreams were filled with Ghoupallesz; with Zaura, he never saw the smoky Underreporter department of the service center in his sleep. In his waking hours, however, thoughts often floated through his head, wondering what had transpired back there, pondering what impression co-workers must have about him being away for so long. He learned on his most recent escape to spy on them that in his nearly six Ghoupalle years and three visits to Earth during that time, only twelve full days had passed in the service center.

He laughed—and *Serpan* Rasek-Kalanou glared at him—at the thought: if he used all of his vacation time from the service center, he could live his entire life on Ghoupallesz, including his retirement. Of course, then he would likely forget all the tax examining rules and procedures.

"*Serpan* Set-d'Elous, *laeforen-tas*!" the cry shot over the field from the commander of the Second *Coraesz*, General Sonel-Timê: 'Come forward!'

He thought the general had somehow spotted his inattention from the viewing stand. But he heard the rising applause and decided not. He marched with stiff, dignified posture, sharp corners on his turns, until he stood before the general, who stood beside the *Berron*. Old Katoum-Armag looked him in the eye, squinting a little from the bright sun. Then his general, Sonel-Timê, presented him with a rolled parchment and a silver statuette of a *Jêpe*, inscribed with ornate words marking the trophy as First Place in the annual cavalry games. His regiment, the 102d, known as the last and least orderly unit in the whole army when he was assigned command of it, had risen from no-shows to the unit which most impressed the generals at the series of riding maneuvers and mock battles played out the previous month in the hills east of Selauê.

He did not know how to respond. The military families, civilian on-lookers, bleachers of other officers were standing and cheering: slapping the hands of people around them instead of clapping their own. The band played the official cavalry song—but he recalled George Custer's 7th Cavalry's tune. He took the awards graciously and stepped back before turning to resume his place among his men.

And yet, it was the *Berron* who called him back to present a merit star to the foreigner who had taken his regiment to heart and whipped them into shape in less than a year. And possibly for the mission of the Special Services detachment up in Sogoê the previous year—though he, naturally, could not be given any public commendation for that action. And the so-called 'Gotankan Campaign' in which his regiment patrolled the area along the northeastern border, preventing refugees from entering the country as the nation of Gotanka was breaking into four separate states following their ongoing wars with Foixe. It was considered a farce, but the soldiers were happy to call it a 'campaign' and laugh about it over mugs of *skual*. And his contributions to cavalry theory in the Academy—as brought out through his 'theoretical history' course—were now adopted as standard cavalry maneuver and battle operations. The vivid history he used as examples of geopolitical situations was fictitious to the cadets but were actual battles from the history of Earth. He taught them military tactics of the Napoleonic era and of the American Civil War, plus some from World War I, thinking those battle situations were most appropriate to the current style of Sekuatean army operations. The only problem was remembering to speak in generic terms, never mentioning that the French had done this, the Germans this, and the Confederate forces that. Otherwise, it might have seemed presumptuous.

Although he had never really intended to join the Sekuate military establishment, living in Selauê posed the need for employment with his *gealan* profits exhausted. Zaura had suggested he apply as an instructor, having credentials from the Queen of Fenula. When he presented himself to the Academy headmaster—the aged colonel, Harax-Brounadar—he was taken immediately to the garrison's headquarters to meet the commander, Sonel-Timê. The general was impressed with the letters of introduction he had, provided by Gina as Jinetta, Queen of Fenula, his previous employer, from the box of documents collected upon her death. He would be allowed to teach military history—considered a basic course that could be taught by any officer—but only on the condition that he take command of one of the regiments for which they were short a *Serpan*-grade officer. He knew then that in the Sekuate military structure the first-in-command served mostly as a figurehead, as policy maker, and as the unit's liaison with higher headquarters. The real work, the daily running of the unit, fell upon the shoulders of the second-in-command. Therefore, it was common to pair two captains, one senior and one freshly promoted. He was offered the figurehead role as well as the teaching position at the prestigious Academy. That excited him. It worried him, too: he might not be able to live up to their high expectations.

Now, with all of his achievements in the five years of his Second *Coraesz* career, he was given his first full promotion. Yes, he had earned merits before—small star patches added to the cuffs of his jacket—but this was a full promotion, up to the rank of *Merzel*, one who commands a *Treskand* of about 1000 men. His papers from Gina stated his last rank as *Serpan-3*—a captain with three merits—and he was awarded one merit for his regiment's superior performance in the Games and one merit for the Sogoê coup (secreted under the guise of his Academy work). Five merits equaled a promotion.

However, he did not want it—even as the old *Berron* leaned down to pin his new rank insignia to his shoulders, breathing out his *skual*-tainted breath. Being *Merzel* would mean working in a headquarters with colonels and generals and not with the 'men who rubbed their hands on the *Jêpe*', as they were called colloquially. They were his men, and he had worked hard to make them the pride of the *Coraesz*. He may have been hired as a figurehead but when he saw just how slothful and undisciplined they really were, he rose to the occasion, asserting his own style of hands-on training. He ran them through cavalry drills day and night, freely punishing them as the law allowed for any hesitancy, and simultaneously rewarding their slightest improvement. No one in Sekuate had ever studied psychology, knew nothing of positive and negative reinforcement. It worked, and his regiment became a crack unit of hard, dedicated *Jêpedor*—'horse' soldiers. Now they had gained such notoriety that the retiring commandant of the Academy had requested his son, a cadet, be assigned to the 102d as its officer-in-training. Harax-Brounadar wanted his son to learn from the 'master of cavalry maneuver'.

He raised his head to regard the *Berron*, thinking the words he had just spoken in his mind had come out 'master of cavalry *manure*'. He fought desperately to hold back his amusement as he saluted them—raising his right arm parallel to the ground and snapping his forearm back toward his chin until his elbow was at a ninety-degree angle. The general gave the responsive salute, extending his arm and bending it at the elbow, drawing it sharply up to his ear.

Turning, he saluted his regiment. He raised the silver trophy and his men threw their red caps into the sky, letting loose a horrendous "*Houla!*"

The band played again as he marched back to take his place with his men. With *his* men. Now he was being asked to give them up? No, he could not do that. But he certainly could not refuse in front of the *Berron*, or the assembled on-lookers. That would not be proper military etiquette.

"Goddamn bastard," Ken muttered over and over as he opened his tenth can of tuna and dumped its contents into a large plastic bag. He had six more, the cheapest brand. The bastard liked tuna so much, he was going to get all he could possibly eat!

He glanced up when he saw headlights coming over the hill, hoping his car would not be noticed parked on the side of the road.

It was a station wagon, he saw, filled with several people. They were loud, too—music, shouting—but he did not give them any lingering attention. That is, not until they slowed ahead, near where the other car was. Probably this was the road for teenagers to make out, he decided. He had not seen any lights from the first car after he parked. When the second car stopped and some of them got out, he decided he was in the middle of something interesting.

He saw five or six people crossing the road to where the chain-linked gate blocked the gravel drive.

"What the...?"

He decided that thirteen cans were good enough. Lucky thirteen, he chuckled. Taking the bag of tuna, he poured in some vinegar and oil to give it as putrid a smell as he could make. Then he climbed out and began waddling down the road toward the other cars, hiding when necessary among the tall grass along the edge of the fields.

❋ ❋ ❋

"Look at'em, not even botherin' to hide their car, just leavin' it parked on the side o' the road like that. They ain't 'spectin' nobody come on tonight for their big party in the woods, huh?"

The girls laughed, trying to quiet each other.

Big Bertha stood back, silent for once, staring at the high metal gate.

"I caint get over that," she said, then cursed.

The others were boosting each other over, feet in hand stirrups, arms hefting them up. Two were already over and waiting on the other side.

"Can't you be a little more quiet?" Kate chided.

When her turn came, the only one to heft her was Bertha. But she was as weak as she was stout, and Kate fell on her back against the gate. The clang shot up and down the road, then died.

"What're we gonna do?" she asked Bertha.

"We caint go on with y'all," was her sorrowful reply. "You go on, tell us all the nitty-gritty details later."

"All right," Vicky called back in a low voice as the others stepping lightly up the gravel path.

"Shoot, I come all the way out here to see the show," said Kate. "Now I'm just sitting out here on the side of the road in the middle of the night."

"Yeah," Bertha sighed. "Woulda been great seein' that orgy."

❋ ❋ ❋

He stood up, admiring his handiwork. The wire grid was back in place—or close. Now came the difficult part. He told Michael and Tammy to keep quiet and not bother him while he concentrated on what he called "tearing the curtain." When he called them, they should hurry to where he stood and without hesitation jump through the doorway they would see.

"Don't take even a second to think about it," he said, "or it'll close on you."

"You're still serious, aren't you?" asked Michael.

"Just keep an open mind."

He touched the wire, sliding his fingers along the intersections, pausing at a few of them. His eyes closed, his ears tuned to the sounds they heard that first summer evening. The tips of his fingers were antennas, searching, feeling for weaknesses in the fabric of space. As he had done before, the air would seem to yield, not the same as when people walked down the street and passed through the air in front of them. No, first was resistance. Then he would know he had found a tangent and, pressing further but with constrained effort, he would find the resistance give way—just like pushing his finger into the folds of a curtain.

But there was no resistance, even after trying for more than ten minutes.

"How long you gonna keep that up?" Michael called after waiting patiently and quietly. "Ya know, man, you look like that French dude—what's his name? You know, that guy that paints his face white and pretends to be pushing against invisible walls. Never says shit, just pushes them invisible walls."

"Shut up, will you?" he snapped.

"Hey, you brought us out here and we appreciate the show, but it's getting late."

"It's a little...cool now," Tammy added.

Michael lifted his arm and laid it casually around her shoulders.

Sebastian said nothing, resuming his efforts. He had forgotten how difficult it could be with others watching, with others disturbing his concentration, teasing, sending out negative vibes. He had to overcome that with greater effort and tighter focus on his objective: the pinpoint of resistance and weakness. He had to meditate first, he decided, to get his mind ready to continue.

Their nervous fingers parted the bushes, their curious eyes

staring through the night into the arena of the quarry, seeing the three figures faintly lit by a lantern in the middle of the open area.

"Look at that," Vicky whispered.

Her three companions—Wilma, Donna Mae, and Allison— were equally fixed on the sight before them. In the yellow glow of the lantern was the Professor, undressing. Right there in the middle of the quarry. There was Michael and Tammy sitting over on the side, watching. Some kind of wire thing stood in front of them. They did not know what it was, but Donna Mae suggested it was probably some kind of sadomasochism device.

"But what do they do, sit on it? lay on it?" eighteen-year-old Allison asked.

"Quiet," said Vicky, poking Wilma to pass down the message.

Michael was standing up, then Tammy, both moving over to the Professor.

"Wait a minute!" Vicky gasped.

Michael was taking off his shirt.

"What about Tammy? I can't see good," said the older Wilma. She scooted ahead, deeper into the bushes.

They watched Michael talking with Tammy, stroking her face with his hand, trying to unsnap her jeans with the other hand. She was not fighting too hard. Then the Professor turned to them— facing the gallery of spies.

"Look at that," they gasped together. They were not impressed or surprised seeing him stripped. What they saw was that he did not have a right arm.

"My God! What happened?" Allison almost shrieked but for Donna Mae's hand quickly clamping over her mouth.

Michael pushed Tammy toward the Professor. They had knapsacks in their hands. Michael was handing clothes to the Professor, who stood in the same spot, not moving, as though he were holding a door open for the others. Tammy stopped in her tracks, and even with Michael tugging on her arm she would not go further.

"They're gonna rape her, I just know it," Allison cried, too quick for anyone's hand to cover her mouth.

"Serves her right, the slut," Vicky sneered, not taking her eyes off the proceedings.

"I can't watch anymore," said Allison, jumping up. She ran back down the trail.

"Let her go," said Donna Mae.

❋ ❋ ❋

With one arm holding the universe open, the Professor was waving his free arm at Michael, getting them to come through. Tammy was stunned by what she saw: sparkling lights around him, outlining his head and body, his arm and shoulder invisible. Michael was pulling her forward. He was hesitating, too. The wind was picking up, it seemed, coming from behind the Professor, from where his arm was missing. A storm was blowing *into* the quarry.

A larger gust of wind swept through the quarry, rattling the bushes outside the stone pillars, causing the flame in the lantern to flicker. It wavered, then went out. Darkness engulfed them— except for the sparkling lights which seemed to grow brighter around the Professor. Tammy could see they were outlining his arm. With his other hand he was pushing the lights apart, but it seemed so hard. She could see something coming into view, there among the lights, like a movie fading in. The lights were dancing in the air—blue, red, gold—like Fourth of July sparklers, she thought.

"Come on, will you?" he called.

Michael's eyes were so wide that she could see how white they were, reflecting the lights. His grip on her arm was tight, and it became tighter the longer he regarded the lights. They were forming a doorway, she saw—it looked like a doorway to her, or a tear in the side of a circus tent—and the Professor was standing halfway through it. His entire right side was hidden. Gazing ahead, she could see different hills rising behind him than the ones she had seen before.

The Professor took the clothing Michael handed to him and dropped it through the lights. The clothing disappeared. He took the knapsack from Michael, followed by hers. She was still hesitating—what was this she was seeing?

"I think it's safe," she heard Michael calling above the whistling winds and thundering roar that was swirling around them.

"What...is it, Michael?"

"It's...," and for once he had no answer to a question posed by Tammy.

She remembered what the Professor told her before in the service center, about going someplace where she could give birth and no one would know about it, and how it would seem like only a flash of time instead of nine months. Was this the place? There he was, standing in the doorway to another world. He said it was another world, didn't he? She was scared, but she had no choice at that moment. She had to trust him.

"Come on, dammit," the Professor called, trying to be heard over the noise of the storm. "I can't hold it open much longer!"

Michael reached forward as if he were going to go through, but just as he grabbed the Professor's wrist, he stepped back. Tammy was still hooked by his other arm. She was pushing him from behind. Which way to go? He was disoriented, overwhelmed by the phenomena. Whatever it was, it certainly did not look safe.

"I can't," he yelled. "We'll all die!"

"No, it's all right," the Professor shouted. "This is normal. It'll stop when I close it."

"I can't...I can't...I can't," he kept saying.

Tammy gave him a shove and he fell off balance, tumbling ahead toward the Professor and knocking him completely through the opening. She looked down, saw only Michael's feet protruding from the lights—only his feet, and still moving, scrambling to get up. The Professor was already gone, but she could see him pulling Michael by his belt—until it broke loose. He dropped it and motioned for her to come on through as the lights faded, the wind dying down.

"Tammy!" the Professor called.

"It's okay," she heard Michael shouting calmly. "Everything's okay, Tammy."

She took a deep breath, closed her eyes tightly, pinched her nose shut as though she was diving into a swimming pool, and leaped through the fading lights.

The two cars on the side of the road, one almost stuck in the ditch there, had left their windows open. It was easy for Ken to sneak along the slope below the level of the road. He had to, seeing some women standing by the gate across the road.

The first car had to belong to that bastard, the Professor. It was the same model but he did not know the license number and, in the dark, it could be the same color. The second one probably was that of his two strange friends, Michael and Tammy. Going to the first car, he took his special tuna casserole and tossed it through the window, hitting the seats with a soft, dull splat. Already the smell was too strong for him and he turned his head to the breeze. The bastard would sure get a surprise, he chuckled.

The smile that spread across his face like jam across bread disappeared when he saw the lights up at the top of the hill, among the treetops. He heard noise from up there—like a tornado. Whatever kind of party they were having, he wanted none of it. But it gave him an idea. Why not make an anonymous call to the fire department? Or the police? They were always looking for wild summer parties to bust up, weren't they? It was his best idea yet. There was a pay phone back at that 7-Eleven store.

"What was that?" Bertha asked Kate, both seeing the brilliant glow, an orange fire rising and dissipating.

"I dunno, maybe some fireworks."

They watched it for a while and listened to the roar of the wind around the quarry walls.

"Fireworks? Musta been cherry bombs, huh? Did you feel that blast—blowin' down the hillside?"

"Sure did. Ya think they're okay?"

"Who—Vicky and them?"

Bertha nodded, worry on her haggard face.

They almost jumped in each other's arms when Allison arrived out of breath, banging against the gate to halt her downhill sprint.

"What happened?" they asked her.

"Oh, it was terrible," she cried, trying to catch her breath. "There was this wire thing, like a rack, and Donna Mae said it was for sado-macho-something, and that guy, the weird one from your department, he took off his clothes, and Michael—he and Tammy were taking their clothes off, too, and—oh, I couldn't watch any more! I wanted to help her—but they wouldn't let me, so I ran straight down here. Maybe it's not too late and we can stop them!"

"Too late for what, Allison?" Kate asked.

"They're raping her!"

❋ ❋ ❋

The three women from the service center stood at the quarry's entrance, stunned by what they had seen, found their clothing torn and dirty. As the winds whirled and roared, they became frightened, too, and rushed out of the bushes into the quarry. They were just in time to see Tammy disappear. To where, they could not see. At that second, the wind battered them and they clung to the rocks and the trees to keep from being bowled over as the pressure wave swept out of the quarry and down the hill.

"I never seen nothing like that!" Vicky declared, still shaking as she gathered her torn t-shirt from where it had been blown off her by the powerful wind.

Wilma, her blouse now without buttons, was embarrassed. They were just going out to peep at little Tammy doing the dirty deed with her two co-workers. She never expected any of this; she was a mother of three and too old for these games.

Behind them, Donna Mae bent down to retrieve her torn tank-top, and held it up for inspection. "You think I can bill'em for this?"

They looked at her, Vicky chuckling.

"I got a t-shirt in the car you can wear. Next time wear a bra."

"There ain't gonna be no next time!"

"Ladies, what did we *really* see here?" asked Wilma, drawing them together.

Vicky stared into the quarry. "I saw the Professor and Michael getting it on with Tammy."

"So where are they?" asked Donna Mae.

"They took off," said Wilma. "Maybe they're hiding from us, or from the storm."

"That *was* a storm, ya know. Just a freak storm that hit us, right?"

"But where did they go to?"

They thought for a moment.

Vicky spoke: "You don't suppose they were sucked up in it, like in the *Wizard of Oz*, do you?"

"No, there must be some cave around here they all dropped into," Donna Mae suggested. "Let's go have a look there."

They walked together, like three gunfighters in Dodge City, but with their eyes on the ground expecting to see a secret tunnel leading to where Tammy and her two comrades were hiding. Instead, they came upon the buckle end of Michael's belt. The opposite end vanished into thin air.

"Where's the rest of the belt?" asked Wilma, stooping to examine it closely.

Standing close, they could feel a faint draft blowing out of an invisible vent.

When she picked up the buckle end, she saw the other end laying ahead, trailing off into something—something like a cloud and yet not a cloud. The quarry seemed to have a sinkhole, she decided, even though she could see clearly that the universe just seemed to stop halfway up the length of leather. She paused, holding it in her hand, not wanting to remove it, and a few sparks seemed to flash at the horizon of her vision.

"Is this your secret tunnel?" Vicky asked her.

"Maybe so."

Regarding the spot where the belt disappeared, she thought she could see movement—or maybe it was a hallucination.

"Let's see," Wilma challenged her companions.

She settled on her knees with the buckle still in one hand,

staring into the void—and seeing something. Then she crawled forward.

"Wilma! I—I can't see you," Donna Mae cried out when her head and shoulders disappeared.

She continued through.

"Wait—" Vicky shouted. "Where're you—going?"

She and Donna Mae shrugged their shoulders and, not wanting to lose her, dropped to the ground and followed.

✳ ✳ ✳

They lay back on the brown, coarse sand, knees and elbows bent, resting under an amber sky with violet storm clouds running fast on the horizon. Michael stretched his arms and legs, felt the energy in them, electricity tickling and pricking like needles. Tammy sat with her face in her hands, afraid to see her new home. And the Professor, their travel agent and tour guide, Interdimensional Voyager Second-Class, stood nearby surveying the landscape, dressed now for a hike, certain that he had matched his desires with the right tangent, hoping that he'd made the correct tear in the curtain.

After they had rested, and the electricity had run from their bodies, he ordered them onward. They gathered their knapsacks, adjusted their clothing for the trek across the desert, and followed their leader. He knew what he was doing, they believed, though they had little choice now. They were far from home. How far, they could only imagine.

Passing a marker of stacked stones he had left on a past voyage, he took comfort in the fact that he had brought them safely through the right tangent. It was difficult, of course, with their negative thoughts and all the other interference, but here they were: the new world, the other universe, the land of make-believe—

"The Dream Land," he announced to his fellow travelers' questions.

As they hiked, he kept thinking of the images he thought he saw as he was persuading Michael and Tammy to come through:

three figures, human forms rising up behind them, between the twin pillars at the entrance to the quarry. He wondered if someone could have followed them there. It was possible, knowing how the rumors of their upcoming journey had spread around the service center like news of a pay hike. But who would go to the trouble of following them out in the middle of the night, into the countryside and up some old abandoned gravel path? If they had come close, they probably would have seen the lighting effects and heard the thunderous roar that came when the universe was torn open. That would be enough to scare them away.

Still, if what he thought he saw were three other people watching them from the quarry's entrance, did they see the flickering lights and experience the whirlwind?

❋ ❋ ❋

"Well, how long they gonna be up there?" Bertha snorted, kicking the gravel by the gate. "It's pert near dawn now."

"I dunno. Must be a good show," said Kate.

"We should've called somebody," Allison moaned.

"Well, why dontcha go check on'em," Bertha told her, "'stead o' cryin' over it." She turned to Kate, "If'n my ol' man do me long as they bin doin' Tammy up there, I'd be in hog heaven fer sure."

"Okay, I'll go," said Allison and started over the gate on her own.

When she was halfway up the hill, already out of sight as the path curved, the two women shared a quizzical look. What was going on up there? After all, it had been almost an hour since Allison raced down to them, shocked out of her shoes.

"Damn, what a long time," Bertha muttered, shaking her head. "Boy, thinkin' about it's making me horny. Biff'll be comin' home soon."

Then they saw Allison walking back down the gravel drive, glancing around in every direction, checking under the trees, stretching up to see over bushes.

"What's going on?"

"There's nobody there," Allison called out, returning to the gate.

"Whaddya mean, nobody's there? Where'd they go?"

"I don't know," she said. "I looked all around where we were watching before, but it's all dark. I even went into the quarry to look—d'you know there's a quarry up there, all hollowed out in a giant circle? But I didn't see nobody. They disappeared—Vicky and them, and Tammy, Michael and that other guy, too. They weren't nowhere."

"Did you call them?"

"No.... It's still dark up there and I didn't know if I should just, ya know, barge in like that. They're still around here—they gotta be—but they're hiding."

"They disappeared?"

"They must've. If Tammy and them went somewhere else, then Vicky and them probably followed. Who knows where they are now?"

"There's no other way outta there but this here road, ain't there?"

"How should I know?"

Allison saw Kate freeze, her eyes widen in the early morning gray. When she spun around, flashing red lights of two police cars were coming down the road. They were slowing, rolling to a halt beside them. Leaning casually against the gate, they got their story straight as the police officers got out of their cars. Their approach was silent, and as they walked over to the women they kept their voices low.

"You the ones who called about the party?"

Chapter 24

Righting Wrongs

On the day his son, Set-*jousta*, marched out of the Selauê Academy with his graduating class, smart in his crimson and powder-blue school uniform, the first snow of the winter season fell. Despite that ill omen, he was proud of the man who bore his name. That he was an instructor was never a factor in his admission, nor in his achievements. His son had scored the highest of his class in the battery of graduation tests and had ranked among the highest in military training. His blood was that of his father, a proven warrior, something important in Sekuatean culture.

And on that day, when his son received his army commission and his *Landor* insignia there on the snowy parade ground, the father knew his own life had been cranked up another notch: another milestone had passed. The stream of life flowed a little quicker. Now that his children were growing up and starting their own lives, he was left behind to ponder his.

Already his daughter, Aisa, had given birth to a boy and a girl, but lost her husband to illness. She moved in with them and added to her daily tasks the caring for her younger brother and sister, about the same ages as her children. Gazing at himself in the star-shaped glass ornament that hung over their dresser, he realized the dilemma he was coming to. He was a grandfather at the age of thirty-two—his real age—though his family and colleagues knew him to be fifty in Ghoupalle years. The stress of his double life was taking its toll on his health.

Afraid to give up his precious Earth forever, he forced himself to venture back there at regular intervals to check on the passing and shifting of time. It was an unusual synchronization that he was living through, where each of his years on Ghoupallesz stole only pieces of an Earth hour. He had yet to reach the next pay day at the IRS service center, though he did not worry too much about it. To make the journey, he left Selauê and headed south to Lyas while telling Zaura he was traveling north to Fenula on military business, a code meaning that he was training the Fenulan army to fight the Zetin. As before.

That it came about the same time each year—he intended it only to assist his memory—made it all the more suspicious for her. As he became further involved in his military career, and as the possibility of his death passed more frequently, she began to steel herself for the day when she would receive news of his untimely demise.

Pregnant with their next child, Zaura cried until she fell asleep, the letter crumpled in her hand like a tissue. The truth was too hard to accept, though she fought to keep it to herself; she could never let her children know his deception. Every year he went away for a couple of weeks, claiming to be working as an advisor in Fenula. If it were not for what she already knew to be true, she would not have worried herself so much. But during the festival back on Karluk, the old woman Uz'A had seen her husband talking with the foreign lady who had come by ferry and departed the next morning. He was never the same after all those years ago, those many painful and empty years they were apart, and the joy of their reunions masked the tension that their union had become. The woman was the same one who came to Lyas to see him, who spoke to him in his own tongue. On Karluk he had pondered her visit—she could tell, her aura still able to sense things in him. She knew his thoughts, especially when she could touch him directly, such as when they made love. It was especially difficult for her to block out the waves of adulterous thoughts.

Then he went away, to be lost at sea. She knew why he was leaving, though she knew of no way to stop him. The customs of foreigners was not her subject, and the customs of Ghoupalle people allowed him such freedom to come and go as he pleased. On that day, she chose not to wave farewell to him until the ferry was beyond the horizon. She might show her true feelings to him. The woman who spoke his language was his destination, she felt—and continued to believe until they next met so unexpectedly in Sairel ten years later.

The time was so swift, their flight so abrupt that she could not allow herself the necessary concentration to read his thoughts. By then, her powers had declined too much anyway, though they seemed to be more effective on him than on other Ghoupalle people. When she returned to Sairel, she saw the notice to visit the communication office. The message explained the circumstances of her husband's death. Yet it came too late to save the poor foreigner; he was doomed. She knew that without being able to read his thoughts.

Their second marriage brought renewed happiness to her life. He loved her, she could feel, even with no substantial *senzena* abilities remaining in her. They had embarked on a furious attempt to make up for lost time, producing two children in two years, and he was able to return to the profession which brought him fame in a previous era. Their life together was complete, and quite fulfilling for both of them. Except for his annual sojourns in the land of his dreams.

There he was lounging in the arms of the women of his heathen land with all the sensual pleasures they could give him, and after he had refreshed himself there, he would return to the dull routine that his life with her had become. He needed respite from her, Zaura accepted and wept silently, unable to believe he was so desperate. She cursed him for lacking imagination, too, always saying he was going to Fenula. She knew that was the land of his lovers, the Lady Jinetta and the Lady Renée. He was obvious about it, and that hurt her even more; if he loved her at all he would try more carefully to cover his deceit.

This time she had hired an investigator to watch him, follow him, report on him. What she learned was contained in the parchment she hid beneath her pillow, pretending it did not exist. Her husband did not go to Fenula, nor was he a member of any council concerned with advising foreign armies. His trips away from her had all been lies. What was he doing then that he had to lie to her?

She rolled onto her back, suffering the anguish of her victimization as she stared at the looping *braji* pattern on the ceiling tiles. Where was he at this moment? Who had him ensnared in welcoming arms?—while she lay bloated and maternal on a *qala* in Selauê, the wife of an officer of the *Coraesz*, alone as always.

Still away with his *regêlad* in the district to the north of Selauê, Zaura knew he was engaged in putting down another episode of civil disturbance. That band of protesters was stirring up trouble again in Kamtan. He was required to take his men into the countryside and arrest the rowdy men and women, taking over for the local constable. The trouble in Kamtan was different, she sensed; it was the third incident, and each time the number of people involved increased. Last time, two soldiers were killed and many more wounded in the clashes. This time, she was worried about him. At least she knew where he was: in the safety of combat.

Her illness deepened during his absence, however, despite her efforts to heal herself from the mysterious affliction which had struck her three times in the past two years. When it attacked her, she could not rise from the *qala,* so weak was she, sweating with high fever and feeling random sharp pains in her chest and abdomen. Being with child only complicated her situation. She was in the hospital when he returned from duty.

He came to her bedside, still in uniform, and knelt beside her.

"*Amo-se n'aven,*" she spoke in the weak voice she forced out. 'We lost the baby.'

He bowed his head and reached for her hand, found it. When he finally regarded her with his teary eyes, a mask of shame had fallen over her. He tried his best to comfort her, saying everything he thought might help, but she clenched his hand tightly in hers and told him to be silent.

"No one is to blame," she said in Ghoupallêan, "but if we are to make another child, we must join our hearts before joining our bodies." She pulled his hand to her lips, kissed it. He felt the rush of blood through the veins she had squeezed shut.

Zaura could never tell him that it was her misery over his unfaithfulness that had wrenched their child from them. That would be as difficult to understand as it would be for him to explain that his supposed visits to Fenula, what she believed were excuses for infidelity, were actually his quick voyages to check on his Earth home through an interdimensional tangent. Who could believe whom more easily?

※ ※ ※

Big Bertha took a swig of coffee and stared across the table at Kate, both of them still feeling the shock. Soon two other women came into the canteen—women who were not able to join the midnight run to Pink Hill.

"Well? What'd you see'em doing?" sassy Sandy asked, dropping into a chair.

"It don't figure," Bertha muttered to Kate, ignoring them. "Where could they go?"

"But what about the clothes they found?" Kate asked. "Some of it had blood on it—that's what the police said."

"Hey, you guys," Sandy slapped the table, "so what *happened* last night?"

Kate turned and took a deep breath. "You don't wanna know."

"I do wanna know."

"No, you don't."

"Stop playing *mind* games. We wanna know—right, Jody?"

Bertha glanced around the canteen.

"I *know* it's gotta be something *awful* to shut *her* up," Sandy said. "I never *seen* her *that* damn quiet."

"Go ahead, tell her," Bertha instructed.

"It's gotta be kept quiet around here," Kate began, "because the police are still investigating."

Sandy's eyes lit up. "Police?"

"Investigating what?" Jody asked.

"Well, we went out to this hill the Perfesser took'em to, out past Independence Center, but it was real sneaky 'cause he parked at the mall and they walked the rest of the way. There was a gate there but it was too high for us to climb over, but Vicky and Wilma and—who else was there? Yeah, Allison and Donna Mae—they went up there, too. Anyway, Allison comes running back saying Michael and the Perfesser are raping Tammy—"

"No *way!*" Sandy laughed.

"Yes, but when they didn't come back—Vicky and Wilma, I mean—and it was getting light by then, Allison went back up there to see what was taking so long, and guess what?"

"*What?*"

"Nobody was there. Not Michael and Tammy, not the Perfesser. And Vicky and them—they weren't up there neither. When the police came and searched, they found some of their clothes—ripped apart, dirty and bloody, like they was beat up or something. But they weren't there. I mean, there wasn't no bodies."

"No *way!*" Sandy cried.

"So what happened?" asked Jody.

"I told you, the police are investigating. They're callin' it murder, or rape-murder."

"Shit, you *sure?*"

"Well, the police didn't say exactly," Bertha cut in, "but that's what they was saying in their radio, and to each other, we heard."

"You guys get asked a bunch of *questions?*"

"Of course."

"Far *out.* Any *TV guys* come to take pictures?"

"No—it was a murder, Sandy, not *Geraldo!*"

"They got murderers on *Geraldo.*"

"Yeah, but these are the same people we work with, and they raped Tammy and maybe the others, then killed them—and hid their bodies up there, in the forest, or under some rocks."

"And to think I *dated* him," said Sandy. "Shit, that coulda been *me* up there—face down in the dirt."

"You know about the Perfesser?" Kate asked her.

"Sebastian Talbot? Sure, I know him. The guy had a *lot* of problems, lemme tell ya. Of course, he used to do drugs, like marijuana and—I dunno—*stuff.* But he was so weird, living alone like that—like a hermit, it was *weird.* You shoulda *seen* his place.

He was *definitely* uptight about sex, I wantcha to know. He *tried* to get it on with me when we went out—I *had* to beat him back—"

"Of course he lives alone," Kate cut in, coming to his defense automatically out of some sense of loyalty. "Didn't you know? His wife was murdered—before he started working here. I thought about everybody knew that."

"Yeah, he *told* me, but he never ever wanted to *talk* about it."

"Sheez, would you?" Bertha blurted out.

"I heard Michael say he was a teacher, at a high school—can you believe it? One of his bad students killed her, so then he killed the student. But he got off jail."

"And came to work here?" Arlene cut in.

Jody laughed. "About the same, huh?"

"Look, he always *seemed* the mild-mannered type," Sandy explained, "but those're the ones that *always* go bonkers and blow *everyone* away. I feel *real* safe with that metal detector up at the front door, ya know. I'll tell you, the guy was a *classic* psycho factory—I mean, he was a schizo-paranoia freak *to the max*. The guy lived in two worlds. Ya know, he really thought he could *walk* through a doorway onto another *planet.*"

"What're you talking about?" Kate asked.

"Just what I *said*. He told me *sometimes* he lives on another planet. *Really*, he said that—just as plain as that."

"Oh, come on, Sandy!" said Kate.

"With all that shit going on, no wonder he's so messed up," said Jody.

"And his fits," Kate threw in to the discussion. "Did you ever see him when he has his fits? He rolls around on the floor like a slug covered in salt."

"That's just epilepsy," Bertha said. "My sister got it, but she takes medicine."

"You *see?*" Sandy stood up, shouting. "The guy's so screwed *in the head*, ya know I *had* to end it. Or it coulda been *me* up there, *instead* of Tammy."

"Vicky and Wilma and Donna Mae, too, don't forget," said Bertha.

Sandy nodded in sympathy.

"You ever sleep with him?" Jody asked, snickering.

"Once. But we *didn't* have sex."

"No?" asked Kate. "Why not?"

"He fell *asleep*. Said beds were for sleeping. Said he had a real *rough* time away on that other *planet* he visits."

Some of them laughed nervously, then fell silent.

"Come on, Sandy," Kate shook her head, "he wouldn't say something like that."

"Not to *you*, or anybody here," she replied, "but with *me*—a few bottles of *booze* empty between us—he'd say *just about anything*."

"That's creepy," sighed Arlene.

"He drinks a lot?" Jody asked.

"Ya know, I'll bet *that's* what was going on with Michael and Tammy," Sandy said. "Suppose they were just *playing* with his *mind*. See, they knew how *messed up* he was, so they were trying to get him *more* screwed up, trying to make him *go freakin' crazy*."

"But why would they do that?" Kate asked.

"Hell if *I* know." Sandy laughed. "But *think* about it: he was acting *so weird* these last two weeks."

"I seen him talking with'em a whole lot more 'an before," Arlene confessed, "like they was busy making plans for whatever happened last night."

"*That's* why Michael and Tammy are missing, too," said Sandy. "Either he *got wind* of what they were up to—figured it *all* out, ya know—and he *got angry* and knocked'em off, or he was *already* so screwed up in the head that it was easy for *them* to knock off *him*—and *now* it's Michael and Tammy who're in hiding somewhere."

"Cassie will be glad to hear that," Kate said.

"Where is she, anyway?" Bertha asked. "She wanted to go along with us but she backed out the last minute."

"She don't wanna know any of this, believe me," said Kate, getting up from the table.

"Then maybe we should tell her," Jody snorted.

"You girls are mean," said Kate.

"No, *listen*," Sandy broke in, "the guy was *fantasizing*, ya know. Like kids who talk to stuffed animals. He's always telling these *big lies.* You know the *big lies* are the easiest to *believe*. Everything he said was *just* a lie. This other planet of his was all *in his head*. He *wasn't* joking around—he really, truly *believed* it."

"But did he, like, go into a trance or something and dream it?" Jody inquired. "Or did he do, ya know, regular type stuff and make it all up later just to blow our minds?"

"I *know* the guy," said Sandy, demanding the last word. "He was *lost* in space, short a *bunch* of marbles, not playing with a *full* deck, fake as a four-leaf clover—just *waiting* for his head to explode, ya know. His mind was *so* filled with his *fantasies*. He was *always* talkin' about'em like they was *real*. Like, he'd *say* he did this and that, he *lived* here and there, married this *girl* and had this many *kids*, and he was in the *army* there and he rescued some *queen* from some freakin' *barbarians*, and he learned their language, and he came *back* here but he missed his fantasy world *so much* he *keeps* going back there. It's all *fake*, I tell ya. Believe me, it's all *in his head*—just one big happy *fantasy*."

Summer breezes blew past them, poised on the long wharf, waiting for the ferry to take them out to Agani Island. In this time zone the island had been swept clean of its witches and was now a resort isle. The sky was a crystalline green devoid of clouds, exactly the beautiful setting he had wished for their first encounter with his world. Whether or not they knew it, they would be enjoying it for several months more. They still believed it was to be a short visit, like a week. Someday he would have to tell them the truth.

"This should suit you for the time you'll be staying here," he told Tammy, helping her settle in at her new home away from home, a cottage on Agani Island, off the coast of Dikondra.

In the boxes stacked beside her were items they had purchased in Lyas, clothing and other essentials, enough to fill both wardrobes and the footlocker sitting under the large *qala*. It was set facing the window, looking out on the pale green sea washing over the fine red sand along the shore. Outside, Michael waited patiently, shirt off, catching some yellow and blue rays.

"I like it," said Tammy, sitting on the foot of the *qala* and swinging her legs like a little girl. "But how long are we gonna stay?"

"Well, it'll be only you that's staying."

"Me…only?"

"Yes. I have to take Michael to another place for his treatment. You are in good, safe hands here. Meanwhile, I will tend to my business elsewhere. But I'll check in on you from time to time."

She was still studying the room, the aqua plaster walls relaxing her, the salty air wafting through the open windows intoxicating her.

"I never been any place outta town," she said while his back was turned. "Are we really…on another world, like you said before?"

He faced her, grinning, unsure how to answer, still surprised she had taken the news so well. She was adapting to the dream land far better than Michael was. Whether she was smarter than he had given her credit for, or she would believe just about anything told to her, he could not say. The way she went with the flow certainly made his efforts on her behalf easier. Michael, was another problem entirely.

"I've told the people here to take good care of you," Sebastian the Professor said. He explained to her his instructions to the islanders. "I've paid them in advance for everything you might need here. They know how to contact me if there is any emergency. There's a well-qualified doctor here, so there's nothing for you to worry about."

"But they…don't talk like us."

"That's no problem," he replied with a reassuring smile. He handed her several notebooks he had brought from his apartment on Earth. "You can study these in your free time—and you'll have a lot of it for a while."

"What is it?"

"It's a dictionary of their language: Ghoupallêan—and it's cross-referenced with English. You can learn to communicate with them in no time at all. They'll be happy to help you, too. One or two of them can speak a few words of English I taught them before."

She thumbed through the notebooks, satisfied.

"You'll have the baby here," he said. Tammy continued looking through the notebooks. "Then you can leave it here to be adopted, if you like, or you can bring the baby back with you. It's your choice. Back home, no one at the service center will ever know you were pregnant."

Regarding him with a pleasant smile, she glanced down quickly at the first page in the notebook, saying "*Daram-se kalmonê*," the Ghoupallêan phrase for 'thank you very much'. The surprised look he gave was all the response needed.

"I'm happy here," Tammy said. "Me and my baby will be happy here."

Her manner was beginning to change, he noticed in the words she chose and her confident face when she spoke. Over the weeks they traveled and shopped, she had become more self-assured. When she stood and went over to him, kissing him on the cheek to show her gratitude, he became concerned about what was happening to her. He knew the air on Ghoupallesz had a higher oxygen content, enabling him—a stodgy being from Earth—to breathe with less effort, providing him with more energy. And the gravity was less than on Earth, giving him the extra step he needed to keep up with the long-legged Ghoupalle people. He never considered that something in the air might improve a person's intelligence.

Waving from the wharf, she saw Michael and the Professor board the ferry, watching until it was lost below the emerald horizon. Her hand fell gently over her belly, her jeans already too tight.

The maid came to her, concerned.

"I'm okay," said Tammy.

Thinking over her new collection of loose, tropical dresses—*porraqê* they were called—she knew she had done the right thing, believing in the crazy Professor, who the others at the service center had despised for being so eccentric. She knew differently now, having entered his dream.

※ ※ ※

"If you want to get back to normal you have to let them do the treatments," said the man who would become Set-d'Elous once he left Michael at the clinic in Lyas. His IRS co-worker refused to be injected with the anti-toxin, guarding his most precious anatomical part. "It's the only treatment for the *moussalaganê*."

The service center playboy was causing him the most trouble of anyone he'd ever brought to Ghoupallesz. From the start, Michael was skeptical, and even up to stepping through the hard-torn curtain he was reluctant and fearful. Michael saw it with his own eyes, felt the energy rushing through him, and yet he still refused to believe. Hiking across the desert, he could survive only by complaining about something every dozen steps. When they stopped at the cache to retrieve items for their arrival in Lyas, Michael had almost set foot in a *tairrag* trap. Fortunately, the AT gun Set-d'Elous kept in the buried strongbox was still charged and he was able to fire a blast into the sand toad's head as it lay buried there waiting for someone or something to step into its gaping, toothy mouth. Instead of being grateful, Michael complained more. In Lyas, he could not read the signs, he cursed. He had none of their money, the food was not what he was used to, people were staring at him—though dressed as he was in his quickly soiled and wrinkled polyester playboy clothes, who wouldn't have stared at him? Now, to make matters worse, Michael was refusing the treatment he had gone to so much trouble to be able to receive.

For his affliction, which was not too uncommon among people who overindulged in *moussalaganê*, the only treatment was regular injections of an anti-toxin. The slow effects of the treatment made the patient never want to overdose on *moussalaganê* again. The anti-toxin had to be administered on a precise schedule: too much or too often, too little or too seldom and the treatment could be quite devastating. The anti-toxin itself had to be manufactured dose by dose as it would not stay fresh for long. Thus, it was difficult to store or obtain outside of a pharmaceutical laboratory. Patients needed to stay in a clinic for a long time. Breeding enough *loñar* for their blood, *fridêr* for their bile, and the *stoupaen* for their *baod* excrement, plus the sap of the *kerron* plant and pollen from *rübas* flowers, was a very involved process. Once the ingredients were measured, mixed with stabilizers, ready for application, the cost was high.

The extra *gealan* he had in his desert cache went for that, enabling him to save the ones he brought from Earth for other necessary expenses. What those might be, he kept to himself. If his accomplices from Earth knew, they might worry about him never returning for them. If something happened to him, they could not return to Earth on their own. It was more than kindness or a sense of righting an unfortunate wrong that persuaded him to wrangle their participation in the expedition.

He had been planning it from the first dream that interrupted his work in the service center over two weeks ago: the Zetin dream. Feeling the icy sensations of the winter in Tebbicousimankalê, he was jolted into super-consciousness, seeing the ghostly images of a time forgotten and forcefully revisited. There was a message there, and a warning, which he fought to drive away. After all, he had already had his conversion—vowing never again to journey to the dream land. He knew that somewhere there was a place where every good turn brought a bad omen and every bad omen multiplied exponentially into the kind of destruction a god of evil wrecks on ignorant people. He just wanted to live his life in peace—several times, if he were lucky—and the twists and turns of the tangent's maze foiled his plans repeatedly. He arrived eventually at the essence of his dilemma: he *had* forgotten something back in that deep, dark winter in the northwestern districts of Tebbicousimankalê, his men sleeping with their *Jêpe*, freezing to death.

After four *peth* he finally persuaded Michael that he had to submit to the treatment, not only to renew his health but to prevent a syndrome—which, unknown to Michael, was fictitious—whereby his favorite digit would become so encumbered by its increased weight that it would block its own circulation, and break off like a lizard's tail.

"Okay, man, I'll do it," Michael cried, shaking his fists. "But you'd better get me some nicer stuff to goof around with if I gotta stay here for a month. Can you get me an Atari system and some computer games?"

"A month?" Set-d'Elous teased him. "No, Michael. It's ten months—every week, every month. You should begin seeing positive results after the second month."

Michael fainted, recovered after the first injection was made.

"I've arranged a place for you to stay during the time you're here. You'll have to come back every week, so you should stay close. And if you forget—if you think you don't need the treatment any longer and you don't come back here on schedule—well, I won't be held responsible for what might happen to your health."

"What do you mean?"

"Some men *have* been known to begin turning female, like growing breasts and losing facial hair, if they stop the treatment too soon."

"Man, what kinda freakin' world you brung me to?"

"It's a nice place, but you have to learn to live within its rules. To that end, I've prepared some notes for you on the customs and language. I suggest you study them all you can. You should have enough free time. Tammy took right to it. You won't have to do anything else while you're here, so you might as well enjoy your stay."

"Yeah, thanks."

"I mean that: you won't have anything else to do. Please, Michael, don't do anything else. Stay here and stay on schedule. When you're fit again, I'll need you to help me with a special project. I needed someone from home, and now you're the only one left—the only one who could possibly be accused of being my friend. I'll tell you more later, when I'm checking on you."

"What choice do I have?"

"Well, you really don't have any, now that you're here. That's why I tried to make your accommodations suitable. For example, when you finish here today, my driver will take you home where you'll be looked after by two private nurses I hired. They will alternate day and night so you always have someone to care for you. I'm sure you'll be able to comply with their therapy."

Then he was off, taking the night KOHAX to Selauê, where he would read the bulletins in the Archives to bring himself up to date.

Settling into a comfortable chair in the main reading room, he began to study all the official reports covering the past fifty years—since he'd last returned to Earth. He had hope that somewhere in all of the pages spread across the table he would find something which might lead him to the fate of his one-time lover and full-time conscience: Gina, Interdimensional Voyager First-Class, Oak Leaf Clusters with Flourishes. Instead, he was drenched in memories of joy and pain: his last years with Zaura-Matousz, when he was teaching at the Selauê Academy and commanding the 102d *Jêpedor-regêlad*.

"So where are we?" Donna Mae asked the wind. Holding her arms tightly over her bare chest, she turned around and around on the sandy plain, looking desperately for something familiar in the dull gray landscape. "We're not anywhere close to the service center, and we sure ain't still in today. Our yesterday was a long, long time ago." She showed the others her watch.

Vicky suddenly began feeling around in the sand.

"We came through some kind of doorway, right? It's gotta be around here somewhere."

"We already looked," said Wilma.

Donna Mae watched Vicky digging then gazed out toward the horizon.

"Look! Footprints!" she exclaimed, and took off at a full sprint.

"Where're you going?" Vicky shouted, chasing her.

She caught her and they fell together against the soft, ash-strewn ground.

"Leave me alone!" Donna Mae cried, tears rolling down her flushed cheeks. "We gotta follow the footprints!"

"They aren't footprints, just the shifting sand."

They wrestled until Vicky gave her a slap and she lay still on her back.

"Look," said Donna Mae.

Vicky's gaze rose. "What?"

"There's *two suns* up there."

Wilma arrived, breathing hard. She dropped to her knees, collapsed beside them. Vicky pointed overhead and Wilma saw the sight. As they regarded the two suns, they silently wondered what they had done to deserve their fate—until the Rouê came upon them, veering from their caravan route, riding their long-necked stubborn *oñacha*.

Spotting the three wanderers, they naturally decided to check on them. Instead, the desert traders leading a team of six pack animals from Sandou to Aivana were surprised to see that the vagabonds were female. Their leader, his face shielded behind his *magal*—the traditional triangular mask which Rouê people used to cover their faces in the desert—spoke with his comrades.

Wilma stood, moved cautiously toward their beasts, followed quickly by Vicky. The women expressed their need of food and water, asking them to call someone for help. The Rouê leader tried to explain, it seemed to them, that there was no roadside service in the vast Zissekap desert. They did toss down a water bag, and another Rouê held up a string of purple meat, not realizing the desperate women would not want to eat the dried twisted entrails of the *lrulru*.

Donna Mae scrambled for the *toop* dangling from the end of the Rouê's fingers. She dropped her guard and the Rouê were startled, laughing at her frantic eating, remarking on her bare chest. They pointed to Wilma and Vicky, talking among themselves. They gestured at each of the three service center employees, no doubt wondering about their tax examining skills, their data entry speed, their accuracy in sorting mail. The women, weary of their ordeal, drank down the water, tried the *toop*, and looked hopeful.

"*A'ajaha lomoha'e mena'aho pefal'le'o ha'ame'e*," the Rouê leader announced in his native tongue, lowering his *magal* enough to display a mouth toothless except the four front incisors.

They must be Ghoupalle, the Rouê leader decided when they

showed no response to his statement. He turned to his left and gave a command. One Roûe climbed down from his *oñacha* and removed from his saddle pouch an amber cloth. Stepping forward, he extended it to Donna Mae, motioning for her to cover herself.

Wilma bowed her head in thanks at their kind act, not knowing that what the Roûe leader had said was: 'The old one we can sell to the villagers for a house servant.'

"O'olama'e fe'ah'pehe'o sama'ame'o sama'bulo'e gama'o," their leader spoke as the other Roûe jumped down from their mounts. 'The other two we'll keep for ourselves until they no longer please us.'

Chapter 25

The Council of Five and the Death of Millions

THE CORE OF THE COUNCIL OF FIVE, the name used by the Gangus family for their National Executive Council after establishing their dynasty, consisted of three students of the Sorêg Academy. Basura-Kanoun, a poet by training... Diert-Gangus, born 1433 in Kolouna... student of political dissertation, he introduced... Rasek-Tifloh to his club of political students....

The current government of Sekuate, represented by the 300-year reign of the House of Sarrêban in Seas, was internally corrupt and isolated by privilege from the people. [The Gangus Political Society] believed that to put authority and power of such magnitude under the control of one person was detrimental to the people. Such power should be delegated, diversified, and divided among several people, each to counter the others. To prevent the interests of a few members from falling into collusion, the minimum number needed as a governing force is determined to be five.

In 1458, Diert-Gangus and Basura-Kanoun married... [in 1460] graduated from the Academy.... [In 1463]... booklet authored by Basura, Diert, and Rasek was published in Selauê... outlining their political concerns. Support grew for the Society... local authorities called them the Gangus Army... concerned that their numbers would become difficult to control.

In Nomat 1466, the Sorêg town leaders requested, then demanded, that the Gangus Army leave. Authorities used the constable's militia to evict members from their headquarters, initiating a riot. They protested in Selauê... distributed their manifesto on the streets but were arrested, charged with inciting treason. Diert was sent to the national prison at Trêpolium for six years.

Rasek worked to increase support for the Gangus Army during the interim, especially in the Kamtan district where their new headquarters was established [in 1470].... Diert returned home [in 1473].... They had a balanced governmental group and began believing... they could be the national ruling council.... An expanded treatise based on the earlier booklet entitled "The Power of Five" was published in Selauê in 1476. Booksellers shunned it. The Gangus Army protested... supporters caused a riot... two Selauê constables were killed and [others] were wounded. The group was outlawed by the city government... and returned their headquarters to Kamtan.

[In 1477]... setting up their own printing press... continued publishing their book... and works of other writers, philosophers and politicians whose ideas agreed with theirs. Basura wrote [in 1478] a sequel to "The

Power of Five"... was published... well received, its political focus thinly veiled by her metaphorical poetry.... Diert was elected to the city council of Kamtan by the town's majority of Gangus supporters....

In 1479, Rasek and Samot went to Sorêg and Croxe recruiting... returning with new supporters numbering in the thousands... officially adopted the name Gangus Army.

With the paramilitary role envisioned by Diert... recruited a cadet... recently dismissed from the Selauê Academy. Banar-Traf became the commander of the military wing of the Gangus Army. [Traf] was anxious to prove that what his teachers had said of his natural leadership ability was true....

Alarmed by the [military] training, the city council voted on Gouo-2:1479 to oust Diert from the council. Public outcry resulted in his reinstatement....

More supporters flocked to Kamtan... population from 98,000 [in 1478] to over 150,000 by 1480... city council voted again to oust Diert, on Terpa-11:1480... rioting by his supporters.... The 2d *Coraesz* was dispatched from Selauê to quell the rioting... five leaders fled the city....

At its new headquarters [south in] Manioug, the Gangus Army continued their activities... preparation for... overthrow of the *Mexas* government... more confrontations with local folk. The city council requested that the Gangus Army leave... went unheeded... requested assistance from 2d *Coraesz*... from Selauê... [they] marched on Manioug... same martial action as in Kamtan: guerrilla fighting, house searches...

seven weeks.

Gangus advance groups raided Lakuar, anticipating their evacuation of Manioug. The citizens and government became hostages in the battle between the rebel army and the Sekuatean Army. Gangus Army members took control of Yiexe [further south] by the end of Nomat. Forces of the Sekuatean Army marched on Yiexe.... With the Sekuatean army withdrawn, the Gangus Army militiamen recaptured Manioug. The 1s *Coraesz* in Seas was ordered to arms. On Laliê-21:1480, the *Mexas* Tomodon-Sarrêban ordered a full-scale, nationwide state of emergency....

—from the legible portions of "A Primary History of the Gangus Revolution" (pamphlet) by Kag-Gangus, member, Council of Five, Seas, 1510

[The torn, stained pages of the pamphlet were found among the personal papers of Queen Jinetta of Fenula upon her presumed death or disappearance in 1441. accompanying maps of Tebbicousimankalê marked with military symbols.]

By early the next spring, he recalled from his days as the commander of the 102d regiment, most of northern Sekuate was suffering open rebellion. Troops from three *Coraesz* were engaged in armed action in a dozen different battlegrounds. With their forces stalemated in diverse locations at the outer fringes of the nation, Gangus Army forces were able to infiltrate Seas, the capital, where they incited riots and caused protests by its citizens. Even the city's sizeable constable force was soon overwhelmed. Across the border in Ilait, the main Gangus force prepared for the major offensive on Seas that their general, Banar-Traf, had planned. They soon marched out of Ilait, to the cheering of peasants and factory workers, directly toward Seas.

The First and Third *Coraesz* waited south of Aithê to intercept the newly expanded Gangus Army. The turning point came when the commander of the Third *Coraesz*, Latol-Secour, turned over his troops to the rebels, believing in their ideology and welcoming the invitation to be the supreme general of the Gangus Army, taking over from Banar-Traf.

That was what he remembered: sitting beside his wife in the hospital in Selauê, listening to the news told by a nurse in the corridor. Before the conflict grew so serious, he was granted paternity leave. He had trusted his second-in-command, Rasek-Kalanou, to carry through with their orders; he would catch up with them later, or perhaps by then they would complete their mission and return to garrison. That was what he hoped; he was not sure how soon he could be released from his vigil. The baby was due that day, but Zaura was too ill to understand what the doctors were telling her.

He listened to the news, as everyone in Selauê did that week, and soon heard the solemn announcement of the capture of the *Mexas* Tomodon-Sarrêban, his family, and most members of the *Pangressus* in Seas. The *Mexas* surrendered control of the government to the leaders of the Gangus Army, knowing that his loyal *Coraesz* would come to the rescue, but history knew he was a fool. Fighting broke out in the city, and there was hope of overthrowing the rebels, but that melted away as surely as the springtime snow was melting in the sunrise of a new government.

A year-long civil war broke out between the Gangus Army and the army units that had refused to surrender to the Gangus Council. The *Berron*, old Katoum-Armag, was seen to smile heavenward when he was finally cut down in battle, at last achieving his hero's reward. Finally, Basura-Kanoun, the spiritual leader and only woman of the Council of Five, called fervently for peace.

* * *

On the second day of winter, the month of *Gouo* in 1481, with the pea-colored flurries drifting down from the Kelly green clouds hovering against the horizon, he had turned away from the hospital window, seeing the suns imprisoned at their final dusk light, and taken her hand once more as he knelt beside the *qala*.

In the darkening shadows their eyes met, able to penetrate deeply into each other's souls. He felt the light squeeze of her fingers, the weak pull of her eyes. He remembered every moment he had gazed into those eyes, and the first time—now forty-one years behind the calm wake of his longboat, sailing the Ghoupalle version of the River Styx: *Fardomn-Iker*. A stroke of a silent oar, a smooth passage, a journey of eternity. So sang the man in the *raelor* robe, extending the "ГП" insignia, hammered out of gold, over her prone figure.

He listened passively, neither hearing the words nor in any way wanting to translate them. To the last couplet he waited, enduring the wait more patiently than ever he had waited before. When that time came, he rose from her bedside and accepted the chalice from the man, drank of its bitter red potion and, as custom dictated—he swore he would never break any custom when her dignity was at stake—he leaned over her *sarroñ*-wrapped body and kissed her lips, allowing the liquid to seep out. The parting kiss. Then the man in the *raelor* robe, now with a silver bowl and a small brush, commenced painting her serene face from hairline to jawline with a similar deep red liquid. He watched it run down her cheeks, maroon streams against her snow white flesh: the marks of love...the marks of life....

Outside, Aisa handed him his new daughter whom Zaura had requested be named for Seasö-Paraxe, her long-time friend. Aisa would take care of her infant sister, she had told him, seeing in his face the distant gaze of a mind filled, overflowing with emotion. Aisa knew that her father needed time alone to consult with the seven gods and nine goddesses.

He did not know where he went that day, lost in a blind stupor, wandering the streets for days. Later, when he had regained his senses, he chose to abandon his adopted world, returning to the steady, safe routine of the service center he knew so well and hated.

Once again wandering the streets of Selauê to his old townhouse, Set-d'Elous paused to stare at the memories pasted on the windows: his children waving as he returned home from the garrison each evening. He smiled, satisfied. Walking farther, he stood before the hospital where Zaura-Matousz had let go her final breath. That same building was today bathed in summer sunshine although he could still feel the dark, damp halls of that winter's day, still hear the dreary tone of the words spoken. With a shudder, he tore himself from his trance and hurried away, content that he had done his duty in revisiting the place where he had reluctantly surrendered half of his heart: First Military Hospital in Selauê.

In the years since he had left Ghoupallesz in 1481, the nation of Sekuate that had been his home in happier times had become the mighty Sekuatean Empire, united by the military fist that had spread from its natural borders to gather in its neighbors. Its territory had tripled, then quickly tripled again, and now extended from the continent of Bæronak on the west coast of the Bær Sea, to the Zet mountains in the far north of Megank, down to the southern ocean of Edyde and Sandou, and east to the Zissekap mountain range, which shielded their civilization from the unexplored wilderness beyond. Nearly half of the civilized world was under Sekuatean control.

Gazing at the yellow sun again—the same sun that had illuminated so many years he had already lived—he felt how the passage of time had become a circle rather than a line. He grinned, embarrassed at his serendipity. A few short years before, as he counted them, back in 1533, at this same time, this same month of *Shae* at the end of the summer, he'd been riding a *Jêpe* with his men, part of the Sekuatean Empire's greatest army, the *Arumê-de-Nog*, slowly burning its way across the heart of Tebbicousimankalê, toward the northwest industrial city of Siaa. His alter-ego, his doppelgänger, lost among the snowfields, could never have imagined he would have any reason to return.

Pressure grew in the side of his head where that memory was stored and he took a deep breath, held it as long as he could, then let it leak out. He reached for his notebook, a pocket-sized record of journeys and adventures, names and dates. He was confused, so with frantic fingers he stormed through the pages until he found the one he needed. He could not be certain what he read, yet he was willing to accept that whatever he had scribbled on the page must be true. He checked his family log for the month of *Shae* in 1533.

AISA-d'ELOUS, born on Karluk Esan on Denio-10: 1445, married with Sartan-Tek in 1472, has two children, six grandchildren; after Sartan's death she remarried: Gushod-Draka in 1483 and has three children with him.

SAMOT-FRÊDIN, son of Zaura's second spouse, born in Sairel on Ahok-4: 1452, married with Gouö-Lavannê in 1484, has eight children, eleven grandchildren.

SET-MATOUSZ, the son conceived during trip from Sairel to Milipour, born after return to Sairel, Keruk-25: 1456, married with Miera-Habarrê in 1520, has six children.

BASHA-d'ELOUS, daughter born after reunion at Aisa/Sartan wedding, Keruk-9: 1475, married with Aroun-Tivas in 1498, has five children.

DUNAS-MATOUSZ, next son after reunion, born on Shae-25: 1476, married with Hafa-Matêsz in 1510, has four children.

SEASO-d'ELOUS, daughter born days before Zaura died, on Ahok-22: 1481, married with Dassex-Metour in 1506, one child, one grandchild on the way.

Today was the birthday anniversary of his son, Dunas, he realized, and wondered where on the planet he might be.

Wartime, he thought, looking over the next several pages: more children whom his children had, and the children of those children, and who they each married, and their children's children's children. They mattered to him. He was not a progenitor who would abandon his family. If he could help them, any of them, he would do so. The first item of business was to get them all to leave Selauê before the vengeful forces of the *Nog-Megank-Ulsinyn* could arrive the next year and slaughter the citizens of his favorite city.

To that end, he had made several trips, trying to find each of them and warn them.

It was a mistake, of course; he did not belong there. He was playing with history, tearing at delicate time lines, playing God. He was god-like, he was beginning to believe, and yet quite likely a god of evil.

So there he was, minding his own business one fine day in a return visit to 1530, and he was pulled into service once again.

As captain of the 102d *Jêpedor-regêlad*, he tried to bring the war to a close by working within, but quite in vain. All the battles, each and every event—from 1530, when he was given the uniform, through 1534, when he escaped—still happened the way he'd read about them in many volumes at the Archives. In fact, he could see now, returning in 1544 with Michael and Tammy along for the ride, that the Archives had built an entire wing to house the collection of records produced by the new government. To start at one end and read his way down to the opposite end might take a lifetime in itself.

Assisted by three archivists, he was able to narrow down his search, finding the passages he wanted in one of twenty-nine official volumes written by the staff recorders of the *Pangressa-d'Elexor*, the Sekuatean parliament.

The text was clear: When the Tebbicousimankalê government, deep in the throes of the 1530 invasion by Sekuatean forces, fiercely defending their country yet pushed to their northernmost extremes to make their final stand, the government-in-exile in Ghoupallæssa, across the sea, sought out the Zetin ambassador ahead of an international conference in the city of Siti. Leaders of the world's nations were meeting to condemn Sekuatean aggression.

"All the nations will call us cowards," the Tebbi prime minister cried out, hearing of the impending negotiations with the Zetin. Deep in his soul, however, he knew there were only two options: embarrassment and survival or strangulation and defeat.

"We have already been following this strategy of withdrawal which our great Marshal Rimsfüt has advised, and we have already earned our reputation as a cowardly nation," the king spoke back at him. "Now we are faced with our very survival. Prime Minister, there is no humiliation so great as total annihilation."

The prime minister bowed humbly, fell to his knees on the steps before the royal chair, daring not to raise his eyes as he spoke.

"We have been following this strategy and have seen its results unfolding: the army of Sekuate chases us across our land, but at a pace too quick for them to solidify any of their positions in the districts they have overrun. They are being drawn into our northern entrapment. All that is needed now are some Zetin mercenaries to hold them there through the winter."

The king rubbed his chin, eyeing the prime minister's lovely wife. He considered the Lady Jinetta's well-known friendship with the legendary warrior Set-d'Elous. It was from him that she had received the clever defensive strategy and passed it on. Rimsfüt had studied the same strategy when he was a visiting cadet of the Selauê Academy.

"Then our forces will strike upon them?" asked the king.

The prime minister responded affirmatively.

"I agree to the negotiations with the Zetin."

Across a long table in a grand palace turned conference center, they made a deal with the Zetin. Tebbicousimankalê offered to return land to the Zetin for their assistance in the war against Sekuate. The land in question was a border area between the two nations, the ring of foothills around the towering Zet Mountains, land which had earlier been colonized by the people of northern Zissekap. It was the culmination of a long history of conflict between the Zetin and the Danid peoples. The subcontinent of Tebbicousimankalê had been the primal territory of the Zetin people. A thousand years before this important day in Siti, when the civil war had ended between the old Zetin priest-king Thoth—T'ᴏᴛ in the Zetin tongue—and his nephew, the evil prince Secour, the land lay divided. The Zetin were weak enough that the ongoing plans of the Danid kingdoms were at last initiated. Staggered groups of warriors and waves of colonists from each of the nations of northern Zissekap arrived across the Tebbi Sea and settled in the cities of the Zetin. They claimed it fair return for the centuries of pirate raiding by the Zetin. The Zetin were forced to migrate to the smaller, northern peninsula. Further expansion of the Danid states in the centuries which followed pushed the Zetin farther north—until most Zetin chose to return to the vast high plateau of Alaun where their ancient ancestors had paused a few millennia to perfect their arctic warrior society.

Now the Tebbicousimankalê government-in-exile, on the advice of its marshal, was offering some of that land back in exchange for military assistance. The Zetin, ever vigilant against the notorious Tebbi treachery, demanded that a hostage be given to them to secure the treaty. Not just any citizen would do, they declared. It had to be someone important, vital to the government, someone whom they would not dare to count as lost to the Zetin, a person of sufficiently high rank or noble connections, and a person who would not fear to be their hostage.

"Gᴠɪx ᴀᴍᴛ'ᴀ-sᴋɴ," said Ut'r-BkanN, chief of the Zetin negotiating team, rising from his *gann* chair and throwing an ornately taloned finger at the elegantly dressed lady sitting at the edge of the room among the official observers.

For the Tebbi negotiators the choice was impossible. The lady chosen was the wife of the prime minister. She could not be a hostage.

"Eᴍ Gʀᴏxᴄ' Sᴇᴋᴜᴀᴛᴀɴᴋ-ᴋᴏᴍ," Ut'r-BkanN exclaimed with a slap of the crisp parchments off the table. 'Then we might as well fight on the side of Sekuate.'

At that crucial moment, the lady herself rose from her cushioned seat and stepped forward to the long table.

"If I can save my people by this act," she spoke in a strong but calm voice, using her most eloquent Ghoupallêan, "then I shall go gladly with these Zetin. However, I warn you now that I shall not allow myself to be the object of abuse, as you may desire. As I am the wife of Arrin-Sassat, the leader of the People's Assembly, I too am a leader of my people. If I am not returned safely in the fulfillment of our treaty, then the people of Tebbicousimankalê will rise up and take me from you. Do you understand?"

Ut'r-BkanN rose, staring into her eyes, and let a grin flicker across his face. Then, sweeping aside the tails of his *gealan*-studded DLAX, he extended his clenched hand to her.

"ZURAM KSA XRA-N," the fat, goateed Zetin ambassador asked, opening his hand to offer the golden *gealan* stone pulled from the bag at his side. He asked her name.

"I will not accept your gift, Sir, but I will tell you my name." She held her head high. "I am Jinetta, of the House of Kish-a-Tek, grand-daughter of Queen Jinetta of Fenula, friend of the warrior Set-d'Elous."

"ZURAM GOP'ZX ZAXC' JLO AS ZAXC' TONNAM-S'RJ," spoke the Zetin ambassador with reverence, bowing to her, knowing the reputation of both the queen and her warrior-consort. 'Lady, we are honored you will be our hostage.'

If the treaty had not been made, he understood, Sekuate might have succeeded in their invasion and Tebbicousimankalê would surely have been conquered. As it was, the Tebbi army was able to beat back the Sekuatean forces with the assistance of the Zetin. After the war, however, as Tebbi forces and those from the other allied nations were tending to the dismantling of the Sekuatean Empire, they ignored the Zetin demand for the agreed territorial compensation. The Tebbi government explained too casually that until the tasks of the great Northern Alliance were completed, they could not afford to be distracted by the complex arrangements necessary to turn over the territory. The Zetin believed in the dishonesty of their neighbors to the south. In retaliation for what was presumed to be a broken treaty, they executed the Tebbi hostage they held and sent her dismembered body back to the Tebbi government council, who claimed never to have fully understood the Zetin's impatience.

Sebastian somebody, also known as Set-d'Elous, would see

that no misunderstanding occurred this time through history. He promised himself that. He promised all the nameless, faceless people of Tebbicousimankalê, and the evil Zetin, and most of all, Gina—whose desperate call from the guise of Jinetta, wife of the Tebbi prime minister, had traversed the cosmos and found him hard at work at his desk in the IRS Service Center.

The next step in this latest journey, he calculated, was to find the former members of his *Jêpedor-regêlad* to fight with him on one more mission. While he stood in the office on Boulevard 25, renamed "Victory Over Bezua-hü" Boulevard, he pondered the ages of men who had been raw recruits when he last commanded them. Some would not be too old to fight again in 1544. He scanned the directory for their names and addresses, and thought sentimentally of his last visit: he, himself, on that previous fateful journey, lost in the snowfields of Tebbicousimankalê, or bogged down in the spring thaws. Then he would return to deal with Michael and Tammy.

It was already ten years past the year of the siege, he knew, adding a dramatic sigh. His heart skipped a beat as he recalled the precise moment when he decided to stop the madness. There he was: far to the north, fighting in Tebbicousimankalê, still in command and regretting it....

Chapter 26

Baptism

Set-d'Elous stood on the edge of the cliff, overlooking the blue sea, a springtime sea, almost seeing the shores of Selauê in his mind, feeling the breeze as it caressed his face like the hand of Zaura, believing that it was a perfect day to die, a day he had long been seeking, when everything was exactly placed to ease his passing. Whether or not he took the final step off the cliff was only a matter of coincidence since he never could step forward and let himself just tumble down the side of the world into the hell that sat beyond the edge of reality. That was his curse: to always want to die, to feel the obligation to die, to be filled with the joy that his death would bring to others, and yet never be strong enough to do it. So much cruelty, so much horror his army had perpetrated the past few years across the subcontinent of Tebbicousimankalê! The cries for justice were ringing loudly in his ears, and the voices speaking to him in the night, when he lay awake imagining another reality at an IRS service center he had once thought dull, were just as cruel.

He groaned, regarding the crumbling dirt at his feet and the white spray of waves crashing against the rocks far below.

"*Serpan-se Ghou-ram sêfam-in el zoulêm,*" his Second asked, coming up behind him yet maintaining a distance, wanting only to know his captain's orders.

He turned then, noticing one of his eight-point stars peeling off the shoulder of his uniform, and forced a grin at the junior captain, Aroun-de-Sotos. Loyal to the end, he thought to himself as the man joined him on the edge of the cliffs—near the end of their days it seemed, still together, effective team that they were.

"*Kanê-se kassera avenk?*" de-Sotos asked.

He was tired of his second-in-command always inquiring about his health, especially when the phrase literally meant one's mental health.

"*Kasser'avâ!*" he exclaimed in an overly enthusiastic manner, claiming he was well, going and clapping him on the shoulder.

Under most circumstances that would have been a simple thing, but his Second did not seem to feel his obviously distracted commander was appreciating their predicament. As it was, the Tebbi army was close on their heels as all Sekuatean forces were in a frantic retreat back across the subcontinent. The bright golden spring day only helped to mask any thoughts of the slaughter to come. They were the trailing end of the retreating Sekuatean forces, used to slow the pursuing Tebbi—though not successfully. Now they were backed against the sea, his regiment literally against the cliffs. And the violet *sangi* were singing, darting, diving among the waves, snatching the eel-like *tondo* from the sea—

"How about the Tebbi forces?" de-Sotos asked him in Ghoupallêan.

"Ah, the Tebbi forces, eh?" his captain answered roughly in the same language.

Captain Set-d'Elous sighed, sucking in the salt air.

"Let'em eat cake," he said and laughed heartily, uttering the phrase in English and watching the puzzled look on the face of de-Sotos. It was well-known that, not born Sekuatean, the captain often enjoyed thinking aloud in his native tongue.

He was about to order a perimeter set to receive the attack and hope for the best—a memorial to the valor of the unit, perhaps—when one of his lieutenants charged up, jumped off his *Jêpe* and stumbled to the captain's side, dropping to one knee and raising his left arm in salute.

"*Kanê-se Ghoum-zu om-da nimorkon-ga Gourran-Arumê kem*

pangra Têfos-am," said *Landor* Baobê in a rush of words, trying to catch his breath. He had come with good news from Supreme Headquarters at Têfos. He continued in his country Ghoupallêan: "You're the most senior captain, so you've been appointed the acting commanding general of all forces in Tebbicousimankalê. You're the *Berron*! Hail to the new *Berron*!"

It could not be true was his first thought, and his next thought was that it would be a short command indeed if it were true.

De-Sotos clasped his forearm, Roman centurion style, and sang out proudly, "Hail to the *Berron*!"

It was technically possible, since he had refused his promotion to *Merzel* previously, that he likely was the senior captain among all campaign forces. What it meant to him was far more significant: all the higher ranking officers had been killed, all of the generals and colonels and majors in Tebbicousimankalê were dead—those thousands of officers of the *Gourran-Arumê*, the massive conglomeration of the six corps of the Northern Army, the mighty Sekuatean *Arumê-de-Nog*, with the four corps of the south, the *Arumê-de-Sotos*, plus other forces from across the Empire and allied nations. They had invaded Tebbicousimankalê by land and sea with a force of five million; now they were cut down to a fraction of that—and no one knew how many survived, so divided were they now.

The original *Berron*, the aged Tomak-Brounadar (who had been a cadet in his regiment long ago in another life) had died from wounds received in the final assault of Siaa, when the Tebbi army retook the city and their retreat began. General Tomaussus inherited the command—until he was killed attempting to reverse their retreat, trying to make a stand in the industrial tri-city district of Debrêk-Cousi-Sentark, hoping to hold the territory they still controlled. Then *Ghexand* Sonel-Timê, the son of the famous general who had been the Second *Coraesz* commander when Set-d'Elous first took over the 102d regiment in 1474, was lost in battle.

Now it was to be him? They had looked all over the theater of operations and could not find a live colonel or major to take charge? What about Tatandelus at the forward headquarters in Têfos, just across the border in Fenula? He laughed. At the past week's pace, they would arrive in Têfos before Tatandelus could come out and take command. He frowned. He did not want the responsibility for the remaining half million men.

He took the tightly rolled parchment that passed for paper on Ghoupallesz and read the text, feeling the gaze of his fellow officers, on that windy cliff overlooking the sea. Sensing the curtain tearing for him, he wanted to step through to the other side and be free. He would gladly hang up his uniform, put away his sword—

Until Tatandelus could be present in the theater, he read, he was the ranking officer. The general was checking defenses in northern Fenula—against the *Zetin*. So the Zetin were coming down through Fenula? He almost gasped; he had never read that in his history book. And if Tatandelus did not live to take over command in Tebbicousimankalê, then he would remain in charge. For as long as he remained.

Ah, that was it! He could see it all so clearly! They had planned for him to be the one in command when the surrender came, so they could put the blame on the foreigner.

He told them the contents of the order and they continued to rejoice that one of their own had made good in his career. He explained to them that it was not a good career move taking over a retreating army backed against the sea. Somehow, they felt more confident of success than ever before. Baobê always was too eager to die, the captain mused. He could not let them down now, he knew, not those men with whom he had fought for several years.

Then, in that silent moment when even the wind ceased to move, he knew he was all alone, alone in a crowd, alone with his fear, alone in his desperation—and the Tebbi army was only a few *radit* away and closing.

Landor Baobê rode eagerly ahead to tell the men, but de-Sotos and he turned slowly to walk back to their camp. Behind him, he heard the roar of the waves and he thought of home—not Earth, not even his adopted Selauê, nor even Lyas, but that brief idyllic year on Karluk Island with Zaura, leading a life of domestic tranquility. He recalled the steamship which they had taken to the island. Then his head became filled with an idea so huge it began to hemorrhage from his skull.

"What are you thinking?" de-Sotos asked, seeing his usually sullen commander smiling against the deep tide of fate.

"I'll tell you tomorrow, if we are alive," he replied, feeling his aura growing, showering his comrade in confidence.

Aroun-de-Sotos laughed uneasily.

To their eastern flank, the Third *Regêlad* was camped, to the west the First, the Fourth to the south. Typical Sekuate military procedure, it was too easy for their enemies to find each and every unit. They always set up in the three-plus-one formation, and always in numerical order. That was something he had criticized and tried to change, but the *Pangressa-Marzag* argued for tradition. It was a wonder they had managed to conquer half of the civilized world following their tradition. No one told them—except the wayward cavalry captain, Set-d'Elous—that Tebbicousimankalê was a very different land, a nation as strong and clever as them. Perhaps that was the challenge of it. That, plus the surrogate wars of the previous decade, where each of the combatant nations fought through other countries, on someone else's soil, spilling some other country's blood. It would be different when the Tebbi defended their own land.

That was what he told them, the words of a *Serpan* who had refused promotion, commander of a *Jêpedor-regêlad*, a unit of two hundred mounted soldiers, important to a battle but not any career position in itself. He did not want to command a *Treskand*—which consisted of three cavalry *regêlad*, three infantry *regêlad*, and two artillery *regêlad*, totaling two thousand men. In place of his *Merzel* promotion, he had been awarded another merit. He had five of them already sewn on his sleeve, the number needed for promotion, earned through various deeds, from the length of service to a single act of valor (there were over five hundred items on the list hung up in every unit's headquarters). Therefore, he became the first in modern history—a relative term to him—to wear more than five merits.

He left for war wearing eight on his sleeve. Somewhere back at the *Pangressa-Marzag* someone had calculated that he had earned three more merits for the Tebbicousimankalê campaign thus far, making him the equivalent of a *Karrond*, or colonel.

In his tent, he waited on his cot until he heard none of his fellow officers nearby. Then he pulled out his footlocker from under his field desk. Commanders were allowed the box for personal items when campaigning, but he kept only essentials and had thrown most of them away during the campaign to lighten it for the two young assistants assigned to him. The most valuable piece of personal gear inside it now was an old, worn book given to him by its author many years ago.

He sat back on his cot and opened the book to where he had left a marker, a page thickly covered in underlined words, notes handwritten in the margins, maps sketched in the corners. He read the page, turned back a few pages and read up to that page he had marked. Ahead to another page, he read, turned to the appendices and checked a list and a map there, and returned to his marked page. There was no doubt that he understood what the book said, but he was suddenly confronted with the error he perceived: his promotion to *Berron*. It did not worry him; most field promotions were recalled once back in garrison and therefore not recorded in authoritative history texts. But he was none the less disappointed. He had based much of his decision-making on facts presented in the book *A History of the Sekuatean Military from 1400 to 1550*, published thirty years after the final surrender of Sekuate's armies to the combined forces of the Northern Alliance in 1534. The book was a gift from the future, and with it as a guide, he still could not change the course of history. Knowing the direction of every battle, of every advance and retreat, he found himself even more tightly drawn into his role, swept along in the currents of that version of history.

This was different, he thought. Maybe he had changed history by appearing in it at this crucial time: just by tripping into the Sekuatean army and playing the subtle role of the *Berron*, the commander-in-chief of the whole campaign. In their present situation, what change could he possibly affect as their supreme leader? Stop and fight, or surrender: those were the only options.

The former was suicide—and yet they had lived through suicide missions before. The latter was personal suicide, he knew, and he would not dare return to his home in Selauê, perhaps not be allowed to live. Yes, his troops would live—what the vengeful victors did not kill—but he would take the fall and suffer the sacrifice.

"What the hell am I doing here?" he cried out in a cold, crisp whisper. "I don't belong here." His English words seemed to hover in the tent, there in the chill of an early spring evening, reverberating around him.

"*Kanê-se kassera avenk?*"

It was Aroun-de-Sotos, entering his tent silently, catching his captain muttering to himself again.

He slapped the book closed in his lap and stared up at de-Sotos, a certain scowl shooting across his face that for a flash reminded him of his boyhood when he was caught looking through girlie magazines. He grinned like a Cheshire cat, casually slipping the book under the blanket on the cot.

"*Famê?*" his Second asked, curious what it was that made the captain so jumpy.

He explained that he was reading a book, became so absorbed in it that he did not hear de-Sotos calling him from outside. That was a good excuse, they both thought for very different reasons. Then de-Sotos asked what the book was about, implying—the commander supposed—that reading a book was not an appropriate activity for an officer, especially during a time of tactical withdrawal. He had to agree, and told him it was a history book—the history of the Sekuatean military. That was all he could say.

That seemed good enough for the junior captain and he went on to state his business.

Remnants of the Fifth and Sixth *Coraesz* of the *Arumê-de-Nog* were quick-marching toward them along the coast, from the southwest. They reached the Sekuate-controlled port of Pontou but Tebbi warships had blocked the harbor with the Sekuatean transport ships waiting offshore to pick them up. They evacuated the city, along with elements of the occupation force settled there. They expected to arrive at Sênich, the main city near their present

317

encampment, in four days.

De-Sotos deciphered the radio message from the coded paper: "Because you are now acting-*Berron*, they are reporting to you; their highest-ranking officer is *Merzel*-3 Katoum-Torek, leading 82,000 battle-ready men." De-Sotos looked up. "Hail to the *Berron*."

Berron Set-d'Elous could only expel a long, weary sigh. Such a big lap he had for them to drop the whole army into! He knew his *Treskand* was relatively safe in their present position, but the march of two brigades would draw the Tebbi army toward them, too. He was surrounded by a small force; the main body—the First through Fourth *Coraesz* of the *Arumê-de-Nog*—were based up the road near the town of Ramous; his *Treskand*, as always, was assigned trailing patrol by the last late *Berron*.

He turned suddenly and retrieved his volume, questions hanging in his mind. Even ignoring the presence of de-Sotos, he flipped through the pages at the end, among the appendices, and read in a mumble the text he found there, translating it in his head—

ROGAR-OMLEN—BORN IN BUISKE, SEKUATE-NOG, 1483; ARMY COMMISSION 1508; GENERAL RANK 1524; COMMANDANT OF SELAUÊ GARRISON 1524-25; COMMANDING GENERAL OF SAN 4T CORAESZ 1525-28; COMMANDING GENERAL OF SAN 5T CORAESZ 1529-34; *BERRON* 1534; KILLED BATTLE OF SÊNICH, WITHDRAWAL FROM TEBBICOUSIMANKALÊ 1534.

—knowing that it was a mistake the first time he read it: *Berron* Omlen, who inherited the command when *Berron* Sonel-Timê died, was already dead. He had held the coveted rank of *Berron* for barely one month—and they had received official word seven days after the fact. The famous Battle of Sênich was designated as his death stage? It would happen next week, when the two *Arumê-de-Nog* corps arrived. The Tebbi would come from the north, down along the coast past their present campsite— ignoring their force, too small to bother slaughtering—and attack the exhausted troops coming from Pontou. What survivors there were would struggle on their own and somehow regroup near Baraxe, one hundred *radit*—about eighty miles—from the riverine border between Tebbicousimankalê and Fenula.

He knew it was going to happen. He knew what the result would be. He knew how many men would die without even a chance to fight back. He knew all of that, and he could do nothing to prevent it. History had already been written, after all; he held it in his hands. That was what made him weep at night when his men could not see or hear him. He knew everything, wanted to forget everything: his single defining moment was approaching.

"*Kanê-se kassera avenk?*"

"If I hear you say that stupid phrase one more time!" he exploded in English, and saw his battle-hardened Second fall back under the sudden outburst of foreign words.

Aroun-de-Sotos stared down at the open book, easier for him to read written in its formal language than for his captain.

"*Fêrag Ghou'n galen temz-se bann?*" de-Sotos asked in a low voice.

The captain told him it was just an old history book, forgetting to hide its cover.

De-Sotos pointed at the book's title, referring to the dates there: *from 1400 to 1550*. The publication date stamped in gold at the bottom of the front cover was 1564. His Second grimaced, afraid to speak. The year for them was only 1534, and they were facing down a battle in four days that would end the campaign.

What difference did such a book make? The junior captain was not easily put off. There were the dates, he insisted, and there was the title. Who would go to the effort to print such a fictional account of their illustrious history? Then he asked his captain, Set-d'Elous, again the question that rang like the blast of a smoking AT gun in his ears: 'Where did you get such a book?'

It was new when he received it as a gift, and over the years he had read and reread it many times, making the notes in it that littered every page. In his mind, he was telling a different story, of how he meant only to return for research, to satisfy the nagging curiosity instilled by Gina concerning the succeeding generations of the children, grandchildren, and great-grandchildren that sprang from his life with Zaura-Matousz. A short, simple journey, he had calculated, a lot of time in the Archives in Selauê, a lot of time reading and looking around.

He only made two mistakes. The first was to return to Selauê of 1530 holding a book he'd been given on a previous trip to Siti in 1572, a book which had no right to exist in 1530, published as it was in 1564. He'd kept it more for sentimental value than for its historical record.

The second was the day he went to the Archives and a woman told him he resembled an officer she had once known but whose name skipped her mind. Instead of running away at that moment, he returned to his studies, allowing her time to retrieve an army officer and bring him to the Archives to identify him. The officer addressed him with proper authority and respect, and he gloated at that, boasting of his past and his military achievements as though the book on him already had been closed. It was not.

Escorted to the garrison, he was re-appointed to the command of the same unit the documents he had in his possession, copied from the Archives, stated he had once commanded. Every retired and reserve officer was needed immediately at the port of Milou, he was told, where the Second *Coraesz* was preparing to set sail. The great invasion of Tebbicousimankalê was at hand.

Although he vehemently denied saying what he had disclosed at the Archives, he was eventually cured of his 'battle-fatigue' by a crack team of interrogators. Then he was able to join the *Coræsz* once more and resume his former command, wearing a new uniform bearing his old rank and unit designation. The fresh-faced young captain who was his second-in-command was Aroun-de-Sotos. That was four years ago—

"*Fan ghexand-d'elous in zaxend-bul temz-se bann,*" he heard de-Sotos asking when he came out of his trance. 'What famous general wrote this book?'

"*Ghexand* Set-Matousz," he replied without batting an eye, hoping the name would mean nothing to him.

He could see De-Sotos mulling the name around in his mind. Of course, over the four years of campaigning, his Second had learned all about him: his Ghoupalle life, at least, and the woman named Zaura-Matousz with whom he had made sons. Finally he found it, however, and laid it soundly before the captain.

"*Ghouram pazar-kal?*"—'Your father?'

The captain smiled for a heartbeat, knowing the same word

was used both for a biological father and a wife's father. He held his hard frown for a much longer time, then spoke solemnly, knowing the time had come to clear his record:

"*Er zam,*" he replied. 'My son.'

When he learned from the commander of the First *Treskand* that the briefly appointed *Berron* Omlen had been knocked off his horse by a low tree branch, breaking his neck and dying almost immediately, he restrained the urge to laugh. That was the reason his death was attributed to the yet-to-be-fought Battle of Sênich. *Berron*s never died except in battle—unless they were formally retired. That was one gratuity the highest military rank afforded: a glorious end. Even if he fell off his *Jêpe* standing in the center of camp, it was due to the battle-stress of the *Jêpe*—that long-eared, bewhiskered, rat-tailed, three-toed, horse-like beast with a long, veiny dewlap and the sagging jowls they rode into battle: an ugly but functional animal, named after the ancient race who first domesticated them.

No wonder his son, the general, had dictated such in his history of the war; it was the only story available to him. It meant also that perhaps he was not mentioned in the history book because he died in a not-so-glorious manner, away from battle.

"They'll die anyway without me," he muttered to no one in particular, ignoring the sudden attention of his interior guard. "So I'm free to leave; history already records their deaths." He expected his guards to ask him if he was giving them an order. "Or maybe, they'll all die *because* of me leaving." He had nothing to live for himself—except his own absurd adventures; they, his men, had everything to live for. "What do I owe them?" he asked himself, shaking his head. He contemplated if the rigors of campaigning could truly bring men together like that, like in the movies.

Now he was the *Berron*—at least until *Ghexand* Tatandelus arrived. There was a small window of slippery opportunity; he could change the course of history, he decided.

Perhaps he could make it happen, by disappearing and being presumed killed, he thought—at the moment his guards let de-Sotos in. His Second was smug, now sharing his secret. He did not understand it, naturally—and the new *Berron* was reluctant to explain more—but to his credit de-Sotos knew when not to ask further questions and just accept. Now, as he entered the tent, he seemed to have news. And it might even be positive by the grin that played across his face despite his best attempts to hide it.

As for the guards who in his new capacity as *Berron* were required to stay close—two inside, four outside at all times, wherever he went, even to the toilet—he feared that one of them might be his assassin more than he feared attack from outside. At this hour, who really knew he was *Berron*? Certainly not the Tebbi army, or they would have swept down on their small camp already.

De-Sotos informed him that his new guard had arrived—his special protective guard, a squadron of warriors to ring his tent. He guessed his promotion might be true after all. Then de-Sotos mentioned that the guard, when nearing their encampment, had intercepted a band of ragged mercenaries who had been closing in. Good, he responded, not knowing exactly how many people were now adding his name to the top of their hit lists. Some of them—wearing no uniform and seeming neither Tebbi nor Zetin—were killed, others wounded, but most captured, about thirty, their leader included. He wanted to know what the new *Berron* wished done with them: interrogate and kill, interrogate and send forward to become prisoners of war, or kill them immediately?

It was a difficult decision for him, whether to follow proper Sekuatean military protocol or his heart. He asked if there was any reason to believe the band was really coming after him, or merely got in the way. Still, they were armed and had no allegiance—mercenaries hired by the Tebbi? Or by the Zetin?

"Hard to say," de-Sotos replied in Ghoupallêan. "Do you wish to see them yourself?"

He was curious, never encountering mercenaries other than the Tebbi-hired Zetin.

"Yes, let's have a look," he said in English. Then, catching himself, repeated it in Ghoupallêan.

De-Sotos said he would call the *Berron* when they were properly subdued for his inspection.

"*Om-se,*" he replied and nodded.

They would be stripped and bound, laid face down on the ground with a guard or two for each prisoner, poised with sword-points at the base of each head. Only then could the *Berron* be allowed to approach.

It took nearly a full *peth* before *Landor* Baobê assailed him. When he appeared from his tent, it seemed that the whole *Treskand* was there to encircle the thirty naked prisoners. His personal guards encircled *him*, walking with him as a moving cage across the ground to where de-Sotos waited.

The *Berron* asked which one was their leader—using a heavy, rough voice that his men needed to hear from him to set them in their places. De-Sotos pointed to the tall one in the center of the front row, two soldiers astride him. At a gesture, one of the guards knelt down and turned the man's face up from the ground, holding him by his long hair. The prisoner grimaced, groaning with teeth clenched.

"Grubby bastard, isn't he?" the *Berron* remarked in English.

"*Fan-se?*" de-Sotos asked, not catching what he said.

He told de-Sotos the prisoners did not appear to be Zetin. They did not understand the Tebbi dialect either, said de-Sotos. What is your will? he asked the *Berron*.

He rubbed his chin. As *Berron*, his whim was the soldiers' life-sacrificing obligation, and any order he gave would be acted upon instantly. If he ordered the prisoners' deaths, they would die before his words could echo once around the camp. He had to be careful, as *Berron*, that he was not misunderstood.

"Interrogate them," he instructed, carefully choosing his Ghoupallêan words, "then tell me what you've learned."

De-Sotos passed the orders to the newly arrived guard company's captain and the prisoners were stood up and herded away, somewhere—that was not something the *Berron* needed to concern himself with.

After dinner in his tent, the *Berron* read in his history book again, looking for any mention of mercenaries in the final days of the retreat. He sensed the curious glances of his interior guard as he read, but he pretended not to notice. He knew the knife was beneath his mattress if he needed it, and any murmur out of the ordinary would be enough to call in his outer-guards.

De-Sotos entered, accompanied by guards who barred his way further with their lances. He called them off and de-Sotos entered, reporting that none of the prisoners had given any significant information. What was his will?

He reminded de-Sotos that he would be leaving in the morning with his protective guards to direct the forces from the headquarters. The prisoners could be taken with them and turned over to the *Coraesz* for disposition. No, de-Sotos argued— he had known his captain-*Berron* for a long time—there were not enough guards available to both watch the prisoners and take care of him.

"I'm the *Berron*, not a nun, dammit!"

Then he translated loosely for de-Sotos, who laughed.

Suddenly there was a commotion outside the tent and the camp was alert.

"Where's that sonovabitch Set?" a man's voice called out, trotting easily into the camp on his *Jêpe* in a decidedly non-threatening manner.

Twenty soldiers leaped up to thrust their lances at him and two others threw ropes over him and pulled him from his mount, dragging him along the ground.

"What kinda reception is this for an old friend?"

It was English—crude English, but still English, sweet language of home.

He tore out of his tent and into the clearing, chased by his guards. De-Sotos ran after them, sword drawn. A line of soldiers from the Fourth *Derrad* who had been cleaning their ATs now had their guns poised at the fallen intruder.

"Who the hell is this bastard lying in the dirt?" the *Berron* exclaimed with a hearty laugh, slapping hands to hips.

"Take it easy! You're the one who told me to watch my language messin' around over here," the tussled, filthy, haggard man shot back, undaunted by his pending death.

The soldiers were suspicious that this intruder knew their

commander's foreign tongue.

He waved off the guards, had to push away some of them who did not believe it was truly safe, and reached down to untie his friend, Jason.

"It's Sekuatean army SOP to greet strangers like this," he replied, raising him up to his feet, one foot still caught in the ropes. "What are you doing here?"

"What the hell do ya think? You didn't come back when you said you would."

"But that was, what?—four or five years ago," said the *Berron*. "What the hell happened? I told you what to do: deny everything."

"Yeah, but—shit—you know me—harder to tell a really good lie to the cops than try to make things right on my own. You shoulda figured that out."

"You're right, I should have."

"You got some men of mine, I hear—didn't come back from lunch. Had that problem back at the plant, too—everybody walking off the line for lunch and not coming back. Wish we had a punishment like they got here—what's it? Setting'em naked on a stake and leavin'em for the *jax* to eat."

"Same ol' Jason!"

They almost embraced.

"*Mu plaeren Ghouram gand-se!*" *Landor* Baobê cried out, sword drawn. 'He speaks your language!'

"*Mu'n pen mek!*" the *Berron* smiled. 'He does, doesn't he?' Then he spoke in his native tongue to Jason: "What did you say you wanted with this man they call Set?"

"I know I'll be damned fer sure, but I wanted to save his miserable freakin' life!"

The *Berron*, chuckling, repeated to his staff what the man had said.

"*Habben sixag-se*," de-Sotos warned. 'Must be a trick.'

"Why do you want to save his life?"

"Sonovabitch! Why does anyone wanna live? Hell, I sure don't—that's why I came here! Where's my men? Hired'em over in—what's that town you went to with Gina? The place you two first lived, back—way the hell back in the future—in Ghoupalle year 1928. You know...over the ocean, in Ghoupallæssa, ya know, allies of these Tebbi bastards."

"That would be Siti. But how'd you do that? You don't know any Ghoupallêan. You don't have Ghoupalle money. How could you enter Tebbicousimankalê with a war going on? And I'm not even going to ask how you found me in all of this mess."

"Questions—freakin' questions! Gimme my men. And something decent to eat—and I'll tell ya."

The slightest twitch of the *Berron*'s hand, down at his side, brought the guards back to full alert. The *Berron* began to turn his back on the intruder who spoke his own language and Baobê jumped between them, protecting the *Berron*'s back.

"They're good, dude. Not as good as mine."

"But your men were captured."

"No—they was just infiltratin' yer ass here."

"Really? I thought they were trying to kill me. That's why we've got all of this security here. In fact, tomorrow they're going to move me to even tighter security. You almost missed me. Think how you'd fare without me to answer your foolhardy call."

"What the hell're you, you need so much goddamn security? Thought you're just some cowboy."

"All of our generals keep getting killed so they made me the one in charge—probably thinking the Tebbi won't go looking for a mere captain as the leader."

"No shit, man. D'you see that humongous army moving down the road?"

"What are you talking about?"

"Don't you have any damn sentries, any lookouts? The whole freakin' Tebbi army's coming down the road, right behind us. We weren't looking fer yer sorry ass, we was getting the hell outta their way."

"I know they're coming, but how'd *you* find me?"

"Shit, all I had to do was ask some dopey farmers where the great Set-the-Illustrious was camped and they all pointed down the road to this dead end. Thought they were pulling my leg—but here the hell you are, crazy dude, up to your armpits in Tebbi regulars—with only me to yank yer hide outta the way. If it was so easy for me, some dumb *foo*reigner, it's gotta be easy fer them!"

A *Jêpedor* stormed into the camp, frantically shouting at Aroun-de-Sotos.

A gesture from the captain to the *Berron* and orders were given to extinguish the campfires, collapse the tents, and take defensive positions. The entire camp rustled for all of ten *pii*, then was silent. Discipline, training, fear. The take-down of a campsite had been practiced too many times in their long retreat.

Merely two *peth* later—forty minutes—they watched from the bushes, guards encircling the *Berron*, Jason, and de-Sotos. The skies darkened into evening as the enemy troops moved through the fields, the shadows of the Tebbi forces, hundreds of them, thousands—and only one flank. They were marching toward the coast, toward the town of Sênich. Deep in the evening darkness, he whispered to Jason what he had read in his history book.

"No shit!" Jason responded in a hush.

The battle was going to happen. As the reluctant *Berron*, he was already too late. Tomorrow, as the troops of the *Arumê-de-Nog* were awakening to breakfast, the mass of Tebbi corps would surround and suffocate them. Half would be killed, the rest randomly scattered, groping for salvation in ragtag bands until they reached the border. He was seeing the cruel future in the naïve present.

Since no moon lit Ghoupallesz, the night draped them in complete darkness—only a faint glow on the underbellies of the clouds, reflections of the lights of Sênich.

"*Lok-se ouran-ga hulgim apê Ghoupallesz, leatas T'hem,*" Aroun-de-Sotos recited just above a whisper. 'The night hides everything on Ghoupallesz, even Heaven.'

Chapter 27

Conversion of Faith

"If I'm not back in a week," he had whispered to his friend, Jason Aronstein, deep in his living room, years before ever meeting Michael and Tammy, "then you'll know that something's gone wrong—"

"That you screwed up."

"Right."

"So whadaya want me to do?"

"What *can* you do? You'll be questioned about me. Just deny everything. You're good at that. Besides the fact of you and me being friends, there's nothing that would incriminate you in my disappearance. Then you can handle my estate—take care of the paperwork, and try to give a good explanation, in layman's terms, of what happened. Not what *really* happened, of course. I mean, what they would really *believe* happened."

"Seems like a whole lotta trouble," Jason said with a grunt.

"I know, and I'm sorry. But you know I have to go. You agree, right?"

"Yeah, you have to warn your son, the general, that the whole damn place is gonna be totally messed up by a helluva war like no one's ever seen."

"And he should take his family to Ghoupallæssa to be safe."

"Yeah, that too."

"Great. You've got it straight. I know what will happen to the world, but I don't know what will happen to my family, so I want to be sure they're safe."

"You know, it's kinda your fault—I mean, you getting into the army like that," said Jason. "Your whole family was living the army life, so what's so strange about your son joining, too. Then little Set-junior grows up to be a general. The family business, huh? Kicked butt in Gotanka, didn't he? Made'em cry uncle in Peror, didn't he? Had a job to do and he did it well."

"But *this* war will destroy him if he's in it. And his family. I have to be sure he and his family are safe. I have to do that. I have an obligation."

"Then you'd better stop talking about it and just do it. It's gettin' late. You gotta be back in thirteen hours, or you'll miss the game. Raiders and Chiefs, man!"

They drove to the quarry, parked the car in the cover of the trees along the road.

He shook Jason's hand under the October moonlight, and for a strange moment he felt something like fear. It was reminiscent of the tenacious pull the aura of Zaura had on him long ago, and it frightened him. He had been in combat before, but never had he entered it trying to stop it. Now the doorway was widening before him, the mystical lights flickering like Christmas decorations. He felt like he was really stepping into the endless void, the bottomless pit, consumed by his final all-encompassing decision.

He pulled back his hand, slung his knapsack on his shoulder, gave a glance at his uniform and leaned forward, staring into the black hole that was his gateway to the future. Stepping through, he vanished into the night.

When Sebastian did not return by the designated time, Jason went counter to his reputation and worried. He drove by the quarry entrance every night for a week. Finally he stopped and went up. He searched around the quarry, thinking his friend might be laying there with some injury. Instead, the rip in the curtain was still shimmering in the night, not closing, and Jason stepped forward, felt the magnetism of the open tangent, and fell through the gap.

Ghoupallesz beckoned, and Jason used the words he knew to find his way to Lyas. That was familiar territory and he set out inquiring after his friend's whereabouts. None knew, and in his former apartment building, the landlord said he had moved out years before. *Years*? He recalled the date his friend had been trying to hit, and learned the present date. Either his friend had been living in the other dimension for some seven years, or he himself stepped through on the wrong day.

Jason managed a ticket on the KOHAX to Selauê and shopped around for his friend. Sneaking past several addresses he had been told about, his poor Ghoupallêan improved with every passing day and uncomfortable encounter. He gained tremendously the day he inquired at the Selauê garrison, where the wartime staff thoroughly interrogated him. His Ghoupallêan proved adequate and he was released. Outside, he was advised to seek information at the Archives.

After painfully slow progress, an assistant located the registry of Set-d'Elous. His present assignment was the Second *Coraesz*, *Sekuatean Arumê-de-Nog*, and it was no secret that they were presently engaged in the war with the five nations of the *Nog-Megank-Ulsinyn*, the Northern Megank Alliance. They were marching on the Tebbi city of Siaa, he learned. The information was backed up by the headlines on the bulletins stamped to the walls of the reading room. Checking carefully, the name of his friend was not among the long lists of casualties.

There was no easy road north, Jason quickly learned. All civilian travel between the two nations had ceased. He needed men, anyway. So he pulled out his notes, his collection of Ghoupalle facts and figures left among his friend's papers—the ones he was supposed to destroy if questioned about his friend's disappearance. There he found an address in Siti, across the ocean in Ghoupallæssa.

Roumak-Torgê, one of his friend's contacts, was very helpful, putting him up in his inn and assisting in locating a few good men.

"Well, of course, he was," the *Berron* remarked, listening to Jason tell the story as they rode along to the new headquarters where he would formally take command. "He's one of Gina's grandsons—getting rich selling arms to the Tebbis."

Torgê was at least superficially interested in the well-being of Jason's friend. Fifteen were hired at first, told briefly the mission, and left to train for it. Jason went with Torgê to hire more mercenaries. Some of them knew the reputation of the warrior Set-d'Elous. Jason never could have imagined it. Their band grew to forty, then sixty, all wanting to get a piece of the action in Tebbicousimankalê. Since the two nations were allies, travel between them was available, but Ghoupallæssa would only supply arms, no men. There was nothing for these mercenaries and freebooters to do; they wanted to fight. Rescue the notorious Set-d'Elous? That was fine for a weekend's amusement. Fight the Tebbi *and* the Zetin? Of course. And the Sekuatean army, as well? Why the hell not?

And they were off, sailing on the morning tide in a freighter stinking of the kind of deep-sea beast that was its usual cargo: the forty-foot sea worm called *stouji*. He was thankful he did not have to see it, much less eat it; the smell was bad enough. They landed in Elêna, a major port city on the far west coast of Tebbicousimankalê, far enough removed that it was not as yet under dispute. From there they took the role of refugees, moving among the Tebbi citizens in their deliberately ragged dress, listening and watching everyone and everything. The Tebbi reported the war news, too, and it did not take long for them to determine the probable location of the Second *Coraesz*: marching to Siaa. They followed them, along with the trailing bands of all the people who lived off trade with the legions.

At Siaa, they could not move any closer, and once the siege began, they were trapped there through the winter just like the armies. Jason chose to abandon the city and found warmer refuge in a southern town. The siege would only be a few days, his comrades told him—but it lasted four full months. By the time the city had finally been conquered by the Sekuatean armies, Jason's band of mercenaries were on the move again, only to arrive at Siaa the moment that the hidden Tebbi army charged down from the north. They lost track of the Second *Coraesz* in the mad scramble to get out of the district. They picked up the trail near Debrêk, the industrial city where the retreat briefly turned into a counteroffensive. They were caught there, too, and lost him again.

After the Sekuatean army split at Loule, the capital, they followed the wrong battle group for more than a month before breaking away to pursue the other group that was racing for the Fenula border. It was just as well, Jason soon learned, because the group that went south was slaughtered against the coast, unable to escape on the transport ships waiting for them. He was glad his friend had been smart enough to keep out of the reach of Death's boney knuckles.

"And here the hell I am," Jason sang out, slapping the rump of his *Jêpe*.

"Here the hell you are," said the *Berron*, nodding.

They were on their way to Karêgosz, together with his personal guard. From their elevated position traversing the ridge, it was easy to see the great encampment on the bluffs to the northeast. The wide grassy moor was the perfect place to meet for battle, the *Berron* mused, running that page through his head from his history book. How could he warn them? They could not outrun the Tebbi army, and they did not have enough forces to fight them and win.

"Don't worry about it, dude. They're history," Jason exclaimed, slapping the *Jêpe* again and listening to its strange giggle-wheeze cry. "Starting to get used to these funny Jeepers."

"Yes, history…," he muttered to himself.

"Hey, it's not like you led them here, or that you made'em sleep in the snow four damn months, or that you're letting them be slaughtered. Don't sweat it, dude. You and me, we're not really here. For us, it's a dream."

The *Berron* turned to regard his friend, still unable to see him as anything more than the grease pit mechanical wizard he was on Earth, always tinkering with racing cars.

"Well, that's what you told me before," said Jason, disappointed at his friend's renewed somber mood.

"And you are right."

"Let's get the hell outta this freakin' place, just you and me, right now. There's gotta be one of yer goddamn tangents around here someplace."

"I can't abandon them."

"Yeah, you're their leader now, huh!"

He turned to face Jason, feeling his guards fidgeting in their saddles, alert to the conflict between the *Berron* and his unsavory acquaintance, refusing to believe the foreigner was so innocent.

"I've lived with them, fought with them, kept them from dying for years—literally years! I can't leave them now to suffer the ravages of the history that will fall around them."

"You can if you wanna. What do you owe them?"

"Owe them? Why is everything always credit and debit with you? Can't you give with no expectation of a reward? Can't you do the right thing—without stopping to see what kind of profit you can get out of it?"

"Take it easy, man—"

The guards charged up beside him, lances brought to bear against Jason's hard leather breastplate.

"You'd better take it easy…while I'm their leader."

Jason dropped his head, feigned humiliation, spoke an apology, and waited for his friend to wave off the guards.

"Listen, I musta played that music box a thousand times before I decided to come after you. The one Gina gave you? That tune you said was from Sekuate—the love song. Now, I've spent almost a year here on this damn world—Who knows how long it's been back home?—all to bring back your hide so I don't have to answer a bunch of stupid-ass questions. Geez, if I'd known it was gonna be this much trouble, I'd—Hell, I thought you were whoring with another gal in Lyas or someplace, that's why you didn't come back. I mean, that's what happened the time you married that Zaura girl. You told me it'd be a short trip, then you stayed a year! How can a guy believe anything you say now?"

"All right, Jason, I've learned a few lessons. What I'm doing now is my payback."

"What the hell you talking about?"

"All that I've done on this world has been self-centered and decidedly *for*-profit. I've taken and taken. And I've seen some of the results of my actions. Now I have this small opportunity to pay back the spirits of this world. By bringing their people safely home. This is my homework. I'm cramming for the big final exam tomorrow. If I pass, everybody gets an A. If I flunk, the whole world will end."

Jason laughed, cruelly artificial.

"What I get, *Monsieur* Berrone—pardon my French—is that you're feeling guilty for using your *gift*—if you wanna call it that—and you think the only way you're ever gonna get away from it is to offer yourself as some kind of sacrifice."

Thankfully, they were met by a welcoming contingent at that time, and he did not have to reply. The thought continued screwing into his mind, however, even as he accepted the rolled parchment formally accepting command of the remaining half million strong army. Together they arrived in the headquarters compound set up in the village market. He explained who the man was who rode beside him, but that did not impress his new staff.

Tebbi spies would know which tent was the *Berron's*: the largest one, in the center of the encampment. That was the first thing he changed, sacrificing defensive strength for the lesser chance that fighting would come. Keep the area looking like it was just a small contingent of retreating troops, only a ragged band of runaways, he instructed. That would cause the Tebbis to think they were not worth attacking. It did not take long for the order to be put into action; he knew they were chewing their hearts out wanting to tell the *Berron* he was wrong but fearing to do so. His senior advisors held back, but he could see the nervousness in their eyes.

"We're gonna do things the American way around here!" Jason barked out from behind the *Berron*.

He winked with his right eye, not even turning his head, and two guards took Jason by his arms and escorted him out. Then he spoke to the head of his personal guard, telling him to take good care of the man but not to let him back in the tent until he gave the order. He needed to be alone, needed time to sort out what to do.

"Do the right thing," he whispered to himself, seeing the interior guards watching him, knowing they would give their front teeth to know what the *Berron* had said in his native language.

That was what Gina had told him countless times: "Do the right thing. You know what it is, just do it. Damn the costs. It doesn't matter what the costs are if it's the right thing." Do the right thing. Release your guilt. See your men safely home. Can't play God. They're history. Do the right thing. He could barely stand Jason's voice shouting through his head and grimaced tightly. The guards took notice but he waved them back.

Jason and his mercenaries had arrived at Elêna on a *stouji* cargo ship. That must have been embarrassing for them. He was beginning to feel that same vague idea growing in his head, shapeless but there. Tebbis would not accept being sent aboard a smelly, rusting vessel like that. Nor would Sekuateans. Karêgosz was a small port which was untended by Tebbi army forces, as far as their intelligence stated. When the Sekuatean forces were turned away from Pontou, a fleet of transport ships had been waiting for them. Karêgosz was a small harbor, with jagged rocks cutting the waves. An idea was taking shape: an elongated form, pointed at each end. A ship. Several ships, perhaps. The port was so insignificant, none would believe they could escape that way. The Tebbi navy would not blockade it; the Sekuatean army would not protect it. He was on his own now, worrying no longer about their retreat or the crazy possibility of a renewed offensive that some secretly desired. He cared only for the men he had served with. These men were his reason for remaining, and once they were safely returned home, he would be free to leave Ghoupallesz.

"Morally free," he quietly mused, attracting the attention of his guards once more.

Then his new chief of staff, *Merzel-5* Iadon-Büsk, entered with news that Tatandelus had finally returned to Têfos. He would soon be on his way to take over command as *Berron*. Set-d'Elous would be returned to the command of the 102d *Jêpedor-regêlad*, to possibly die in battle at Sênich or, worse, survive it.

✻ ✻ ✻

In the bottom back corner of his battered wooden footlocker, beneath the cracked picture of his deceased wife wrapped in silky *habal*, was a small leather pouch that once held marijuana when he and Jason had driven around searching for secluded places to park and smoke. Now it held a collection of individually wrapped *gealan*. Most were a dark, hazy orange—ordinary grade—yet a few were emerald green, and there was the silver-purple one he had given to Zaura when he proposed marriage the second time and received back at her funeral. It alone was worth double everything he owned in the universe. With care he set it down in his palm, shielding it from his inner-guard with his back. It glowed in the dim light, its silvery sheen reflecting how haggard his face had become. He looked ten years older. But the *gealan* still shone. The others were also in good condition. He never intended to bring them, but he had them with him when they were packing for the voyage across the Tebbi Sea in the great invasion. He had only spent one of them, at Siaa, to buy stoves for his troops.

He replaced them in the pouch and slipped it under his coat. Standing, he asked one guard to get his chief of staff and the other to have his *Jêpe* readied. The guards hesitated, not knowing if they should leave him alone, fearing punishment for obeying his orders and for disobeying those of the Sekuatean army: the *Berron* must never be left alone. He assured them it was allowed, and they believed him.

In the moment they stepped from the tent and others could replace them, he slipped out of his tired uniform and into dirty clothes taken from the captured mercenaries. With his pouch tied securely to his belt and weapons hidden on him, he slipped out the back of the tent, dodged his exterior guard who saw only one of the ragged men tagging along with the *Coraesz*.

He was free, he sighed, stopping to catch his breath in the shadows of the market. He never wanted to be held like a prisoner in the headquarters tent or be interrogated about what he would do to save them, tortured until he could come up with the correct orders to bring victory to the Sekuatean armies.

✳ ✳ ✳

Hidden in his ruffian clothes, he pulled Jason out of a sound sleep, pressed his finger to his lips, and led him away in the darkness.

They took a pair of *Jêpe*, threw off the military saddles and rode away. Crossing the moors, he caught sight of the lights of Karêgosz, down the steep slope, perched at the sea's edge between tall, rocky cliffs. A short, narrow spit separated the harbor from the ocean waves, and inside the port were three small cargo ships and a dozen fishing vessels. He studied the harbor, feeling the *gealan* dangling in the pouch at his side.

In the darkness, reality dissolved, and the two arcade foosball players from Earth set aside their differences and worked for the common good of the strangers in their care. Using their powers of persuasion, they hired almost all of the ships that were in the harbor that night. The fishermen and merchant marines were never so concerned who was hiring their ships. The magnificent price offered was their fixation: the bulging pouch of *gealan*— distributed among the ship owners and the captains—were dreams come true to men weary of their daily routine.

It took all he had but it was done. He left his friend to see to the ships' preparations and made his way back to his headquarters alone. Dressed as a country ruffian, being of no value to anyone, he was not worth a second look. Besides, he knew that history was set; nothing that could happen to him would change that.

His staff was in shock when he told them his plan, so certain they would all be executed upon their arrival in Sekuate.

"We are not fleeing from the battle," he explained to them. No, they were not deserting. They would be escaping from the Tebbi forces at Sênich, to fight again another day. 'Tactical withdraw' was not in the vocabulary of the *Pangressa-Marzag*, of course. They would regroup at Têfos, on the border, where they were already scheduled to march. There they could reorganize and, as he stated to enlist their enthusiasm for the idea, they could then counterattack back across the Klub River.

His Chief of Staff, *Merzel* Iadon-Büsk, protested as strongly as he could—beyond the point a less genteel *Berron* would have tolerated. The *Berron's* command was their sacrificial obsession, he knew—'*Toun-i-Stae Sartuxen-da T'hera*' was how it was said, literally their 'current and continuous sacrificial duty,' the oath taken upon induction into the military. Yet Iadon-Büsk feared the disgrace of the army, of the empire, or at least his own staff— which he had ruled since crossing the Tebbi Sea with *Berron* Tomak-Brounadar.

"If you want to stay and fight, be my guest," he barked at Büsk, whose uniform carried patches of higher rank than the field-promoted *Berron*.

The room fell immediately silent and the *Berron* tried to gaze into the eyes of his staff members but most heads were bowed.

"So my orders shall be carried out at once," he spoke in a calm voice, then added a brief, confident oratory about how his own *Treskand* would be first, to show the others he feared no reprisal from the *Pangressa-Marzag*.

Satisfied, the *Berron* turned to exit—a single step—and his next heartbeat was elongated into what seemed like five *peth* as the angry Chief of Staff Büsk drew his sword and started after him and the *Berron's* two inner-guards rushed to intercept the crazed officer, one guard lunging with sword in hand, the other grabbing the available sword of another staff member, the three of them hurtling toward the apex of death: three swords colliding, the guards' two flashing blades coming together like scissors to clip the tumbling Büsk's head off at the neck. When the *Berron* turned at the commotion, he found the head between his feet, pale face staring up at him, still defiant.

The headquarters staff hurried to spread the new orders—and the text became mixed with rumors about the *Berron* cutting off his Chief of Staff's head when he had protested. The troops were marched down to the harbor of Karêgosz where Jason waited, directing them on first one ship and the next, filling the cargo ships and turning to the fishing vessels. By midday, the first ship was heading out of the harbor into the Tebbi Sea.

In the afternoon, the news began filtering in about the slaughter at Sênich. A few who had escaped made it up the coast to Karêgosz and described the battle. It was an attack in the predawn hours, the Tebbi forces killing men in their sleep, in their tents. The *Treskand* on night duty counterattacked and held them off for nearly three *peth*, long enough for the other units to organize and join the battle. They were partially protected by the sea on one flank and a ridge of hills on the other side, limiting the Tebbi army's attack. Later the Tebbi forces circled around the hills, catching the Sekuatean forces in a pincer and pressing them back against the same kind of rocky cliffs that squeezed in gloomy Karêgosz. Soldiers forced from the cliffs littered the sea below. Those that remained above were captured and routinely slaughtered. Of the 82,000 troops reporting to him three days earlier, only a few thousand would survive to the Klub River.

"Did you read of this in your history book?" his former Second, Aroun-de-Sotos, asked him angrily upon his arrival in Karêgosz with his *regêlad*. He did not use the polite speech required when addressing one's superior officer, the *Berron* noticed. "And if you did, why did you do nothing to help them?"

He translated for Jason, standing beside him.

"Yeah, I got that much," Jason responded with a smirk. "What do these fools want? You're trying to save *their* necks and whadaya get? Pissing on your parade."

"Nothing I do will change anything," the *Berron* muttered, watching the men of his former *regêlad* boarding the *stouji* freighter. He felt that he was watching them be forced to commit suicide. They wore that look on their faces, leaving their *Jêpe* behind in the camp as instructed, leaving their tents set up as usual to distract the Tebbi forces marching on them. There was the future, trudging up the plank onto the stinking vessel.

He heard Jason laugh, and looked up.

"Look at these guys!" Jason chuckled, then put on his best clown face. "Just who *is* this man and why the hell're we listening to him?"

"Quiet!"

"That's what they're thinking, ya know."

More reports of the battle at Sênich staggered in through the evening, as more of the hired ships set out into the sea.

Near midnight, overseeing the boarding of the last boats, he was given a rolled parchment by a lieutenant—no one of higher rank wanted to be the one to deliver it to him. It was from the theater headquarters in Têfos, signed by *Ghexand* Tatandelus himself. He regarded the words there, listening to the sounds of ships preparing for launch and the whistle of the wind in his ears. Then he rolled it up and slipped it in his jacket pocket.

On board his own ship with the troops from his 102d *Regêlad*, he leaned against the starboard bow railing, observing the water below as the ship chugged its way out to sea. He sent for de-Sotos. The noise of the engine was hypnotic and he nearly became entranced by the time the junior *Serpan* came to him, reporting with a formality not seen since they first boarded the invasion fleet in Milou.

"I'm your captain again," he spoke in Ghoupallêan, retrieving the rolled parchment from his pocket and offering it to his Second for inspection.

"No, Sir," de-Sotos replied, refusing it. "You always have been."

The lights of Karêgosz left them far behind as they chatted uneasily about some of the events at the 102d *Regêlad* camp while he was away being *Berron*. De-Sotos asked about his friend, the one who spoke his language, and the one-time *Berron* explained that Jason was staying behind to gather his own men, disguised as vagabonds, and look after the Sekuatean troops who could not fit on the ships they had. Once they docked in Têfos, he explained to de-Sotos they would return to Karêgosz to evacuate the remaining troops, including Jason's forty mercenaries. He had promised that, he told de-Sotos and the man laughed.

He asked why, received no reply, but believed it was because his promises had never really meant much. He planned to change that—in another time and place, of course. Then, holding up the parchment, he realized he had been clenching it in his hand as they talked.

"I won't need this once we land," said *Serpan* Set-d'Elous, "I'll be out of a job." He allowed the crumpled scroll to slip out of his hand, down into the dark waters.

The first cargo ships had made it to Têfos, the radio message came back, but the next group alerted a task force of Tebbi warships off the coast of Rox and they were steaming to intercept the Karêgosz ships. Before dawn, they spotted the Tebbi warships on the gray horizon, and turned toward the open sea. They lost them for the next few hours, then were caught again. The former *Berron's* ship and two other vessels continued south, drawing off the Tebbi ships long enough for the others to make Têfos safely. In the stormy weather that broke upon the Tebbi task force and hid the evacuation ships from them, they approached the port of Milou. There, in the city from which they had first struck out for the Tebbi coast, sent off by cheering crowds, they returned grim and sober. The surprise arrival wore off quickly and the weary troops were taken ashore.

Serpan d'Elous ordered *Serpan* de-Sotos to stay in Milou with their troops and tell their story to the *Pangressa-Marzag*: they were all under the orders of the acting-*Berron*, who had no doubt gone mad in their retreat. Then Set-d'Elous, shed of his uniform, set out in a fishing vessel, and steered north back across the sea, trying to find the tiny rocky harbor of Karêgosz. Tebbi warships paraded around the points, awaiting Sekuatean ships that might attempt any further evacuations as the renegade *Serpan* had done. Already the main Tebbi news bulletins marked his feat with a mix of restrained applause and not-so-subtle cursing from the office of Marshal Rimsfüt in the re-captured capital. As for the *Pangressa-Marzag* in Seas, his commission had already been retired; final disposition awaited only recovery of the body, dead or alive. That was the order given by the head of the Council of Five, the quite elderly Kag-Gangus, son of Basura-Kanoun and Diert-Gangus, two of the original leaders of the revolution. Kag would soon be murdered by his nephew, the insane Jurian-Gangus, who was the real power on the Council.

Sailing the wretched trawler into Karêgosz late in the evening, disguised as a fisherman, Set-d'Elous searched the town, inquiring after his comrade from Earth. None knew of him, though one harbor pilot acknowledged that the Tebbi army had swept down upon the town from the moors to plug the leak of

Sekuatean troops. The man could not report on the results, but it was not difficult to fill in the blanks: his friend, and the remaining men left behind, had been slaughtered like the unfortunate soldiers at Sênich.

He turned to go, pausing at the sight of the green-grey sky overhead and blanketing the rocky hillsides, featureless plaster buildings perched precariously on the rocks around the harbor. The sky was filled with flecks of lightning, and he thought he saw the flash of a dragster peeling rubber, heard the roar of Jason's famous 456 cubic inch V-8 engine with the 800 CFM Holly doublepumper in the thunder that crackled around him.

He scanned the craggy shoreline for any sign of his friend's ghost as they sailed off under the brooding, charcoal clouds. Exhausted and distressed, the captain recalled the last words they had shared in Karêgosz as they supervised the boarding of the final boat:

"You know, I've been looking into these funny steam-powered cars they have here," Jason had said. "I think I've just about figured them out, I mean, like, how to make'em really haul ass, not that dinky thirty-miles-an-hour shit. I got one of them ETUR hidden in a barn back in—whatever the town's called. Worked on it all last winter, waiting for you to get done with your siege. Then you guys blew it, and had to retreat! Anyhow, it was just about finished—my modifications, I'm talking about. Should really burn some rubber down these Tebbi highways."

"You never could resist toying with whatever strange machines you find."

"Better'n your hobby."

"My hobby? What's that?"

"Gettin' yourself in a helluva lotta trouble all the time!"

Anticipating the shoreline of Milou and dreading the arrival, he carried his official report securely in the upper left chamber of his heart, there to burn him the rest of his life. His best friend, whom he had tried to protect from the wild twists and turns of Ghoupallean fate; who had risked all the horrors by returning to save his interdimensional mentor; who had formed his own army just to fight across Tebbicousimankalê in the midst of someone else's war; who had actually reached him and who was only a day away from escaping the ravaged land for the safety of the sea—was now gone. And he, victim and victimizer, stood stock still with that realization, knuckles white as he gripped the railing. He watched the sea, knowing that never again would he allow another person to pass through the tangent to Ghoupallesz. Of that he was determined. He'd had his conversion, sworn his bloody allegiance, and the oath was cut clearly into his brain: *never again.*

Jason Aronstein had died a noble death—in the service of those gods who love to gamble, who live to play handball with human heads, who laugh at the folly of men.

PART FOUR

I will show you fear in a handful of dust.

T. S. Eliot, *The Waste Land*

Chapter 28

When the Gods Played Handball
With Human Heads

In those days when the yellow sun bled crimson and never cleared the smothering horizon, the man who fancied himself the God of Evil from the Western Sky broke with tradition and strode through the snow fields from temperate regions of the south, firm in the belief that he carried the power to cleave the universe and meld the spirits of warriors long-sacrificed into a fighting force of tremendous ferocity. And as the storm wind crashed into his face, poised there on the bow of the ship out from Milou, he mocked the gods and dared them to give him their best shot, throw up their hardest obstacle, set his way full of danger and intrigue—hah! something interesting for a change. He heard in reply only the thumping of the engines far beneath him in the rusty steel hull.

—from *Tarag-d'Er Pazar* ("*Tales of my Father*") by Metour-d'Elous, 1562; translated by Sebastian E. Talbot

The memory of his last crossing of the Tebbi Sea filled him with remorse, and he cursed the gods for taking him up on his challenge. Busy netting their rackets on the court of the universe, they were using their cruelest burden on him: the razor's edge of events long past—ten years on Ghoupallesz and the endless stacks of tax returns on Earth. Those memories, like slivers and chips off porcelain tile artwork, cut into his eyes and sliced into his brain, severing the tenuous grasp he already had on reality. To those frayed ends he clung, willing them to hold through just one more mission. With Tammy on Agani Island and Michael stowed away in Lyas, he could concentrate on the mission. Only then, he hesitantly promised the seven winds and the two suns, he would relax his grip and allow his sanity to fall to the whim of those athletic gods. His only wish was that such a new life would take a different turn and find a more fruitful, pleasant existence than one that he could ever dream.

"Sometimes dreams can come true," he heard the northwest wind laughing, feeling the cold salt spray on his face, his hair tossed around like demons fighting to be free. But it was a human voice he had automatically translated from Ghoupallêan.

He turned to his comrade there at the railing and offered a callow grin, as though he had caught himself being too serious and wanted to hide the fact from his friend. No longer in the *Gourran-Arumê*, nor in *Jêpedor-regêlad* number 102, they were simply friends on this last of all missions: he and his former Second, Aroun-de-Sotos.

"And sometimes dreams become nightmares," he replied finally, in Ghoupallêan.

Aroun-de-Sotos was not referring to the dreams of his ex-captain. He meant his own heroic desires, which the return of Set-d'Elous had unleashed. Ten years before, on that misty morning in the new springtime, de-Sotos was the last to disembark from the freighter in Milou. He was immediately taken into custody to answer for his men. They were all under the orders of *Berron* Set-d'Elous, just before he was relieved of command, he told the military court in Selauê. He explained that the *Berron* had thought it the best course of action given the approaching Tebbi forces. Acting-*Berron* they corrected him. The acting-*Berron*'s all-consuming attention to getting his own men away, the court argued, had left other units of the *Arumê-de-Nog* to slaughter. There was nothing more he could say, no words with which to defend himself, de-Sotos knew. The explanation could only come from his captain—who was *Berron* for three days—and from his strange words, and from his history book. De-Sotos had seen its worn pages with his own eyes: the date of printing, the name of the *Berron's* son stamped on it as the author. The events his commander had described to him had actually occurred—the Battle of Sênich, the succession of Tatandelus as *Berron*, were but two examples. He *had* to believe—though he had still protested as he boarded the ship in Karêgosz.

Set-d'Elous—whose full story de-Sotos would not know for several years—returned to Karêgosz for the remaining troops but found none, so he had steamed back toward Milou. Another vessel they met passed the news that the harbor was closed. They sailed on to Biznuik but were again turned away. He elected to sail on to Selauê, and there they sneaked into the harbor at night like ghosts. At that time Selauê was not a safe place to remain. As the closest major Sekuatean city to the recaptured Tebbi bases in Adanê, his beloved Selauê—city of fountains and landscaped boulevards that was his Ghoupallean home—would become the first victim of aerial bombing in their history—a method of warfare up to then considered cowardly and ignoble by the nations of Ghoupallesz.

He made his way along the coastal roads, alternately hiding and begging for food as many did during the war years. By the end of the year, as winter blew across the southern chaparral country, he finally arrived in Lyas. He paused only to take a look at the old apartment building where he had first met Zaura-Matousz. Then he rushed to the tangent outside the city, lost on the fringes of the desert, and returned to the quarry he knew so well.

It was just before dawn there. On the calendar he kept sealed in plastic between two rocks, he'd marked the day of his departure; a fresh look showed him he had missed three days. He vowed right then and there *never* to return to that world where so much had happened, so much good and so much evil, and he knew he was responsible for some of each.

During his nearly year-long journey across Sekuate he had lost weight, and when he showed up for his shift that night, Joyce remarked how fit he looked, asked about his diet plan. He was still new there. He did not know Michael yet. And Tammy was that skinny blonde girl at the end of the row who was always giggling.

The Trêpolium High Penitentiary, east of Selauê, was reserved for the hardest of criminals and all military ones. In his cell there, Aroun-de-Sotos, stripped of his rank, had time at last to finish reading the infamous history book his captain had left while transferred to the headquarters near Karêgosz. He did not steal it; it was his duty as Second to secure his commander's papers should they be important for military records. As precious as he believed the book to be, he feared losing it if he offered it as evidence at his trial. He found it among his personal effects in his cell, however, and there he read its aged pages, veritable lists of events now as familiar as the back of his hand. And more of the history was happening with each day that passed: the retreat of Sekuatean forces through Fenula and Rox, their eventual surrender before the expected final battle at Milipour in Bezua-hü. He told the court what would happen and was called treasonous. How dare he predict the fall of the Empire's great army!

Then the terms of the treaty were spelled out—the main points exactly as prisoner de-Sotos had stated—limiting Sekuatean forces to their original territory as measured after annexation of neighboring countries. So he was brought before a special committee of the *Pangressa-Marzag* and questioned.

After the liberation of the northern states of Zissekap from Sekuate's grip came the massive invasion of the Empire by the vengeful forces of the Northern Alliance. Sekuate was cut into quarters and a noose tightened around the capital of Seas. When the great palace was stormed, the last two members of the Gangus Council (now the "Council of Two") were found hiding deep in the ancient dungeons. Brutal Metour-Gangus and his wife, Mourta—the "Butcher and Baker of Seas," the "Devil and his Consort"—were executed. The scaffolding was erected in the same square fronting the palace's impressive facade where earlier had stood the hundreds of thousands of soldiers to receive the Council members' farewell salute before marching off to their deaths in foreign lands, far from home.

Sekuate was then ruled by a governmental council from the Northern Alliance. A Redistribution Conference was convened in 1540 to carve up the Empire, diplomats attempting to form again several small nations that had ceased to exist during the Gangus government's reign. Many of those former governments had not survived; those that did demanded large concessions as their just compensation. The eastern city of Sairel was given to the reconstituted nation of Ilait, an otherwise barren plateau. In protest, the Sekuatean army, reorganized but designated as a defensive force, moved to occupy Sairel district. Troops of the Northern Alliance stationed in the newly formed nation of Arêsz in the northwest were ordered across the border into Selauê district. However, Selauê, in older times its own kingdom, city-state, and republic, and was originally settled by Danid rather than Rouê peoples, began asserting its independence from the tainted rule of Seas.

Everything happened exactly as prisoner RG-17181, Aroun-de-Sotos, had stated. Kept completely isolated from all news bulletins, they knew he could not have formed his conjectures solely from recent information, the courts concluded. Therefore, on the first day of *Keruk* in 1541, he was finally released from prison, a parchment of pardon in his hand signed by the newly appointed *Berron*, Katoum-d'Airen. He returned to Selauê where he continued to be banned from military involvement and, having no family since the war's end, he settled in with a new one, working in their carpentry shop.

The sudden appearance of Set-d'Elous had sent equally powerful jolts of hatred and joy through him. After a fist fight and a night of drinking *skual*, his captain asked him to enlist in a mission. The weary warrior signed on gladly. There was not a board to saw or a peg to be hammered so important as the chance to get his old blood-lust flowing again. Damn the army of Sekuate! Praise to Set-d'Elous, who returned to him his sullen dignity with a vengeful purpose!

Sailing now in sight of land along the rugged, foggy Tebbicousimankalê coast, the two ex-*Jêpedor* turned to rejoin their band of mercenaries below, final plans yet to be made. As they descended the stairs to the main deck, Aroun-de-Sotos took the shoulder of his captain and held him back a moment, telling him he believed everything he had said about future events.

"What have you read about this mission of ours?" he then asked.

"There is no book written about this," Set-d'Elous answered, continuing down the stairs.

* ✳ *

Twenty hills to Poxantium—the city at the great bend of the mighty Qanlê River that split the subcontinent in two like a narrow, snaking sea—they rode after landing at Pontou. The land was bursting with a spring-like delight, as though fields of daisies spread from horizon to horizon, sunflowers sprouting at every turn, laughing children at every crossroad, welcoming strangers at the inns where they stayed, the people joyful of war's end. And there in the brown six-floor plaster-walled townhomes of the eastern Tebbi city, they arrived on *Ghulad-25*, a warm autumn evening in the uneventful year of 1544, at the appointed place. As expected.

"*Kalmonê-se*," the white-bearded, leather-skinned man spoke clearly and with reverence when Set-d'Elous and his men entered the house.

Aroun-de-Sotos, immediately cautious, had no idea why this old man would address his captain in such a stilted manner. He stayed back, listening to them talk, watching their every gesture. Again he felt excitement, the duty of protecting his *Serpan* from harm. It was true that he was nothing more than a carpenter without Set-d'Elous to bring him back to adventure. Without him, he could never hope to find his way into Zetinê for the mission of his dreams. Not even his former captain could possibly know the remarkable secret he had drawn from his prison reading. There in the book his captain had tried to hide from him, the Book of the Future, he had found his destiny as sure as he could see his face in a mirror.

They sat with the old man of the house, Set's trusted confidant for hundreds of days tossed across a hundred years. Dorgat-Ouvaxe was as gracious and informative as always, Set-d'Elous noticed, but this time he began to feel uneasy at the man's overly polite speech. He began to wonder if Tebbi police were even now in the closets ready to pounce upon them and arrest them as former Sekuatean officers of the Invasion. He had to trust this last remaining partner of the earlier mission to free Queen Jinetta— long ago, when he had gotten the *gealan* business from Renée as a reward and moved to Lyas and met his darling Zaura and....

The woman who had opened the door to them, his rotund wife, poured them *drül* and let them drop in a few crisp *juni* for flavor. He knew she would not be so kind if they were mere pawns of the national security forces.

"She's there," old Ouvaxe said in his most polite level of Ghoupallêan, "held in the castle of the high priest T'UN-DAX. It's common knowledge in the capital, but it's not reported officially in bulletins. My contact said there is talk of war with us"—with Tebbicousimankalê, he meant—"because of our delay in settling the treaty. They are serious about the terms and won't hesitate to kill the Lady Jinetta if they suspect those terms will not be met."

"And will they be met?" the captain, Set-d'Elous, sat up and asked, taking one of the hot *jol* offered by the stout, jovial woman.

"In the capital, people have no constitution for the hostage situation, because the Lady Jinetta is the wife of a man forced from office."

"What...?"

"It was a shameful act," and he bowed low as though it were all his fault. "Our prime minister, Arrin-Sassat, who faced the Zetin at the negotiation table and forged the treaty which helped us defeat the bastard Sekuateans—pardons, My Lord, whom I know to be different from the Invaders—the man who willingly gave his wife over as hostage of the barbarian Zetin—was found in a *qala* with a Lady of the *Oustarrê*."

"The *Oustarrê*?"

"A member of the royal house," Ouvaxe explained, using a hushed voice which again alerted d'Elous. "She was a sister of the *Mexas*—by a concubine, though, not by his true spouse. Still, they used it to force him from office. They were separated for seventeen days, as is required, and he was forced to apologize to the *Mexas* before the full Assembly. He performed a fine and dignified dance of penitence, but in the end he was still dismissed."

"Without his rank, he has no power to effect policies which would settle the treaty. He has no way to return his wife safely."

"Yes, My Lord. It is beyond his control now. The royal house has no fortune invested in the foreign-born wife of a scandalous man. They would prefer to see our mountainous territory remain in our family rather than save the life of one woman."

"There's the scandal, Ouvaxe!" the captain cried. "They have no idea who she really is, or all that she has done on this world. The fools would let die an angel who—"

"We are fools, the people of Tebbicousimankalê," he wept, bowing.

"Tell me the rest."

"She is held there, in the castle called KVANN-STA' PO'CIX—near the city of S'AM. It is said she is kept in comfort, yet her life is directed by *utê*—boy eunuchs—and the other servants of the *Ghêrata*. She is paraded before the Zetin people on holy days, as a symbol of Southern treachery. Rumors say she lives in chains, and brought out for display at formal dinners presided over by the high priest whenever he visits. Whenever he is not in residence...there are tales of abuse."

"Then we must rescue her at once."

"That is the critical factor, time being a very limited commodity. If your schedule is correct and your prediction true, the Lady Jinetta will be taken from the castle and executed in twenty-nine days."

"Twenty-nine days?" He pondered a moment, then turned to de-Sotos at the end of the table. "No need to wait until the last moment just to be dramatic. We'll leave in the morning."

* * *

Breakfast was a bowl of *tabli* and a tall stack of *sebal* to dip in it, washed down with bottles of *gor*. Then he turned to his men, de-

Sotos at his side, all of them dressed for battle, armed, clothed in their rough, northern garb, and spoke to them of their mission. In Selauê he had found three former *regêlad* members who had been mere lads when he commanded them during the Tebbi invasion. Out of the army now, they were forced into retirement with the banning of the military by the *Nog-Megank-Ulsinyn* occupational government. Outside the garrison, he enlisted a few more who remembered him as a hero who had tried to save his men from certain death. They were nine when they met Dorgat-Ouvaxe in Poxantium—and he added two of his strongest partisans, muscle-bound monsters with obedient faces. Also his nephew, Zaran-Ouvaxe, a mechanical genius on par with the captain's friend Jason. The elder Ouvaxe would arrange everything and meet them at the mission's end. Now they were thirteen: Set-d'Elous and his twelve apostles.

Upriver from Poxantium where the shoreline narrowed at the town of Qanlê, they found the first bridge to cross; being wider, only ferries were used further downriver. It was northeast of Qanlê that the river of the same name turned sharply up into the mountains—cutting through the lofty *Zet-Saer*. The 'Wall of Zet' it was called, so sheer and towering were its ramparts. On prior visits to Ghoupallesz, he had converted the elevations on a map from *mest* to meters and found its tallest peak to be more than a mile higher than Mt. Everest in the Himalayas. Swirling like a frozen hurricane of rock and ice around the Alaun plateau, it could still be breached by traveling between the great curving arcs of mountain peaks. The most prominent passage was along the Qanlê River. When the grade became too steep, they would have to strike overland, walking the snow fields and skirting glaciers pocked with crevasses. Despite the treacherous passage, the steep gorges had long been feared as a gateway of invasion for both directions and it was patrolled and guarded with religious fervor.

Snow-smeared peaks shredded the blanket of clouds, twisting the world into a kaleidoscope as he was thrown down on his back, thunder roaring in his head, ears ringing and eyes filled with horror. His opponent's spear was beside his outstretched hand. Quickly, he grasped the staff and flung it up just in time to catch the breastplate rushing at him, hurling its mass up and over his own body, letting the warrior crash behind him.

As he rolled over in the snow, he saw a trail of crimson essence and strings of organs dissected by the blade. The warrior still struggled to escape: crawling, one hand trying to hold in his seeping guts. The spear stood out from the chest, slapping back and forth with every shaky step. He jerked the shaft free with his blood-stained fists and the warrior folded against the icy ground. As he raised the lance, it caught a glimmer of sunlight, and he brought the lance down hard, splitting the rock.

The warrior still defied death, so he again removed the spear, preparing for another stab. Then he stopped, seeing the Zetin warrior wrenching the stubby knife from its scabbard and flinging it up to the face. Blood splattered the snow with fat globules as the warrior finished his death mask.

Set-d'Elous, satisfied he had done his duty, sank to his knees as his men rushed down the icy slope toward him, calling him by his former rank: "*Serpan, Serpan!*"

With his men gathered around him and de-Sotos checking his nicks, he scanned the circle of faces, thinking of home and friends who did not speak his language.

"This is *here*?" he asked, dazed, in English. "On this mission? Not the siege of Siaa?"

De-Sotos, having learned a few words of his captain's language during his prison study, responded: "Here, now, one-five-four-four year, in *Zetinê*."

Set-d'Elous struggled to his feet. "But I've done this before."

On the high slopes near the Zetin temple of TJANN-DAX, a crisp green noontide embraced them. With broccoli clouds drifting innocently overhead, their thoughts were tempted away from their mission. A Zetin border patrol met them on a traversing ridge and opened fire. Two of their men were immediately struck down but the mercenaries from Selauê, wearing air masks for the altitude, quickly returned fire and in less than a *peth* had them down. Coming back to their dead comrades, they arranged the bodies in straight lines, set the severed heads atop the necks, burnt ends together. As they regarded the injuries from the Zetin Tnx-103 gun—a heavier version of the Sekuatean army's AT, they chose to leave them for the next snowfall. They would be buried soon enough; burning the corpses, as was Ghoupalle custom, would alert other patrols.

Continuing, the captain was sullen. Too many bad omens, dreams coming true. He was lost in a time and place which for all he knew could be inside his head. And he could not get out of it. If he were only trapped within his imagination—as many in the service center already suspected—then he might never save Gina. He had to believe she really was in danger and that he and his men were the only ones who could rescue her. The Tebbi government had given up on her—so how could he?

Before them on the horizon stood the Pinnacles, the mile-high needles of bare rock that sprouted from a vast mountain dome, called *Rn-Jarr* in the Zetin language and *Zet-prix* in Ghoupallêan, the top of the Wall. A sky filled with spires, stretching up to puncture the suns, slicing the sky into slivers. There, within sight of the glorious *Zet-prix*, they left the body of another member who died from lack of oxygen from a faulty mask. The cathedral of stone towers would serve as a fitting memorial, he decided. Skirting the Pinnacles, they began their descent to the somewhat less high Alaun plateau.

Young Ouvaxe reminded the captain that the castle was to the east of where they would break from the mountains. Perched on the foothills of the north side of the Zet mountains, they had a spectacular view of the entire plateau. The castle Kvann-sta' Po'cix was not one that would be strongly guarded, Young Ouvaxe told him. Positioned on the foothills outside the city of S'am, it was already protected from three sides. Only the mountain side was vulnerable—yet only from adventurous mountaineers. As it was the occasional pleasure palace of the ambassador Ut'r-BkanN, there were likely to be many concubines and servants. In all other days it served as the high temple of T'un-Dax, so their *Ghêrata*—the legion of priests and attendants—would also be present.

The thirteenth night out of Qanlê, the wary de-Sotos watched his captain prepare to walk among the Zetin. Picking up some of the language years before while living on Karluk Island, he could produce the rough, guttural sounds with astonishing accuracy. "Because I clear my throat a lot," he joked. His appearance needed changing the most. Zetin were of stocky build, with thick trunks and muscular limbs. Their hairy faces were wide, cheekbones pronounced, foreheads high, heads square—unattractive by Ghoupalle standards. Then there were the marks every Zetin man wore called Zk'ra—prominent tattoos or cuts made across the cheeks under the eyes. The reddish wig he produced from his pack would transform his short, clean-cut Ghoupalle look into the arctic warrior's long, frazzled battle mane. The small *süggor* they killed would provide blood for striping his beard in warrior fashion. The sharp-hooked *Kalêf* shoulder epaulets taken off the dead warrior would make him authentic. Other decorations were lifted from the Zetin patrol they had encountered: the flowing feather arm bands, enameled leather breastplate, shin guards of *rênar*, and a heavy necklace of *jalo* claws.

In the morning, his men thought their camp had been invaded by Zetin warriors.

✳ ✳ ✳

Out of the mists, like a spirit condensing into view, she rose above the gray *papê* grass at the crest of the slope, behind her the autumnal sky billowing over the plateau, a charcoal gray streaked with pink lightning, like the beast she rode, wild splashes of black across its rump and a shaggy mane of auburn dreadlocks. The maiden—she must have been to be so posed—rose on her *Jêpe*, scanning the stark landscape before her, seeing him watching her, perhaps considering whether or not he were to be her mate.

He glanced away from her, deciding her familiarity was no accident. She had ridden her *Jêpe* before on a hill similar to this one, he recalled. The thought disturbed him.

"*Kanê-se pokem parten ga,*" de-Sotos spoke, urging him to keep moving.

Young mercenary Secour-Atisz suggested they capture the girl for themselves, wanting to get back at the Zetin for the crimes of generations past.

De-Sotos saw his leader entranced by the girl. No doubt she was wondering why this Zetin warrior was traveling with men who appeared, despite the distance, to be Tebbi.

"*Kanê,* mission is go—we go," de-Sotos called to him, impressing his captain with his English studies.

"I've been here before," Set-d'Elous muttered. He squinted hard to see her in the dim light. Turning to de-Sotos, his eyes desperate, his was voice strained: "This is happening now? Not in the days of the siege?"

"Yes," de-Sotos replied, puzzled. "New mission."

Then, as the lustful young recruit with the big mouth started forward on his *Jêpe,* the captain ordered him back. Before he could take further action, Atisz pulled his AT from his saddle holster and fired a shot into the forehead of the Zetin girl. She fell from her *Jêpe* in slow-motion, the crash against the hard earth heard only in the minds of her witnesses.

Returning to the others, the stubby barrel of his AT still glowing, Atisz smiled, expecting thanks.

"*Klux-bane-durren bretu alat zamas-sekâm-Zetin-klux stae,*" Atisz crowed proudly. 'That bitch can't make any more of them little Zetin bastards now.'

In a heartbeat, the captain had his own AT directed at the man and squeezed the trigger with no hesitation. The orange plasma burst against his throat, burned a passage through, and fell to the ground behind him, followed two *pii* later by the man's body, sliding from his saddle.

Off they rode then, as fast as they could, hearing on the arctic wind the anguished scream of her husband.

Their final plans were made when the gray stone towers of KVANN-STA' PO'CIX swung up to meet the dark emerald clouds settling over the vast plateau. In Zetin style, dungeons were at the top. The lord lived on the ground floor, and each lesser ranking resident stayed on successively higher floors. The number of stairs residents were obliged to march up each day was testament to their rank: the fewer steps, the higher the rank. Underground rooms were used to keep the lord's intimate guests close at hand. The mercenaries did not know whether to seek the Lady Jinetta in the high tower or the concubine rooms set in the depths of the hillside.

The captain lay back against the rocks, watching the small blue sun setting, thinking it was the full moon he had left back in Earth's sky. In that solemn flicker of contemplation, he could feel the gravity of the dream land encroaching steadily onto his private domain. He wanted to be called the Professor again, he decided, preferring his days teaching at the Selauê Academy to his days commanding at the Selauê garrison. Looking over to see what de-Sotos was doing, he remarked to himself that here was a true soldier, a man destined to die fighting. And Samot-Angêron. Here was a man so wrapped up in his plots and conspiracies that were the world to go straight he would die of boredom. And the now middle-aged Pan-Dossar, the youngest member of his regiment when they marched off to Milou for the Tebbi invasion, now looked positively drained after their twenty-day journey through the Zet Mountains. Some of the others stood gazing down at the lights of S'AM in the distance. And old Ouvaxe's nephew, Zaran, definitely was no soldier but a scientist, busy unpacking the special equipment they had carried with them, some mechanical thing he saw unfolding.

The dream land now was a government-issue metal desk stacked with two weeks' backlog of tax returns waiting for him to check for accuracy and determine the amount of tax which was underreported by the free-loaders and cheats he loathed. Perhaps there would be overtime work, at time-and-a-half pay, to clear it all out. He closed his eyes, listened to the murmur of his men for a while, and allowed himself to slide effortlessly over the edge of reality.

The desks were arranged the same when the door swung gently aside and he entered. He was afraid his Zetin disguise would alarm them, at first, but no one seemed to notice. Typical. He was nobody.

As he walked down the aisle between the gray metal desks, it seemed most of his colleagues were away at lunch. Joyce was at her desk, talking on the phone. Felix had his head buried in an *Omni* magazine. Ahead was Fat Ken's desk, and the smug tax examiner pulled his sneakered feet off his desktop, swiveling the squeaky chair around to face him.

"Gotcha purdy good last night, didn't I?" laughed Fat Ken, folding his newspaper.

The Professor paused, wondering what he meant, then turned toward his own desk, there in the corner. The top was cleared of tax returns, file folders, the miscellaneous forms he needed. Didn't they need him to help with the backlog?

He went to the metal shelving nearby to retrieve the next bucket of files to work on. The woman standing there was Cassie. Her surprised smile flipped to an angry grimace. She brought her hand up to slap his face but he caught her wrist.

"Where's Michael?" she asked.

"He's in the hospital," he answered without thought.

"What happened to him?"

"He had an accident, you might say. Tammy, too. She's in the hospital, too—"

"Tammy? *And* Michael?" Cassie shrieked, drawing Joyce's attention.

"Well, yes. I thought you knew."

"I didn't *mean* to blow'em up," she cried, and threw her hands to her face. "It was...an accident. Really! I was only gonna scare'em!"

The Professor did not know what she was talking about. Neither did he know what to say to console her—or what he had already said but should not have said. Either way, he decided he'd better get something for lunch. There was not much break time remaining.

"How about some more tuna?" Ken called.

He wondered what Ken meant by that, finding another door

and pushing it open.

Chapter 29

Love

Stepping into the corridor, he saw the walls set with huge gray stones like a Medieval castle, long tapestries of Zetin gods and great warriors hanging on the walls, torches set in slots at regular intervals. A chilly draft sailed through the corridor and he pulled up his stiff, studded collar, shaking his head.

The door had already closed behind him. As he paused to wonder whether he had actually just walked through the service center department, he felt a presence and spun around. It was Aroun-de-Sotos and Samot-Angêron, whom he had let in. After walking in as one of the castle guards, he had made his way according to the floor plan Ouvaxe had obtained from historical records, and opened a side door for his partners. With everyone's responsibilities clear, he left for the main hall.

There, high rafters stretched overhead, made of some material like elephant tusks, the walls were lined with polished logs, and *jalo* heads were set on spears about the room. The floor was a patchwork of shiny yellow tiles he thought were *grangi* shells. Momentarily in awe, he regarded the rustic symbols of Zetin culture.

A team of temple attendants distracted him from that fierce collage, clad as they were in their pure white loincloths and open vests that tied at the throat. They were down on their knees cleaning the huge floor with vile smelling sticks of soap, rolling them along the tiles and wiping after. The echo of the soap sticks hitting the tiles and the swishing of their towels made him think of the nightshifters back in Code & Edit, stamping numbers on endless stacks of tax returns.

One girl straightened up, bowed until her short hair brushed the floor, whispering plaintively, "Z'"—which he knew meant literally 'man' but in context was like 'my lord'.

He ignored her, trying to remember Ouvaxe's directions so he would not have to retrieve the sketch hidden inside his jacket. The passage he wanted was to the left, he calculated—left, that was, when facing the giant statue of the ancient Wiseman DNT'O-KRA', who had been born with three eyes, all of which worked.

The cleaning girl looked Ghoupalle, and when he approached she eyed him suspiciously. He remembered that he wore the appearance of a Zetin. Naturally, she was wary of him.

"Z'ITAC'...GZAX," he muttered gruffly, trying to act Zetin, pausing before the great statue, and gazed curiously down the side corridor. 'Don't worry, I'm tired.'

"AS-RUNN," she spoke, bowing low. 'Wise one.'

"Aaa...umm...HA-CINN-ST-GLÜ," he responded—appropriate to spoken words of humility, an invocation of their gods: 'Many good spirits to you.'

A real Zetin would not have been so polite to a mere slave girl, he cursed himself. But it was too late to take back his kind words.

Stepping past her, she resumed her work, hitching up her loincloth which had slipped during her consternation.

He entered the wide, torch-lined avenue, moving with tension—acting as a Zetin would act. He saw another guard ahead in the corridor. The Zetin was fondling a slave girl. So he grabbed the next maid he saw and gave her rump a playful squeeze. She did not resist his advance, but fell limp in his arms—as was required, he presumed. He felt ashamed. He wanted to free all of the prisoners in KVANN-STA' PO'CIX. There was only room for one, though, and that thought began to burn through him.

Down the corridor, two other guards passed him, spoke to him about a party or meeting that night and how many slave women there would be. He chuckled with them but spoke only "KR"—an affirmative response. That was not uncommon, Zetin being people of few words; the language gave meaning to single phonemes rather than the usual combinations of sounds needed to form words in Ghoupallêan—or English.

In a dark alcove, he paused to check his sketch map, and saw that he had to pass through the banquet hall to continue to the staircase leading below ground. He had decided to search for Gina among the concubines first, despite the anxiety he felt at the possibility she was one. A team of guards passed him seconds after he put away his sketch.

"DK'RAL," he said, a warrior greeting, literally 'cold heart'. Saluting each other, they continued on.

Once down to the next level, he shoved his hand inside his jacket for the sketch but it was missing. He realized that he had probably dropped it when the guards surprised him. It was too late to retrieve it. He was deep inside the castle and too far into the mission to jeopardize their carefully timed plan. His means of escape, provided by the younger Ouvaxe, would be in place at a certain time. If he were to get away cleanly, there would be only a few *pii* of opportunity.

The second level below the main floor was simple: long corridors with rusting metal doors set in its walls, each containing the private chamber of a concubine, locked from the outside, comfortable but spare inside. He knew which door: the eleventh one on the right. Ouvaxe's contact in Zetinê had reported the Lady Jinetta was kept in that room. The woman the spy had seen was a Ghoupalle, and had long, blond hair down her back. True blond hair was uncommon even among Ghoupalle people, but the Zetin lord reportedly prized it above all her attributes. Peeking through the barred window, he had no doubt it was her.

There in the center of the dimly lit chamber he saw a woman standing, her arms stretched up and over her head by chains attached to her wrists. Her toes barely touched the tiled floor. In the flickering torchlight, her unclothed figure was taut and the curve of her back faced him. Spilling down her shoulders was the cascade of blond hair.

He examined the lock, a bolt that could be opened by anyone. Testing the door a crack, he glanced up and down the corridor before swinging it open. He rushed in with knife drawn, coming up behind her and cupping his hand over her mouth to silence her scream as he ran the blade up her arm to the leather cuff at her wrist. She squirmed wildly, fearing whatever she had learned to fear.

He spoke into her ear, "It's me, Gina. I've come to save you—like I always do."

She relaxed a little, and when he had cut the second wrist cuff loose, she collapsed in his arms. He lowered her to the floor, brushed her hair away and gazed down upon the face of a stranger. The woman, a girl of twenty or so, opened her eyes and regarded him. She brought her arms up to cover herself. She was weak and the sight of another Zetin warrior caused her nearly to pass out.

"I'm not Zetin," he spoke to her. "It's my disguise."

She did not seem to understand, and he realized he had spoken in English. But repeating it in Ghoupallêan brought no better response.

Their eyes met again: she was not Gina.

"*Fan-se gumai*?" he uttered. 'Who are you?'

The girl still did not seem to understand him so he repeated his question. He asked about her health, if she could walk, and how long she had been in the castle. None of his words registered on her face and he thought she was too dazed to understand him.

She lifted her hand to his face, caressing his cheek, and something like a smile slid quickly across her face.

"Thank—you," her words spilled out. It was English, he heard. "Who—are—you?"

He sat her against the wall.

"I came to rescue you—or someone like you." He looked around the room for something to cover her. "Are you Ghoupalle?"

"Everybody—" she started, then paused to catch her breath, "—keeps asking me that. Just what the hell—is a 'Goo-pull'?"

"I guess you're not. By your accent, I guess you're from Earth—America, right?"

"From *Earth*? What're you talking about?"

❈ ❈ ❈

Dressed in a *kuiparra* robe from the hook on the wall, she threw her hair back over her shoulders and stood before him with some measure of confidence.

"We had car trouble," she began, then paused to load more words, "and my boyfriend pulled off the road, said he'd go to a gas station, about a mile away. It was across a field. It was dark. I didn't want to stay by myself. We walked through this field. We took a step and it was like we walked through some invisible door. We saw it only at the very last second. We didn't even have a chance to go around it. It appeared right there as we stepped into it—just like magic!"

The land they found themselves in was Zetinê, and the ones who found them were Zetin. The next few months she described as a hell she never could have imagined from her worst nightmares. She and her boyfriend were separated from the day they arrived at the castle. Although she knew him to be held in the next cell, she never saw or spoke to him. She got a break when the Zetin lord discovered she spoke the same language as the hostage from Tebbicousimankalê. Only a sophomore at a private college in Iowa, she found herself the personal maid to the Lady Jinetta. They did not speak often, always being under surveillance, but her new job did free her from the nightly assaults. When she allowed the Lady the comfort of a footstool to take the weight off her arms when she was once strung up like her—punishment for refusing to honor the lord's request—the girl herself was taken to a cell and stretched to the ceiling, left exposed for any warrior who might want her.

"I don't know how long I've been here, because there's no time in this place. Feels like three, maybe six months—I don't know."

"It's probably longer than you think, because of the time differentials between the two worlds," he said, helping her up. "We still age at Earth speed while we're here. What do you remember?"

"Well...I remember Jimmy Carter was president when we got

lost and ended up here."

He was about to tell her how American politics had gone since then, but the approaching footsteps stopped him.

"AS-SKN!" the guard snapped.

The Zetin warrior who on weekdays was a quiet tax examiner regarded the intruder and immediately jerked the girl to her feet. As the guard stared through the partially opened door, the Professor took her arm and spun her around, flinging her down on the floor. He turned and growled at the guard: "AMT'A GLZAX EM KAX-HOH'!" He raised his fist to strike the woman. 'This one's mine, so get lost!'

The enraged stream of utterances that shot back from the real Zetin's mouth he did not understand, but he got the meaning. The warrior stormed into the chamber, KL drawn, saliva running off his tongue—a nasty habit of Zetin warriors when they were filled with bloodlust. Something like 'How dare you speak that way to me when I'm your superior officer' was the Professor's hasty translation, drawing his own KL.

The girl fell back, scrambling to the corner as the Professor moved to intercept the attacking warrior, catching the KL with his own blade and pushing the Zetin back against the metal door jamb. The Zetin growled and promptly bit the Professor's arm. They slid back into the chamber, collapsing on the floor and rolling across the tiles, wrapped around each other, hands holding their blades from each other's throat.

"If you want—to get out—of here—" he called to the girl as he struggled face to face with the Zetin, "why don't you—give me—a hand?"

She sprang up and grabbed the loose end of the chain and began hooking it around the Zetin's extended foot. When he was fastened, she rushed to a lever in the wall by the door and pulled it. The chain began to rise, winding around a recessed wheel in the ceiling, dragging the Zetin away from the Professor.

He jumped up, kicked the Zetin's KL away, and positioned his knife at the warrior's throat. As the Zetin was lofted toward the ceiling, the Professor slid his blade between the warrior's black breastplate and spiked choker, piercing the collar. Blood shot out like an opened soda bottle. The Zetin was left dangling from the ceiling, blood forming a pool where the girl had once stood. The girl took the knife from the Professor and thrust it into the Zetin's groin. There was no cry; he was already dead.

They listened at the door. Then the girl directed him to the next cell where they found her boyfriend. She could hear him when he screamed, she said, but the walls were too thick to talk to each other. She had been so close to him and yet separated the four Ghoupalle years they had been imprisoned.

The young man was strung up nude in the same manner. They immediately cut him down. His arms dropped to his sides, limp, drained. As his girlfriend held him in her arms on the floor, the Professor grabbed the robe from the hook. Recovering, the youth saw that someone had come to free him, but he had no words for his saviors. He rolled on his side, facing away from his girlfriend, pushing her back as she tried to kiss him.

"We've come to rescue you," he told the boy. "Can you walk?"

"Yes," he mumbled, reluctantly.

"Let's go, then."

"I'm not leaving without *that*," the young man, skinny and haggard, demanded.

His gaze almost levitated the stout bottle on the shelf in the corner. They understood at once. In the bottle, buoyed in a blue liquid, was a set of male organs.

"Take care of them," he told de-Sotos when they reached the designated place.

Giving them two additional captives to spirit out of the castle—the hallways flowing with guests, servants, and guards—was not what they expected. Hidden among the shadows of a little used corridor, the girl and her boyfriend waited barefoot on the chilly stone floor, clothed in rough woolen robes, still in shock at their cruel imprisonment and their sudden freedom. Being with men who looked more like themselves than Zetin, they began to relax. One of them spoke broken English and said they were part of the same team, mercenaries from Selauê. Angêron boasted they were a crack unit of the Special Services battalion of the Second *Coraesz*, but the collegians cared little about details. In their minds was the single question of whether they could, once free of the castle, return to Earth.

Their mission was very critical, Aroun-de-Sotos stated, especially after hearing that a battery of warriors was on their way to the castle as official escort for the Zetin ambassador Ut'r-BkanN. They needed to be leaving the castle at this very moment instead of starting to wait for their leader, the impossible Set-d'Elous, to find the Lady Jinetta.

"But I know where she is," the girl interrupted. "I didn't know she was the one you were here for. I was her personal servant."

"Where—room—*Kalmonê* Jinetta?" de-Sotos asked.

"It's on the tenth floor. You can't miss it—the end of the hall—the one with the guards outside. She's always watched, you know—"

"Guards?" de-Sotos asked, wondering about his captain.

"Yes, about a dozen of them—always."

Listening carefully to his instructions, Angêron turned over the extra AT, assuring de-Sotos he would see to the safety of the two beside him. Then de-Sotos was off, running down the corridor after his captain, wearing only his courage and his Ghoupalle face in the Zetin world.

❈ ❈ ❈

The Professor raced up the long staircase to the fourth level, checked it, went on to the fifth, heard a banquet in progress, went to the sixth, then to the seventh.

Pausing for breath, he had to kill a guard who questioned his sloppy dress. He hated being told how to wear his Zetin uniform. They wrestled, his hand clamped tightly over the Zetin's mouth to keep him from calling out. Then he swung the KL up from his belt and pulled it out through the Zetin's throat. When he was agitated, he did not know his own strength in the lighter gravity of Ghoupallesz.

On the eighth level he found a warrior hovering over a

Ghoupalle woman on the floor and jerked his head back by his kinky red hair. The startled woman crawled out from under the Zetin, throwing her loincloth back into place. He lowered his KL and slit the lusty warrior's throat. The girl's eyes never left him, shocked to see Zetin kill Zetin. He tried to shake her off, telling her to 'get lost' because he had business elsewhere, but she pursued him, watching him from around each corner.

They had just arrived at the ninth floor when he turned suddenly at the sight of a guard column standing stiffly at attention against each wall. Retreating to a side room that was unlocked, he took the slave girl in his arms to better control her. Still shocked, her eyes were wide as she stared into his. He pressed her up against the wall, light from the torches on the corridor walls streaming through the bars, and clamped a gloved hand over her mouth. He whispered in Ghoupallêan: "I'm really Ghoupalle, from Selauê—so tell me—if you know—where is the room of the Tebbi woman called Jinetta?"

He waited, saw her eyes bulge with amazement. His grip relaxed, testing her desire to flee and she remained still. She brought her hand gently up to his face. Then, in a flash, she had examined his face with her fingers and discovered that the ZK'RA marks under his eyes were fake. A crooked, toothy smile suddenly reflected in her eyes.

The Professor spun around to confront the guard coming into the room.

"As..." the warrior spoke, curious.

He repeated his phrase about the girl being his and for the guard to go away, but the guard only laughed at him, turning to go.

With his attention fixed on the departing guard, the girl twisted free and shouted, "SEKUATANK-ZAX!"

The warrior rushed back, catching the girl against the wall, and shifted his gaze over at the man in Zetin garb with one eye mark smeared by her finger. His KL was immediately drawn, but instead of him the Zetin slashed at the girl. The Professor saw it was his only chance to escape and cursed the girl for insulting him, calling him a Sekuatean. He watched her die under the warrior's KL, as other guards rushed to the doorway to see the murder. He tried to hold his heartbeat in check, surrounded by the five Zetin warriors. The bloody loincloth was ripped from her body and he glanced down and saw her gut cut open. The guard offered him a string of intestine, dripping with sticky blood and waste, as satisfaction for her insult.

He was ushered from the room, the guards slapping him on the back, encouraging him to take another girl while they still had time—before the ambassador arrived at the castle. He shrugged it off, then realized he was not acting as a Zetin warrior should act. He became enraged, broke from their circle, and stormed down the corridor, presumably toward the concubine quarters.

Turning the corner, he faded into the shadows, letting his heartbeat return to normal.

Up on the tenth level, he heard the guards before he saw them, a large contingent, and he backed away from the bend in the corridor. It must be Gina's chamber, he thought. Heavily guarded, it was the main room on the floor. The words he could make out from their chatter told him the ambassador was due at any time. Then the Lady Jinetta would be brought out.

He sat on a bench at the top of the stairs, his heart racing too fast to continue. Their schedule had been shot, he knew, wondering if he could even get out of the castle himself. And Gina? And the lives of his men? It was all for him to decide; it was his dream.

"As-GLXE?" he heard a deep voice booming behind him. 'What are you doing?'

By the time he had translated the words in his head, he had been picked up and tossed down the stairs, tumbling to the bottom and crashing against the wooden railing there. His eyes focused on the giant, barrel-chested guard stomping down the stairs toward him, repeating the question. This Zetin was probably the Captain of the Guards, he surmised by the uniform, seeing he wore a band of extra long *jalo* claws around his forehead and his epaulets were more sharply upturned than those of the other guards.

"Here, commanded me, to wait-and-watch for ambassador," he tried to explain in his poor Zetin, once more being picked up.

The big Zetin, holding him up face to face, gave him a toothy, bitter-breathed grin. From kissing distance, the Zetin declared that the Professor was dumb, talked like someone's idiot son, and was too drunk to do his job. He was ordered back to the barracks. Then, just as he was about to ask why or where or how, he was told there would be no sex privileges for six nights.

The guard captain dropped him on the floor, gave him a firm nudge with his boot and stomped back up the stairs.

The Professor lay still for a moment, then he pulled himself up, his back against the railing, fearing to see the guard captain return and find him still there. With more concentrated effort he was able to get to his feet, feeling lightheaded, steadying himself. The sounds coming from upstairs sounded as though they were underwater. His head was swimming. His mouth tasted of blood; he had bitten the inside of his cheek. The pain in his side worried him. Ribs? Liver? He forced himself to take a step up the stairs, and with each step the loud chatter of the guards lessened.

At the top of the staircase, he heard nothing. He saw only two guards there when he came around the corner, one on each side of the huge double doors. They stood rigid, facing each other grimly across the *jalo* rug. Because it was the entrance to the chamber of a very important person, they were careful to stand with great discipline. It was a room in which resided the object of his love. He mentally slapped himself: it was the room where the ambassador Ut'r-BkanN was about to visit. That was the reason all of the guards had cleared out.

And here he was, staggering down the corridor toward those double doors, probably only a few *pii* ahead of the most important Zetin in this half of the kingdom.

Before reaching the guards, he stumbled and fell face first on the puke-yellow carpet. At the instant it happened, he did not know whether it was accidental or if it was part of his master plan. Every second was being improvised now. If it were his plan, the first step would be for the two guards at the door to realize that, with the ambassador coming, they could not allow their drunken comrade to lie there in the middle of the hall....

Chapter 30

Service

The chamber was paneled in dark *ghêqir* wood, ornately trimmed with gold and *beq*, all richly polished. In its center was a large *undon-qala*, suspended by marbled *mâk* columns rather than chains, and supported from beneath by an upright *jalo* pelvis. Ferns he thought were *ulassi* were growing out of raised planters along the sides of the room. Overhead a nine-pointed chandelier held a ring of bulbous candles. The curved floor, rising toward the walls, was strewn with *jalo* and *fenk* skins, and on the six walls hung abstract Zetin paintings of the mythic forces of nature. On shelving in the corners squatted pottery of Zetin design: stout bodies with long, narrow twisting necks. At the head of the *qala*, a delicate bronze *lann* doe knelt in submission. The nightstand held a thick book he saw was written in Ghoupallêan script rather than the angular Zetin characters.

As she climbed sensuously off the *qala*, rather like the *lann* herself, she turned to receive the chamberlain. In that moment, he knew it was really the Lady Jinetta—his high school sweetheart, Gina Parton. The golden hair that streamed down her back, the figure suggested beneath the filmy *borlan* gown, the gold rings on her toes, and the slanting *fleran* comb that rose with the locks swept up from her forehead in Zetin style—all served to anoint those features which he loved most.

But he had to wait.

Stepping nimbly across the thick-furred skins, she knelt on the large, circular cushion set down by the chamberlain's assistants on the entrance tiles. Her ankles folded beneath her, rocking on her knees as if in prayer. With her hands clasped in her lap and her head bowed, she could only listen. The lord's chamberlain opened his message book and read, standing before her, over her. The ambassador, Ut'r-BkanN, would be attending her this evening. In her honor, a gracious dinner would be prepared consisting of twelve dishes of the finest wild and domesticated flesh, garnished with imported fruit and vegetables. And to assist her in the necessary purification and dressing, extra *utê* would be provided. Tonight was a special occasion, the chamberlain stressed, and her cooperation was humbly requested. He bowed and stepped back. She rose from the cushion and an assistant gathered it up, and the door was closed between them.

She knew the meaning of the overly eloquent Ghoupallêan words of the chamberlain, but she could not imagine an occasion that would be special to her. Every time the old Zetin ambassador came to visit her, they had dinner. That was not special; she had even come to like some of the gourmet Zetin dishes, despite their highly carnivorous diet. The evening always ended the same way: with his amorous advances. She was his hostage, but he had always treated her as a guest of utmost respect. He had never forced her physically though he could have. She wanted only to hear the news that the long war with Sekuate had finally ended, and that the treaty between their two nations would be concluded and she would return to Tebbicousimankalê.

She let out a long sigh, one which on a high balcony of the castle might have swept snow off the *Zet-Saer*. Sinking on the huge *qala*, she embedded her face in the furry G'PA pillows. Her time was so restricted, always measured, her actions never her own. The time spent with the ambassador was a respite of sorts, a fine dinner in an elegant hall, the chance for some witty repartee and clever conversation with an intellect equal to her own. But it always ended in the same way—and it began the same, with the *utê*.

Rolling onto her back, she stared up at the hooks in the ceiling, counting the *pii* until they came to make her presentable.

"I remember another time when I had to help you escape from a gilded cage," a too-familiar voice spoke out from inside the wall. "Or was it a padded cell? Do you remember? The time you returned to Earth and were picked up by the police. I can't recall what you did, some kind of car wreck? They took you to the Eastwood Psychiatric Center when you insisted you were Queen Jinetta of Fenula and not simply Gina Parton, college student and dope smoker."

"But I *was* Jinetta, Queen of Fenula, then," the Lady responded, thinking it was her conscience speaking.

"I visited you at the hospital, then came back pretending to be an orderly, and gave you a rope and a screwdriver—"

"And that night I unfastened the screen and tied the rope to the bed and slid down the wall outside to where you and Jason were waiting in his dragster."

"We sure burned some rubber that night getting the hell outta there—and got away clean. Nobody came after us, and you were back through the tangent before anyone knew you were ever in town. It was a masterful plan from the start, and we pulled it off without a hitch."

Nodding her head, she remembered pleasantly.

"And what about this time?" she asked. "Will you pull it off without a hitch?"

"We'll have to see."

She looked up when the voice did not continue and saw him peeking out from behind the wall panel. Seeing his Zetin face, she had to crack a grin. She shook her head in disbelief, climbing off the *qala* and stepping toward the closet where he was hiding.

"Oh, dear Sebastian. You're always coming to rescue me. We really have to change that. Maybe I could rescue you—if you would be a little more adventuresome. Get in trouble, why don't you?"

"I will," he grinned, "someday...when I have nothing better to do."

He closed the panel, wanting to go and embrace her, but fearing to touch her with the Zetin guards so near.

"I never suspected it would be *you* my guards hid in the closet," she said with a laugh. "You look just like one of them—at least bent over like that. How did you get them to put you in here, in the closet? I thought it was some kind of practical joke—poor, drunken bastard wakes up to find himself in deep shit when the ambassador arrives."

"Well, it's a long—I mean, *long*—story, so let's get you out of here first."

"But the *utê* will be here any—"

He watched from the closet as the Lady was becoming the object of art, the center of attention, and the oracle of inhibition. Ten *utê*—the boy eunuchs—encircled her, bathing her in ritual style. The Zetin religion did not permit water immersion and so bathing was done by applying the liquid to the body—in ritual fashion, one touch at a time. A team of trained *utê* could bathe a nobleperson in about two *peth*, with each one assigned a particular part of the body. The small hands worked delicately and with precision, their shiny *mâk* tongs pressing the dampened pinch of HRT to her flesh. No swirling or brushing, only a single touch to one spot.

The HRT, pinches of hair from a mountain sheep called ST'XO, were dampened in a shallow basin filled, as custom required, of pure rain water sterilized by a blast of solar radiation from ZI'RA, the larger sun, then quick-frozen on a north-facing mountain slope for nine days, collected at first light on the tenth day by a temple priestess who had enjoyed sex with her lord on the first of those ten days under the light of *Am-ra*, the smaller sun, while facing to the north at climax. If any of the specifications were inexact, a terrible pestilence would strike the one being bathed by the impure liquid. For the Lady Jinetta, nothing was too good.

It was never an inconvenience to order the ritual purification whenever he visited, the ambassador had explained to her. When the time came that she would finally accept him, when they would be joined in a holy union beneath a fountain of Family Blood, the HANN-S'H—the spraying of a valued slave's essence over the couple as they mated—she would understand the need for every ritual to be performed completely and flawlessly. Besides, he often mused to his chamberlain, the rumors of how unfragrant Ghoupalle women were lingered among the Zetin. Who would respect him if he joined with one and did not first have her properly purified?

To that end, the Lady Jinetta complied and raised her arms toward the ceiling, taking hold of the padded rods from the box overhead. Allowing her body to stretch taut, the *utê* poked and probed her bare figure, pressing the HRT into every crack, crevice, and orifice. They cut and trimmed all hair from her, in every corner of her body—except her head. In Zetinê, married women went hairless, but being a foreigner and a respected one—and given that her hair was a most attractive shade of gold—the Lady Jinetta was permitted to keep it.

Later, a nearly transparent ceramic bottle of TLAUT was brought for her to drink from, cleansing that filthy haven of germs, the mouth. An *utê* then received the liquid back in a basin straight from her lips, and dabbed her lips with HRT as six more *utê* arrived with four adolescent girls, initiates of the *Ghêrata*, bringing her elegant dinner gown.

Together, the party dressed her in the satiny, pink S'LARI outfit the ambassador had chosen. This one was of a particularly fine-woven fabric like silk, resembling a three-piece pajama set. The shirt extended slightly below the hips but the pants were in two sections, each slipped individually up the leg and fastened at the hips by strings. The effect was a dubious fashion but the Lady Jinetta was delighted by the cheerful colors, the smooth touch of the fabric, and the subtle though intriguing Cubist patterns on it.

Stepping into her FN'TA slippers, made of seashell overlaid with gold, feeling the weight of the tall, ungainly KLM'ES headdress set on top with her long hair wrapped around it, supporting it, she was ready. Her escort moved as one down the long corridor, descending to the second level where the ambassador awaited her in a private dining hall. Behind them moved a quartet of fierce Zetin guards, one of them really a tax examiner.

* * *

Set-d'Elous was glad Zetin architecture decreed that formal dining halls be ringed by an outer corridor where waiting servants could easily anticipate their lord's whims, overhearing both conversation and command. It also provided a place for him to wait for his move. The servants thought he was one of the lord's personal guards and, having served the meal, he was left alone to plan. As he waited behind the LM, the paper-thin walls which hid him, the ambassador's rough baritone droned on, trying to entertain the Lady.

"I met a man once, on my early travels north in the state of Zevêna," he said in his most polite Ghoupallêan, down the long table to his guest, "and he sat under a broken ILX tree, in a position of meditation, and when I stood over him, blocking the sunlight from his upturned face, he opened his eyes and gazed at me. In those days, I was a young man, and wore not a warrior's marks upon my face. This man—I guessed him three times my age—stared at me for a while. I felt discomfort at having disturbed him, and so begged him to allow an apology—it was before I wore the ZK'RA, as I said. This man, certainly a holy man and perhaps a follower of TJANN-DAX, spoke to me then in words which were a riddle to me—they were neither ZETIN-GAM' nor Ghoupallêan. This was strange to me, because I was in Zevêna, which is a northern province and far from any other cultures. But the words he spoke were heard in my head, not my ears—yet I understood them perfectly. He said I would become a man of peace in Zetinê; I would be a respected politician, a kind diplomat; I would be sought for my wise counsel, and worshipped for my accomplishments. Please do not laugh, as I know you must wish to do. It is all true! Naturally, his words surprised me, for I was on my RE'KL—my Youth Trek—seeking to become a warrior and obtain the ZK'RA of a warrior. It was not in my mind to be a man of peace, certainly not a man of wisdom! But those were the words this man spoke to me. And now you see, it has come to be."

He raised his goblet to her, as if proposing a toast, and waited for the Lady to likewise sip, then took a gulp himself.

"Dear Lady, what shall I do?"

She spoke not, but communicated with her eyes, asking him what he meant.

"You do not know what day this is, I guess. It is the anniversary of our TKTKA—the meeting whence began our relationship. It is the one-hundredth dinner for us—and it falls this time amidst the high holy period of S'EK-CONN, which is a good omen. My priest has given me assurance that anything I attempt tonight will succeed. You would not wish to call my priest a liar, would you?"

Gina sat back in her strange mechanical chair, as well as she could with the restraints that kept her legs and back tight against the chair but her arms free for partaking of the meal. It was not her usual position for dinner but Ut'r-BkanN had insisted, and the lord always got his way in his castle.

"That depends on what you attempt," she replied, the sugar in her voice coating his anger.

"I have only the most honorable intentions, My Lady, because I am an honorable warrior—a man of peace, as I told you—and as I have demonstrated to you by the alliance negotiated between our two countries. And you are an honorable woman."

Set-d'Elous pressed his ear against the LM, feeling his moment of action approaching.

"Dear Lady, since you have been my guest, we have had such delightful times together. I enjoy our visits, and until tonight—and except for the first few—I do believe you cannot be a liar concerning your own pleasure. Each visit I have brought a gift for you, and you have rejected them all. Tonight, I have brought one more gift. There will be no others if you refuse this one, so I beg you to indulge me in this gift. It is our anniversary."

A cute but solemn blond *utê* appeared immediately from behind the LM, presenting a round metal tray with a small maroon cushion on it. The sudden motion of the boy caught the Professor by surprise and he almost tripped as he stepped back out of sight.

"You now have one hundred *gealan* in your collection. If I release you, you will be a rich woman. If you stay, you will be a richer woman. I am begging you that either way you will accept this token of my appreciation."

"Appreciation? I'm your hostage."

"My appreciation is of your candor, dear Lady, and your honesty, your sense of humor—especially in those moments when I know you wish to be in anger—and not the least do I appreciate your superb Ghoupallean beauty and refined manner. I cannot find that among my own people, and our laws keep me from indulging my fantasies in that regard."

The *utê* withdrew, leaving the cushion with the *gealan* sitting on the long table, halfway between them. The creamy white spherical stone reflected the light of the chandelier and the wall torches.

"Do you not find it beautiful? You know we have no word in ZETIN-GAM' for 'beauty,' the closest being E'H—but it really means only something that is desirable due to its appearance; if you desire whatever you might call ugliness, it is also E'H."

"In my homeland, we also find beauty in ugliness, and we also use the word 'beauty' to describe it."

"Ah, we are not so far apart after all, are we? For these past two years you have been my guest, dear Lady, I have studied the Ghoupallêan language. And so I speak even now to you in your own language. This is because I wish to converse with you in detail—and, because our Zetin language is not a beautiful language, not appropriate being uttered by as rich and gentle a voice as yours."

Gina eyed the huge *gealan*, two inches in diameter, admiring its creamy luster but dreading the favor which always followed a gift.

"Has it been only *two* years?" she asked. "I've counted the days—despite all your attempts to shut me up inside where I cannot see the suns and—"

"It is only two years, My Lady."

"And the war against Sekuate? Is it still not won, even after two years?"

"It is not. The Sekuatean armies are stronger than any imagined. The war continues, and our own borders are threatened. You should never fear for your safety, certainly. For you are my guest, whom I would protect against any foe."

She resisted the urge to press her argument, still believing it must be longer than two years. No reflection in her mirror could strip away the illusion: the Earth years still lay upon her, age slipping past slower than on the people around her.

"I am pleased you are not alarmed," he said, a moment of silent contemplation passing between them. "The war shall come to a successful conclusion soon."

"Then you will be returning me to my husband in Tebbicousimankalê."

"That is our treaty, dear Lady, and I agreed to it on behalf of my country. But tonight I would wish instead to negotiate a new treaty."

"A new treaty?"

"Yes, My Lady. With you."

"With me? What sort of treaty could I have with you?"

"Dear Lady, I would like you to stay with me after the war is won—please hear me out before you decide—and for this honor I will give you anything you desire to seal our 'treaty'. I know that you have a husband, but those laws do not bind you here in Zetinê. And you think I have a wife—which is true, because I have told you—but a wife in Zetin is different from a wife in your country. It is only a legal union, I told you before. What I desire is a woman with whom I can enjoy my life."

Her first reaction was to chuckle politely under her breath, leaning back in the strait-chair she was strapped into. She realized she was not in a position to refuse any demand, so she simply smiled at him, playing with him as she usually did—for her own amusement, to pass the time, and to fend off his potential anger.

"Lord Bkann," she spoke, carefully choosing her words, "I am genuinely honored that you wish me to join your family, but it is too soon for me to answer."

"I know you worry about your duties in this new relationship, so let me explain them. Of course, the natural order decrees that a male is able to have several mates at once, yet a female cannot carry more than one mate's child. This is the way it was intended. The twelve gods have written this on the side of Mount HJAK-L'RA—though I have never seen characters there. That is why our women fulfill their duties in our society—and do not rebel, as they do in the Ghoupalle nations. My wife is only the head of my family. To her I pay my money, to you I pay my respect. If I could, I would make you my legal wife, but you are not Zetin, so I can only have you as my First Consort. Besides, I cannot talk to the woman; she is Zetin and will give me anything I ask. I want a woman who will fight with me—and sometimes win. To such a man as I, who has everything, it is a rare pleasure to have a companion such as yourself. I have other concubines, yes—I told you of them—but do not be concerned that you would be as one of them. As my First Consort, you can bear me many children; I am old, but you are young. I will decree that you and your children will be my heirs after only my wife. She has no children—it was a mistake, this marriage, and I have always regretted it. I have no legal heirs who can take my position as ambassador."

"You introduced that young man—the one with the blood-tipped beard—as your son, didn't you?"

"Oh, that boy? He's a bastard. And an idiot. He cannot be my heir by law. His mother and I, we—we met in battle and took a rest together, that is all."

She lowered her gaze, showing disapproval by severing eye contact with him, and scanned the long dinner table for a vegetable dish. The feast of meat entrées was certainly overwhelming but she always craved some fruit and vegetables. Lord Bkann usually had such delicacies imported at great expense from Skiy, where the Zetin diaspora had settled in tropical Bæronak; there was almost no growing season for plant foods in Zetinê.

"I can give the children of my concubines whatever riches I have, to help them make their way in the world." He pulled out a rolled parchment from under his end of the table. "I have already written it, you see. All of my wealth shall go to my concubine families upon my death—that is what I signed here!"

She spied a dish of orange, corn kernel-like seeds of the oblong *haptig* melon grown in Skiy. It was not a favorite, being somewhat bitter and a little salty as they prepared it.

"You will certainly find another, younger woman, Lord Bkann, when I grow older—and I will be pushed aside as you are pushing aside the ones you now have to make way for me. Is this all the vegetables you had prepared this time?"

She frowned, waiting patiently as her lord spoke.

"Dear Lady, it is not true! I will not live long enough to find another. I could die tonight—and my dream would be unfulfilled. I desire to father a child with a woman who draws these strange sensations from me."

"Are you saying you love me?"

"We do not have that word in ZETIN-GAM'—but as we are speaking Ghoupallêan, I can use it. I warn you: if my colleagues hear this word spoken by me, they will see it as a sign of weakness, and then all will be lost that I hope to gain. My Lady, do you mean to trap me into expressing this word with my own voice?"

"Yes, I do," she laughed.

The Professor, behind the LM, reached for his KL blade, sensing growing frustration as Ut'r-BkanN rose from his chair.

"That cannot be. They are a fool's words."

"Then I cannot be your First Consort—or your First anything. I am still married to the Prime Minister of Tebbicousimankalê, with whom you are allies. I cannot turn around and be your sex slave!"

The Professor stepped forward, transforming himself back into the warrior Set-d'Elous, and the floor creaked. He froze. The ambassador was too absorbed in discussion to notice.

"Dear Lady, you must think on this matter further. The holy period of S'EK-CONN will last but six days, and when it ends, so will your chance. For now, we must salvage our pleasant dinner engagement. This is the reason I am living so long—and longing for the opportunity to see you, and converse with you, and see the smile of your face and the sparkle in your eyes, and the blush of your cheek, and the rising and falling of your breasts beneath your dress—and the feelings I sense in you…what is it called? In ZETIN-GAM' we have the word E'z—to 'sense sexual arousal in another.' I sense it in you—"

Set-d'Elous saw the ambassador moving down the table toward the Lady, captive in her chair.

"—and despite wanting to show my restraint on yet another

visit, I have sworn to myself that I absolutely must have you tonight—for this is our anniversary!"

The ambassador lunged at Gina, ripping open the silky jacket of her S'LARI costume, expecting her to spit at him or do some other repelling act which Zetin women never did. Instead, she did nothing to discourage him and he paused, staring at her chest and her sly, twisted frown—a curious facial expression he had never seen her wear before. He rolled forward the lever on the side of the chair and watched as the chair's mechanical panels begin to move apart, pulling her legs open.

"My Lady, you shall now become my First Consort, and our new child shall be my second heir. You will be honored among the members of my House."

His hand went to his belt to slip the catch free—but at the sharp sound of tearing behind him, he spun around, ready to curse the *utê* for disrupting him.

Chapter 31

Match Point

"Ja-SKN!" the warrior Set-d'Elous exclaimed as he broke through the LM screen, his KL sword drawn for battle, his cry measured to startle the ambassador but not to alert those outside the room. He promptly spilled on his side as he landed, miscalculating how much the floor was recessed.

"KSAN? GZAX-JAN?" asked the ambassador, more startled than fearful. 'What?—I'm a maiden?'

The Professor righted himself, stood facing the ambassador, sword leveled.

"I meant to say you are a pig, Ut'r-BkanN," he spoke in Ghoupallêan, correcting himself.

"AS-KSAN?" the ambassador asked, knowing that this man could not really be one of his guards, speaking to him in Ghoupallêan. 'Who are you?'

"Set-d'Elous ZAX!" he declared.

The ambassador laughed, hands on his hips.

"You are the famous warrior-consort of the Lady Jinetta's mother? You wear your beard with an incorrect battle stain! Look at yourself: a true warrior would know how to paint the blood stripe on his beard—but yours, it looks like you dunked it in a bottle of red ink! And your Zk'RA: if you put HRT to your face those marks would melt from your cheeks. I'm not impressed—least by your command of our language. The word you want is J'A; the word JA is 'maiden'; the word JA' is 'death-throttle', and JA'A is 'ripe fruit' or a woman's sexual area—small but vital distinctions."

"Thanks for the grammar lesson, Ut'r-BkanN, but I've come to free the Lady Jinetta from you and your castle. It's been much too long for her to stay in one place. She's more at home traveling through space and time. We thank you for your hospitality, but now she must be leaving you—especially since the war ended ten years ago!"

"Ten years ago?" Gina cried out, wanting to jump up but held back by the straight-chair's restraints. The mechanism which moved her legs apart had reached its maximum extent and had stopped automatically. "I've been here for ten years? Is it true?"

"Not at all," the ambassador said, gathering himself and returning casually to his end of the table. "This intruder obviously cannot be the warrior he claims to be, so I doubt what he says."

The warrior stepped forward, blade raised and pointed at the barrel-chested man in the elegant robe.

"Release her," he ordered the ambassador.

"I shall not—and neither shall you."

Set-d'Elous jabbed his KL in the direction of the ambassador, who seemed unimpressed with his amateur swordsmanship.

"Have you noticed I am not frightened of you, young soldier?" Ut'r-BkanN grinned. "This is my castle, and you will meet a hundred guards before you exit. It is only my amusement which prevents me from having you dispatched immediately. Now, tell me about yourself. How did you come to be hiding behind the LM in a poor Zetin uniform?"

The ambassador pulled out his chair, sure that the impostor was no threat to him.

"I *am* Set-d'Elous!" the Professor insisted.

Ut'r-BkanN waved him away.

"I thought you would be taller—and older, too. You stole the Lady Jinetta's mother from the castle of KVANN-STA'GR-TJA, correct? And killed the high priest LANN-KDE in his mineral bath? That was more than one hundred years ago. How is it that you can be so young and spry?"

"Because, Lord Bkann," Gina burst out, straining against her bonds, "he did *not* rescue my mother from the Zetin barbarians. It was *me*. I was the woman he rescued. I'm not her daughter, I'm *her*. He and I are not like you, the Zetin and the Tebbi. You think we're the offspring of our parents, but we're not. We are special. We are gods. We must change our careers to change our lives; we don't age and we don't die!"

"Can it be so?" the ambassador exclaimed, rising from his seat. He had never heard such assertive talk from the Lady Jinetta. It was as though she had taken on a new persona. "It is as the holy man told me long ago, when I was on my RE'KL," he spoke—and the warrior Set-d'Elous took the cue to press his position, pointing his sword at the ambassador, "and I—I blocked his sunlight and he—he told me I would be a man of peace who—would be sought for counsel. Then he said—"

"What did he say?" Set-d'Elous demanded, moving the blade tip against the ambassador's throat, resting it on his studded collar, pushing him back against the LM.

"He—said—when I—" he dropped to his knees before Set-d'Elous, hands thrown together as if deep in prayer, "he said, 'You will be wise and many will seek your counsel—but when you take the woman of golden hair who claims to be a god, hold her and keep her, she will pray to the two suns and the seven winds, and on the day the God of Evil'—I now remember it, it's true—'when Set dines with you it shall be your last day in this world.' And you, Lady Jinetta—you are the woman of golden hair, and now you claim to be a god, and he—*you!*—are Set, the God of Evil from the Western Sky, here in my dining hall?"

The great warrior stepped forward, pulling off his red frazzled wig, showing his true facade.

"Yes, and I've come for you."

The ambassador let out an explosive sigh and the room was filled with a vile scent as he clenched his gut.

"PM-TRA," he moaned in a harsh voice, feeling his robe soiled.

The ambassador looked up at the man who often was a god, and in his Zetin eyes was the shock which Set had hoped to see there. And he, the warrior Set-d'Elous, who certainly could not remember the future very well in those critical moments, knew that he would someday come to rest under an ILX tree in the northern state of Zevêna where a scrawny youth would happen by in search of the warrior spirit, and he would speak his wisdom in simple riddles, and that youth would grow to manhood and lead a nation into and out of war, and die on the day he dined with Death. However, on that day long ago, not knowing how the future would ultimately go, he had just been jiving the kid. Sometimes he got lucky.

"I see now the truth in what you say, Warrior, but if the Lady is who she says she is, and you are who you say you are, then you know my fate already."

"You're a pathetic man, Mister Ambassador," he cursed in good, colloquial English. Kicking over the chair for effect, he was glad it crashed loudly beside the man kneeling on the floor. "I'm just a man, only an hourly employee of the Internal Revenue Service. I examine people's tax returns to see if they're correct, see if they've followed the rules, see if they've paid their fair share. And if they haven't, I send them a nasty form letter! It isn't that I'm a god to you, Mister Ambassador; it's that you think I am a god—and that *makes* me a god to you."

"Ten years..." Gina was muttering when he looked over at her. "Ten years...."

Set-d'Elous turned to the ambassador, nudged him with the toe of his boot.

"Tell her what's happened these ten years."

"It dishonors me," the ambassador replied.

The ambassador reached for the stubby knife at his belt and Set kicked his hand away.

"Tell her!" he demanded.

"The war is ended," Ut'r-BkanN began, rising up but bowing his head low.

"When did it end? Tell her!"

"The Sekuatean armies were driven from Siaa, were chased into Fenula. Many soldiers were killed. They were pursued into Bezua-hü, and at Milipour they surrendered. The year was fifteen and thirty-four."

"Two years after I came here!" Gina gasped.

"Two years after. Tell her about your plans."

"What do you mean?" asked Ut'r-BkanN.

"About the treaty with the Tebbi."

"The Tebbi—well, they are your people—they do not seek your return."

"What!" Gina cried out. "Why not?"

"They do not wish to fulfill their part of the treaty: the foothills of *Zet-Saer*—our payment for fighting the Sekuateans. They prefer their land to your life."

"What about my husband? Surely he wants me to be returned," asked Gina.

"Tell her!"

"He was the lover of your king's sister. So he was publicly rebuked, and he later killed himself."

Set turned to her, seeing tears fall from her eyes.

"The reason, Gina," he explained from old Ouvaxe's words, "was that when he was forced to resign, he was so distraught, thinking he could never get you back."

"You bastard!" Gina screamed at the ambassador.

"We were waiting for the Tebbi to fulfill their part of the treaty! You—you cannot blame us—me. *Your* people abandoned you. And *I* protected you."

"But I was your hostage—compensation for a treaty that was broken. And you—"

"Tell her about the holy period."

"I cannot say it."

Set pushed him over on the floor, the KL again at his throat.

"On the last day of S'EK-CONN...you will be taken from the castle and executed. It is the Death of Nine Cuts: feet, legs, arms, waist, groin, then head. We have been communicating with the Tebbi government, trying to conclude our treaty, but they always tell us to wait. Wait for what, you wonder? They say we must be patient as they finish the reorganization of Zissekap. We have given them many opportunities, and a fair warning, and—*I beg you*, believe that I have tried to save you—my government will not wait any longer. After ten years our land remains in Tebbi hands, and all we have is a woman whom the Tebbi do not want."

"And tonight?" Gina asked him. "Is that why you wanted to add me to your harem? Were you really trying to save me, or was it your personal interests being served?"

"I want you to live. They want to send you back on the same day our armies invade—but you would already be dead. Your body would be divided—in the custom for traitors or criminals—and packed into a cloth bag. The Tebbi will know the seriousness of our claim then."

"Send my body back in a sack?"

"Not I, but the War Council."

"But you are a member of the War Council!"

Two *utê* appeared from behind a side screen, one carrying a tray of the rare jLIX fruit, the other a pitcher of *jalo*-blood wine. They stared at the man dressed as a Zetin guard but with short, dark hair. They saw the ambassador on his knees and the Ghoupalle woman with her jacket torn open. Then, as the boy with the pitcher stepped back in his consternation, he fell against the LM and dropped the pitcher. The purple liquid ran thickly across the tiled floor and the boy scampered up on the raised back stage corridor and away. The fruit boy set his plate down timidly on the table before Gina, backed away, and followed the first boy.

"Quick, Gina, we have to get out of here," he called. "There's got to be a release to this machine somewhere."

"It's on the back of the chair," said Ut'r-BkanN.

Set ran to the double doors, throwing the huge bolt down across them, then rushed to Gina's chair and slapped the lever forward. The clamps began to slide loose as he stomped over to the kneeling ambassador.

"It's time for your treaty to be fulfilled," he said, taking his KL and raising it over his head, showing his angry teeth in Zetin fashion and feeling the saliva build in his mouth, becoming a Zetin warrior at last.

"Ko'L," the ambassador cried—'Stop.'

The blade halted in mid-swing.

"I demand the right to the Zetin honor-death."

Set knew what he meant from battling the Zetin in the mountains and in his dreams. As he watched, the ambassador straightened up and quickly retrieved the short, stubby knife that was sheathed on his belt. He lifted it to his face.

The pounding on the door took his attention away from the

ambassador. In that moment of distraction, the Zetin lord leaped up and slashed Set-d'Elous with the knife meant to cut off his own face. Set fell against the table, grasping his right shoulder as the ambassador ran for the door.

Gina, still fastened to the chair but with her arms free, reached up and pulled off the KLM'ES headdress she wore. The ornament, representing a sword piercing flames, slipped into her hands and as the ambassador lunged for the door, she thrust the sword-like headdress at him, catching on his breastplate and tripping him. He fell onto his back and slid across the tile floor, crashing against the hard wooden doors.

Set-d'Elous pulled himself up, his shoulder red but still holding tightly to his sword. He stumbled to Gina and cut the straps that held her in the chair. She jumped up, stretching her limbs while he turned to the ambassador.

The pounding on the door ceased, but only for an instant.

Gina held her breath, not believing the guards had really gone.

A sharp crunch broke the silence and the thick wooden door split open, the shiny blade of a KM'VA penetrating it. The battle axe was withdrawn and once more swung against the door.

Gina sprang back, splintering wood flying into the room.

"Is there another way out of this room?" he asked the ambassador.

"The *utê* door behind the LM," Ut'r-BkanN replied, content to remain safe on the floor. Let them flee then if they must, he seemed to be saying. He was already disgraced, and his death would only free him from the publicity. He also wanted to escape from the room, before his guards could see him in his present state.

The Professor grabbed Gina by the wrist, his mind racing like an accountant with a long list of figures to sum. They vaulted up onto the raised LM platform and broke through the screen. Two *utê* waiting there ran and they followed the boys.

Echoing through the winding corridor, they heard the final crunch of wood as the thick bolt was severed and the doors fell open. A storm of Zetin guards rushed into the room. Pausing a moment to tend to their lord, they took up the pursuit, racing through the narrow, low corridors where the *utê* went to and from their business. The guards, tall and wearing spiked helmets, continually bumped their heads on the low ceilings, and caught their swords and axes on the thin paper walls, slipped on the polished wood floors, and crashed into each other going around the corners.

Gina and Set came out into the kitchen area, startling the cooks and servants. Throwing some pots and pans down from the overhead racks as a distraction, they ran on.

Out in the exterior hallway, where the massive stone walls cooled them from the heat of their flight, they found themselves alone. Gina took a look at his shoulder and told him it was not too bad. He thanked her, hoping he would not need to use it in a fight. Then she opened her hand and showed him the large, white *gealan* she had snatched in the confusion. The ambassador said it was hers, didn't he? They stepped toward the closest intersection in the wide hallway.

Condensing from the shadows ahead, at the far end of the corridor, came a man running wildly, swinging a red-stained sword through the air over his head.

"*Serpan, Serpan!*" cried Aroun-de-Sotos.

He rushed toward them as a guard squad marching in formation entered the intersection from the adjacent corridor, unaware of the escaping prisoners. Seeing them, the sergeant concluded they were not the usual guests and gave the order to capture them.

Set held up his KL and took the first guard in the gut, slipping the blade through the narrow opening in the joints of the breastplate. Then de-Sotos, who was out of place on this mission and away from his post but damn glad to be seen now, slashed his way through the squad from behind, joining his captain. They hit the guards with the torches off the walls, swinging their blades at them until all were dead or fatally wounded. The sergeant survived and ran to get help, his cries ringing against the stone walls.

"For your safety, I come," spoke Aroun-de-Sotos in his most polite Ghoupallêan, out of breath but kneeling down before the Lady Jinetta.

"No need to be so righteous," said Set, helping him up. The

Lady Jinetta was just his old girlfriend from high school.

The man could not stop being humble before her, even as they rounded the corner and jogged along the hallway looking for the exit. Turning to Aroun-de-Sotos, a few paces behind, he saw his sword was drawn and an AT was in his other hand, watching the rear.

"The plan—are we still on time?" he asked in English.

"Zaran did—ready now," de-Sotos replied in English, "no time—we wait and—go there."

"Good, then we'll head straight up to the tower. And you better get back to your post, or you won't be able to get out of the castle."

He dipped his head quickly in acknowledgment, but he continued with them.

"I said you'd better get down to the basement," Set shouted as de-Sotos fell back.

Then he saw why. Another squad of guards came around the corner, this group knowing about their escape and expecting to find them. Swords drawn, they did not hesitate to charge them. Gina and her rescuer shifted to a sprint, leaving de-Sotos behind. They had presumed he would follow, too.

"Wait, Gina!" he yelled, and stopped.

With his sword firm in his hand and the blood from his shoulder wound running again, he listened to the growling of the guards behind them.

Suddenly, de-Sotos plunged around the corner.

"Here—take!" he cried, throwing the AT to him at the same instant the guards rounded the turn.

Set flipped on the AT, checking the number of pulse rounds, frantically eyeing the temperature gauge, then focused on the bulky beast-men before him. His finger squeezed the trigger and a fire of molten projectiles shot out at the guards, striking them, burning through their breastplates or landing directly on their faces like meteors striking a planet. The explosions of flesh and cries of anguish from the guards halted them where they stood or fell, moaning on the floor.

Gina ran up to de-Sotos, pulled him back from the fighting, sitting him against the wall.

"Are you hurt?" she asked him in Ghoupallêan, then saw his wound.

The small puncture in his chest belied a wound which had erupted out of his back, a sign of the HK'REG, a Zetin weapon resembling a lance which, once stuck in an opponent's flesh, shot an explosive bolt on through the body.

"Can you walk?"

He nodded, then looked over at his captain, setting the cooling switch on the AT.

"Come on, let's go," he called to them.

"He's wounded," Gina told him.

"We really have to go now," and he bent over to pick up his comrade.

De-Sotos gritted his teeth. They pulled him into a side room where they could rest. As Set lowered him onto the floor, Gina closed the heavy door behind them. Under the torch light they could see the thin trickle of blood down his chest from the hole, and the sopping pool under his back.

"You—go," de-Sotos groaned.

"We can't leave you here," he responded.

"You—no carry—dead man—"

Gina knelt beside them. "You *must* live!"

"I live...enough...."

"Nonsense! Come on, we can make it—all of us, together."

The man who had studied his captain's life for ten years shook his head in disagreement, digging into his vest as Set motioned for Gina to go to the door and watch the corridor.

The paper he retrieved was crumpled in his hand, but he thrust it at his captain.

"What's this?" asked Set, taking it.

"This only remains...from book."

"Book? What book?"

"*Your* book...future book."

"You read it?"

"Yes—forgive—important gift for I—ten years. Read—here page—"

"You shouldn't have read such a book, you know."

"Read—about *Serpan* Aroun-de-Sotos—in Second *Coraesz*, of

Second *Berêlad*, Second *Rasselad*, Fifth *Treskand*—the great *Jêpedor-regêlad* number one-hundred-two, soldier number...."

As he began rambling, Set quickly scanned the wrinkled, dirty page of Ghoupallêan and found the name of his comrade. The paragraph, he read, told the circumstances of his death: *killed in Special Services mission, in Zetinê, during the rescue of the Lady Jinetta of the House of Sassat in Tebbicousimankalê, who...'* and he paused, knowing the rest.

"*Kanê*—I know—go Zetinê," said de-Sotos, looking away. "When I go to prison, go to Archives—look about you, *Serpan* Set-d'Elous. I know—I go Zetinê."

"But, dammit, why? You didn't need to come on this mission; it's *my* problem to rescue her. She's just my old girlfriend; it's not worth *you* dying. If you knew about it, why did you come? I mean, we've already been through so much, you and I—"

"Save her—*Kalmonê* Jinetta."

"I am. That's why we have this mission."

"Hah, you don't know. I don't know—read book. She don't know—my mother—her baby—and we go lost."

It must have been time for her to move on again, he understood then, so her lack of aging would not be noticed. He knew that name from a list of names locked in his desk drawer in his apartment on Earth: Lirêa-Katoum. The baby daughter whom Gina left behind was the woman who grew up and married Ralad-de-Sotos and had a son named....

"Then you are—" the Professor took his dying comrade in his arms "—her grandson."

"Yes," de-Sotos responded, a grin playing on his lips.

He closed his eyes and clenched his teeth, fought his pain; he had to finish his dying thoughts.

"Set-d'Elous, I want—go with you—be in—mystery land," he pumped out the words with the final heaving of his chest. "I want go—from this world—fly away—fly your world—walk streets of *Ur-tha*—like you—and—be a god—like you—"

He rolled over slowly in his captain's arms.

"You will, Aroun-de-Sotos," whispered Set-d'Elous, water collecting in the corners of his eyes.

"It's clear out there," Gina called from the door. "I think they're looking for us in some other part of the castle. Or maybe Ut'r-BkanN told them to let us go. He might do that, you know. Sentimental old fool."

He lowered the body onto the floor and stood up.

"Gina, come here."

"What is it? He died, didn't he? He was one of your mercenaries?"

"No, Gina. He was more."

* ❋ *

It sounded like there was a riot in the main hall, below them.

"Bmxi var kvannbru-skn!" one of the guards was shouting. 'The slaves are running out of the castle!'

"Bmc'a kruhet em Zuram-Jinettao' Drbu zax gkiL'va-gn!" another, deeper voice soared over the other noise. Ut'r-BkanN was ordering his guards to forget about the slaves escaping; the Lady Jinetta and her warrior were more important to capture. "Em z'icorr tonn!" he added.

Gina glared at the Professor. "That was Bkann. He ordered them not to kill us."

"We have to get to the top. Our only means of escape is there."

"No, not the top," she insisted. "It's a dead end. That's why the worst criminals are put there—the only escape from there is straight down."

"Exactly, Gina. My men are running interference."

Suddenly the hall was filled with the barking of orders again and guard squads appeared, searching every room in a routine manner, moving quickly up the corridor.

"They're coming," she said.

He took her in his good arm and pressed his lips to hers.

"Not a good time for making out," said Gina.

"It's for luck," said Set-d'Elous. "Now, we have to get up to the top of the tower."

"How many times do I have to tell you? We'll be trapped up there."

He grabbed her by the arms and shook her.

"No, we won't! That's precisely why they won't look for us up there. If we hurry we can get past them. Then they'll never find us. We'll be gone from this castle."

Clenching her hand, he pulled her out of the room, checking directions and running into the long shadows of the endless corridor, the din of destruction moving after them.

"I hope you trust these friends of yours."

"With my life," he responded, leading her along the corridor.

"That's all you have to give, isn't it?"

Up the stairs to the twelfth level, then the thirteenth level, no sign of guards.

"They have the worst criminals up here," Gina said. "They just lock them up and throw away the key, no need for guards this high up."

On the fourteenth level, she ripped her hand away from his, and fell against the wall beside him, gasping for breath.

"Let's take a second—to catch—" he also halted, sword drawn, "our breaths."

Checking the corridor behind them, he listened to the shouting below. He sheathed his blade and slumped against the wall next to her. Breathing deeply, she lifted her hand to his face, brushed his cheek, mouthing the words 'I love you'. He laid his free hand on her waist, the urge to pull her close strong.

"Look!" she cried out in a hushed voice.

A shadow appeared on the opposite wall. It had to be a guard sneaking down the stairs. The guard either already knew the reason for the commotion below or was curious about it now. The shadowy figure descended the same stairs they were about to go up. The figure moved slowly, shadow growing, expanding—but there was no silhouette of the standard Zetin spiked helmet.

He unslung the AT, sliding it into his hands.

"Wait," Gina whispered, placing her hand on his, "use the sword—it's quieter."

He studied the monstrous shadow.

"The AT is more certain," he replied. "No one can be that big, unless it's the captain of the guards—that ugly brute who threw me down the stairs earlier."

He stoked the AT, finger weighing on the trigger as the giant shadow staggered around the corner.

"Oh, man, what the hell *is* this place?" the shadow cursed in English.

The Professor opened fire, sending a hot blaze of plasma at the—

He wore his usual Fleetwood Mac t-shirt, not quite reaching his waistband, belly flab hanging out over his belt, the black and white beard, the toothless grin that always preceded his insulting remarks. It was Fat Ken. His hands went to his stomach, feeling the burning flesh there. When he dropped to his knees, a loud crash exploded around the stone walls and the floor cracked.

"Ken!" the Professor exclaimed. "What are *you* doing here? I didn't know it was you. We're being chased by those big Zetin bastards."

"Hey, Professor, what're you *doing* here?" Ken mumbled, a stupid look rolling over his bewildered face. "And what're you all dressed up as? some *Star Trek* Klingon?"

The Professor shook his head, lowering the AT.

"Wait a minute! You're not here—you *can't* be here! You're just an illusion—some hallucination I'm having because I'm under stress!"

Fat Ken spit up blood then, which ran down his beard onto his t-shirt. He wavered on his wide knees, like a redwood that had been cut, and fell to earth, smashing against the stone floor like a demolition ball, sending a quake up the hallway.

"Ken!" he cried. "I didn't mean it—really! It—was an accident!"

"Come on," Gina urged him, "he's already dead. Let's not join him."

Up to the sixteenth and seventeenth levels, around a corner and down a dark corridor feebly lit by torches.

"This way," Gina told him at the next intersection, tugging his hand.

"You been up here before?" he asked.

"No, why?"

"Do you know where you're going?"

"Do you?"

They raced on up the narrow flight of stairs to the eighteenth level but the Professor stumbled against the top step and fell on his wounded shoulder. The cry that shot from his mouth caught them both by surprise. It was partly the anguish of shooting and killing his service center colleague—no matter how he came to be in the Zetin castle this night. All he could think of was that Ken had fallen through some doorway between the two worlds, maybe one broken open by his presence in the castle. It was not just anybody, but someone he *knew*, someone he did not like.

"You saw him, right?" he asked Gina.

"Who, the fat guy?"

"Yes—I used to work with him."

Their talking aroused the prisoners locked up on that level. They came to life, crying out for food, for a drink, for a neck to wring—anything. He took Gina's hand and they hurried down the hallway, fearing the noise would call attention to them.

They ran up the stairs they found at the end of the corridor and came to a different level, losing count which one it was. A long carpet ran down the hall and along the walls stood twin rows of *jalo* skulls set on upright lances as marks of rank for the ambassador. The gaping jaws, opened wide enough to swallow him whole and spiked with teeth as long as his fingers, stopped them as the torch light flickered eerily across them.

At the end was a set of double doors like the ones which guarded her own suite.

"This is it," she said, "the way to the top, to the balcony."

They tried the doors, found one that moved free. Then they saw the scratches on the wood and knew that someone had been there before—and recently. The door had been locked and then forced open. Their eyes stared hard at each other: was it the Zetin guards or his own mercenaries?

The doors swung open.

"Zuram-o' Drzi caxog gdam."

"Lord Bkann!" Gina gasped.

"Welcome, Madam and your consort, to the final *peth*," the ambassador repeated in Ghoupallêan.

She grabbed Set's arm but he shook her off so he could be free to fight.

"If you're trying to escape, you must run down, not up," said Ut'r-BkanN in a steady, calm voice, back in control now. "It is a mistake many guests make. Understanding that faulty logic of the Ghoupalle mind, we have chosen to wait for you here."

Gina led Set as they stepped backward, the light of a dozen torches spilling out over the spiked helmets of the Zetin guards accompanying the lord of the castle.

"Dear Lady—and you, Set-d'Elous, the God of Evil from the Western Sky—do you think the other gods will save you this time? With a moment of contemplation, even this old warrior can overcome his fear of gods. I said before that my priest told me whatever I do this night will succeed. I cannot lose."

The guard beside the ambassador spoke to him and he laughed at his two visitors.

"We found this man inside and dealt with him in a rather conservative manner. Perhaps you know him?"

One of the guards tossed out a body, its limbs almost completely severed, including the head, all flopping around like a rag doll and dripping with blood. It was a Ghoupalle man, they saw: Zaran, the nephew of old Ouvaxe.

"We thought he might be one of your conspiratorial band. So you see, tonight I cannot lose."

Set-d'Elous stepped forward, KL drawn.

"Then I have nothing *to* lose!" he shouted, lunging ahead, running the blade into the unsuspecting Zetin ambassador, taking him by surprise despite the guards on either side.

The ambassador fell off the blade and dropped to his knees. The guards mulled a beat, wondering whether to tend to their lord or kill the prisoners. Set had the AT unslung from his good shoulder and switched on, checking the remaining shots. By the time the guards decided what to do, he had the AT's stubby barrel directed at them, squeezing the trigger. Burst after burst flashed across the widening space between them, igniting the hair and beard of the guards, burning through their shirts. He did not have time for it to heat up fully, he knew at that moment: the shots were only hitting like hot popcorn.

Gesturing to Gina, they fell back down the hallway, stalling while the AT grew hotter—but there were only a few shots left anyway, he saw.

The guards pursued cautiously, battle axes swinging, but the

AT was blinding in its fury, setting the guards aflame, searing through their enameled breastplates. Their muscular bodies dropped like sacks of cement. Ten of them—no, fifteen, sixteen—seventeen—until the gun clicked wildly and no molten pellets came out. He let the AT slide onto the floor, burning his hand on the hot barrel.

Alone, the ambassador lay on the floor, his hand-picked ceremonial guard destroyed. He struggled to pull himself up, first to his elbows, then to a sitting position against the wall, as the God of Evil returned to him. He knew that if he somehow survived the night—as his priest told him he would—he would strike down the rule forbidding firearms inside the castle. The enemy always seemed to have them! Of course, the enemy seldom traversed the Wall of Zet to attack him from the silent hillsides, under the guise of his own castle guards, in the blackness of night, when he had drank wine with his heart's companion, and lay vulnerable.

When Set-d'Elous stood before him, the ambassador pulled himself to a wobbly upright position, holding on to one of the lances crowned with a *jalo* skull. He grinned at the warrior, the embarrassment of defeat. Then, breathing heavily, holding his chest, his mouth open, he tried to speak but could not and cleared his throat.

"Your KL has pierced me," he said, "and since I am an old man it may be fatal—but it is not so deep that I will die soon."

Set-d'Elous regarded the ambassador, baffled.

"In fact, I might live a long time yet. You see, tonight I cannot lose. I can only *win*!" and the ambassador thrust up his short LA'D dagger hidden in the folds of his robe, striking Set in the front of his hip.

Gina shrieked.

The two warriors stared at each other, eye to eye, as Ut'r-BkanN held him close, hooked on the end of his blade, his opponent feeling the grooved, triangular metal digging around in search of an artery.

Fighting the pain, Set-d'Elous clapped his hands on the ambassador's shoulders and raised himself up, pushing on the Zetin, lifting himself off the blade, pushing himself away from the ambassador.

Landing on his back, he felt the blood rushing from his hip, the four inch gash pointing toward his groin.

The ambassador, astonished that it happened so quickly, maintained his grip on the *jalo* skull lance, exchanging his victory mask for one of desperation. His apologetic chuckles fell over the warrior's shoulders like his thickening blood, as he watched Set-d'Elous retrieve the AT. It was empty, he knew. Puzzled, he was not ready when the warrior took the AT by its extended shoulder support and swung it against the ambassador repeatedly—until the LA'D rang on the stone floor and the ambassador toppled. The lance was still in his hand but the *jalo* skull had slipped off it and fell beneath him as he landed, its wide fangs sitting open like the same sharp-toothed trap that caught the beast, catching the ambassador between its white, silent jaws with a crisp snap.

"KO'L!" Bkann shrieked, laying still. "You will have to use your KL to finish me."

"I don't have to finish you off," Set-d'Elous slowly responded. "You're already done. I only need wait—an hour or two. The time you take to die is up to you."

"No, you can't do that!" he cried. It would not do for his servants find him with his face locked in a grimace of pain. But he knew that he would not be allowed the ritual act again, having used it deceptively before. "I cannot die this way! I cannot move! My back is broken! I cannot move my arms or legs!"

Gina dropped beside the fallen ambassador.

"He's right," she said. "If we leave him like this, he'll be dishonored and disgraced before all Zetinê."

"He held you hostage for ten years, didn't he?"

She stared at the man, feeling a twinge of sentiment, a flicker of nostalgia for those pleasant times they did have before. Perhaps it was not entirely his fault, she wanted to believe. It was an impossible situation which he had tried to make a little more tolerable.

"Help me, dear Lady! I cared for you! I imported vegetables for you at great expense! I'll even say the foolish words!"

She smiled warmly. "Say them."

"I—love—you."

404

"I'll grant your wish, Ut'r-BkanN," she said solemnly, hovering over him on her hands and knees.

"Are you crazy?" asked Set.

"I don't want him to be disgraced."

She took the stubby knife from the holster on his belt, weighed it in her hands, and stared into his dark Zetin eyes, thinking back to the morning in Siti when he selected her as hostage. Then she laid her hand over his face, prompting him to close his eyes, and took the knife tightly in her hand and cut.

When his dripping death mask lay properly in his open hand, his other hand curled into a clench of the knife she had set there. The double doors beckoned and they entered. She grabbed a torch from the wall. They stepped among the many torture devices occupying the room. Skeletons and decomposing bodies hanging on and in the machines did not distract them from their destination.

"I'm really bleeding now, Gina," he groaned, trying to maintain his strength a little longer. "We have to get out of here."

The draft blew through the closed doors ahead: the balcony.

They gazed upon the multitude of stars painted across the canopy of night. The winds of Zetinê blew against them as they admired the vast plateau. The package hidden in the corner shadows was what he had expected, the gift of Zaran-Ouvaxe.

On its exterior were the words *Tasan-de-Qannor.*

"'Wings of a bird'…?" Gina translated.

He tore open the elongated sacks and saw the struts and springs, the panels and flaps inside, and carefully slipped them out of their wrapping.

"It's a hang glider!"

They worked frantically to assemble it, and had just finished securing the great wings to the frame when a new giant stormed out onto the balcony behind them.

"As GLXE KSAN?" the burly guard captain shouted, picking his way around a side ledge where a slave girl's head quickly ducked down. 'What are you doing up here?'

The guard captain jumped down onto their balcony and continued cursing him: 'Didn't I tell you to get back to the barracks and sober up?' and 'Your sex privileges were canceled, so you have no excuse for being up here with this female.'

When he did not show proper deference to the captain, the enormous Zetin picked him up by the arm holes of his breastplate and threw him against the stone battlements, almost tumbling off.

"Ko'L!" Gina cried for him to halt.

The guard captain grabbed him again and dragged him off the stone ledge. Just as he dropped Set on his wounded hip upon the pile of empty sacks near the doorway, the guard captain noticed the contraption sitting against the ledge: something like a kite, a thing of curiosity. He strode over to it.

Set-d'Elous pulled himself up, blood running down his leg.

When the guard captain turned to ask what the thing was, Set-d'Elous cranked up his remaining strength and sent himself hurtling like a missile into the broad belly of the Zetin. He slammed the guard captain back against the stone ledge and together they rolled over the side. Only Set's feet saved them from the fall below: twenty floors down to the ragged cliff face, and five hundred *mest* further to the stinking marsh there at the bottom.

Below hung the Zetin guard captain, clinging desperately.

Above, Gina held tightly to her high school sweetheart's ankles, seeing the hang glider on the opposite ledge rocking precariously at the whim of the breeze.

Chapter 32

The End of Reality

Soaring through the vast starry night like the great *Anaxoustiq* bird it imitated, riding the thermals off the Zet mountains, they hovered over the Alaun plateau like gods. Now the rising of the larger sun was melting the cool winds which buoyed them; things seemed to work differently in high Zetinê, as Zaran-Ouvaxe had proven. They shifted their weight and the glider slid into a gracious curve, below them the lakeside resort town of Qêsserta rising up to meet them, excited people standing among the trees, beside a broken and unpaved road cut through the forest, waving hands greeting them, shouting praise, prostration of worshippers spreading like a wild fire through the crowd alongside the line of wagons. A final updraft held them a moment suspended over the congregation like angels descending from the heavens, their heads haloed by the rising dawn, the larger sun and its blue sister.

Settling among his mercenaries, he allowed them to unhook him from the contraption and carry him off to the medic waiting in the front wagon. As he lay frozen from the high altitude winds, his blood caked and dried down the length of his leg, he learned he would live. He could even love again. The dagger of Ut'r-BkanN had missed the artery in his hip by a fingernail's width. And the noble lady he had come to save had in the final hour saved him.

He could not hold back his satisfied grin. Safe in the woolly robe thrown over them when they landed, he faced his comrades who beseeched him to explain what had happened. He pushed them back, too exhausted to relive the adventure, but to his lady he whispered the words that perfectly described his emotions.

"I love you, too," she whispered back, and when no one was looking, kissed him.

Samot-Angêron came to him with his report: their mission had saved fifty-eight people from the castle KVANN-STA' PO'CIX—including the two lost youths from his homeland—all while the Zetin guards were chasing them up to the top of the castle.

The former slaves bowed as a group, thanking him and his men, weeping in their joy. Others were still too shocked by their sudden and unexpected release to believe it was true. Old Ouvaxe had arranged for his contacts in Fenula to bring wagons to take them down through the rugged mountains. They would be treated at Fenula city and sent to their homes—if they could be found. By then, the mercenaries had already agreed to share their part of Set's reward with Dorgat-Ouvaxe, already busy with the resettlement of those freed slaves who had no homes awaiting them.

He told them of the heroic death of Aroun-de-Sotos. In private, he clasped Ouvaxe's shoulders and informed him of his nephew's death. The man was unmoved. His grim face told his thoughts, and he remarked only that he was glad the youth could die in the service of the Queen of Fenula, as Gina was known upon her return.

"He was grabbing my wrists, hanging dead weight," explained Set-d'Elous deep into a night of drinking and laughing around the long tavern table in Fenula city. "But while he was twisting in the wind, I saw one of those *Kalêf* shoulder hooks dangling there on my torn uniform, so I stretched over to it and chewed the thread until it popped free—and it shot straight down and hit him in the eye. He cried out, lost his grip, and that was all there was to it. Then Her 'muscular' Majesty pulled me up!"

With a fresh round of *skual* ordered for everyone, they thanked the genius of Zaran-Ouvaxe for his careful studies of the Alaun plateau's intricate wind patterns, and for inventing the contraption they used to escape the infamous KVANN-STA' PO'CIX.

Now they were free to live again and fight another day, to be lovers and friends, and drink the night away in the good company of those famous souls who had risked their lives for the good of the goal.

When he and the Lady Jinetta went to bed in the inn—after putting their comrades out to sleep away the day—they stripped each other of their nobility, and made love passionately. By the greening of the dawn, they had sworn their undying love, as they had once done on the shore of a rain pool in the circle of an abandoned limestone quarry where the silent universe opened for them...opened for her...for him....

Already the warmth of morning sunlight was spreading across his head where his arm curled under his jaw. In the dawn air he heard the sweet chatter of birds on the telephone lines, the bark of a hungry dog and the din of morning rush hour traffic on the highway, reminding him that he was safe at home after working his usual night shift.

"Dontcha think you slept long enough?" a woman's voice spilled over him like cool spring water.

He brushed her off, willing his lover to let him sleep a little longer. Then, feeling a hand nudge his shoulder, he surmised the end of reality had come at last.

"These gentlemen here'd like a word with you," the woman persisted.

Surrounded by his crossed-arms fortress, his head lowered to seal in his secrets, his eyes popped open in darkness, listening for the enemy outside. He knew it was not Gina's voice but that of Joyce, the section manager. Deciding it must be important, he raised his head and stared mole-eyed up at her.

"Sorry to bother you during lunch break," she said.

"What is it?" he asked.

"You're Sebastian Ellis Talbot?" one of the men spoke, "of fourteen-ten East Seventy-first Street in Raytown, apartment three-B?"

"Yes…why? Who are you?"

"Would you stand up?" the second man instructed.

He noticed then they were both wearing suits—out of fashion for the night shift—and visitor badges were clipped to their lapels.

The Professor stood, glancing at Joyce for an answer. His manager was retreating to the safety of her desk. He looked around, saw that no one else was there, probably all away at their midnight lunch.

"I'm Sergeant Wilson," said the first man, "and this is Sergeant Drummond. We want to ask a few questions. Down at the station. Would you come with us?"

"What about?"

"Mister Talbot, you're under suspicion of murder. Please hold out your hands."

"*What…?*"

"You have the right to remain silent," Wilson told him, then turned to his partner, "Cuff him," and back, "If you give up the right to remain silent, anything you say can and will be used against you in a court of law…."

They bent him over his desk, the gray metal government-issue furniture he had called home for the past few years. As they placed the handcuffs on him, his co-workers, hearing the news, began rushing back into the department. The two men straightened him up, then escorted him out. He would have been embarrassed if he'd really felt guilty of something, but all he could do was give that sly grin he usually extended to all the strange people with whom he worked, something neither evil nor devious but decidedly plotting.

"It's very simple, Mister Talbot. We just want to know where the bodies are. That's all we want to know. Can you tell us? There's nobody else, nobody for you to cover for. Why not just tell us?"

The prisoner remained stoical.

"Okay—once again," Detective Henderson conceded, seeing the

morning evaporating, becoming noon, "one *last time*—for your memory: On the night of August third, you and two co-workers, Tammy Sue Tucker and Michael Randolph Fenning, went to the property on Pink Hill Road, the abandoned quarry you own. They have not been seen since. On the same night, six other people, all employees of the service center, followed the three of you to the Pink Hill location. At or near there, four of these people witnessed the assault upon Miss Tucker by you and Mister Fenning. One of them informed the authorities of the assault. The three who stayed have not been seen since: Donna Mae Maggs, Victoria Liliana Sanchez, and Wilma Faye Murdock. Are we clear so far? Now, earlier that night, while you were in the service center, another employee was heard by others in your department to say he would 'get you'—perhaps for some perceived transgression. Later, this same person, one Kenneth James Davenport, was found shot dead outside your apartment. The manager there reported no other persons present, nor were any shots heard, only a flash of light. Whatever weapon was used on Mister Davenport, gutted him," and he turned to Sergeant Wilson, "like one of those goddamn creatures from *Alien* burst out of him—"

"I bet they heard *him* scream out in space," Sergeant Drummond snorted.

Henderson continued: "The time frame, however, would have allowed you to return from Pink Hill to your apartment for the second act. And *soooo*, the list of victims numbers six, Mister Talbot. All employees at the service center, four of them working in your particular department. They all at one time or another spoke, or heard others speak, about behavior of yours which they called eccentric, or weird, or shall we say, sociopathic. They all at one time or another expressed doubts about you being in a stable frame of mind. Now, we can certainly understand how it might have been their *taunting* that produced the sudden burst of rage that may have caused you to plan some kind of retaliation. Then the others, uh, they got in the way, right?"

The detective paused, waited for the prisoner's reaction.

"Do I have it straight?" asked Henderson.

The prisoner remained motionless and silent.

"Now, one remaining thing has yet to be resolved and that is that none of the bodies—other than Davenport's, have been found. Can you—*will you*—before we need another pot of coffee—*tell us where they are?"*

Sebastian Talbot stared at the three detectives—Henderson, the office geek, Wilson with the drooping mustache, and Drummond with the big shoulders and double chin—and the two uniformed officers trying not to act bored, and a couple of men in suits he guessed were either lawyers or news reporters. Sipping his decaf coffee, holding the paper cup with both hands, he tried to warm himself against the October chill outside. The cold front had moved in quickly; it was warm when he'd arrived at the service center to start his night shift as usual. In the dark he could hardly tell the difference.

When he was ready, he set the cup down and raised his head to gaze out the window, seeing the dull autumn colors, knowing now that instead of a short weekend away he had been gone for three months.

"First of all, I didn't kill anyone." His voice was normal, calm, too exhausted to be nervous. "And second, the people I'm accused of killing were my friends—even if they did insult me on occasion. Third, I never knew those girls who supposedly were spying on us."

"Then where are they now?" asked Henderson.

"Michael and Tammy are living in their new homes, far away from here. I don't know their addresses. Fat Ken I don't care about, but I didn't kill him. The others I don't know. Whatever happened to them while they were out in the middle of the night, hiding in the forest playing secret agent is anybody's guess. I never saw them, never heard them, never even knew they were there, and some of them I never knew *period*."

"What were you doing up there, Mister Talbot?"

He sighed, shivered momentarily, and sat back.

"I saw I was running late for my shift so I didn't even stop by my apartment to change clothes. I just rushed in to work, saw it was lunch break and sat down to catch a few winks before I had to start. I was tired, all right? Then you guys wake me up and I have no idea what you're talking about."

The fatigue of staying up all day following a night shift was weighing on him.

"I didn't kill anybody." He took a deep breath. "I was helping them with a personal problem, that's all. Those women at the service center wouldn't tell you that, because it's their friend who's involved. Michael was hooked on Tammy, but his girlfriend wanted me to get him away from her. Cassie Dorfman's her name. Did you talk to her? Probably tell you the same story. Anyway, I was sort of trapped by her, all because—well, I'll tell you: the three of us—Michael, Tammy, and I—we *did* do a *little* recreational drug use. Cassie saw us and she threatened to tell on us if I didn't help her get Michael back. Well, I never cared about that; it was the right thing to do. Cassie thought she was his girlfriend, not that it mattered to me. Maybe he never considered her his girlfriend, but she did."

"So what were you doing up there in that quarry?"

"It was just a place to be alone, you know, without prying eyes to invade their privacy—to say goodbye, finally. That was the plan, anyway."

"The plan? You had a plan, huh?"

"Not a *plan* plan, just an idea how to, um…solve the problem."

"Problem, huh?" asked Drummond.

Henderson cut him off: "And what about the explosion later? Was that part of this plan of yours?"

"What explosion?" the prisoner asked.

"The whole hillside exploded—some natural gas thing, we're told. Pieces of clothing were found there. Geez, what were you *doing*? We know you studied physics; was it some kind of experiment you were doing?"

He shook his head wearily, disgusted with them but too fatigued to fight back.

"Look, guys—I'm beat, okay?—I just finished visiting my daughter and her son. I was on my way to see my other son but he died. My girlfriend walked out on me. She was pregnant and left me a note. I remembered Michael and Tammy so I went to each of them and tried to get them to come back with me but they wouldn't, so I came on back myself. I got to work, like I said, just trying to forget about everything, trying to just straighten out my life."

"Just a simple day in the life of, huh?" snickered Wilson.

"You know, if you had the truth to tell but you knew everyone would say you were lying, would you still tell the truth?" He watched them thinking. "Let's put it another way: one person's truth is another person's fiction. I have not lied to you."

"Go on, then. How many children *do* you have?"

"I don't know. With Zaura, five—and I adopted her other son." He was distracted by Wilson whispering to one of the suits in the room that his wife's real name was Linda. "Any others I can't really confirm. But my eldest son wrote a book about the wars, so I wanted to see him, talk with him, but he—"

Wilson cleared his throat, going over to the one who looked like a psychologist.

"—died. Before I could arrive."

Everyone was staring around the room at each other. Then they focused on the prisoner.

"Now what?" asked the prisoner.

Henderson waved him to continue.

"I was planning to take a trip and visit him and his family—"

"*His* family?" Henderson asked.

"How old are you?" Wilson asked.

"How old do I look?"

"Never mind. As you were saying?"

"Well, Gina was pregnant—about four months I guess—when I remembered that I left Michael and Tammy back...well, umm, back where I left them—"

"And where's th—?"

"Shhh, let him talk."

"So I thought I could kill two birds with one stone—it's only an expression—by swinging over to Selauê to see my daughter, Aisa. She didn't recognize me, of course, because I was disguised, acting like I was a reporter interested in her famous father's career. She was very kind to this stranger—*me*. And she looked very well for her age. So did her son, Metour, who had just become a grandfather himself. She told me all I wanted to know about the family, answered all of my questions, so I left. Even then, I wanted to go see my son. I checked the ship schedules, planning to sail over and visit him after I settled things with

Michael and Tammy. But then I got word that he died—he got old and died."

"Your son got old and died?" asked Drummond with a squint.

Henderson continued: "So you met Michael and Tammy where?"

"Down south. Well, they weren't living together, so it was a hassle going to both places. But then everything started going crazy. I mean, I went out to the island where Tammy was supposed to be living but she wasn't there. In fact, the islanders told me she had left about nine months before—"

"Nine months...?"

"The case is only three months old, but *let the man tell his story*, Sarge."

"I was able to trace her back to Zissekap, strangely enough. Tammy was staying on the island until she had the baby, which was Michael's—you know, so no one would know she was pregnant. Now you see why it was all a big secret. But then, while she—"

"Wait a minute," Drummond interrupted, holding up his hand. "Sorry, but let me get this straight, okay? At the quarry that night was all a ruse to get Tammy away secretly so she could have the baby in some other town?"

"You finally got it!"

"Okay, then. Now...what island was this 'down south'—Florida Keys? Virgin Islands? Barbados?"

"It's called Agani by the natives, off the coast of Dikondra. About forty miles. Oh, crystal clear waters of pure turquoise—"

"Was this island in the U.S.?"

Sebastian the Professor shook his head.

Wilson poked Drummond in the ribs to cut him off.

"Okay," said Henderson, "Tell us the rest."

"Well, she was there for a few months, anyway, but then a ship came and she went with them. I don't know if she was kidnapped or they simply persuaded her to go. I don't know if they were pirates or merchants. Anyway, I tracked her to Zizebran and from there to Aivana where I discovered she had married the king. She was completely changed. I mean, she was dressed like a queen—dignified, intelligent, refined."

"Can you be sure it was her?"

"Oh, yes. She recognized me—*I* hadn't changed. She invited me to have an audience with her and she told me about her adventures. She had the baby—a girl—and was about to have the king's child. You should've seen her, all decked out in silks and jewels, like one of those princesses in the *Arabian Nights*. She was skinny before, but she had put on about thirty pounds—besides pregnancy weight—and looked very healthy. But then, when I reminded her it was time to go, she said she wanted to stay with the rich king."

"Go figure," Drummond snickered. Wilson grunted.

"I even reminded her about her son, the one she left here with her mother. She said she thought about him but if she went back for him she would lose her new life. She asked me to get him and bring him to her, offering me money."

"So that's it? You left her there. With the rich king—in the Persian Gulf? Some tiny Arab state?"

"Not exactly."

"So what about Michael?" Wilson spoke up.

"I went to get him next, wondering just how much trouble he would've gotten himself into during all this time. I left him in my house in Lyas, near the hospital—oh! I didn't tell you about his, um...injury. He was undergoing treatment there for...well, withdrawal, you might say. Anyway, I arrived in Lyas and not only was he not in my house—I paid the servants to take care of him— but he had stolen a lot of my things. Well, I tracked him down— thank goodness he was still in Lyas. There he was, living it up with his nurses! I mean, the two nurses I hired to help him with therapy between hospital visits. They were living in an apartment in what would pass for a red-light district, near all the gaming houses and brothels. He wasn't too glad to see me, you can bet. I apologized for being away so long, said it was time to go back. So what was his reaction? 'Screw you,' he said. He was having too great a time to go back to...well, he called it by the name he always used: the 'Sewer' Center. We argued about what he stole and he paid me back for most items—from his gambling money."

"Turned into a playboy, huh?"

"And then some! Seems as though he didn't even finish the

treatment, so he wasn't, aaa...back like before. He said that was what the nurses loved about him. I never would've thought that— I mean, I know what kind of person he was before: he *did* have some kind of moral streak running through him, but.... I guess absolute moral decay decays morality absolutely."

"Let's get this straight, okay?" suggested Wilson. He turned to the quiet man sitting across the table from the prisoner. "You getting all of this down, Doc?"

The all-too-familiar psychologist, stroking his beard, nodded.

"So, let's see," Henderson started, "Tammy had the baby and married the king. She didn't want to come home. Then Michael fell in love with his nurses, became a gambler."

"Don't forget, he stopped his treatment," Drummond interjected.

"And that's why neither of them came back with you. You sure you don't have any address, phone number, some way to reach them? It'd really help us."

He shook his head, then rubbed his tense forehead with his hands, feeling a headache ballooning inside—this one from his fatigue, not from the approaching alignment of tangents. When the next one would be he could only dream, wanting it to open immediately.

"And then what happened?" asked Wilson.

Sebastian slouched in his chair, a long sigh trickling out of his dry mouth, continuing to shake his head.

"I returned to Kipzon and I found the house empty, and a note tacked to the wall over the *qala*—that's what a bed's called there. This was what she always did, her whole life—hah! in each of her lives. She just walks away. I could expect that with her Ghoupalle lovers, but me? I go way back with her, to high school. I thought she couldn't leave me, not after the experiences we'd been through together. Anyway, the note said something about how she had to be moving on—'but don't worry,' she wrote, she'd be a good mother to our child. *Our child!* She even promised to name the child after my late wife, Zaura. Oh, I could've looked for her, but she might be in a hundred places. I risked my life to save her from Kvann-sta' Po'cix! That's where the Zetin warlord, Ut'r-Bkann, was holding her hostage. I had to cross the *Zet-Saer* with the mercenaries I recruited from my old cavalry regiment, then fight the guards—all to be with her again, to finally have the life I always dreamed of with her. Everyone was running away from me—the more I helped them, the faster they ran. So I ran, too— back here to my little metal desk in the corner, where I can just do my work and not be bothered by anybody."

Chapter 33

Mythology

"I've asked Detective McElroy to sit in because he's been working on the Aronstein case, another missing person," said Detective Henderson. He turned to the beefy man with the biceps stretching out his short-sleeve shirt, his tie loose around his thick neck. "Would you fill the others in on the case?"

"Jason Paul Aronstein was Talbot's best friend," said McElroy. "He disappeared almost three years ago. No signs that he planned to move away. He left his prize-winning dragster parked in his garage, the VCR set to record a late movie, fridge well-stocked, and a music box playing. You get the idea: same as your current missing persons. But his neighbors often saw him and Talbot talking, with some arguing, in the three weeks before his disappearance."

"Thanks," Henderson said. He turned to the suit. "And this is Deputy Barkley of the U.S. Marshal Service. You were sent here concerning a previous incident involving Talbot?"

"Yes," the smartly-dressed Barkley responded, standing and gesturing around the table. "It's all in my report, which you have a copy of before you. Another case of some mild-mannered fellow suddenly exploding, taking some of his colleagues down with him. But this one didn't go and blow away everyone in the office. From the reports you gentlemen have prepared, it would seem that he was even more clever than your run-of-the-mill psycho. This guy didn't have to shoot up his office. He simply lured all of the people he wished to kill out to a secluded location in the middle of the night and did away with them there. It's efficient."

"Doctor Liebowitz?" Henderson called to the man in the corner.

The spectacled man sat up, stroked his beard, glanced over his papers.

"Ah," the psychiatrist intoned wearily, nostalgically, "it seems only yesterday that we were discussing the unusual dreams he was having, trying to interpret them. I remember one in particular, a matter of months ago; it sticks in my mind even now: something about him becoming frozen, stiff like a board, then breaking apart, like those bananas that are dipped in liquid helium. He thought it was an omen of unforeseen troubles, of friends cheating him, of hurtful gossip. It seems that he finally acted on his paranoia. I wish I could have spoken with him before this unfortunate incident occurred, but he stayed away from our sessions. Perhaps his absence was due to the fact I also assist the police department with cases, such as today, and he didn't want me to have the opportunity to talk him out of it. It's clear he doesn't know the difference between the real world and his fantasy world. They run together, mix and merge sometimes, and often are completely separate, almost as though he believes he can exist in two separate worlds and travel effortlessly between them. It's not as though he is pretending, or making it up to win an insanity plea. He *believes* what he says. He *is* telling the truth. The details of his fantasy world are quite astounding, actually, far more intricate than I've ever encountered."

"He *won't* get off on an insanity plea," said Wilson.

Barkley grinned. "That's why I'm here.... Didn't you read my report? He's one of ours—Federal Witness Security Program."

"He's in your witness protection program?"

"That's correct." Barkley glanced around the room with a tick of amusement. "And so...we'll be taking him off your hands for you."

"Why is he in the witness security program?" asked Wilson.

"He's a witness, of course."

"Yes—but for what?"

"I can't tell you. It's classified. That's the point of the program."

"But we're his cops," Wilson said, using his whiny voice. "You'd think we, of all people, would have a right to know. We're practically family now."

"For his own protection, we can't tell you. I know it seems a bit—"

"For *his* protection? What did—" Drummond exclaimed and was quickly cut off by Henderson's hand slapping the desk.

Wilson picked up the question: "So he saw someone do something to someone some time. So what?"

"I'm sorry, but I can't tell you," said Barkley, then paused and narrowed his eyes. "But I *can* tell you he was a teacher when he went into the program. I can tell you where he used to live. I can even tell you that his wife died after being beaten and raped by a freaked-out punk who was never convicted. That was what sent him down the path to witnesshood. As for the suspect, the long-haired hippie-freak radical-type piece of crap kept saying he was 'Son of Luther'—something like that. His name was Victor, I recall. Victor Buchanan. As in the son of Luther Buchanan. Does that name ring a bell?"

"Not especially," said Henderson.

"Okay, who's Luther Buchanan?" asked Wilson.

"Only one of the underworld's most notorious henchmen—part of the—whoa, *shit!* I *can't* tell you the crime family's name."

"Are you saying *our* Sebastian Talbot, mild-mannered tax clerk, witnessed some crime by some wiseguy, and that's why he can get away with murder *now*?"

"Close. Anyone could have connections to them. Even Detective McElroy here—"

"Hey!"

"Sorry. But that punk who killed his wife has sworn to get him. We have to protect him from any attempts. We're obligated to that. He fingered the crime family for us. In the long-run, perhaps, we *can* resolve this, *er*, awkward situation and he can be returned to his former life."

A pregnant pause, then Drummond delivered the baby: "I *know*!" He jumped up. "Yes! I *heard* of him. But it wasn't any

'Luther Buchanan.'"

"What are you talking about?" asked Wilson.

"It was *him*—the, aaa, *you know*: the one keeping his girlfriend hostage. *That's* what he was saying—you don't remember? All last night he was going on and on about that guy. How he'd gotten back from a trip where he had to fight not the son of 'Luther Buchanan,' but a name closer to 'Oother Buckang.' Right? That's what he said. He called him *Ut'r-Bkann*."

Wilson chuckled in disbelief and Henderson smiled cynically.

"Gentlemen," said Barkley, "I'm sorry to rain on your parade but it was the real Luther Buchanan he witnessed, not some fantasy character he's got you believing in."

"But it all fits," Drummond said. "Don't you *see*?"

"He's possibly right," Doctor Liebowitz joined in. "It's not uncommon for a traumatized person to twist an unpleasant reality into a fantasy which he can more easily control. We all want to have more control over our lives. He made it so with his. He became the master of his world. It's just that his world didn't exist."

"How does this real criminal match his fantasy?" asked Henderson.

"Simple," said the doctor. "If a real Luther Buchanan was after him, a threat to him in real life and he could not deal with it, he would reprogram his mind to think of Luther Buchanan as a warlord in a fantasy world and he some fantasy warrior. Switching makes it easier for him to deal with the situation. His reality then becomes unreal and he can dismiss it. Conversely, his fantasy—which represented a comparatively pleasant environment—becomes real and he can enjoy his life there. It seems as though his friend, this Gina woman, and his supposed other wife, this Zaura-something, and his supposed children, grandchildren, and so on—were all twisted representations of his reality, too. He made them up, created them the way he wanted them to be. However, as always happens in these cases, the complexity of the fantasy world eventually gets out of hand and he tried, therefore, to make his fantasy life and his real life merge—trying to make the fantasy into reality. That's probably why he went to so much trouble to bring in his co-workers: to validate his fantasy. A fantasy becomes more real to a person the more people he can get to also believe it."

"Is that so?" asked McElroy.

"Sometimes a person takes a break from reality," said the doctor, "and forgets to come back."

"I see now," said Drummond, nodding his head thoughtfully. He glanced around the room, gathering their expressions of agreement, then turned to Henderson's grim facade. "You see, don't you?"

"I see we still got the Davenport case to tie him to, that's all I see," Henderson said. "We don't know where he buried the others—or how he disposed of them. But we've got one body: Davenport. As long as he's away from society—just get him the hell away from everyone. Call him crazy and let him rot away in some cushy federal institution—I don't really give—"

"Sure would be nice to find the bodies," Wilson muttered. "If we could find one body."

"We have enough," said Wilson. "I think we got our case."

"But—just supposing," Drummond began, breaking from his moment of contemplation, "suppose Talbot *was* telling the truth. I mean, about him going through some hidden door to a new world? If it *was* true, then all those people could really be trapped there. And if we put him away, they'll be stuck there—I mean, without him to bring them back."

"Sergeant Drummond," said Henderson with a sigh, "have you been watching that goddamn Sci-Fi channel again?"

In the only shadow he could find in his bright cell, he curled himself into a fetal ball and tried to sleep. But the only dreams that came to whisper in his mind were of days past: the days that made up Ghoupalle years, when life was grand and the lady he loved lay beside him, and there were no questions. He remembered a dark night long, long ago when he had stayed up, shaking with anger, feeling his confidence draining.

The words echoed in his cell, but he need not have worried;

only he could hear them:

"Take any moment in time, from any place you've ever been, at any time in your life. Narrow it to one brief second—a blink of an eye or beat of your heart. Choose it and freeze it—stop it in your mind—step out of it, turn around and look back. What were you saying or doing at precisely that moment? Who were you with? What sights did you see? Or did you even notice them? Examine them. What do you see? What is it that makes the moment special? What if you knew it would be the last moment of your life? How would you want to live it? Would you miss any of it? Like the way a tree bends or a bird swoops? The way the clouds boil overhead in July; the gurgling of your empty stomach, the laughter of children? The touch of your baby daughter's hand on your knee, and the warmth you feel inside when you see the pale sun on a winter's day? And the chill you feel when the open pasture is suddenly still and you think you are the only person on Earth—and the shiver that runs down your spine when you realize you're not? A single perfect flower you find in your hand, and all of the ways the same scene can appear at different hours and in different seasons? Moonlight illuminating a first kiss, and quiet summer rain with the sun shining? All of that and more. What memory would you take with you —if it were your last? Step out of yourself and see it, feel it, imagine it—now. That's the defining moment: when time absolutely stops so you can step back and see it from every possible angle, like a statue you can walk around. That is what my life is like now. At any time, without warning, the whole universe stops dead and I see it frozen around me. I'm fixed in a loop and all I can do is wait it out. When the universe begins to spin around me once more and all memories fade into the cacophony of life, it becomes more than a memory of a moment: it becomes a photograph of my soul. And I know another moment will come—but never when—and I'll have to deal with it. You think it's driving me crazy? Is that why my head is so screwed up? Is that why I'm telling you all of this? And do you really care?"

"I care," Gina had whispered graciously, leaning over to kiss him, running her fingers through his tussled hair.

When they finished making love, he remembered, and the twin

suns were rising between the lofty spires of Mount Jilam, Gina gave him the gold and emerald ring her husband had given her on their tenth anniversary. In exchange, he gave her the jeweled pins his wife, Zaura-Matousz, had used to fix scarves around her golden head. It was perhaps greater in its sentimental value than Gina's ring was in monetary value, but they called it even.

"It's not over for you," she assured him, "not for a long time is it finished for you."

"As long as I fight it."

"Then fight on, as you say. Live long and prosper!"

"That's what you want then, is it?"

"Yes."

"Then fight, I shall," he had exclaimed in a hushed voice before kissing her feverishly. "For you, Gina. I'll fight for you."

"And I'll give you reason to fight."

"That is all I can ask of you. Or of anyone."

※ ❋ ※

First came the chill.... Then the numbing cold.... He broke into laughter, knowing that his life was over—the quick impending death, feeling the police van rolling over and over, down into the ditch leading to hell: first dripping gasoline, then explosion, the fireball blazing, the inferno, release from the body's endless entrapment. His guards were tossed around like a pair of dice, landing snake-eyed and silent. He, being chained to the wall, survived.

The doors were torn open and, instead of medics, a great hulking figure stood there, the afternoon light casting its muscular form in terrifying silhouette.

"You...!" the stranger growled, and raised the sword he carried in a scabbard over his shoulder.

The Professor did not cower, had no space to do so.

The stranger snapped the great blade down at the prisoner, severing the chains, then yanked him out of the police van and tossed him roughly on the ground like a duffel bag.

Out in the sunlight the Professor gazed at the statuesque

young man: red frazzled hair falling to his hips, the last handful caught up in a leather band; clothing American grunge: ripped dungarees and red plaid lumberjack shirt. It was the toothy grin which caught the Professor's eye.

"At last, I have found you," said the maniac, taking the prisoner by his handcuffs and leading him around the side of the police van, over to his own vehicle—somehow no longer bound for the Eastwood Institute for the criminally insane. Hanging out the doors of the van were the slain bodies of the driver and a guard. Across their faces were burn marks like tire treads. He noticed the smooth hole in the windshield.

"Get in," the big man ordered, opening the back of the beat-up Wagoneer.

Then they were off down the highway, maniac in search of a wreck, passing quickly through subdivisions and onto an old country road. The 7-Eleven store he recognized, also the new shopping mall perched on the edge of farmland, the fishing lake. The hill rising from the fallow cornfields, and the downshifting of his driver, gave him some hope that he was really being rescued. He dared to believe the stranger was an angel sent to lead him to a heaven he could only imagine. But angels did not carry firearms.

"Who are you?" the Professor asked again as he was ordered up the gravel path.

He continued his questioning, pushed and prodded up the hillside to the entrance of the abandoned quarry. There, his escort halted.

"I am known to you," he snarled in some bastardized dialect of English, raising his weapon like an extended finger, pointing, accusing. "You are the warrior Set-d'Elous. You are the God of Evil, the Destroyer of Worlds. You are the consort of the Lady Jinetta—"

"Yeah, yeah, all right, I know who *I* am. But who the hell are *you?*"

The tall, red-haired maniac laughed and the hillside roared with him.

"*You* are the murderer of my father."

The so-called warrior Set-d'Elous, feeling rather humbled in his quaint prison garb, searched his memories as his captor

426

continued.

"It is not unusual for a warrior to forget his kills when they be so many. You shall not escape punishment, however. To avenge my father's death, I went on the High Holy Day of S'EK-FOP' before the Council of His Excellency, the Lord-High Governor of the Seven Nations of Zet, and swore before all of them to return honor to my father's wavering spirit, who was cheated of his full life."

"Wait a minute," he said, raising his cuffed hands.

"No—there is no waiting! I am VK'TU-BKANN, first son of UT'R-BKANN, and I will make *you*, the warrior Set-d'Elous, my sacrifice!"

"Why me?"

"You killed my father!"

"I didn't kill your father. Sure we fought, but he was—"

"The woman Jinetta was not so strong. She died soon after my impregnation, and so a child could not be born of her to be a worthy sacrifice."

"Gina isn't dead. Not yet, anyway—"

"I have tracked you to this strange barbaric world you call *Urtha*. I have studied your people, learned your language, tolerated your customs, and I have waited for the Seven Winds to grant me their counsel. When the convergence was near, I went to the dwelling where you lived and I took her. I filled her with *moussalaganê* until she begged to be impregnated. Then it was easy! She died soon after the sex; she was weak. My plan was defeated. I have been forced to wait four years more to capture you, to make you my sacrifice, that *your* slain body shall honor my father. Although yours is a lesser sacrifice than the offspring born of rape, I have pledged to add my first wife and my chief concubine to his honor. My father will be pleased, and bare his red fangs in the winter sky, when his murderer has been slain and eaten by his son!"

Recognition suddenly swept through him and the years collapsed into a heartbeat—

"*You!*" he exploded, and lunged at the Zetin.

The son of Ut'r-BkanN fell back under the onslaught: the Professor beat his face with his handcuffs, cutting through the fire-hardened flesh to bring boiling blood to the chilly autumn air, gouging new ZK'RA marks across the Zetin's wide cheeks. He must kill th-this-this *thing*! Coming through the tangent in a different time loop, it was *this* monster who attacked Linda in the guise of a high school punk—all the time believing it was Gina who was his victim. And yet, with his many years on Ghoupallesz, through many personas, it really did seem like a hundred years since that ugly day. It was this Zetin monster's plan to avenge his father's murder—*now*, when he had not even known that he would go to save Gina from the castle KVANN-STA' PO'CIX!

The Zetin scrambled to his feet, stood back to raise his weapon: a TNX-103. The Professor saw his opponent stoke the heater with a flip of his thumb, and he froze there. He had exactly twelve heartbeats before it would be hot enough to fire a fatal shot. Charging head first at the Zetin, the son of Ut'r-BkanN swung to the side and slammed the gun's metal arm support against the Professor's head. His crashing body cut a groove against the soft, rain-wet clay. The Professor lay dazed. He could smell the TNX growing hotter but his head was spinning too fast to know which way was up.

Suddenly the air was filled with the wailing of police sirens, and the dilemma of who he should let be his rescuer spilled over him like a bucket of offal.

The Zetin grabbed his prey and dragged him to the center of the quarry—to the spot where he and Gina had first torn the universe and stepped through.

"You know about this tangent?" asked the Professor.

"My people have always known of these doorways. You, as a perfect fool, stumbled through this one—"

"And bought myself a shitload of trouble!"

As the sirens came close, he could hear doors slamming and the scurrying of boots up the gravel drive.

"It is I, son of UT'R-BKANN, great ambassador to the Unclean Nations, who has been granted this special power. I passed through the Portal of Hell, there in the Inner Sanctum of the Temple of T'UN-DAX—which has not been permitted in many generations, not since the age of our Lord T'OT. I followed your filthy scent across the deserts of your Egypt and over the polluted ocean to this land called America, where you fled."

"Home of the brave, land of the free—"

"Not for you!"

"And here we are. Now what? How can we come to an equitable resolution?"

The Zetin plopped the Professor down on the large stone at the exact center of the quarry, the altar of sacrifice, and positioned himself to cover the entrance with his TNX gun.

"I will take you to Zetinê and there you will be a sacrifice to my father!"

Arriving at the quarry entrance, the uniformed police officers ordered the scraggly vagabond to raise his hands, but he did not obey.

"Shoot him!" the Professor shouted to the officers.

Instead, the Zetin faced them with ferocity in his twisted face and defiance in his heart. He slipped his free hand through the jagged rip he had made in the invisible curtain in the middle of the air. The Zetin hoisted the Professor onto a shoulder, arms and legs flung in every direction, and stepped into the gap.

"Halt!" shouted Detective Drummond through the bullhorn. "Don't move! Put down the man you're carrying!"

"I'm being kidnapped!" cried the Professor.

The Zetin warrior stared at the meek, weak Earthlings.

"Put your weapon down!" ordered Drummond.

Vk'tu-BkanN took a calculated step backward, gave them a hateful sneer and a boisterous guffaw, then let loose a covering volley of molten pellets from his TNX-103 as he disappeared into very thin air.

On the ashen plain where the eleven universes met in balance, he saw they were not alone.

Mounting the slope before them stood a line soldiers, all armed. His big Zetin porter, surprised by the welcoming party, dropped him hard on the sand.

Hearing the order to fire, the son of Ut'r-BkanN roared his disapproval: a string of jagged words which by Zetin custom were never allowed to be written.

"It is not finished, Set of *Ur-tha!*" the Zetin shouted in English, shaking his fist and rattling the hot-glowing TNX weapon.

The Zetin warrior spun in the sand and bounded off like an enraged *jalo*, back through the torn curtain in the air. Right into the waiting arms of the police, the Professor guessed as he picked himself up and brushed off his dirty clothes, hearing the faint echo of gunfire.

A silver-haired man broke through the line of soldiers and slid down the shifting sands to meet him. The twinkle in his eye was the same as it had been years before. Saluting, they took a long look at each other.

"It *is* you," his old comrade, Samot-Angêron, now a general, laughed.

Angêron grinned. His former captain was on time. It was exactly as Ouvaxe had said. When the orders came through from headquarters, he knew it was true; he did not even need to see the royal seal. The prophecy was fulfilled!

"Who sent you?" he asked, in a suddenly foreign-sounding Ghoupallêan.

"You do not know?" Angêron responded, surprised. "It was the Prince."

"The Prince?" he quizzed. "I don't know any princes."

"The Prince knows *you*."

"How can that be?"

"His Majesty died several years ago, soon after I found employment in his service, and it was the wealthy inventor, calling himself Jason Aronstein, whom the queen then married. You knew him long ago—the retreat from Tebbicousimankalê— before he escaped from the Tebbi army in a fanciful ETUR machine of fantastic velocity—"

"You mean his *dragster*?"

"That is how he called it, I believe. Alas, it is for him to tell you the tale."

"Well, in the dream land, anything *is* possible."

Then he ordered his men to detonate an explosive at the crux of the tangents, the blast forever mending the curtain, sealing the doorway. There would be no more travelers, no more misguided adventures by unwilling strangers. And in time, his sins would all be forgotten, by him and everyone else, just as surely as he would eventually endear himself to all his Ghoupalle brethren, serving as the gentle and generous god they had so long desired.

Epilogue

Fixing a Hole

Hell is other people.

Jean-Paul Sartre, *Huis Clos* (No Exit)

Reclined on the cushions, sipping the shimmering *halê* from the long-necked pitcher, the *Mexas* gazed up at the tall Roûê girl rhythmically waving the fan over him, stirring the tepid air. Nearby sat the rotund Prince, fattened on the gourmet dining of his royal family, laying back and drawing on the long, coiled silver tube of his hookah, the piquant scent of *jafêle* wafting up around them. In the corner of the room a pleasant tune floated among them. The machine was one of a host of inventions which bought them the titles of prince and king, lords of the palace: a rotating device producing music from the flat circular disks spinning atop a peg.

"What's the meaning of this song?" the Prince asked, already two or three *jafêle* bowls beyond his tolerance.

"The song's about fixing a hole," the *Mexas*—in private hours called Set-d'Elous—responded to his closest friend, Prince Jason. "But that's only on the surface. Most songs have deeper meanings—just like life does."

"Life has deeper meaning?" Jason chuckled, rocking on the cushions and nearly rolling off them. "Like what?"

"Well, Gina once said 'Life is for the experience.'"

Jason Aronstein, the Prince of Aivana, who had married the widowed Queen Tammy, stretched on his pillows and let loose a wizened sigh. He offered the hookah to his friend, who refused it. With his mind consumed by the *jafêle*, he uttered a sacred affirmation of the universal powers which neither he nor anyone else could ever truly hope to understand. He said: "Yeah...."

"I think she meant that there's no heaven, no hell, only the ones people make for themselves. She believed we're all here by a quirk of nature—like the quirk that our two worlds could be connected as they are. So, if we are going to be here, we might as well enjoy ourselves." He smiled, frowned. "But if some people enjoy themselves *too* much, then the universe gets out of balance. We all have to get along with each other. That's all there is."

He adjusted himself on the cushions and pondered how he would spend his time during the next ten years as he awaited Gina's arrival. It was recorded in papers given to him upon her death long ago. She would be visiting Aivana soon. He would meet her again.

"I'll tell you, Jason: there's a whole lot of difference between *being* a god and living like one. In the dream land, anything is possible, but let's not forget how lucky we are. I mean, you never would've expected the King of Tebbicousimankalê would take a fancy to that old Ghoupalle ETUR you suped up—even though you did manage to escape from the whole Tebbi army in it. But to be a prince and have your own country—that's too much!"

"He came through, didn't he?"

"Yes—look around us! You have your wife and your children. I have my endless freedom. However, let's not take ourselves too seriously: *we* know who we are. Fortunes bigger than ours have been made and lost in a single game. Tomorrow we could be out on our butts, a couple of dumb flunkies, smokin' and jokin', and rolling in the gutter like we used to do. Look at us now, the way we just sit around every day...."

And as he paused for breath, he spied one of the guards eyeing him curiously.

"You! What are you staring at? Back to your duty!"

When the guard snickered, the angry *Mexas* rose to his feet and stormed over to the bars but was reminded that, as *Mexas*, he was too precious to be exposed to the dangers of life outside the palace. He was genuinely thankful that they cared to protect him so well. Smiling, he changed his tone.

"As long as you're here, would you bring another pitcher of *halê* and a fine plate of *ulae* for the Prince and me?"

The guard chuckled, shaking his head, moving away down the corridor.

"Why didn't he obey my command? Why didn't he salute?" he asked the Prince, busy with his hookah.

The *Mexas* could never understand the servants. He shook off the guard's disrespect and returned to their conversation, as casually as if they had never been interrupted.

"So look at us! What are we doing here?"

His companion did not answer, only grinned. That upset him and he plotted to go to his corner of the room and partake of his daily nap. He knew that after he went to sleep and awoke to the bright sun of another world, everything would make sense.

After that restful pause he would realize that living in a gilded cage was better than having no cage at all.

THE END

Acknowledgements

Any work of imagination necessarily draws from a variety of sources. For inspiration, insight, and where applicable the gift of insousiance, I am greatly indebted to Roger Zelazny, Michael Moorcock, Robert Silverberg, and Gene Roddenberry. Special thanks go to my daughter who not only endured hearing all the tales of the Dream Land but produced the cover art.

About the Author

Stephen Swartz grew up in Kansas City, Missouri where he dreamed of traveling the world. His writing usually includes exotic locations, foreign characters, and splatterings of other languages—strangers in strange lands. After studying music, even composing a symphony, Stephen had planned on being a music teacher before deciding to turn to fiction writing.

The Dream Land was born from various childhood games, then forgotten until reignited in adulthood by the music album *The Celts* by Irish singer Enya. No correlation between the novel and that album is intended; the music simply evoked the necessary soundscape to allow interdimensional voyaging to occur.

After countless voyages, Stephen now teaches English at a university in Oklahoma and continues to write fiction late at night.

THE DREAM LAND

Book II

Dreams of Future's Past

WHEN YOU'VE CONQUERED A NEW WORLD, DO YOU CHANGE HISTORY OR CHANGE YOURSELF?

After his adventures in Book I, Sebastian Talbot (a.k.a. Set-d'Elous, legendary warrior and Sekuatean cavalry captain) has exiled himself to a desolate island, content to laze away the days writing his memoir. Until the emissary from Queen Tammy arrives with a mission he cannot refuse. Tammy, the IRS clerk he took to Ghoupallesz along with Michael in Book I, wants him to go fetch her son who she left on Earth. How could she return for him? She married the King of Aivana.

That mission raises desperate questions for Sebastian: If he can go back and forth through these interdimensional doorways and arrive in different time periods, perhaps he can do something to prevent the big war he fought through, the war that destroyed his family and millions of others. So he returns to his Ghoupalle wife Zaura. While on patrol duty, he comes upon a young poetess he knows will become the rebel leader who helps overthrow the monarchy and causes the wars. What would you do?

Meanwhile, back on Earth in another timeline, Sebastian awakens from a coma and is helped in his recovery by Dr. Toni Franck. An affair develops—just as his opportunity for escape comes along. Later, as Sebastian/Set escorts teams of mercenaries back and forth to conduct their history-changing business, he tries to meet up with Toni again only to realize the police are still in pursuit. Desperate to see her, he arranges a meeting only to have a SWAT team show up, cornering him. Can he escape through an interdimensional doorway this time?

THE DREAM LAND trilogy continues in Book II with parallel time lines, world domination and world destruction, and as always the minutiæ of heroic minds playing god without a rule book.